The ROYAL
Station Master's
Daughters at War

Ellee Seymour is former journalist and PR professional living near Cambridge. *The Royal Station Master's Daughters at War* is the second book in a WWI trilogy inspired by the life of Harry Saward. Ellee was inspired to write the series after meeting Brian Heath, the great grandson of Harry Saward, who was the royal station master at Wolferon for forty years from 1884 to 1924 and whom the novel is based on.

Also by Ellee Seymour:
The Royal Station Master's Daughters

The ROYAL
Station Master's
Daughters *at* War

ELLEE SEYMOUR

ZAFFRE

First published in the UK in 2023 by
ZAFFRE
An imprint of Bonnier Books UK
4th Floor, Victoria House, Bloomsbury Square, London,
England, WC1B 4DA
Owned by Bonnier Books
Sveavägen 56, Stockholm, Sweden

This is a work of fiction. Names, places, events and
incidents are either the products of the author's
imagination or used fictitiously. Any resemblance to
actual persons, living or dead, or actual
events is purely coincidental.

A CIP catalogue record for this book is
available from the British Library.

ISBN: 978-1-83877-682-4

Also available as an ebook and an audiobook

1 3 5 7 9 10 8 6 4 2

Typeset by IDSUK (Data Connection) Ltd
Printed and bound in Great Britain by Clays Ltd, Elcograf S.p.A.

Zaffre is an imprint of Bonnier Books UK
www.bonnierbooks.co.uk

This book is dedicated to Brian Heath, the proud great-grandson of royal station master, Harry Saward, who wanted me to share his extraordinary story. I hope I have done him justice.

Prologue

'In the name of the law, stop that woman, the one there in the red jacket!'

The cry came from a short man with puffed-out cheeks who was wearing a bowler hat. He waved a stick in the air, panting as he pursued a young woman across the platform at Wolferton Royal Station.

As the woman glanced over her shoulder, she tripped, her bag flying from her hand, and she fell heavily to the ground. The station master's eldest daughter, who was also on the platform, rushed over to assist her.

'Are you all right?' asked Jessie anxiously, unaware of the man's cry behind her due to her hearing impairment.

The woman stared straight at Jessie and recoiled, her face turning white, her lips trembling. Without a word, she rose quickly, picked up her bag and pushed past Jessie, running off down the platform.

Jessie watched as she fled the station, her lips pressed together. *What a rude woman. That's the thanks I get for offering to help.*

Her father suddenly appeared at her side, his jaw clenched. 'Jessie, Didn't you hear the call to stop that woman?' he asked.

'Stop her? But why?' Jessie asked, narrowing her eyes.

The man with the bowler hat rushed over, his face red and his brow sweaty. He panted, 'Why did you let her go? Didn't you hear me raise the alarm?'

'No, I didn't hear you. What alarm?'

The man pointed his stick towards the end of the platform. 'Quick, we can't let her get away. She's wanted by the police.'

Jessie's eyes widened. She had only seen the woman for a split second but she didn't look like a criminal, though her manner annoyed her. Thinking back, she recalled the woman's frightened expression and wondered why she had come to Wolferton, a hamlet near Sandringham House on the royal family's country estate in Norfolk.

Harry Saward rubbed his neck. 'You'll have to chase after her yourself. I can't just drop everything and leave, I'm the station master.'

'You have to help me,' the man insisted. He beckoned Harry towards him. 'There's something you need to know, something of a confidential nature.'

Harry moved close to the man, who whispered some words in his ear. The station master straightened instantly, his eyes showing concern.

'Very well. I'll help you. We must find that woman immediately. We can't have fugitives on the loose on the royal estate.'

Chapter One

'She's a slippery one, that's for sure.'

Harry stroked his moustache as he sat at his kitchen table later that evening with his wife, Sarah, and daughters, Jessie and Ada, deep in thought.

'You're far too old to be chasing after villains, Mr Saward, especially young 'uns,' his loyal housekeeper gently scolded.

Harry noticed how Betty bent over more these days, rubbing her back. She was no spring chicken herself, but she was one of the family after being with them for more than twenty years.

'I was just doing my public duty, Betty, but she was too fast for us.'

Sarah's lips were pursed. 'I agree with Betty. You should leave the police to do their own work. Magnolia was at the station and couldn't wait to call in at the post office and tell me about it. I could hardly believe my ears when she said you flew out of the station at a great speed, as if your life depended on it.'

Jessie commented, 'But, Ma, this gentleman wasn't a police officer, he was a private detective. Someone must have employed him to pursue this woman here. She looked so young and frightened. What could she have done that was so terrible? And where can she be now?'

Ada, at twenty-five years old, was the station master's youngest daughter and the fairest, most resembling her father. She looked thoughtful. 'She came here for a reason. Jessie has a point. Do you know what she is supposed to have done?'

Harry cleared his throat. 'Bigamy and theft, and possibly more, even worse if what the detective says is correct. That's not all, I'm afraid. This woman claims to have some connection with our family, though I'm darned to know what.'

Betty almost dropped the cup she was holding. 'That's impossible. You don't have any bad 'uns in your family who would do such terrible things, do you, Mr Saward?'

Harry shrugged his shoulders. 'Not that I know of.'

Sarah thought for a moment. 'You say you have no idea who she might be. Could she have anything to do with Maria or Ruth?'

'The same thought had occurred to me. I must call in to warn them, just in case this person is on her way to see them.'

Sarah asked, 'Oh dear, can't it wait till morning?'

'I'm afraid it can't. This is the royal estate and we can't have fugitives or suspicious strangers on the loose here.'

Betty shuddered. 'What does she look like, just in case I should cross her path?'

Jessie spoke up. 'As Father didn't see her, I can tell you. I'd say she's in her early twenties with auburn hair.

4

She was wearing a smart red jacket with a black skirt and white blouse. I couldn't help but admire her outfit, and I thought how striking she looked.'

Sarah retorted, 'Looks can be deceiving.'

Harry nodded in Betty's direction. 'Yes, they can, and she's a wily one for sure. I advise you to search your outhouse when you get home.'

Sarah commented, 'There is more concerning news, I'm afraid. I take it you've heard about the terrible daylight air raid in London yesterday? If I recall rightly, Ruth's brother, Gus, lives in the East End, which suffered the most. You might want to ask her about that while you are there. She'll want to know if he's all right, and his daughter Nellie too.'

Harry rubbed his chin and looked thoughtful. 'Yes, you're right. I don't believe Ruth and her brother are close, but I'll certainly ask.'

He rose from his chair.

'Are you going out already? You haven't finished your tea,' Betty fussed.

Harry eyed the cold meat pie and pickles on the plate. 'It will have to wait. This is a more important matter that can't wait. I need to deal with it right now.'

'Very well. I expect Beatrice will be peckish when she is back from the hospital,' said Betty, referring to the station master's third daughter as she removed the plate from the table. 'We can't waste food.'

Sarah glanced at the carriage clock on the mantelpiece. 'Speaking of Beatrice, it's five to seven, she was due home a while ago. I'm not surprised though, she tells me they are short staffed at Hillington Hall.'

Harry replied, 'You know Beatrice. She won't leave until she is satisfied she has done everything she can for her patients.'

Sarah walked into the hallway with Harry where they saw a newspaper lying on the floor. It had been pushed through the letterbox.

He took the paper into the kitchen. 'That's strange, I wonder who left this for us?'

A headline in bold lettering stood out on the page – BIGAMIST AND THIEF NELLIE JEACOCK HUNTED BY POLICE.

Harry's jaw dropped. There was also a small black and white photograph with the article.

Jessie peered over his shoulder. 'That's her. That's the woman I saw. It says her name is Nellie Jeacock.'

'What does this Nellie Jeacock have to do with you?' asked Betty.

Sarah stated with a steely glint in her eye, 'It's as clear as night follows day. This woman has nothing to do with us, but we're not the only Sawards around. I bet my life that she's come here to see Maria or Ruth.'

Harry's voice was firm. 'I doubt they would have a part in all of this. Look how well Maria has settled in as a maid at Sandringham House, with her family here too. She wouldn't risk losing that.'

Sarah blurted, 'I want no part of it. And if you have any sense, you will keep out of it too. Just say your piece and leave. They can sort out their own problems.'

Ada spoke up, 'But Maria and Ruth are good people. They have been so thoughtful and caring towards Leslie when I wasn't up to it,' she said, referring to her son, a toddler of almost three years old.

Harry's eyebrows furrowed, 'I agree. I do feel responsible towards them. After all, they are family, like it or not. I have a duty to see they're all right. It's what my father would have wanted.'

Maria's sudden arrival two years ago had turned the station master's family's lives upside down. Harry was one of ten children and after his mother had died, his father Willie remarried at the age of seventy-one. He wed Ruth, his housekeeper, who was considerably younger than him at just twenty-eight. Their wedding caused much tongue wagging, especially as they had three further children – Maria, Freddie and Archie.

Ruth found herself homeless after Willie died. In desperation she had brought Maria to Wolferton to be looked after by Harry, while Freddie and Archie went to stay with Ruth's brother, Gus, in London.

It hadn't been the easiest start, but Harry and his family had warmed to Maria, who was a natural at caring for Leslie. They were shocked to discover later she had a young son of her own, Joey, conceived when Walter Jugg, the landlord of the inn where Maria helped out, raped her when she was only fifteen.

Maria and her ma and brothers Freddie and Archie, now fifteen and fourteen years old respectively, were now reunited and all living happily together with Joey at

7

Honeysuckle Cottage in Wolferton, a tenancy that Harry had secured for them, when usually only men were allowed to hold tenancies on the royal estate on the understanding they would leave when the estate workers fighting for king and country returned from war.

'You're too soft,' Sarah called out, as Harry bolted out of the door. 'Mark my words, I can sense trouble ahead.'

Chapter Two

Maria Saward stepped gingerly into the Dowager Queen's lavish drawing room in Sandringham House. It was her first day as maid to Queen Alexandra and Mrs Pennywick was giving her precise instructions about what could and couldn't be touched. Maria's chest had puffed out like a fat bird's when informed by Mrs Pennywick that due to the usual maid falling sick she was required to take her place and assist in cleaning the Queen Mother's private rooms.

The small drawing room was filled with valuable royal treasures. All around were decorations of a musical or floral theme. A magnificent Dresden porcelain chandelier hung above her head. It had been a wedding gift to Queen Alexandra from the Kaiser, nephew to her husband, when he was Prince Edward.

The housekeeper remained glued to Maria's side as she walked around the small room, just off the main spacious drawing room, taking it all in. Maria felt as if she was walking on air and wished her ma could see her surrounded by so many handsome objects.

The housekeeper pointed to an occasional table and instructed Maria to gently pick up a delicate Meissen figurine of a girl wearing a white and gold crinoline dress and dust it.

'Be sure to hold it with the lightest of touches. But firm enough not to drop it,' she was instructed.

'It's so lovely,' gushed Maria, as she brushed the duster over the exquisite ornament. 'Just look at her sweet face and blue eyes. They're the same colour as the cornflowers we have in our garden.'

Her eyes rested on the matching male figure next to it. 'And just look how finely dressed the man is, in his white breeches and gold waistcoat. What a handsome pair they make. They must be worth a small fortune.'

Mrs Pennywick bristled. 'It's not your place to comment like that, Maria. I would ask you to keep your mind on your work and your thoughts to yourself and you won't get into trouble. Now put them back where they were and tidy up the table and newspapers in the corner.'

Beneath her strict exterior Maria had observed a softness in the housekeeper's expression on occasions, feeling that Mrs Pennywick was keeping a kindly watchful eye on her.

The sound of a bell ringing from one of the rooms nearby stopped them in their tracks. They glanced at each other as it rang again, and then again, with increasing impatience. Mrs Pennywick, her lips as straight as a pencil, shook her head.

'I suppose I'll have to answer it. You can't rely on staff these days to be where they should,' she complained.

Hazel Pennywick was tall and trim, her hair tied back neatly at the nape of her neck, and her appearance and boundless energy belied her age. Now in her early sixties, with retirement beckoning, she had been persuaded by Queen Alexandra to stay on until a suitable and trusted replacement could be found.

The widowed housekeeper had readily agreed; with no one at home to answer to, she would soon be bored. She regarded Sandringham House as a second home as she had spent more time there in the last forty years than under her own roof, and it made her feel good to be wanted.

Mrs Pennywick paused at the door. 'Did you hear what I said?'

'I'm sorry,' spluttered Maria, returning to her senses.

In a stern tone, the housekeeper instructed, 'I will repeat my instructions one more time. Please *do not* touch anything else until I return. I suggest you just familiarise yourself with where everything is, so you can remember next time. Everything you see here is of great value and personal significance to Her Majesty and must be treated with the greatest care and respect.'

'Of course, Mrs Pennywick. I daren't touch anything anyway, in case I drop it. I'm a real butterfingers.'

Mrs Pennywick's eyebrows arched as she swept out of the room. 'I don't like the sound of that. I hope you will not disappoint me after the trust I have placed in you.'

Maria smoothed down the folds of her black dress and grinned to herself. Everything she did was to prove to

Harry and his family that she was deserving of their faith and trust in her, and to make her Joey proud of her.

What would they think if they could see her now in this grand room, walking around the fine Sheraton armchairs, her fingers trailing over the floral fabric?

What would Eddie, her sweetheart, think too? A faint smile curled at the corner of her lips as she saw Eddie in her mind's eye, with his mop of black hair and cheeky grin, and a look in his eyes that showed he was besotted with her. The porter at Wolferton Station had courted her patiently while she held back, unsure if she returned his feelings and how he would feel about her if he knew the truth about her past. Then the eighteen-year-old surprised her by telling her he had enlisted to fight for his country and would soon be leaving Wolferton.

Although this was almost two years ago, Maria could remember it as if it had happened yesterday, how anxious this had made her feel. Her stomach clenched like a tight fist and her throat dried. A tear pricked her eyes and she realised then for the first time she had feelings for Eddie too. The evening before he departed they had walked hand in hand along the dusty lanes lined with cowslips and green hedgerows, where rabbits darted in front of them and swallows dived low as the sun began to set. They turned by the church and followed a track that led up into the woods where they sat under an oak tree.

Maria sobbed, 'Please, promise me you won't do anything foolish, Eddie Herring. A dead hero is no good to me or yer ma.'

'Or little Joey,' he whispered. 'I'm doing this for us. I have to fight for my country, for our future, and, with God's blessing, I will return.'

Eddie pressed his finger against her lips and smothered her face with kisses. Maria pulled away, her face creasing. 'I mean it, Eddie. I couldn't bear it if anything happened to yer. I'll pray for yer every night.'

Eddie pulled her towards him and dried her damp cheeks with his fingers. 'You do that, my sweet. Remember. And remember this, no Hun or anyone else is going to get the better of Eddie Herring.'

She pressed her lips hard against his with a burning urgency. She then felt his lips on her neck and she tossed her head back, her thick auburn hair hanging loose down her back, listening to his moans and sensing his arousal as his hands lightly stroked the softness of her breasts.

Maria pulled away. 'That's enough. Just hold me a moment longer, Eddie. I just need you to hold me tight, without . . .'

Eddie looked shamefaced. 'Oh, Maria, I'm sorry. I didn't mean to take advantage. I lost myself for a moment. I would never . . .'

'I know that, silly. Not every man is like that monster Walter Jugg.'

'I don't know how you can even say that man's name after what he did to you.'

'He can't harm me anymore. Although he forced himself on me, I wouldn't change Joey for anything. He ain't going to be anything like that man, even though he has his blood coursing through his veins.'

13

'I'll help look after him, if you'll let me. He's a smash-ing lad.'

Maria nestled her head against Eddie's chest and felt his heart pound as she rested under the crook of his arm. 'Joey has taken to you too. I know you have the best heart, more than I deserve, after what happened.'

'Forget him. Walter is dead now, he can't hurt you anymore. He was a wicked man, a liar and a blackmailer who snatched an innocent child and got what he deserved when the train killed him.'

Eddie was referring to the day when Walter snatched Harry's nine-month-old grandson, while entrusted to Maria by Ada, from the station master's garden. Eddie had chased him down the railway line and snatched Leslie from him, but Walter's foot became trapped in the track and he couldn't free himself in time before the train turned the bend and hurtled towards him.

'None of what he said about me was true. He came here to blacken me name and made false accusations,' Maria said softly.

'Shush, my sweetheart. I don't want to hear that man's name anymore. This is our last night together for God knows how long. How about another kiss?'

Eddie took Maria's chin in his hand and lifted it towards his face. She opened her lips to speak, but he pressed his finger to them, before kissing her gently.

Thinking back on that tender moment now, Maria could recall the musty smell of the damp moss where they sat and the fragrant pines as they watched the sun disap-pear over the horizon.

'Will you be my girl then? Will you wait for me till I return?' Eddie had asked, as they parted company that evening.

'Of course I will, I promise,' she grinned, her face breaking into a wide smile. They sealed their promise with a final lingering embrace.

'I may not be the best letter writer, my sweet Maria, but I promise to write when I can,' he told her, gently stroking her cheek, pressing his lips on hers for a final kiss.

'Just a few lines to know you are still alive, that's all I want. I promise to write back, my darling Eddie,' were her parting words.

She watched him walk away, turning his head every few seconds until he was out of sight.

As the weeks and months passed, Eddie's letters were infrequent, and she treasured every scrawling word when news from him reached her, but the last one she received just a month ago filled her with dread. It had been written by a nurse on his behalf in the Middle East in Gaza, a place she had never heard of, where he was being treated for a severe leg injury. She couldn't stop thinking of him suffering in a far-off land, wondering how he was.

Today, her hair was tucked neatly out of sight under her mop cap. Her olive skin, large brown eyes and high cheekbones attracted admiring glances from some of the male staff at Sandringham House, but Maria shrugged them off. She meant it when she said she would wait for Eddie. It was his kindness that had won her heart, seeing how he treated Joey as his own, and men like that were few and far between.

Maria tentatively ventured into the adjoining long and handsome drawing room with a painted ornate ceiling and intricate panelling on the walls. Her eyes feasted on the hoard of valuable objects displayed before her. Glass cabinets were built into the walls to house Queen Alexandra's treasures and they were crammed with a collection of figures in semi-precious stone, jade and amber. Her exquisite collection included many precious works by Fabergé, who had secured the patronage of the royals in the early 1900s. There were also many more delicate Meissen figurines and ornate occasional tables crammed with silver-framed family photographs and life-size family portraits adorned the walls too, their eyes staring down on her. Maria whistled under her breath, awed by the splendour and riches of the room that filled almost every space. She found herself walking softly towards one of the large bay windows that looked out onto the green and luscious grounds. The huge window stretched the length of the room and gave the room its light and airy feel. A grand piano with a mature potted plant on it was positioned in front of the window.

An object in the corner of the window caught her by surprise. Her heart seemed to freeze, then beat like a drum, and her eyes widened as she stared at the magnificent sight in front of her. She tiptoed over to a striking gold cage. Standing three foot tall, the cage was topped with an ornate golden tower and a crown had been crafted onto its domed pinnacle. It was positioned on a pedestal, meaning her eyes were at the level of its inhabitant. The corners of her mouth curled as she gazed at its feathered occupant, a bright green parrot with long vivid feathers down its back, almost reaching the bottom of the cage like a cascading bride's veil.

Maria shot a sideways glance at the door. As there was no sign of Mrs Pennywick returning, she leant forward and peered inside the cage, a sense of incredulity filling every fibre of her body. The exotic feathered creature appeared to be dozing on its perch, its smooth head lowered into its chest, which gently fluttered in and out.

She could barely believe the sight that befell her eyes – an exotic creature with a pink throat, bluish crown and rump and bright green shoulders. She knew from what the servants had told her that its coral-red beak and longer tail feathers were a sign that this was a male bird. She couldn't resist sliding the tip of her slender finger between the bars, enthralled by this striking bird.

'Well, ain't you a pretty sight?' gasped Maria, entranced. Her hand shook as she inched her finger further inside the cage, intending to stroke its plump tummy.

The bird cocked its head and squawked, 'Aint you a pretty sight?'

Maria's eyes widened. 'Did you really say that? That's what I said earlier. I can't believe you can copy my words just like that.'

'Who's a pretty boy then? How do you do? It's a great pleasure to meet you,' the bird shrieked, ruffling its feathers and arching its neck. Its black beady eyes stared straight at Maria, her jaw dropping wide open like a trap door.

Maria shook her head and gazed in disbelief as the bird spread open its green plumage and shuffled along its perch towards her finger.

'Cor, blimey. You can really speak. Just like a human,' Maria gasped, swiftly snapping her finger back before it was pecked. 'What else can you say then?'

'Good morning? May I offer you some tea?' the bird screeched.

Maria stifled a giggle. 'Oh, yes please. Two sugars please. And shush, not so loud. You'll get me the sack.'

'Shush. Not so loud. You'll get me the sack. God save the King, God save the Queen,' squawked the bird in a high-pitched cry mimicking Maria's words, relishing the attention. It cocked its head to one side, staring back at Maria, who raised her finger to her lips.

Maria had longed to see this wondrous bird, having been told about it downstairs in the kitchen. She grinned as she realised the bird was repeating words it had previously overhead spoken in its presence.

'So it's true. Mrs Pennywick wasn't pulling me leg. You're Emerald, I've heard all about you. You are a clever bird. I only hope she ain't 'eard you, else I'll be for it,' Maria muttered under her breath.

Maria realised this was the famous Princess Parrot that one of the kitchen maids had told her about. She recalled Annie telling her the bird was named in honour of Princess Alexandra following her marriage to Prince Edward. When Edward was crowned king the bird's name changed accordingly to Queen Alexandra's parrot.

Her curiosity got the better of her and she momentarily forgot the advice given to her by Annie to stay well clear of the bird if she should see it.

Annie's warning words were ringing in her ears now.

If anyone lays a finger on Emerald, woe betide the consequences. Never mind all the riches and treasures in this room, that bird is irreplaceable and means a great deal to Her Majesty, more than you can imagine.

She grinned. 'I ain't ever met a parrot named after a princess before, let alone a queen. Wait till I tell Ma and Joey all about it.'

She looked towards the door and fretted, half expecting the housekeeper to storm in having heard the bird's squawks.

Deciding there was no point in standing idle waiting for Mrs Pennywick to return, Maria set about tidying around her, being extra careful not to pick up any delicate ornaments that could slip through her fingers. She spotted a copy of the *Daily Mirror* on a chair and picked it up. It was open at one of the inside pages and she was about to close it and fold it neatly when her eyes were drawn to a headline and a black and white photograph of a woman. BIGAMIST AND THIEF NELLIE JEACOCK HUNTED BY POLICE.

Maria's eyebrows knitted. *I know that name. Nellie Jeacock. Now where have I heard it before?*

The penny suddenly dropped. *I'm sure Uncle Gus's daughter is called Nellie. I'm sure I heard Ma mention the name Nellie Jeacock once, something about her niece getting married. She was sent a newspaper cutting about it and the name Jeacock stuck in me head 'cause I thought she said Peacock. Oh dear, I must let Ma know. If this Nellie's on the run, and she really is Uncle Gus's daughter, she could be anywhere. What if she turns up here, in Wolferton?*

Chapter Three

'I just felt something wasn't right the moment I set foot on the platform,' said Jessie. She had toffee-coloured hair and fair skin, and at twenty-seven she was a year older than her sister Beatrice, who had just returned home from her nursing shift.

The station master had left the house moments before to visit Ruth and Maria.

Some people said Jessie was gifted with a sixth sense as a result of the hearing impairment she had had since suffering a virus as a child. She seemed to have a well-honed intuition that others lacked.

'Every day I see more families grieving, wearing black bands. When will it all end?' she asked.

'I know only too well,' Beatrice replied softly. 'I see the suffering from war among my patients. It's hard to believe that the cause of all of this pain is the King's own cousin, Kaiser Wilhelm, who used to visit Wolferton on his way to Sandringham. Though it was always said the King found him rude and arrogant. So tell me, what was this uneasy feeling you had?'

Jessie's eyes narrowed. 'I felt I needed to be on my guard, that something untoward was about to happen.'

At first, I wondered if it was to do with the terrible news about the daylight air attacks in London yesterday. It was all people were talking about at the station. But then I saw her, and my eyes followed her every move.'

'Followed who?' quizzed Beatrice.

'The girl, Nellie, the one who is in the papers. I spotted her leaving the train and running along the platform before she tripped up. I thought she was afraid, I could see it in her eyes. She ran off the platform with Father and a private detective chasing after her, but she gave them the slip.'

Ada passed Beatrice the newspaper, her finger pointing to the article. 'Someone pushed this through our letter box. It turns out this mystery woman is connected to the Saward family.'

Beatrice's eyebrows arched. 'Maybe this Nellie Jeacock is the reason for your sense of unease, Jessie. It never fails you.'

'I think you're right. I hope Father can get to the bottom of it.'

∞

Honeysuckle Cottage was half a mile away from the station master's house. The tied cottage was similar to many tenanted to estate staff, resembling picturesque gingerbread houses, built from the local sand-coloured carstone. The pretty front garden had sweet-scented pink honeysuckle clinging to the door frame, presenting a chocolate box image that warmed the heart.

'Everyone's talking about the daylight bombings in London yesterday, Ma. I know yer don't have a fondness for yer brother, but do you think Uncle Gus is all right? What if his house has a hit?'

Ruth shrugged. ''E's 'ardly likely to send me a telegram, the tight-fisted wastrel. If it did have a hit that would do us all a favour. Good riddance to bad rubbish.'

Maria appeared shocked.

Her mother added in a softer tone. 'I don't mean to sound harsh. It's unsettled me hearing his name after so long. You're a good girl. It's typical of you to be thoughtful and ask after 'im, Maria. I've not heard word though, so I would guess 'e is all right. No news is good news though, as far as 'e's concerned.'

Ruth had washed her hands of her brother after discovering he frittered away the money she gave him for Freddie and Archie's keep when she was unwell, spending it on drink and treating them like skivvies. She had known leaving the boys with him was a risk, that he was renowned for drinking, but had been desperate and hoped he had mended his ways. She wanted to give him a second chance, for Nellie's sake, the daughter he was bringing up alone.

'What is it?' queried Ruth, seeing Maria's anxious expression. 'Why do I get the feeling there is something you want to tell me? And what's that behind yer back? It looks like a newspaper. Come on, spit it out, what's on yer mind?'

Unable to hold back any longer, Maria spread the paper on the table and pointed to the headline. Maria gave her mother a few moments to read and digest the report. She

23

saw Ruth's hand fly to her mouth as she read the headline stating Nellie Jeacock was being hunted by police.

Maria blurted, 'Do yer think it's Uncle Gus's Nellie? The one you were sent a wedding announcement about?'

Ruth looked closely at the paper. Her jaw dropped open. 'Yes, it is, that's her. I can't believe it. The poor girl, what trouble has she got 'erself into?'

'What makes you so sure it's 'er?'

Ruth screwed up her eyes and pressed her face close to the page. 'Because this woman's face 'ere staring up at me is the mirror image of 'er dear mother, Maggie, God bless 'er soul.'

Maria's jaw dropped. 'I feared as much. These are very serious charges, Ma. Bigamy? That means she were married to two men at the same time, it makes 'er sound like a con woman. And it says she's a thief too. Why, Ma, she could go to prison. Maybe's that's why she's legged it. Do you think she'd come looking for us?'

'I did write to 'er, so she might know of our whereabouts, though I never 'eard back. Gus also knows about the Sawards and their royal connection, she could 'ave learnt about us settling here from him.'

Maria felt her chest tighten. 'I'm scared, Ma. I have a bad feeling about this.'

'Let me think for a moment. I can't take this all in,' sighed Ruth, slumping into a chair and holding her head in her hands.

Maria placed a comforting arm around her mother's shoulder. The silence in the room was almost deafening.

Joey plonked himself on the floor by Ruth's feet and sucked on his thumb in silence.

After a pause, Maria blurted, 'I don't think we should be too hasty in jumping to conclusions. I know what yer think of Uncle Gus, but what do we know of Nellie? We don't know if what the paper says is right. Who is this man she married? She is your niece, yer own flesh and blood, after all, and my cousin. Just think what a tough time she must 'ave had when she lost 'er ma. Yer can remember what it was like for us when Pa passed on. We were homeless and desperate when we came 'ere and you begged Harry to take me in. I can't help but wonder what kind of tough life Nellie has with Uncle Gus.'

Ruth nodded. 'Maybe the girl married for security, I can't blame 'er. Cousin Helen bumped into Gus who bragged about Nellie marrying this older man who wasn't short of a pound or two and she sent me the newspaper cutting. Truth be told, I fretted about Nellie, that's why I tried me best to keep in touch as she grew older. She were only four years old when the angels took 'er dear mother. I did me best for 'er at the time, but I'm ashamed how cruel me brother turned out. Losing Maggie was the undoing of 'im. Poor little Nellie cried for 'er ma every night. It would break Maggie's heart to see her Nellie in this kind of trouble. She would turn in 'er grave if she knew the 'alf of it.'

Ruth picked up the paper and read the words on the page again. Her face paled. ''Ave you read it all? There's more to it than bigamy and theft.'

'No. I didn't have a chance to read the whole thing. What else does it say?' Maria pressed her mother.

Ruth shook her head. 'I can't believe this.'

'What is it? Tell me.'

In a faltering voice Ruth read the article aloud. '"*A warrant has been issued for the arrest of Nellie Jeacock, twenty-two years old, after she failed to appear before Bow Street Magistrates' Court this morning on the felonious charge of being an accomplice to the attempted murder of Stanley Jeacock, a charge of bigamy and the further charge of theft of a silver locket containing a lock of hair from Admiral Lord Nelson. Anyone with information about the whereabouts of Nellie Jeacock is urged to do their public duty and contact the police immediately.*"'

Maria's eyes widened. 'Attempted murder? Stanley Jeacock? That's Nellie's husband. Oh, Ma, it's saying she was involved in trying to kill him.'

Ruth buried her face in her hands. 'None of this makes any sense. I can't 'elp thinking about Gus, though, if 'e's behind any of this.'

'And if she shows up 'ere, what will we do, Ma?'

Ruth bit her lip, her eyes falling into her lap where her fingers were knotted. She answered after a long pause. 'If Nellie were so bold as to turn up 'ere, me head tells me we would 'ave to inform Police Constable Rickett. Harbouring a criminal, family or not, could land us in deep water, and we can't risk losing everything we have built up 'ere in the last two years.'

'I suppose yer right, Ma,' Maria replied with a heavy heart. 'I wonder what she's really like, this Nellie, if she is as bad as they say.'

'That's what I'd like to find out. Me 'eart tells me she's the daughter of me dear friend and me brother and the least I could do is give 'er a chance to explain herself.'

Maria had never met Gus's daughter. She knew her mother had cut off ties with her brother two years ago after discovering how hard he worked Freddie and Archie on his rag-and-bone round when they were just boys. Nellie had never been there when Ruth had called in to see them, she believed her brother when he told her she was out working, so Ruth hadn't seen her niece since Nellie was a little girl either. Maria was a baby when Nellie's mother, Maggie, died. Ruth left Maria at home with a kindly neighbour when she made her visits to London to see Gus and Nellie following her friend's death.

'You've not spoken about Maggie before, Ma. She sounds like a lovely person. I'd like to 'ear about 'er.'

Ruth sighed and inhaled a deep breath. Maria listened agog as her mother told her how as a young man in his late teens Gus had impressed their family with his business head and bargaining prowess, saying he could turn a farthing into a shilling. He always had long queues at his market stall where he sold second-hand clothes and bits and pieces he picked up from house clearances.

Maria smiled. 'Gus was a real grafter back then. We were living near Audley End in Essex at the time and one

27

day Maggie called round and I noticed 'er cheeks blush when Gus entered the room. She asked if he had a girl, and I let on to Gus that Maggie was sweet on 'im.

'The next Saturday night a big May Day dance was being held in our village and he asked her to go with 'im. She looked so sweet with flowers in her curly fair hair. Gus was instantly smitten with Maggie's fresh face and innocent ways.'

Ruth paused and shook her head. 'You'd hardly believe I was talking about the same man. She were the making of 'im. He could 'ave a temper from time to time, but she reined in his fiery nature. He made Maggie laugh and she softened his rough edges. He was always keen to please her, he worshipped the ground she walked on and she hung on to his every word.

'They wed on her nineteenth birthday the following May Day, a halo of daisies crowning Maggie's fair hair. I could see from the way that Gus's face lit up as she walked down the aisle that he were very much in love. This was a new side to Gus, and it warmed me heart to see them happy.

'Gus had the idea of moving to London thinking the streets were paved with gold, so they started married life in the East End of London. He bought a horse and cart and went from door to door buying any old tat and selling it on. He did very well and built up a tidy little business.'

Maria asked, 'I never knew Gus with a soft side. What 'appened?'

'I went to see them a couple of months after they wed and was shocked to see the state of their lodgings. They lived in just one room in a house full of shifty characters reeking of stale alcohol, dirt and urine. They made eyes at Maggie and the filth that came from their mouths made it clear they thought she were a prostitute. I could see she feared for 'er safety, but she never spoke a bad word about Gus, saying they needed time to save up so they could move somewhere better. I gave Gus a clout around the ear that night and told him to find somewhere more suitable straightaway.

'A few weeks later a chance came for them to rent a dilapidated terraced house around the corner in Whitechapel. Maggie didn't like the idea as the area was tainted with the memory of that killer, Jack the Ripper, who murdered them poor women on the streets, but 'e told her not to be so daft, that the killer was long gone, and this was a golden opportunity for them to have their own house.

'It were little better than a slum and Maggie scrubbed it from top to bottom, wrapping a cloth tightly across her mouth and nose, as the smell was so foul, cleaning the walls and floors of animal faeces in one of the rooms where the stench made her stomach heave. She threw open all the windows to air the rooms, despite the chilly November air, and, thanks to Gus's rag 'n' bone trade, they had the pickings of furniture, curtains and bedding, though not the best ones, as Gus insisted they would have to be sold on. The small bricked backyard was just big enough for his hard-working old nag to be tied up where they could keep a good eye on it.'

Maria said softly, 'Maggie sounds like a nice lady. I wish I had known her.'

'She was the best,' Ruth agreed.

She continued her story, telling Maria how hard Gus worked then, trawling the streets from dawn to dusk, while Maggie took in washing to make ends meet. When Ruth visited the house Maggie could be found in the outhouse boiling water and scrubbing dirty linen on a washboard and she noticed how red and sore Maggie's hands were.

A year later, their daughter was born and Gus and Maggie felt their happiness was complete. They named her Nellie. Although money was tight, Gus started staying out late and drinking, complaining how Maggie was tired every night and showered all her affections on their daughter.

Ruth berated her brother for his jealousy and by the time Nellie celebrated her fourth birthday, Ruth could see that she would one day grow into a real beauty with her thick auburn hair, violet eyes and soft peachy complexion.

It was just after Nellie's fourth birthday that Ruth noticed her sister-in-law was increasingly tired, her face pale and etched with pain whenever she doubled up with stomach cramps. Gus had barely noticed, being so tied up with his own work and spending much of his free time supping ale. Maggie's frame had become stick thin and she ate very little. When she became too weak to stand and took to her bed, her daughter kissed her mother's face, willing her to wake up and play with her. Gus had to pull her off her fading mother, and within a couple of days, Maggie took her last breath. The cause of death was registered as dysentery.

Gus was overwhelmed with grief and guilt for his neglectful ways towards his wife. Ruth visited more frequently and offered to help care for the child, at least until her grieving brother had decided on his future plans. Nellie clung to her father, refusing to be parted from her only remaining parent. Gus's grief was all-consuming and his young daughter sat on the floor next to him, staring up at his sad face.

'Poor Nellie,' murmured Maria.

'It hit Gus 'ard. He rarely left the house and neglected his rounds. I stayed with him for a while, but he turned to ale to drown his sorrows. One night he returned from the Black Cat Inn in a drunken state and a foul mood and told me to clear out. He marched me out the house and told me I was never to cross his threshold again. He told me to leave them alone, to make their own way.'

Maria's eyes widened. 'That was a terrible thing for 'im to do for no reason. Was that the last time you saw Nellie?'

Ruth nodded, telling Maria that Gus had wrenched the crying child from her arms. A tear pricked the corner of Ruth's eyes as she described hearing Nellie's whimpering sounds behind the door, her cries becoming more pained, as she was frogmarched out of the house.

She sniffled, 'I left them to it as she asked, but I should have done more for the poor girl. I wrote to her every Christmas and birthday, but never 'eard back, so I stopped writing after a while, thinking Gus just tossed me letters on the fire.

'Mine and Gus's paths crossed again just over two years ago at a family funeral. I were surprised to see 'im there and I asked after Nellie. He told me she was picking up work where she could, but didn't go into details.

'When I was about to leave Gus came over. 'E apologised to me for his past behaviour. I could see 'e were a changed man and felt 'e was genuine. A short while later, Willie died and I became ill. That was when we came here to Wolferton, and I turned to Gus. I was desperate at the time and I asked 'im if Freddie and Archie could stay with 'im awhile, thinking Nellie were there to help. But he lied to me. I would never have left the boys if I had know Gus was going to work 'em so hard.'

'Oh, Ma, I'm sure you did yer best. You mustn't blame yerself, Uncle Gus is the one at fault.'

Maria felt Joey tugging at her skirt. She took him into her arms and squeezed him tight, stroking his hair and kissing the top of his head.

Ruth said, 'I think that's enough chatter for one night. I'll heat up some milk for Joey.'

She walked over to the window that looked out onto the side garden. 'Shouldn't Freddie be back from the station by now?'

Maria's fifteen-year-old brother, Freddie, had been taken under Harry's wing and was working at the station as a porter, doing odd jobs as required and helping out in any way he could.

Ruth straightened her back. 'Speak of the devil, here 'e is. 'E's stomping down the path at quite a pace and looks excited about something.'

Freddie flung open the kitchen door and blurted, 'You'll never believe what's happened.'

'What do yer mean? What are yer in a state about?' Ruth queried.

'There was a right old ding-dong at the station this afternoon. Uncle Harry chased after a woman with a private detective. It turns out she's on the run from the police. She came on the train from London and everyone's been told to look out for 'er.'

Chapter Four

Maria and Ruth had been shaken to their core after hearing Freddie confirm their worst fears.

They were still absorbing this turn of events when they were jolted by a knock on the door. Harry Saward stood on the doorstep. Maria invited him in, her brow wrinkled.

'Judging by the looks on your faces, I guess you've heard the news then, about this woman called Nellie Jeacock turning up in Wolferton. Does the name mean anything to you?'

Ruth nodded. She rubbed her hands together and cleared her throat. She poured out her suspicions to the station master about Nellie being her niece. 'I can scarcely believe what the paper says about 'er.'

Harry seated himself at the kitchen table. The house was as neat as a pin, a large table taking up most of the room in their kitchen where he was seated. The shelves of a dresser were filled with decorative plates, a few with the faces of cats which Harry recognised as coming from Magnolia and Aggie Greenstick's cottage.

As he sipped his tea, he commented, 'Somehow or other a connection has been made linking her with us. It didn't make sense to me as I had never heard of her. It came as a shock when this private detective informed me she was connected to the Sawards. What is she really like, this Nellie Jeacock?'

Ruth recounted to him the sorry story of Nellie's early life. He rubbed the back of his neck and shook his head.

'That's a very sorry tale. I suspect she has come here to see you, maybe to ask for refuge. You would be ill advised to take her in. You must immediately report her to the police if you see her.'

Ruth and Maria exchanged glances and nodded. They gave their word that they would do so. Harry continued, 'I don't suppose you've heard any news from Gus about how he is after the daylight air raid. That's where Gus lives, isn't it?'

Ruth pressed her lips together and shrugged her shoulders.

'Don't you care about him at all?' he pressed.

'It might seem shameful to admit, but no, I don't care in the slightest, and, no, 'e's not been in touch, an' is unlikely to.'

Joey squirmed, tugging at Maria's skirt demanding her attention. The station master bent down and ruffled his hair, before rising from the table.

Ruth asked after Harry's daughters. 'I saw Ada and Jessie the other day at the station. We went to King's Lynn one afternoon, and Leslie was playing up a bit. Who can blame him? 'E must miss his pa.'

Harry replied, 'Ada's been involved with the women's group that Queen Alexandra started and Jessie is spending more time at Lizzie's farm, you know how good she is at growing things. You'll see more than pansies and pinks in our garden now. A row of carrots and spuds can sit nicely along them, and a good thing too.'

'It sounds like your Jessie could teach us a thing or two, being born with green fingers. I imagine she's a blessing for the lady farmer.'

Harry smiled. 'Jessie has always enjoyed helping me in the garden. And Beatrice has surprised us all with how well she has taken to nursing after working in the post office with her mother.'

'She has, and she can't stay away from the place from what I've heard. She stops off sometimes on her way home from the hospital and is full of it. She is made of stern stuff hearing what she has to do for those poor soldiers.'

Harry commented with a wry smile, 'Who would have thought three years ago their lives would have changed this much.'

Maria piped in, 'And our lives too, though not just because of the war. I'll always be grateful for how yer took me in when I had nowhere else to go.'

'That's all in the past now. You've done us proud, you've done yourself proud,' Harry said. 'I'll be on my way then. But don't forget to heed my words. Nellie Jeacock is a wanted woman. You should inform Police Constable Rickett if she turns up here.'

Ruth nodded, but kept her lips sealed, distracted by Joey, who was bawling.

Maria had been about to settle him in bed when Harry arrived, and all the commotion had excited him.

After Harry had left, Maria heaved Joey onto her lap as she slumped on the wing chair in the corner. 'Tell me a story, Mama. I want a story about animals.'

Maria sighed, 'Very well, but it's going to have to be a quick one. Look at yer, yer can barely keep yer eyes open.'

Joey snuggled his flushed cheek against his mother's chest.

'Now shush and listen. How would yer like a story about a bear? A big brown bear who was so tall that his head would touch the ceiling.'

Joey's heavy-lidded eyes stared upwards. '*A real bear?*'

Maria ruffled Joey's thick mop of dark hair and smiled. 'It's a true story too. Can yer believe two grizzly bears once lived at the Big House?'

Joey's eyes widened. 'No! Can I see them?'

'They ain't there any more, but it's true. Cook told me after I asked 'er about the ornamental bear Queen Alexandra has in one of 'er glass cabinets.'

She paused to see the interest register on Joey's face and gave him an affectionate cuddle. Harry told her he was a bright boy as he soaked up everything he was told like a sponge.

'My, my, look at your plump rosy cheeks. I bet you've been eating double Grandma's apple pie, Joey Saward. No wonder yer are growing bigger by the day.'

Ruth murmured under her breath, 'Truth be told, he's been off his food this last day or so. But we can be sure he's going to be a strong lad, no doubt just like his . . .'

Maria's eyes darkened. 'Please, Ma, don't say it. I know what you're thinking. I see the likeness of that man in my Joey's face every day.'

Joey's eyes opened slightly and he murmured, 'Tell me about the bears, Mama.'

Maria's lips brushed against Joey's forehead, a choking feeling rising in her throat. She felt fiercely protective towards her lad and dreaded the day he faced taunts and cruel jibes from others for being a bastard. It seemed unfair that he should suffer this stigma when he was not to blame for the circumstances of his birth.

Ruth pressed her hand reassuringly on Maria's shoulder. Maria glanced up at her mother's eyes and acknowledged her silent apology.

'Well, Joey, did I hear yer ma mention bears? I want to listen. I've not 'eard this one before.'

Maria beckoned her mother to sit closer, brushing aside their disagreement. Joey raised his eyes to her face and was about to speak when Maria pressed a finger to her lips.

'It must be true as Cook told me, and she was 'ere when it happened. A few years back there used to be a bear pit at the Big House near where the kennels are now. In his younger days, the Prince, Edward, before he became King, would go off on his travels to far-off countries and had a fascination for the exotic. 'E saw these two brown bears on one of his trips and arranged for 'em to be transported to Sandringham to amuse his guests. They were called Charlie and Jenny.'

Ruth's eyebrow arched. 'Are you sure this isn't one of Cook's tall tales?'

Maria's expression was serious. 'She swore on 'er life and knows for sure as her pa was one of 'em that had to search for the bear, and she was a new kitchen maid. 'Er ma worked in the kitchens afore her too and told her all sorts of larks would go on as the Prince liked to play practical jokes on his guests, and his daughters too, the Princesses Louise, Victoria and Maud. One day one of the Prince's guests decided to get his own back, and released Charlie from the pit, thinking he would head towards the house, but he didn't. He ran around the parkland instead and seemed to be enjoying his freedom.'

'Oh my goodness,' exclaimed Ruth. 'He could have caused untold damage.'

'It certainly caused a great ding-dong. There were search parties out hunting high and low for Charlie, concerned 'e might stray too far or hurt someone. The Prince and Princess Alexandra were furious. Thankfully, Charlie was captured and no 'arm were done, except for some trampled flowerbeds. As yer can imagine, that guest was not invited back.'

Joey's eyes filled with fright. 'I'm glad he didn't eat any children. How did they find Charlie?'

'The gardeners spotted him in the parkland far from the house and spent the morning with sticks and nets rounding 'im up. One of 'em managed to get close enough to throw a net over his head and they brought 'im back on a cart where 'e was chained up in the pit.'

Ruth was alarmed by the tale. 'I'm glad the Big House is more orderly these days and doesn't have fierce animals there anymore. I wouldn't like to think of yer working there with wild bears in the grounds.'

'You mustn't take it to heart, Ma. Cook says the escape even made headlines in the papers at the time, asking what would have happened if the bear had stumbled across a healthy young Norfolk nursemaid in charge of a plump and inviting baby.'

Ruth shuddered. 'Oh, my goodness, just imagine that.'

'Well, Princess Alexandra, as she was then, was horrified by the jape and said it was fortunate nobody was killed. She insisted the bears had to go and they were given to London Zoo.'

'That's the best place for them. Your cook, she knows a lot. I'm surprised she has time to prepare any meals if she is jabbering away with you all day. Mind you, that is a good tale.'

'It makes the day go quicker to chat and I like hearing what it was like 'ere during days gone by.'

Joey pulled an impatient face. He tugged at a loose strand of his mother's hair. 'Tell me another story, Ma. Please!'

Maria stifled a yawn. 'I think it's way past yer bedtime, and you do look very sleepy. I need to turn in too if I am to be up at five thirty. Did I just hear the church bells ring nine times?'

Joey pleaded in a soft voice, forcing his eyes to remain open. 'Just a little story.'

'You look as if you are ready for bed, sleepyhead. But maybe just one more.'

'Is this another of Cook's stories? Are you giving in to him again? You spoil that boy.'

Maria's face broke into a smile. She enjoyed her bedtime stories with Joey, the one time of day she could enjoy his company.

'I don't suppose another couple of minutes will do us any harm.' She smiled.

Joey nestled against his mother's chest again and gave a contented sigh. Maria stifled another yawn and noticed Joey's eyes beginning to close against the warmth of her body. She spoke softly, spilling out some more yarns that Cook had heard from her father.

'The young princesses enjoyed playing hoaxes and horseplay too. They would stuff bullseyes and other sticky sweets in their Uncle Affie's event clothes, trap guests with buckets of water and pass around soap as cheese at the dinner table. It's nothing like that now.'

Ruth interjected, 'Uncle Affie? Who was 'e?'

Maria smiled. ''Is real name was Prince Alfred, 'e was the brother of Prince Edward, but they called 'im Affie. I like that name.'

A faint smile formed on Joey's lips. Maria glanced down at Joey whose eyes had shut firmly and his chest was rising with his deep breaths.

'I'd best carry 'im upstairs. I hope 'e's not going down with something. 'E's feeling a touch warm.'

41

She lifted Joey gently and when she reached his bed she removed his clothes. As she pulled his nightshirt over his head she saw a cluster of faint blotches on his skin, which was warm to the touch.

Her forehead creased as she kissed his, pulling the sheet over his tiny chest in his small bed in the corner of her room. By the time she had settled him, she heard the sound of his soft snores and she crept out of the room, hoping he would be better the next day.

∽

Nellie Jeacock's quick thinking and nimble footedness had enabled her to shake off her pursuers. She'd noticed the bowler-hatted man sitting opposite her on the train from London, his eyes peering over the top of his newspaper to observe her, then dipping them when she stared directly back at him. He sat wedged between an old maid, whose elbows spread out as she knitted socks for the troops, and an elderly man sporting side whiskers whose snoring turned into gurgling sounds when he cleared his throat.

She glanced at him and thought his face looked familiar, but couldn't put her finger on it. She buried her face in a magazine, but barely read a word, her heart pounding. When they approached King's Lynn the knitter packed up her needles and wool and reached for a basket in the rack above her seat. She moved a briefcase next to it and Nellie caught sight of a name that sent shivers coursing through her – 'G. Cheddars Esq.' – engraved in fine bold gold lettering. She realised it was *Gordon Cheddars*, the private detective who had halted her wedding and destroyed her dreams of happiness with the man she loved.

As the engine had drawn in at King's Lynn Station, she'd swiftly scooped up her bag and left the compartment, switching to another seat further along the corridor, leaving it to the last possible moment so the bowler-hatted man wouldn't have time to ease himself out of his seat, pick up his briefcase from the overhead rack and follow her. She swiftly settled in her new seat next to the window, a burly man next to her whose bulky torso she could hide behind if she pressed her back against the seat.

She chided herself for not being on her guard when she finally arrived at Wolferton Station. The destination signs at all stations were removed to confuse spies who might be lurking, but a fellow passenger sitting opposite, a pleasant mother with her young daughter, was getting off at the same station.

As Nellie alighted, her eyes scanned in all directions for the bowler-hatted man, desperate to give him the slip before he had a chance to spot her.

She'd heard the private detective call out that she was wanted by police and fled the station. She watched with great relief as Harry and the detective turned in the opposite direction.

Her plan was to ask for directions to Honeysuckle Cottage. She clutched an old letter from her aunt with her address that she had found at her father's house. It was Aunt Ruth she had come to see, determined to prove her innocence. Her arrival had already attracted unwanted attention and she wondered how she would find her aunt's house when she saw a figure she recognised a few feet away walking towards her. It was Freddie, who she had seen when he and his brother Archie had been staying with her father.

It was easy to trail Freddie from a discreet distance and she observed him lift the latch on the wooden gate at Honeysuckle Cottage and walk along the side path. A tear pricked her eyes when she saw Freddie burst in, he was a good hard-working boy. She tiptoed to the side of the house and through the kitchen window she could see him chatting animatedly to his mother. She remembered the kindness her aunt had showed towards her when she was a young child, and had only recently discovered the full extent of this.

She bit her lip as she pictured them sitting around the table later to eat together as a close-knit family, exchanging stories about their days, laughing together. These were things that had been missing from her life.

She brushed away a tear as it slid down her cheek. She needed to find a hiding place nearby while she thought through her next step. She wandered around the lanes, her eyes soaking in the views of the glorious countryside, stretching to the distant fields that met the blue sky on the horizon, with the sun beginning to dip low. The grassy edges of the lanes were lined with buttercups bursting with bright yellow petals, delicate white daisies and cob-web-patterned cowslips, while birds fluttered overhead. It was a different world to the dingy one she had grown up in, the sounds and foul smells making her choke. Pigeons were cooing on the church roof when she stepped through the pretty lychgate at St Peter's Church as she made her way along the stony path.

She walked into the porch and gazed up at the elaborate hexagonal cast iron lantern with coloured stained glass sides hanging overhead. She tried the church door and it was locked. Staring at the stone seat in the porch, she sat down to reflect.

After a while she decided, *There's no point in putting it off any longer. I must see Aunt Ruth now. I'll throw myself at her mercy.*

When she approached the cottage she saw a dim light on in the front parlour and could make out the silhouette of a male figure pacing backwards and forwards. She held her breath as she tiptoed towards the front window, crouching low so she could not be seen.

Inch by inch, she raised her head until she could see inside the room. She ducked back down as she recognised the station master from earlier. She looked in again and her heart skipped a beat when she saw her aunt showing him a page in the newspaper. Freddie was there too, and another young woman and a toddler. She wondered if this was Maria, Freddie and Archie's sister they had mentioned to her, though she had no idea who the small boy was.

Harry moved towards the window holding up the paper in front of his face, clearly showing her photo and the story of her alleged crimes.

Her heart pounded as she spun around, knocking over some terracotta flowerpots by the front door as she clumsily hastened away. She disappeared out of sight just as the front door opened and Harry left.

Stumbling down the lane, she cried, 'How can I prove my innocence? Will anyone believe me?'

Chapter Five

Beatrice buried her face in her hands, gulping back the sobs that welled up within her.

'It never gets easier, but you couldn't have done more, Nurse Saward.'

Beatrice dabbed her eyes with the handkerchief Matron handed her. 'He was only twenty-one, and I really thought he would pull through.'

It was the first time Beatrice had been called upon to assist Dr Butterscotch on a major operation. He was Matron's father and one of the country's most distinguished war surgeons at King's Hospital, London. Frances Butterscotch had persuaded her father to attend to her patients once a fortnight and operate on their most serious cases.

The second of Harry Saward's three daughters, aged twenty-six, and the most confident and strong willed, Beatrice was uncommonly lost for words when Matron had suggested she should assist her father on his next visit. As a volunteer nurse, she was not expected to take on such an important role, but two of the trained nurses had been taken poorly that day and Beatrice was asked to step into their shoes.

Beatrice had taken to nursing like a duck to water and fitted in well at Hillington Hall, a large medieval country house set in parkland, which was being used as a military hospital during the war, and a convenient twenty-minute cycle ride from Wolferton. She had volunteered as a VAD nurse to serve wounded and sick soldiers. The Voluntary Aid Detachment was run by the Red Cross and Order of St John and they were desperate for volunteers in both their emergency medical facilities at home and in field hospitals overseas.

Beatrice wore her nurse's uniform with pride, cocking her head in the mirror to check she had correctly adjusted her stiff white nurse's cap, ensuring her hair was tucked away neatly. She always smoothed down the folds of her long starched white apron, with its distinctive red cross on her chest, which she wore over a grey cotton dress with its detachable white collar and cuffs. Each day, she was moved by the dedication of doctors who did their best to save limbs shattered by shrapnel and bullets.

'You are more than capable, my dear. I know I can count on you,' Matron had reassured her.

Beatrice had the darkest features out of the three Saward sisters, inheriting her mother's hair and eyes. She had no regrets giving up her work at the post office, which her mother ran with brisk efficiency. The loss of a patient always deeply saddened her, but they were surprisingly few as the wounded were given the best medical attention and had been brought to Hillington Hall for rehabilitation.

The station master's daughter brushed off her nerves, knowing she should seize the opportunity to show off her skills. She did her best to hide her lack of confidence and remain composed as she stood alongside the eminent surgeon. She could see Matron had inherited her father's flame-coloured hair and square jaw.

Beatrice was pleased at being singled out by Matron, a tall, striking woman in her forties with arched eyebrows, who didn't miss a thing. Beatrice had heard the other nurses gossiping about her saying she had no interest in men, that she was married to her job after the man she had once been engaged to died from tuberculosis shortly before they were due to wed. Matron remained at the hospital all hours, long after her shift had finished.

Beatrice was preparing the surgical equipment, taking the greatest care to thoroughly sterilise it, wondering what the operation would be and who the patient was. Dr Butterscotch and Matron were deep in discussion, reading patients' notes while walking from bed to bed.

'I hope you have a steady hand, Nurse Saward,' the doctor told her solemnly, peering over his spectacles. 'My daughter has recommended you as the most suitable VAD while I perform a delicate brain operation on Private Peabody, and I am relying on you to assist me well with a steady hand.'

'Of course. I want to do whatever I can to help.'

Beatrice had attended to Private Peabody when he arrived at the hospital a week ago. His head was swathed in bandages, only his eyes visible. At first he was thought dead, after being shot in the head on the front line in France, but he was carried by stretcher bearers to the camp's hospital where doctors had patched him up, saying it was all they could do for him, recommending urgent specialist medical treatment in England. Beatrice had seen the fearful expression in his moist eyes, and wondered if that was how her Sam had felt too, far away from home, when he stared death in the face.

She hoped Dr Butterscotch's celebrated surgical skills would succeed in removing the shrapnel embedded in Private Peabody's brain. Beatrice steadied her shaky hands as a hole was made into the young soldier's brain, her heart pounding so loud she thought the doctor would hear it.

Dr Butterscotch instructed Beatrice where to shine the torch into the cavity and at first she flinched when he suggested she look inside. But not wanting to appear squeamish, she leant forward and quickly pulled away having viewed the brain pulsating. Dr Butterscotch nodded in her direction, then bent over the patient and probed into the skull. Beatrice held her breath and gripped the torch tightly. She froze as the surgeon triumphantly removed three pieces of shrapnel and proceeded to quickly stitch the opening in the soldier's head.

'Will he be all right?' Beatrice enquired tentatively, her stomach in knots after the operation was over.

'It was more challenging than I thought and some brain fungus is evident. I'm afraid I can't be certain, but if the chap pulls through the next twenty-four hours then there is a good chance he will be OK. Poor fellow.'

Beatrice's voice wobbled. 'At least he now stands a better chance of surviving, thanks to everything you have done.'

'We'll know soon enough. I expect you are all done in now. That was a pretty gruesome first operation for you to assist at, and you did remarkably well for a VAD, Nurse Saward.'

'That's very kind of you to say, Doctor. But it's very little compared to what our boys go through.'

Beatrice completed the rest of her shift, ensuring her patients were as comfortable as possible, her mind constantly on the condition of young Private Peabody. At the end of her shift she sought out Matron and asked if she could stay on and sit by the young Tommy's bed throughout the night.

'I feel attached to him, in the most professional sense, of course. I'm of the mind that if he roused and saw a familiar face, a friendly face, it would comfort him.'

Matron frowned. 'You look exhausted, Nurse Saward, and our best nurses must not form these attachments. You won't be any use to me tomorrow if you are not refreshed. Please do not fret over our young private, our night nurse will keep a good eye on him.'

Beatrice protested, 'But you're always here, Matron. I really don't mind staying on, in a voluntary capacity.'

Matron would have none of it and Beatrice reluctantly assented. She stopped by Private Peabody's bed before leaving. She sat in a chair next to his bed and gently stroked his arm, whispering encouraging words urging him to pull through, even though his eyes were closed, hoping it would somehow get through to him.

At home that night she thought of nothing else. She barely listened as Jessie spoke to her about her day at Blackbird Farm digging up potatoes and onions, or Ada fretting at waiting for news from her husband Alfie, who was away fighting the war.

She couldn't wait to return to the hospital and the next morning she rushed to his ward. Her eyes searched the room for Private Peabody, but she saw only an empty bed.

Matron approached and placed an arm on Beatrice's shoulder. Taking her aside, she told her, 'I'm sorry, Nurse Saward, but I have some bad news. Private Peabody didn't make it. His heart wasn't strong enough. We are deeply saddened at his passing, but you must take comfort from knowing we did everything we could, and he is now at peace.'

Beatrice's eyes moistened. Matron seemed to take it in her stride, but every death on her ward knocked Beatrice sideways. Despite Matron's reassurances, she questioned if there was more she could have done.

'But ... I thought ... oh why? Did I do something wrong? Why did he have to die? He was so young,' cried Beatrice.

Matron spoke crisply. 'Private Peabody's death was most unfortunate, Nurse Saward, and you must not blame yourself in any way. From what I hear you carried out your role in the most exemplary fashion, but we have to carry on.'

Matron's eyes met Beatrice's as she dabbed at a stray tear and inhaled a deep breath. 'Of course, Matron. I do apologise.'

'You couldn't have done more. We have new patients arriving today and I need you to be on best form. Can I rely on you?'

Beatrice forced herself to smile as she continued with her duties. She had set her heart on nursing following the death of her sweetheart, Sam Peters, in Gallipoli, on Turkish scorched soil in August 1915. She could still see his cheery face in her mind's eye as she waved him off from Wolferton Station, watching him proudly wearing his khaki uniform and marching alongside his comrades with the Sandringham Company of the 5th Battalion in the Norfolk Regiment. He was the apple of his mother's eye and had taken over as head of the house, working as a stable lad on the royal stud and becoming the family's main breadwinner, after his father had died suddenly in an accident at work.

When news reached her that Sam had been killed, Beatrice put her own grief aside to console Sam's heart-broken mother Edith, whose nerves became increasingly frayed, his sister Florence, fifteen, and twins Roly and Ben, thirteen.

If she could have helped save Private Peabody she felt as if it would have, in some way, made up for the loss of Sam, and others like him, all good men whose lives had been horribly ended in the most brutal fashion.

Now another grieving mother would endure the most painful heartache for the rest of her days. Private Peabody's death sharpened her resolve to continue doing whatever she could to save the lives of people's sons, fathers and sweethearts.

'I want to save as many heartaches as I can, the heartaches of those left behind who grieve for the rest of their lives. After all, a broken heart can never be stitched up,' Beatrice asserted.

Her main concern when taking on her new role was one shared by many new nurses – overcoming her nerves at seeing a naked man for the first time when giving a bed bath. Some frowned that an unmarried woman should see a naked man, but she quickly realised she had to get on with the job, and it was a task that needed to be done repeatedly.

Matron placed a comforting arm on Beatrice's shoulder. 'How would you like to assist in the needlework class today?'

Beatrice smiled. 'Yes, I would like that. Thank you, Matron.'

They made their way to the day room. Beatrice never failed to be moved by the staunch resilience and humility of some of these men who had lost limbs. The silent heroes, she called them. Some of those who had lost arms were now learning embroidery as part of their rehabilitation. She felt humbled to see their faces shine with pride after completing an intricate piece of sewing, the circular wooden frame positioned rigidly on a stand so the disabled soldier could lean over it and stitch carefully on the canvas with their one hand. Word soon spread about the high standard of craftsmanship that these disabled servicemen accomplished and Matron quickly became a staunch advocate of the Disabled Soldiers' Embroidery Industry.

'Here, let me help you,' Beatrice offered Private Bertie Bowers as she watched him grapple with the needle and thread.

'I'll never learn if you 'elp me, but thank you all the same,' the young private replied earnestly, his mind focused on the challenging task.

Matron whispered in her ear. 'It's marvellous, isn't it? Private Bowers' confidence has increased immensely since taking up needlework.'

'It is,' Beatrice agreed, watching him concentrating hard on his sewing using only his left arm, his pinned up pyjama sleeve where his right arm had been.

He looked up from his work and said cheekily, 'I don't mind a pretty nurse sitting alongside me though. You are the prettiest one here. Has anyone told you what lovely eyes you have?

Beatrice drew in a sharp breath at the private's self-effacing humour. Her cheeks flushed at his compliment.

Matron tutted. 'Enough of that kind of talk Private Bowers. We are here to do our duty, not to be ornaments for you to ogle at.'

Private Bowers winked at Beatrice.

'I'm sure he meant no offence,' Beatrice murmured.

'That may as well be, but I would prefer it if our patients concentrated on their needlework. It is doing wonders for rehabilitation. I am so grateful Father suggested we introduce embroidery here. He really believes it helps improve injured men's morale and will help put some money in their pockets too when they are back in the outside world. God knows they are going to need every chance to earn a living when they leave. I heard that some men are so skilled that a commission has been secured for them to sew an altar frontal for the royal family's private use in Buckingham Palace. What better patronage could one ask for?'

∞

Beatrice stepped softly through the former dining room, now converted to be one of the wards, to assist with the arrival of new patients. An ambulance train carrying one hundred sick and wounded men had arrived at King's Lynn railway station and patients were dispatched to hospitals closest to their homes whenever possible. Stretcher bearers carried the wounded, many swathed in bandages. Others were carried in cots or on chairs, and those who were able to walk did so, some with the aid of crutches, some without.

A cheering crowd would gather at the station on these occasions, giving the soldiers a heroes' welcome and dishing out sweets and cigarettes. It was a touching scene that

Beatrice had witnessed once when asked to assist with arrivals at the station when they were short of orderlies.

Beatrice's ears suddenly pricked up. 'Give bed twenty-seven to Eddie Herring.'

Eddie Herring? Could it be the same Eddie Herring who was a porter at the royal station? Maria's Eddie? She stopped dead in her tracks, looking straight ahead at the bed where Nurse Jennings was fluffing a pillow.

She was cheerily chatting to the new arrival. 'Welcome to Hillington Hall, Private Eddie Herring. I hope you're not going to give us any trouble, like some of the others.'

The patient spoke dully. 'Huh. Some chance. I only wish I could.'

Nurse Jennings tried to raise his spirits. 'Enough of that, you saucy so-and-so. I bet you have a sweetheart, and what will she say if she hears you talking to me like that?'

On hearing Eddie's name, Beatrice strode over to the bed. Her jaw dropped, a smile curling on her lips. 'Eddie Herring. It's you! I can scarcely believe my eyes. Wait till Maria hears you are home. She'll be so thrilled!'

Chapter Six

Eddie stared at Beatrice, his eyes incredulous. 'Beatrice? It's so good to see you. Maria told me you was a nurse now. How is Maria?'

'She's doing very well for herself. I'll stop off and see her on the way home to tell her you are here. Why are you here though? Ah, I see, it's your leg.'

Eddie screwed his face tight and winced. 'Some bastard in Gaza shot me in the thigh, but he came off worse. I wrote to Maria about it, but my leg has worsened since then.'

'I'm sorry to hear that, Eddie. We have the best doctors here. Try not to worry. They'll sort you out in no time.'

Eddie winced again, his face contorting in pain. He arched his back and tossed his head. 'Ouch, ooh. A bone is shattered and was operated on in a field hospital, but it may need more doing to it. Oh, Beatrice, it's going to be all right, isn't it? I'm not going to lose me leg, am I?'

'Shush, Eddie. Not if I can help it. Our doctors really are excellent. We even have a surgeon who comes from a top London hospital to oversee the most complex cases. Everyone will do their very best for you.'

Eddie's eyes moistened. 'I'm sorry, I didn't mean to sound like a sissy. Only, well, I want to marry Maria one day and be a father to Joey and she won't want to wed a cripple.'

'Don't even think such things. You know Maria thinks the world of you. She is doing well for herself and working at the Big House as a parlour maid. In fact, I was told she now helps in Queen Alexandra's private rooms. She will be so pleased to know you are here and will want to visit you as soon as she can.'

'I hope so, and I'm so pleased for her. It's no more than she deserves. There's nothing my Maria can't do if she puts her mind to it. I only hope I'll be good enough for her, and that she won't pity me if I'm a lame dog.'

'Don't be so daft, Eddie Herring. Maria was really worried when she heard you had been injured.'

Eddie's face brightened. 'Really, Beatrice? I know she cares for me, deep down. I'm all at sixes and sevens since being shot.'

Beatrice leant over and whispered, 'Now listen to me, Eddie, you'd better call me Nurse Saward here if people are within earshot, and I must call you Private Herring. Just think about getting better. And try to keep your spirits up. We'll do all we can for you here.'

Eddie grinned. 'Very well, I'll try my best. Nurse Saward, may I ask a favour of yer?'

'Of course. What is it?' Beatrice grinned.

Eddie stuttered. 'It's about Maria. If yer have a chance, will you ask her to visit me as soon as she can?'

Before Beatrice could reply Matron bustled over and paused at Eddie's bed, her eyebrows knitted together and her arms folded across her chest. 'Nurse Saward, could you please attend to your patients and leave Private Herring in the capable hands of Nurse Jennings. His condition does not require the attention of two nurses. It's important he rests and does not become overanxious.'

Beatrice demurred, speaking softly to Nurse Jennings when she returned. 'Jemima, please take good care of this patient. He is very special to me and my family.'

'Thank you, Beatrice . . . I mean, Nurse Saward. I hope I haven't got yer into trouble,' Eddie uttered. 'If you have a chance to call in on Maria, do ask her to come and see me as soon as she can. I can't wait to see her.'

'Of course I will. And I will call in on your mother too. Now you must do as Matron says, and rest.'

Nurse Jennings smiled sweetly at her patient. She had blonde curly hair and blue eyes and, like Beatrice, was very popular with patients due to her friendly manner. She leant over Eddie's bed and smoothed his ruffled sheet.

'I'll look after Private Herring as if he were the King of England. Now let's make you nice and comfy again. You need to rest, Private Herring, else Matron will be after me, and you wouldn't want to get me into trouble, would you now?'

Matron turned. 'Did I hear someone mention my name? I hope you are not taking my name in vain with idle chatter.'

Eddie and Nurse Jennings shared a conspiratorial giggle. 'We have a cheeky one here, Matron,' the nurse replied with a serious expression. 'But don't worry, I think he'll behave himself, especially as he wants his sweetheart to visit, and he needs to be in good shape for that.'

Matron fixed Eddie with one of her stern looks. 'Well, we had better make sure he is on top form, and I hope he will not distract my staff while he is here. I'll be back to see you later, Private Herring.'

'Yes, ma'am ... I mean Matron,' Eddie replied, saluting her from his bed and pulling a face. Matron clucked and turned, shaking her head. She concealed the upward curl of her lips from both nurses and patients to retain her air of authority.

When Beatrice had finished changing a dressing on another patient's arm she glanced back in Eddie's direction. He was tossing from side to side, unable to settle. Nurse Jennings had stepped out of the ward, so Beatrice walked over to him.

Sitting by his bed she lightly stroked his brow and made soothing sounds to calm him, watching closely as his heavy breathing eased and his eyes closed, drifting into a deep sleep. She recalled Eddie's kindness towards the young lad Robbie Bucket, how Eddie and his mother had taken the thirteen-year-old boy into their home after he was sentenced to a birching for his involvement in the theft of food parcels intended for soldiers overseas. The whole of Wolferton turned against Robbie and his bullying father, who had forced his son to steal. Without the love and affection of a real family, Robbie would have ended up in the workhouse.

Eddie's kindness touched Maria's heart too and he worshipped the ground she walked on. Beatrice couldn't wait to see Maria's reaction when she broke the news to her of Eddie's arrival.

Later, as she was preparing to finish her shift, she glanced towards the end of the ward and became aware of Matron standing in the doorway looking in her direction. She was talking to a well-dressed gentleman and pointing at her.

Beatrice stared at the male figure coming towards her. In his early thirties, he was dressed smartly in a dark suit, white shirt and tie. His movements were laboured, short and shuffling, and he leant on a silver-topped stick for support. She recognised his gait as he walked towards her. Her pulse quickened.

'Mr Perryman. What an unexpected surprise. What brings you here?' Beatrice was surprised to feel a slight fluttering inside as she extended her hand.

Before the man could reply some of the patients made whistling sounds.

'Shush. Don't be so silly. Mr Perryman is just a friend,' she told them, her cheeks flushed.

'Throw us a ciggie!' one of the patients called out.

'And over here. Me too, if you can spare one for a Tommy who's done his duty. I didn't get given any at the station.'

The ward suddenly burst into chaos with outstretched hands demanding cigarettes.

Mr Perryman threw his hands in the air. 'I'm sorry, lads, I don't smoke myself. But I promise next time I come I'll bring a few packets for you.'

Beatrice caught his smiling face. 'Shall we find somewhere quiet for a moment, before Matron accuses us of causing a riot?'

Mr Perryman laughed and followed her out into the entrance hall, stopping by the foot of the beautiful curved marble staircase. She couldn't help noticing that his limp, caused by polio as a child, had worsened since she had last seen him two years ago, when he had been the solicitor representing Robbie Bucket.

The solicitor beamed. 'Oh, Miss Saward, I can't tell you what a pleasure it is to see you again.' His expression was one of pure delight. 'I was called here by Matron to perform a sad duty. Captain Willoughby is not expected to last the night and he wanted a new will drawn up. I was happy to oblige, and while I was here another two patients asked me to do the same for them. I was just saying farewell to Matron when I turned and saw you. I had no idea you worked here.'

'Oh yes, I've been here over a year now.'

Beatrice's cheeks turned a pretty pink, her eyes shining. She had brushed aside the fluttering sensation inside her that she experienced when she first encountered George acting as duty solicitor and speaking up in court for Robbie. She had been pledged to Sam at the time, who had been posted overseas, and even though she was unsure of her true feelings towards him, she knew she had to stand by him.

She discovered later that Mr Perryman had paid Robbie's doctor's fees to treat the searing wounds from his birching, and it had touched her heart to learn that he could be so caring towards a boy who was a victim of his father's bullying.

George Perryman may never be a hero on the battle-fields. His limp made him medically unfit, but the way he could speak up for those who had no voice of their own made him a hero in her eyes.

George fixed his gaze on Beatrice's face. 'I hope you don't think it forward of me to speak truthfully, but I have wondered about you frequently since we met that day in court.'

Beatrice gulped, twisting her hands in front of her, her throat clenching tight. She lowered her eyes. 'It's not been easy for me, these last two years, losing Sam . . .'

'I heard about his death, and I know how dreadful it has been for Mrs Peters. I'm so very sorry for your loss. If there is any way I can assist the family with my legal expertise, please don't hesitate to ask.'

Beatrice nodded. She stood awkwardly.

George smiled, his whole face lighting up. 'So you are a nurse now? No longer assisting your mother in the post office?'

'That's correct, Mr Perryman. I feel I have found my vocation and it is very rewarding. I wanted to do something more to help with the war.'

'I do so admire your resolve and dedication here, and your desire to help those in the greatest need, Miss Saward.'

Beatrice felt her cheeks flush again. 'Oh, please, call me Beatrice.'

'And you must call me George. I feel so pleased that our paths have crossed. And hope they will do so again very soon.'

Beatrice hesitated. 'I'm sure they will. Only, I'm afraid my nursing duties leave me with very little free time.'

He persisted gently. 'Maybe if you have a half-day off we could meet one afternoon for a stroll. I do so enjoy your company, and I think you do mine.'

Beatrice turned her head away and bit her lip. His invitation had taken her totally by surprise and she felt conflicted. Would Sam's family feel betrayed if she agreed to spend time with George? Was she ready for a new romance, with her nursing duties now a priority in her new life?

Her mind was made up. She wanted to keep her life simple and uncomplicated for now.

Beatrice tried to put him off tactfully. 'I'm grateful for your attention, George, perhaps another time?'

The hurt showed on his face. 'Very well. I won't detain you any further. Good day, Miss Saward.'

The formal use of her name cut through her. She watched as the solicitor shuffled out of the front door, leaning on his silver-topped stick, and almost had a change of heart.

She was shaken to hear a voice behind her. 'You are a fool, Beatrice. Anyone can see he's madly in love with you.'

'Oh, Jemima, I didn't see you there. Don't be so daft. Of course he isn't in love with me. You must be mad to think such a thing.'

Jemima gripped Beatrice's arms and stared straight into her face. 'Oh, come on. Surely you don't want to be an old maid like Matron? You have to live and love for today and grab what happiness you can. None of us know what the next day will bring. Why, a bomb could drop on us anytime here again in Wolferton and blow us all to smithereens. Remember the bombs dropping at Dersingham on the edge of the Sandringham Estate the last two years? Poor Violet Dungar died in the last attack, and she was only thirty-six.'

Beatrice, her eyes moist, spoke falteringly, 'That's what I worry about. Loving someone and losing them again, after Sam. We see it happen every day. Isn't it better to not love at all?'

'No, you silly thing, it most certainly isn't. You should count yourself lucky to have a second chance and should love while you can. I'm sure Sam would have wanted that.'

Chapter Seven

Beatrice looked in on Eddie again, but he appeared restless and Nurse Jennings was attending to him. His condition was concerning, and she knew it could go either way. She hoped a visit from Maria would help put him at ease.

She pulled up on her bicycle at Ruth and Maria's house on her way home from work that evening, anxious to deliver Eddie's message.

Maria answered the door and invited her in. Beatrice blurted out almost immediately, 'Maria, have you heard? Eddie's home. He's at the hospital. I saw him today and he asked after you.'

Maria's face shone. She clasped her hands in front of her chest. 'E's home! That's wonderful news. But why is 'e in hospital? What's happened to 'im?'

Beatrice paused. 'It's still early days, and we can't say for sure. His leg is badly injured. His mood is low, which is perfectly natural. Those poor men, the way they have suffered. If you could visit him, it would cheer him up no end.'

'Of course I'll go. Does his ma know 'e's home? If not, I must let her know. I'd go now, only Joey is under the weather and I need to stay with him.'

'Oh? What's wrong with him? Would you like me to see Joey?' asked Beatrice.

Maria shook her head. ''E's in bed now, I'm hoping 'e will sleep it off, but thank yer for offering.'

That day's newspaper was on the table, spread open on the page showing Nellie's face. It was in Beatrice's clear view, but Maria remained silent, not wanting to burden Beatrice with their woes.

After Beatrice had informed Maria about visiting hours on Sunday afternoons, they walked down the path together. 'Eddie will be thrilled to know you will visit. I'll let you know if there are any changes.'

'Tell Eddie I'll be there as soon as I can. I can't imagine what he's been through, and I ain't ever going leave him on account of a bad leg. Tell him I love him, whatever happens to him. He is the truest, most kindest man I know.'

∽

Maria slept fitfully that night, her mind spinning with thoughts of Eddie. She couldn't wait to see him and in her dreams she saw his face looking pained. She awoke with a start. The morning sky had a thin pale blue gossamer glow and a golden globe rising on the horizon showed the promise of another warm summer's day.

She gently slid out of the large bed so as not to disturb her mother and glanced at Joey, who had his eyes closed, his chest rising and falling. She walked to the jug of water on the marble-topped stand and poured some into the matching bowl, decorated with pink rosebuds. She shivered as the cold water splashed against her smooth skin, tingling and refreshing, forgoing the warm water she usually fetched from downstairs to save time. She slipped into her camisole and black stockings and pulled the black dress down over her head, smoothing the folds in front of her.

She glanced again at Joey. He was still lying on his back, his lips slightly parted. Her concerns from the previous night weighed heavily on her mind. She bent over and noticed a pink colouring to his cheeks.

'Ma, come quickly and you look at Joey? His cheeks have an unusual flush to 'em. It don't look natural to me.'

Ruth rubbed her eyes and roused instantly. Maria's face was strained with worry.

'Now yer mention it 'e woke up in the night and complained his throat was hurting, but I didn't want to wake yer,' her mother told her. 'I thought 'e might sleep it off.'

Maria knelt at Joey's side, tears stinging the back of her eyes. Her voice wobbled. ''E's going to be all right, ain't 'e?'

Ruth placed the back of her hand against Joey's forehead. His skin had a rosy glow to it and was hot.

'Is everything all right?' asked Freddie, stumbling in bleary eyed.

'I don't know.' Ruth asked him to bring up a fresh bowl of cold water and a flannel with great haste.

'We need to sponge 'im down to reduce the heat in his body,' she advised, her eyes showing concern.

'Oh, Ma. I can't leave Joey like this. I'm expected at the Big House soon, but it don't seem right to leave. I'll be fretting about 'im all day.'

'It's most likely just a childhood ailment. Try not to worry. Joey is a strong lad and a fighter. I'm sure 'e'll be fine very soon. You go off and I'll take care of him.'

Maria pondered. 'I hope yer right and this is nothing worse.'

Maria had her own fears for her mother's well-being and didn't want to burden her with a sick child. Ruth brushed aside concerns about her own health. She suffered from a wheezy chest brought on by heightened emotions that could make her gasp for breath, her lips sometimes turning blue. Maria noticed how weary Ruth looked these days, much older than her forty-eight years, and felt it wouldn't be fair to pile an extra burden on her.

Freddie appeared with the cold water and flannel. 'I can at least do this before I leave,' Maria said, gently sponging her son's warm face. She undid the buttons on his nightshirt and winced as she gazed at her little Joey's tiny body. It was bathed in sweat and covered with an unusual redness. Joey groaned and turned his head towards his mother, half opening his heavy eyelids.

Ruth paced the bedroom floor, her hands clasped together in front of her. Her face paled. 'What is it, Ma? Why do you look like that? Is there something you're not telling me?'

'I don't want to alarm you, but I can't hold back now, seeing his little body red and blotchy. I fear he's burning a fever.'

'But you said a moment ago there was nothing to worry about!'

'I think differently now. We need to send for the doctor, without delay.'

The urgent tone of Ruth's voice shook Maria. 'Oh, Ma. Please tell me 'e'll be all right.'

Freddie offered, 'I'll go for the doctor. I'll go now, as quick as lightning.'

Maria quaked, 'Thank you, Freddie. Please ask 'im to come as quickly as 'e can. Tell 'im Joey's skin is getting hotter.'

Freddie fled from the room, pulling on his trousers and shirt as he went.

Maria's hand flew to her mouth. 'I've made up me mind. I'm definitely not leaving Joey like this. I need to inform the Big House that I can't go in today. I don't care what Mrs Pennywick says. My place is 'ere with Joey.'

'You're right, Maria. Perhaps Archie can drop a note off for Mrs Pennywick and explain the urgent circumstances,' Ruth suggested.

Maria rubbed her watery eyes and stared tenderly at her ailing son. 'Oh Ma, what if . . . what if Joey doesn't pull through?'

'Stop talking like that, right away,' Ruth snapped.

Archie stood at the doorway. 'Freddie's just told me what's happened. Of course, I'll let Mrs Pennywick know. I'll do anything to help.'

Maria was thankful her brothers were on hand when she needed them. Freddie, though in his mid-teens, was a tall strapping lad with handsome dark features. He enjoyed being the man of the house and wanted to take

71

care of them. Harry frequently complimented the way he was shaping out. He praised Freddie's courteous manner, desire to learn, and how well he got on with everyone, passengers and staff alike.

Archie, at fourteen, was one year younger than Freddie, fair haired and freckled, and the quieter of the two brothers. He had a reserved nature and was happy with his own company. He found it hard to talk about the suffering he'd endured under Uncle Gus's care, keeping the memory of those dark days bottled up inside him. He enjoyed spending time with Lizzie Piper, the woman farmer at Blackbird Farm, a friend of Jessie's.

Maria hastily scribbled a note for Archie and instructed him which door to go to at the back of the Big House. After he had left, Ruth urged Maria to eat some porridge before the doctor came.

'I couldn't eat a thing,' Maria retorted, her expression anxious. 'But I do have a thirst. I'll make some tea and bring up some fresh water to sponge Joey while you sit with 'im.'

She went downstairs and poured water into the kettle and paced the room while she waited for it to boil, glancing out of the window for sign of the doctor's arrival. She quickly poured drinks for herself and her mother and took them upstairs. Tears pricked the corner of her eyes as she gazed down on Joey's reddening cheeks.

'I can't bear the wait. I'll stand outside by the gate and look out for the doctor,' Maria told her mother.

Maria stepped out of the front door and inhaled a deep breath of fresh air, perfumed from the honeysuckle that clung to the front wall and the sweet peas. She glanced down at the terracotta plant pots on either side of the front door that Jessie had given her filled with tender geranium cuttings that she had nurtured with Joey. She stooped down and picked up some broken fragments; three of the six pots were smashed, the sharp jagged edges of pottery scattered on the path with piles of soil and the twisted remnants of the baby geranium shoots.

She examined them closely to see if they could be replanted, but the roots were too badly damaged and it was clear they were beyond saving. Believing a stray cat was to blame, she cursed it under her breath. A white jagged edge peeked out from under some of the disturbed soil. It was from a Great Eastern Railway ticket showing it had been purchased for travel from St Pancras Station to Wolferton.

Maria stood up, her eyebrows furrowed. She stared at the ticket. *How did this end up here with the broken flowerpots? Who could have left it?*

Then it dawned on her. A shiver ran down her spine.

It must be Nellie. She's been here!

She was so deep in her own thoughts that she didn't hear her name being called. The man's deep voice repeated, louder this time. 'Where is Joey, Maria? Take me to him straightaway.'

She jumped back as the doctor spoke, his shining Daimler parked outside. Besides the King, the doctor was the other person in Wolferton to own this sleek model. It was greeted half in awe and half with suspicion by village folk who felt it wasn't a natural and safe way to travel, preferring to get about by foot, bicycle or horse and cart.

'I came as quickly as I could. Take me to your boy.'

'Oh, Doctor, I am so pleased to see yer,' Maria gulped, shoving the ticket in her skirt pocket. He followed her briskly into the house.

Dr Fletcher was well liked in Wolferton and had served patients for the last thirty years, following in his father's footsteps. He was kindly, turning a blind eye if patients couldn't afford his fees. He accepted payment by way of fresh bakes or vegetables, a chicken or two and even embroidered cushions. He had a tall and imposing presence and his dark moustache was greying, matching his thinning hair and sideburns.

Ruth called out from the top of the stairs, her voice tinged with anxiety. 'Doctor, please come up. Joey's just been sick. 'E's shivering, 'e's taken a turn for the worse.'

The doctor dashed up the stairs two at a time. Joey's cheeks were a deeper crimson. He lifted Joey's nightshirt and drew in a deep breath, his shoulders dropping. Joey's tiny body was covered with a scarlet rash. He examined the toddler's reddened eyes and looked deep into his mouth. He had a reddened tongue, which the doctor held down using his tongue depressor, and used a small mirror to stare into his throat. He could see it was inflamed. Maria stood anxiously at the end of the bed, biting her lip and repeatedly making the sign of the cross over her chest.

74

'What is it, Doctor? Why has 'e turned this colour?' Maria asked, her eyes fearful.

Dr Fletcher packed his medical equipment into his bag. 'How long has Joey been like this?'

Ruth told him, her eyes narrowed, ''E started to go off his food a couple of days ago, I didn't think much of it at the time. The redness on his skin has just appeared and worsened overnight.'

'I'm afraid Joey has scarlet fever.' The doctor's expression was serious. 'I'm hoping we have caught it in time.'

Maria's knees buckled under her. 'Will 'e pull through, Doctor? I beg yer, please tell me Joey will be all right.'

Dr Fletcher spoke kindly. 'We'll do everything we can. I will contact the hospital to see if he can be admitted as soon as possible.'

Maria gripped his arm. ''E's not going to die, is 'e, Doctor?'

'Please be assured everyone will do their best for him. He looks a strong lad to me, a real fighter, and that is what he needs to be right now. I would like Joey to go to the fever hospital in King's Lynn where he will be given the best specialist treatment. Is there any way you can take him there to speed up his admission? We have to hope a bed will be available for him. I'll call them as soon as I return home.'

Ruth thought for a moment. 'I could ask Old Abel who lives down the lane. 'E has an old horse and cart and is a good sort. I will go now and ask 'im.'

'You look exhausted, Mrs Saward, you stay here. If Maria can get Joey ready, I'll call in on Old Abel after

I leave here. As you say, he's a good man and I'm sure he'll oblige.'

'What do we owe yer, Doctor?' whispered Maria, as she followed him downstairs. 'We're so grateful, only we don't have much . . .'

'Don't bother yourself about that for now. I'm sure we can sort something out. I've been looking after the Sawards for many a year now.'

Maria wept with gratitude, drying her eyes on her sleeve.

The doctor raised his eyebrows. 'I'll have to notify the local authorities about the infection, of course. Tell me, has Joey been in contact with any children who live in overcrowded or unhygienic conditions? That's how scarlet fever tends to spread.'

Maria shook her head. 'Not that I know of.'

She saw her mother look away and bite her lip. 'Ma, what is it? Do yer know something?'

'Well, now you mention it. Do yer recall the travelling accordion player and his young 'uns that camped up in the woods last week? Joey heard the man playing his music when we passed by and begged me to take 'im back. They invited us in, and when I declined as I had jobs to do, they said Joey could stay the afternoon. He begged me to let 'im stay and I didn't see the harm in it. I was grateful at the time as it meant I could get on with me jobs without 'im being a hindrance. He had a very jolly time, but when 'e came home he said two of their young 'uns were sick. You don't think . . .'

The blood drained from Maria's face. 'Oh Ma! That must be where 'e got it from. They're not there anymore, they left a few days ago. Do yer think we'll catch it now, Doctor?'

'It's more common in young children,' the doctor informed them, as he left. 'However, if you do feel unwell and notice symptoms similar to those Joey has, then you must stay inside and isolate.'

Within twenty minutes, Abel pulled up outside Honeysuckle Cottage with his horse and cart. Maria wrapped her sickly son in his bed sheet and with the help of her mother they carried him down the stairs and into the cart. Maria gently scooped her sick son in her arms and seated themselves as far away from the old smithy as possible, so as not to put him at risk of infection, and within a flash they were off.

Abel was well into his seventies with white bushy sideburns and gnarled hands that resembled the twisted ridges of an ancient tree trunk. He cracked the whip, turning round from time to time to check on Joey's condition. Every now and then his old horse, Starlight, named after the star-shaped marking between his deep brown eyes, would shudder to a sudden halt and stubbornly refuse to budge. It took considerable coaxing from Abel, who whispered reassuring words into Starlight's ears, before he gently trotted on again, then gathering speed as if the wind was behind him.

''E's a clever old thing, you know,' Abel told Maria. ''E were going to be slaughtered at the knacker's yard in

Dersingham when I retired and his working days were over and all 'e were going to do was cost me money I couldn't spare. I took 'im there, and as soon as we reached the slaughterer's he reared his back hooves and bolted back to Wolferton. I ain't ever seen 'im move so fast. Ever since then 'e's been on the nervous side. I ain't ever gonna take 'im to the slaughterers again, 'e's staying with me now until 'e claps out the way nature intended.'

'Poor Starlight. He is very dear to yer, I can see that. I'm glad he ran off. We would be lost without him today.'

Maria gripped Joey's limp frame tightly as the cart rocked from side to side. She gazed at the sleeping bundle in her arms, at his hot red face, her eyes filled with fear.

'Can yer go faster, Abel? Joey's eyes are shut and I'm afraid I might lose 'im. Every minute counts,' she pleaded.

Abel turned to see Maria's anxious expression and flicked his reins, urging Starlight to pick up speed. ''E'll only go as fast as 'e wants, that's his way now, I'll do me best to giddy him along.'

An hour later, the longest hour of Maria's life, they arrived at the hospital on the outskirts of the town. Abel steered the horse towards the front door and pulled up the reins sharply. Maria stepped off the cart carefully, tightly gripping her son against her chest. A porter indicated the entrance for the isolation wards around the corner, but seeing her distressed face, he told Maria to follow him and he ushered her through the side entrance. A nurse wearing a long starched white apron, her dark hair tucked into a short white headdress, sat at a desk at the end of the corridor. She took over, speedily making a note of their details and instructed Maria to leave Joey with her. Maria watched numbly as another porter was called and he wheeled Joey off on a trolley. Maria promised Joey, in a broken voice, that she would return as soon as she could.

Another kindly nurse appeared and placed a comforting arm around Maria's shoulder. 'Come back on Sunday, that's our visiting day. There are no promises you can see him then, but we can let you know how he is. He will be given the best care here.'

Her reassuring words fell on deaf ears as Maria fought back a rush of steaming tears and gulps.

She stumbled outside and found Abel standing alongside Starlight. 'Poor lass, yer look all done in. Why don't you put yer head down for a few minutes while I get yer back home. I'll try not to go over too many bumps.'

She stifled a sob and climbed into the cart, curling up on the wooden surface, shaking from one side to the other as the wheels spun around and jerked as Abel swerved to avoid an obstacle in his path.

'I won't want to live if Joey dies.'

'Now stop those nonsense ideas whirling round yer head. This is Joey yer talking about, and 'e's a tough little lad.'

Chapter Eight

'Is there any more news about this woman on the run?' Betty asked Ada.

'You mean Nellie. No, not a whisper, and I know Father spoke to Maria and Ruth about it yesterday. Maybe she's left Wolferton,' the station master's youngest daughter replied.

Betty's eyebrows arched. 'Maria has more than enough on her mind. I hear that Joey was rushed to the fever hospital today. Poor little boy, I hope he pulls through.'

Ada shuddered. 'It's very worrying. I hope Leslie doesn't catch it. Did you hear the news that Eddie is home? Beatrice mentioned last night he is on her ward, but his leg is in a bad way.'

'Our poor men, how they suffer. Beatrice will take good care of him.'

She cocked an ear. 'I just heard the postbox. I'll just see what there is, and then I must press on with our lunch. How does braised oxtail sound? Jessie is out helping Lizzie on the farm, and Beatrice is at the hospital, so it will just be you and Mr and Mrs Saward today.'

She manoeuvred around Ada's toddler Leslie, who was on the floor playing with a wooden engine. 'And Master Leslie, of course,' she added.

A couple of minutes later, Betty returned from the hallway clasping an envelope. 'It's for you, Ada. It looks like it's from your Alfie.'

Ada grabbed the letter, her face lighting up. Before war was declared Alfie was a talented organist and choirmaster in the seaside town of Cromer on the North Norfolk coast. It was here that he and Ada started their married life. When war was declared Alfie quickly signed up with the Artists Rifles, which attracted recruits from musical, artistic and theatrical backgrounds. With Ada suffering terrible sickness during her pregnancy, Alfie urged her to return to Wolferton, telling her he had to take up arms.

'What kind of man am I if I cannot fight the Hun to protect my wife and the child she is carrying from their clutches, if they should succeed and invade our country?' Alfie had declared.

Like everyone in the land at the outset of war, they expected the fighting to be over by the end of the year. That was 1914, and she never imagined that three years later they would not be reunited as man and wife.

Leslie tugged impatiently at his mother's skirt, bringing her back to the present moment with a jolt. 'Is it from Papa?' the toddler asked, his large blue eyes staring up at his mother as she devoured the lines.

The boy had only seen his father once since he had been born and Ada prayed that he would not become a fatherless child. Holding the rank of lieutenant in the Artists Rifles, Ada appreciated it would be difficult for him to return as soon as she hoped.

Betty spoke softly. 'I know he'll be home as soon as he is able. He must miss you and the little 'un terribly.'

Ada raised her eyes from the letter, her face showing alarm. 'Alfie says he's had a narrow shave. A sniper shot right above his head and a shell burst in front of him, killing six good men. He doesn't know how it missed him, and thanks my prayers for sending a guardian angel to watch over him. He says morale is low, the men are hungry, and he is doing his best to keep their spirits up.'

Ada paused, her eyes moistening. She pressed her hand against her chest. 'When he feels low he looks at our photograph and pictures me and Leslie, seeing our faces and imagining we are together again. He asks me to keep praying for his safe return.'

Betty placed a comforting arm around Ada's shoulder. 'There, there, my lovely. Your Alfie is alive. He has a clever head on his shoulders and is made of stern stuff. All being well, it won't be long till we win the war and beat those blasted Huns once and for all.'

Ada sniffled. 'I only wish that were true, Betty.'

'Is there news on when he can take leave?'

Ada shook her head. 'I'm afraid he says it's not possible yet, they are too short of men. But he hopes he can sometime in the next six months. He doesn't feel he can leave his men, that's the kind of selfless man he is. It also depends how long his leave is. If it's only for a few days, that won't be sufficient time for him to make the journey home and back again, which is what happened last year and the reason he stayed on in France.'

Ada also knew her beloved husband wanted to protect her from the gory details of war and the awfulness of his life on the battlefield. He was a sensitive soul and deeply felt the shock of losing any of his men.

She knelt down to cuddle her young son. His face was crumpled. 'A sniper shot my papa? Will he never come home again?'

Ada tenderly wiped away a tear from his cheek and pressed him to her chest. 'Oh, my darling boy, Papa wasn't killed. The bullet missed him. Of course he will come home again, and when he does we will go to the seaside. How does that sound?'

Leslie's eyes popped wide open. 'Oh yes, I would like that very much. I want to see Papa.'

'You will, as soon as he can come home. I promise, cross my heart.' Ada smiled, making the sign across her front.

Her face crumpled. 'Oh Betty, I don't know how much more our men can take. It must be so dreadful for Alfie, more than we can possibly imagine, watching good men killed in front of his eyes, the battlefields turned crimson with their blood.'

Betty wiped her moist eyes. 'You're setting me off now. I know how much you miss him, but you must take comfort from knowing Alfie is alive. Our King and government are doing right by standing up to Germany. They're doing their best and we can't be beaten by them.'

Last year in one of his letters Alfie described a visit from King George, who was accompanied by the young Prince of Wales, Prince David. There was a guard of honour for a visit at a French château and the corner of her lips curled as she recalled him describing how the men placed their tin hats on top of their bayonets and gave three cheers as His Majesty drove off. Alfie said it had boosted his men's sinking morale as the war seemed even more entrenched, rather than nearing an end.

Ada placed a comforting arm around Betty's shoulder. 'You're right, Betty. You are such a blessing and always find the right words to say.'

'I'm a silly old thing. It's me who should be consoling you, not the other way round. Tell me, does Alfie say anything else?'

Ada picked up the letter again and continued reading. The housekeeper raised an enquiring eyebrow as Ada's eyes scanned the lines on the page, mumbling the words under her breath.

She looked up from the letter. 'Alfie's asked me to visit an officer he knows, the son of a good friend who is stationed in King's Lynn on a training exercise. He is due to leave at the end of the week and asks if I will call in and visit him, should this letter reach me in time.'

'Who is this officer?' queried Betty.

'It appears Alfie knows his father well from his musical circle. He says it would be an enormous favour if I could see him to pass on his very best wishes to him before he leaves. He says it would mean a lot to him.'

'I see. So are you going to see this chap, what's his name?'

'Yes, I think I will as Alfie requests it. His name is Captain Charles Hopkins-Handley, and it appears he is an actor. Alfie says that Charles's father regularly entertained King Edward at Sandringham House and was very highly regarded by him, though this was a while ago.'

'When were you thinking of going? I have just done a bake. You can take him a Betty special, if you like.'

Ada gladly accepted the offer. 'I shall go this afternoon, and will write straight back to Alfie, if you wouldn't mind keeping an eye on Leslie for me.'

'You don't need to ask, of course I will.'

'I'm so grateful, Betty. I'm sure he'll be on his best behaviour for you.'

The housekeeper reassured her, 'We'll be just fine. It's to be expected that little ones will have the odd tantrum. I'm sure he will be happy playing on the new swing Mr Saward put up for him in the garden. Or we can go up to the bank with a picnic and watch the trains come and go.'

Leslie did a little jig, flapping his arms. 'Oh yes, I'd like that.'

༄

Ada packed Betty's bake into her bag, grateful that she was not going empty-handed. That morning, the housekeeper had baked a tray of thick gingerbread biscuits, grateful for the eggs and large jug of milk Jessie had brought back with her from her visit to Blackbird Farm, a thank you from Lizzie for her help in tidying up. Betty knew the recipe off by heart, and it couldn't be easier, just mixing all the ingredients together: 1 lb of treacle, 12oz plain flour, ¼ lb butter, ¼ lb coarse brown sugar, 1 oz ginger, ½ oz ground allspice, 1 teaspoonful of carbonate of soda, ¼ pint warm milk and three eggs.

Betty gave the package of biscuits, neatly wrapped in brown paper, to Ada, who also added a packet of cigarettes, knowing Charlie would appreciate all the home comforts he could get.

Ada clutched the address she had been given by Alfie. When she arrived at King's Lynn railway station, it seemed that every other person wore khaki; the place was teeming with uniformed men marching through the streets or lugging heavy kitbags over their backs, the town being a major centre for training soldiers. It saddened her to see how many townspeople wore sombre expressions and black armbands over their sleeves, the pain in their eyes mirroring the heartache of their loss.

She stepped cautiously along the uneven cobbled footpath, past a row of grand-looking terraced houses with wrought iron canopied balconies on the first floor overlooking the town's park. Some young boys kicked a ball inside the bandstand while an elderly couple shuffled past.

After a few minutes, the streets became narrower, the houses more tightly huddled and narrow alleyways wound their way towards the wide river. The high-pitched squawk of seagulls swooping down in the search for food, diving over Ada's head before taking off again, made her duck out of their reach. Some women scuttled past carrying the catch of the day that fishermen had hauled in that morning, and skinny cats darted in front of her like greased lightning, their noses twitching at the fishy smell.

Ada paused at the address she had been given, 15 Fisher Mews. It was part of a group of buildings in an enclosed courtyard used by the army to house officers. Two soldiers stood stiffly on guard at the entrance. Ada explained the purpose of her visit and the more senior one, a sergeant, allowed her to go through after she smiled persuasively and showed them Betty's bakes.

'You will find the captain's room on the first floor, over in the corner on the right,' indicated the sergeant, pointing to the room.

As Ada ascended the wooden steps, she looked down on the noisy quadrangle. Officers were barking their orders, running through a drill with their men, at least three hundred of them. They marched in unison, standing to attention and raising their bayonets; the noise was almost deafening. She walked past a maid carrying fresh sheets, a large bundle of keys secured around her waist. The maid nodded as Ada passed, confirming that the room she was seeking was further along the gangway.

When she reached the door, Ada knocked. There was no response, so she knocked again louder, and then for a third time. After there was still no response she pressed her ear against the door and knocked again, calling out Charles's name.

She was unsure whether to leave the biscuits on the doorstep with a hastily written note, feeling this wasn't the best moment to trouble him, but was curious to see this friend of Alfie's family. She peered over the balcony down in the courtyard, wondering if the captain was there. She was still pondering this in her mind when the maid approached.

'Can I be of assistance?' she offered.

Ada explained the circumstances of her visit and the maid fumbled with her keys. 'He's most likely out with his regiment. I'll be cleaning the captain's room soon. If it helps, I can let you in and you can leave the biscuits on his desk. I'm sure he'd be most grateful for them.'

'That's awfully kind of you. I was hoping to see the captain and don't mind waiting for a few minutes, but if he is otherwise engaged, then I shall leave the biscuits with a note.'

The maid's eyebrows furrowed as she stood alongside Ada outside the door. 'That's a rum 'un, his curtains are still drawn. The captain usually leaves them open in the day.'

'Perhaps the captain is unwell?' queried Ada.

The maid knocked sharply. When there was still no answer she fumbled for her key and unlocked the door. She stepped aside, allowing Ada to enter the room.

Ada's eyes rested on a bed in the corner, its sheets and cover crumpled, and a washbasin next to it. Some clothes were strewn over an armchair and a couple of books were scattered on a small table with a plate from where he had last eaten, the cutlery neatly placed across it.

Suddenly her heart skipped a beat and her knees buckled. Slumped across the desk under the window was a man's figure dressed in military uniform. In front of him was a photograph of a beautiful lady with long wavy hair cascading down her shoulders, a string of pearls gracefully adorning her long neck and resting on the front of her white lace blouse. Ada couldn't help but notice a leaflet on the desk advertising a new play in London called *The Pacifists*.

The maid's hand flew to her face. She cried out, 'Is he dead?'

Ada's face turned ashen and she felt the hairs lifting on the nape of her neck and arms, her mind scrambling to understand.

Her heart raced as she eyed the man's motionless body. She stepped forward tentatively in jerky movements, slowly extending her hand out to touch the captain's shoulder. His head rolled to one side, his eyes wide open and staring straight at her face. Blood streaked his face and hair. A revolver rested near his hand.

A piercing scream filled the room. Ada realised it was coming from her.

'Oh no. He's dead!'

Chapter Nine

Maria rubbed her eyes as the cart drew up outside Honeysuckle Cottage. 'I don't know how I can ever thank yer Abel.'

'Just to see the lad on his feet will be all the thanks I'll need,' he replied. 'I'll come for yer on Sunday if yer like. Now take care of yerself.'

'I don't know how I can wait a whole six days.'

'Yer 'ave to take care of yerself, for Joey's sake. 'E needs a strong ma to look after 'im when 'e comes back 'ome.' Abel winked and set off down the lane with Starlight flicking the dust up.

Maria stood at the front gate and glanced up at the windows. They were flung wide open and as she stepped along the path she saw sheets and bedding pegged out on the washing line. She entered the kitchen and saw her mother slumped in an armchair, her eyes half closed.

Aggie Greensticks was standing at the kitchen sink, her sleeves rolled up. Maria's jaw dropped as her eyes took in the room.

'What's happened 'ere? Everywhere is so fresh an' sparkling.'

Ruth blinked and rose quickly. 'We have Aggie to thank. She's been wonderful. But first, tell us, how is Joey? What did the hospital say?'

Maria updated them, and when she finished speaking Ruth and Aggie promised to pray for him that night.

'There's nought more we can do,' Maria sighed wearily. 'He's in the hands of the doctors now.'

As Maria's eyes glanced appreciatively at the clean-up that had taken place while she was out, Ruth told Maria how Aggie had arrived shortly after she left for the hospital, having heard about Joey's condition from Freddie after he alerted Dr Fletcher. She'd got stuck in, ignoring Ruth's protestations, scrubbing all the surfaces in the bedroom, boiling the bedding and clothes they had been wearing.

Aggie stared at Maria. 'If you give me the clothes you're standing in, I'll wash them while the water is still boiling and hang them out on the line before I set off. You should scrub yourself down too with hot water and salts.'

Maria realised she was still wearing her maid's working clothes. 'I couldn't possibly expect you to do that. You've done more than enough already.'

Aggie insisted, saying it was important to do this as quickly as possible in order to stop the infection spreading. Maria obediently carried a bowl of warm water to her room and washed herself quickly before changing into a clean skirt and blouse, returning downstairs and placing the clothes she had been wearing in a copper in the outhouse.

Maria wrinkled her nose. 'Everywhere looks and smells so fresh. Aggie, how can I ever repay yer for yer kindness?'

Ruth rose feebly. 'She's beaten the rugs too and washed down the carpet and walls in Joey's room using a solution of chlorinated lime to make everything as fever clean as possible. I told 'er to stop, but she wouldn't hear of it.'

Maria said, 'I'm very grateful for everything you've done for us, Aggie. You and Magnolia have been so kind to us since we moved 'ere.'

The two sisters had taken Maria under their wing. Once Maria's secret about Joey and the fact he was illegitimate was known to them, the Greenstick sisters revealed their own secret to her – that they had also both been born out of wedlock.

Maria could barely believe what she was hearing. Magnolia and Aggie always appeared to be so well-to-do and snooty. She assumed they looked down their noses at her. She could still remember the shock she felt when the sisters blurted their truth to her, *We are more like you than you think, we weren't born posh.*

They confessed that their mother had been a maid at Sandringham House when she fell pregnant by one of the guests, someone loosely connected with the royal family. He had set her up with a house and made financial arrangements to look after them all, even after his death. This revelation had helped form a bond between the sisters and Maria.

'As you know I have a great fondness for Joey and yourselves. He makes us chuckle and brings some joy to our childless lives,' Aggie told her with a wistful tone, pulling out a chair at the table and mopping her brow with a handkerchief.

'I just need to take the weight off my feet for a moment.'

'Of course. How rude of me not to offer you a seat after everything you've done,' Maria replied. 'Joey loves going to Kitty Cottage and playing with yer cats. I hope he ain't too rough with them.'

'Oh, don't worry, they will let him know if he grabs their tails too hard. When Joey is better maybe he would like to come for tea. I know Maud and Jasper would be happy to see him again,' Aggie grinned, referring to Joey's two favourite moggies.

Maria's face broke into a faint smile. 'Oh, yes please, Aggie. Joey will really look forward to that.'

She reached across the table and placed a hand on Aggie's arm. 'May I ask you a personal question?'

Ruth shot a querying glance at Maria. Aggie replied, 'You can ask, by all means.'

'It strikes me that yer a good person, kinder than many people know. I was wondering, well, why have yer never married?'

Ruth's jaw dropped. 'Maria, that is quite enough. Aggie's personal life is none of your business.'

Aggie pondered for a moment, deep in thought, then raised a hand. 'I don't mind telling you. Yes, there was someone dear to me once, a long time ago ...'

Maria's eyes widened. She spoke softly. 'Who was he? Can you tell us what happened to him?'

Ruth interrupted and raised her hand. 'Really, Maria, this is none of yer business.'

Aggie sighed, her eyes falling to her lap. 'There's no need to be cross with Maria. I'm of the age now that I care less about keeping details of my past life secret. Why should the ghosts of the graveyard be the only ones to know the feelings that once filled my heart?'

Maria stuttered. 'Ma is right, it's none of me business. I don't mean to pry if it upsets you to speak of it.'

Aggie's hand reached up to her right cheek and she placed it over a large brown birthmark. 'When I was a child and went to church, I heard one woman say this was the sign of the devil, that I would be stained for life due to the sins of my mother because she chose to fall in love and have two daughters out of wedlock with a married man above her station. I was always being made to feel as if I didn't fit in with society. Wherever I went I felt fingers were pointing at me and people saying, *There goes the girl who carries the mark of the devil.*'

Maria stared wide eyed in disbelief, taking in Aggie's words. 'I understand how you feel. I fret that Joey is suffering now, that his illness is punishment for 'im being born out of wedlock. It's always the children who suffer for their parents' sins.'

Ruth gasped. 'How could you even think such a ridiculous notion?'

Maria's tone was heated. 'I can't help it. That's the way I think. Some folk can be cruel and I worry too about Joey being taunted 'cause 'e was born with no father's name on his birth certificate. It ain't his fault that Walter Jugg forced himself on me and I have never regretted a day that I decided to keep 'im rather than give 'im up. It weren't yer fault either, Aggie, to be born with a mark like that. If you ask me, it's not the mark of the devil, but the mark of an angel, 'cause that's what you are.'

Aggie's eyes moistened. 'Not everybody thinks like you, Maria.'

'We don't want to upset you,' Maria replied tactfully.

'It would be good to tell someone about him. His name was Percy and I've often wondered about him and how our lives would have turned out if we'd stayed together.'

'Percy, that's a nice name. What was he like? How did yer meet?' queried Maria.

'Fate brought us together. Our paths crossed quite by chance at King's Lynn market one Tuesday when I stopped at a stall to purchase a meat pie. I had just had my thirtieth birthday, so this would have been twelve or so years ago. Percy was standing behind me in the queue and as I turned I bumped into him, dropping my pie on the ground. It made such a mess.'

A faint smile curled the corner of Aggie's lips as her mind recalled her past love. 'It was not the most romantic first encounter, but Percy was very apologetic for his clumsiness. He insisted on buying me another pie and bought himself one as well. When he invited me to join him at the park so we could eat them together on a bench by the bandstand, I was over the moon. The hour passed in a blur as all I could think about was how wonderful it was that this man with the kindest face wanted to spend time with me.

'I saw him there again the following Tuesday, quite by chance, though I had secretly hoped our paths would cross. After that we arranged to meet there each Tuesday on market day. Percy worked as a clerk at an accountancy firm on the Market Place. I hadn't told Magnolia about Percy in case she thought I was being a silly fool.'

'Surely she wouldn't have minded?' queried Maria.

'No, maybe not, I realise that now and wish I had told her as, unbeknown to me, someone from Wolferton had spotted me with Percy strolling arm in arm in the park. The following Tuesday Magnolia followed me into town. I was so giddy at the thought of seeing Percy that I didn't notice her. She saw us together and came over to us.

'Percy was very polite and courteous and told her he loved me. I was speechless and overjoyed that he returned my feelings. It was the first time I had heard him say those words. Magnolia asked Percy if he knew the truth of our birth. I had told him about it the week before, and he said it didn't matter at all. We all three sat together and Magnolia became acquainted with Percy. Afterwards, she told me I had her approval and she was happy for me.'

Ruth pressed, 'So surely there was nothing to stop you and Percy being together?'

'No, there wasn't. We talked about how Percy would come to Wolferton to live, that we could still, somehow, all be together.' Aggie choked on her words.

Maria's eyes welled. 'It sounds like true love.'

Aggie nodded. 'I had never felt so happy in my life. Sadly, I wasn't to know that this would be the last time I saw him. When I arrived for our usual rendezvous the following week, he failed to turn up. Neither did he appear the week after, or the week after that.'

'There must 'ave been a reason. Did you find out what happened to 'im?' asked Maria.

Aggie shook her head. 'After a month, I plucked up all my courage and went to his place of work. When I mentioned his name to the lady behind the front desk she asked me if I was family. When I told her I wasn't she said I should speak to them about him, that she couldn't divulge personal details about their staff. I became flustered as, unfortunately, I couldn't remember his address. He did tell me, but it slipped my mind and I spent days walking around in circles looking for him in the area I thought he lived, hoping our paths would cross. For weeks, I turned up to meet him on our park bench at the usual day and time, but to no avail. To this day, I have no idea what happened to him. I cannot believe he was not sincere.'

Maria pressed gently. 'Maybe he was taken ill, or someone in his family suffered some misfortune. I'm sure there must be an explanation.'

Aggie croaked, her eyes moist, 'Magnolia wondered if Percy was married. I never for a moment imagined he was. Whatever the reason, it wasn't meant to be. While that might be true for me, at least Magnolia now has a chance to right the wrongs of her past where her gentleman is concerned.'

Ruth gulped. 'I beg yer pardon. Are you saying Magnolia has a gentleman in tow?'

'That could be the case. Isn't it funny how life turns out? Seeing as we are close, if I can rely on your discretion, I will tell you what's happened to Magnolia in the last couple of days.'

Both Maria and Ruth swore themselves to secrecy.

'Very well,' Aggie continued. 'Two years after Percy's unaccounted for disappearance, Magnolia became fond of a gentleman called David Fellowes. He was a teacher in Wolferton and a cousin of our vicar. They sang in the choir together and her fondness for him grew, but it appeared to be one-sided as she never let her true feelings for him be known. I noticed how jittery she became in his company though and I could see he was fond of her too, but she kept him at arm's length.

'Within a few weeks, David told Magnolia he was leaving Wolferton having accepted a promotion, a deputy head's post in St Albans. A few months later, Jane Rumbelow, the vicar's wife, informed us that he had married a teacher. Poor Magnolia, she fell to pieces and suffered from the most painful unrequited love.'

Aggie paused, inhaling a deep breath. 'The thing is, David Fellowes is back in Wolferton. I overheard his name mentioned in the butcher's and my ears pricked up. I could scarcely believe it when someone said he was widowed and renting Dove Cottage. Apparently, he'd enquired after Magnolia. As I left the butcher's, I saw him a few feet ahead of me, turning the corner towards the church. I couldn't wait to tell Magnolia.'

Ruth's eyes were wide with disbelief. 'How did she take the news?'

'She's been on edge ever since. She took to her bed for the rest of the day and her nerves are still jangled. I don't expect it will be too long before their paths cross, and suspect he will call on her, as an old friend. For me, seeing David again, ten years after he left Wolferton, rekindled my cherished memories of Percy too.'

'That's sad,' Maria muttered. She rested her hand on Aggie's arm. 'If Joey comes back to us, I mean, when 'e returns home, I would like to have him baptised in the church 'ere to thank God for answering our prayers. And I would like to ask you, Aggie, to be his godmother.'

Aggie's face broke into a wide smile. She brushed aside a tear. 'That would be such an honour. You know I love little Joey as if he were my own.'

Aggie rose, stifling a yawn. 'I feel quite exhausted now, and I can see you are too. Please do keep us informed about Joey and don't hesitate to ask if there is anything we can do.'

Maria yawned and followed Aggie to the door. She watched her leave and was about to close the door when a rustling sound from the back of the house made her ears prick up.

Suddenly a woman's figure stepped in front of her. She appeared anxious and her eyes darted in all directions. 'I've come to see Aunt Ruth. Is she in?'

Chapter Ten

Maria stared incredulously at the figure standing on the doorstep. 'You're Nellie Jeacock, ain't yer?'

The young woman in front of her appeared jittery, glancing over her shoulder anxiously. Her hands tightly clutched her embroidered carpet bag.

'I'm looking for me Aunt Ruth. Ruth Saward 'er name is. Is this where she lives?'

Maria turned her head to call her mother to the door when Ruth suddenly appeared. She jerked her head back. 'Nellie! What in heavens name are you doing 'ere? Yer know you're wanted by the law.'

Nellie's eyes locked on Maria's face, and then Ruth's, her face turning pale. Suddenly, she swayed to one side, her bag slipping from her fingers. Maria rushed forward to steady her. She shot an anxious glance towards her mother as they supported Nellie and led her into the kitchen, placing her in the armchair in the corner of the room. Ruth returned outside and walked a few steps along the path, her eyes darting in all directions to see if anyone was passing and had spotted the fugitive on their doorstep. Breathing a sigh of relief that nobody was in sight,

Ruth picked up the carpet bag Nellie had dropped and dashed inside.

Maria stared intently at their unexpected guest. She sensed an air of vulnerability about her, with her porcelain pale skin and clear violet eyes. Nellie looked up when Ruth entered the room and reached out quickly to grab the carpet bag – a little too quickly, Maria thought, wondering if it contained something precious to Nellie. She pressed it against her chest.

'Yer must be wondering why I'm 'ere. Forgive me, Aunt Ruth, for turning up out of the blue like this, but I had nowhere else to turn. I'm scared and I wanted to go somewhere I could feel safe. Somewhere I would be listened to, and not judged harshly.'

Ruth's eyebrows knitted together. 'We wondered if yer might turn up. We heard yer were at the station and the station master chased after yer. I know you've had it tough, Nellie, but I can scarcely believe what the papers say about yer.'

'I saw him with the private detective on me tail, like I'm some sort of common criminal, but I swear I ain't. If you give me a chance, I'd like to tell yer my story, and ask a favour of yer too.'

'What do yer mean, your side of the story? Are yer saying what's in the paper ain't true? We 'ave to be careful too, seeing as yer wanted by police,' Ruth replied, a worried look on her face. 'We don't want no trouble.'

'I've not seen the papers, but I expect what's in there is a pack of lies.'

As Ruth rose to fetch the newspaper, Nellie's eyes settled on some toy soldiers spread on the table. She tilted her head, raising an eyebrow. 'These look fine wooden soldiers. Who might they belong to?'

'They're my Joey's. He's me little 'un, coming up to three years. He's taken ill at the moment and is in hospital with scarlet fever,' Maria told her.

Nellie stuttered. 'I'm sorry, I had no idea. Yer 'ave enough worries of yer own without me troubling yer at such a difficult time.'

Ruth jerked her head back. 'She has. Her Eddie is ill too, just back from the war and the poor fella risks losing his leg. We're worried sick about them both. Take a look here at what the papers are saying about you.'

Ruth handed Nellie the paper. Nellie placed her bag on the floor and took the paper in her hands. As her eyes took in each word, her face reddened. She sniffed, wiping her cheeks dry with the sleeve of her jacket. Maria fished in her pocket and passed Nellie a handkerchief.

Nellie looked directly at them. 'What it says 'ere, it ain't true. I can prove it, or rather me father can vouch for me innocence, if I can find him. 'E's the only person who can save me from these terrible lies.'

'How do yer mean?' pressed Maria, curious to know Nellie's side of the story, forgetting Harry's warning about informing the police if she should turn up.

Ruth frowned and Maria whispered in her mother's ear, 'I know we should ask her to leave right now, but you can see how pitiful she looks.'

Ruth whispered back, 'You've got yer Eddie to think about, as well as Joey. But I feel the same. Shall we give her just five minutes? It sounds like my brother Gus is behind this too. Let's 'ear what she has to say.'

'It won't do any harm to hear 'er out,' Maria replied.

Ruth turned to Nellie. 'We'll give yer five minutes. I can't turn me niece out the door just like that. I wish I had done more to stay in touch with you over the years. I feel I let yer down, and now yer in this terrible mess.'

'Oh no, Aunt Ruth, please don't blame yerself. I know yer tried over the years. Look, I found yer letters. Pa hid 'em in a box under the stairs and I found 'em one day when 'e was out. They had yer old address on but I knew from when Freddie and Archie stayed with us that you were 'ere in Wolferon, so that's how I knew where to find yer. I could tell you cared for me and I 'ad nowhere else to turn.'

Nellie fished a bundle of letters tied in string out of her bag and handed them to Ruth. 'Well, I'll be blowed. These are my letters. What a scoundrel that man is!'

'I know I did wrong to run away from the court, but I had to. I promise I will give meself up once I can prove me innocence, otherwise they'll bang me up and throw away the key, or worse. I need to find Pa. 'E told the police a pack of lies to save his neck. I 'ave to somehow get 'im to confess the truth and clear me name.'

Ruth fumed. 'How are yer going to do that after the air raid in his street. We don't even know if 'e's still alive. You need to find yerself a good lawyer. In fact, maybe we can help yer there as the station master's daughter, Beatrice, is friends with a legal man. You can try to run away from trouble, Nellie, but yer won't get far. It always has a way of catching up with yer.'

Maria asked, 'Ma's right, but how can we mention this to Beatrice without implicating ourselves? Perhaps it's best not to say anything just yet?'

Ruth asked, 'Yer mentioned you had a favour to ask. What might that be? I don't see how we can help.'

'It will help just to get it off me chest. I swear to yer on me life that what I am about to tell yer is the truth.'

Nellie dug deep into her bag, tossing clothing onto the floor as she did, until she found what she was searching for. She held up a pillowslip and fumbled inside, bringing out a small ebony box with a shiny gold clasp. 'This was given to me by Aunt Millicent. May I leave it in your safe keeping? It's very special to me.'

Ruth raised an eyebrow. 'Aunt Millicent, you say? I thought she died many years ago. What does she have to do with this?'

'I swear that I am the rightful owner of this locket. I promised Aunt Millicent I would always remember 'er by it. I would like yer to take care of it for me, just in case anything should happen to me, and if it does, then I would like yer to keep it.'

'It's not what I think it is, is it? It's not the stolen locket that's mentioned in the paper?' asked Ruth. 'We can't take in stolen goods.'

Nellie's eyes flashed. 'I told yer, it's not stolen. It's mine!'

Ruth and Maria watched as Nellie gently undid the delicate clasp, their faces incredulous as her fingers lifted out a silver locket. She smiled as she opened it and their eyes rested on a small curl of hair tucked neatly inside.

'Please 'ear me out,' Nellie said. 'I haven't told you me story yet. As yer know, I didn't have an easy life with Pa. It was after Ma died that he changed to the man 'e is today. Yer saw the difference Ma's death made to 'im, didn't yer, Aunt Ruth?'

Ruth nodded, a wistful look in her eyes. Nellie continued, 'After she passed on 'e turned against me. I soon learnt I had to get out his way sharpish when he came home from The Black Cat the worse for drink.

''E found companionship with a woman called Doris. She had no children of 'er own, and, at first, she showed some kindness towards me, but not for long. She would go off for long spells, telling Pa she had to go away with her ol' man to visit family. Yes, that's right, she were married. Pa's rages worsened when Doris weren't around and he fumed with jealousy. When she returned they would leg it to The Black Cat and I would crawl onto me mattress on the floor, afraid of their screams when they returned and fought like cat and dog, and I made meself scarce so I didn't get clobbered around me ears.'

Ruth dabbed a moist eye. 'Oh, Nellie, I'm so sorry, I had no idea things were as bad as that.'

Nellie continued, 'One night I heard Pa babbling to Doris about how 'e couldn't bear to look me in the face as I reminded him of Ma and how 'e wished I was out the way.

Ten years had passed since the angels took Ma. I was well developed for a fourteen-year-old and Pa's drinking pals had noticed; I could tell by the looks in their eyes. Doris told Pa she'd found work for me as a cleaner in a house of respectable women, only it turned out to be a house of women who sold themselves, if yer get my meaning.'

'She never did?' gasped Ruth.

'I stormed out and took refuge in my local church. The vicar there was kindly and by a stroke of luck it was then that Aunt Millicent appeared out of the blue. I had no idea who she was, this genteel lady with a kind, soft voice, but with steely eyes so you knew you couldn't mess with 'er. I could scarcely believe my ears when she came home with me one day and told Pa she was going to take me under her wing out of the goodness of her Christian heart in exchange for me 'elping out around the house with some light chores. She wanted to 'elp with me education too seeing I 'ardly went to school as Pa kept me at 'ome. She was recently widowed and in need of companionship too.

'She told Pa she preferred the company of younger ladies than old maids. I giggled when she said that. Pa put on an act and told 'er how much 'e would miss me. She saw right through 'im and told 'im 'e was a disgrace. She was quite magnificent, telling Pa she wasn't leaving without me. In the end, Pa said, "Take 'er, she's useless."'

''E never did! What a brave person yer Aunt Millicent sounds. Fate must have brought you together,' Maria exclaimed.

'Or my mother's guardian angel,' muttered Nellie wistfully.

Ruth rubbed her chin. 'Well, I'll be blowed. I've not heard of Aunt Millicent for many a year. How fortunate for you that she turned up like that. I often wondered what happened to 'er. She was my own mother's sister and we lost touch over the years, more's the pity. She was always very fond of yer ma.'

Nellie continued, 'Yes, she told me as much. She said it was only by chance that she learnt of my dire situation from her vicar when he happened to be in London and met the incumbent of my parish at a church gathering. He urged my aunt's vicar to inform Aunt Millicent about my circumstances without delay and 'e in turn implored Aunt Millicent to act with God's speed as 'e feared what plans Pa might have for me.'

Ruth and Maria exchanged shocked looks.

'That man! What a rotter me brother turned out to be,' exclaimed Ruth. 'Our parents would turn in their graves if they knew the half of it.'

Nellie lowered her eyes. 'I couldn't believe me good fortune. I was truly blessed to be placed with such a generous and caring aunt. I felt the angels had sent her. She lived in a comfortable house in Margate with white-painted walls, facing the seafront. It looked like a palace to me. I've never been so happy, strolling along the sandy beach and pier. I felt Ma was looking down on me. I didn't do any housework either, I was just 'er companion. She had a housekeeper, Mrs Biggs, who kept the house in order. I felt all me troubles had passed.'

Nellie shifted in her seat. 'The vicar had tea with us one Sunday and told Aunt Millicent what a great difference 'e noticed in me appearance, how my cheeks now had a healthy pink glow and my eyes sparkled like crystals, like the sun shimmering on the waves that I spent hours gazing at out of my bedroom window.'

Maria said sympathetically, 'I know how yer must have felt. I was in trouble meself once and the Saward family kindly took me in and it's thanks to them I am reunited with my family and have Joey with me. I will tell yer about it another time.'

Tears pricked at the back of Nellie's eyes. 'I would like to hear all about it, Maria. I'm so happy to have found you and Aunt Ruth.'

Ruth probed, 'So how did things work out with Aunt Millicent?'

Nellie dabbed her eye. 'I was very fond of her and grew to love 'er. She helped me with me reading and liked me to read to 'er from the Bible as she had failing eyesight and I accompanied her to church on Sundays. She also enjoyed telling me stories of folklore, shipwrecks and pirates, smugglers and great battles that had once taken place on the sea. She was so knowledgeable.

'Of course, I realised that one day I would 'ave to leave 'er, that I couldn't stay there forever. But I didn't expect it to end so suddenly the way it did and I blame meself for not being at 'er side the day it 'appened.'

Ruth's eyebrows narrowed. 'The day what 'appened?'

'Poor Aunt Millicent was short-sighted and on more than one occasion I caught 'er arm just in time when she missed the step at the top of the stairs. One day, she sent me out on an errand and I was delayed returning as I was assisting a neighbour carrying in 'er shopping and she insisted I stay for refreshments.

'When I returned home, I found Aunt Millicent lying at the bottom of the stairs. I'll never forget the sight of her eyes wide open staring up at me. I touched her and she didn't move. I could see she was dead.'

'Poor Aunt Millicent. What a terrible shock for you,' consoled Ruth.

Nellie continued, 'We think she tripped over the hem of her long skirt and fell down the stairs, breaking her neck. It was a new skirt that she intended to take to the dressmaker; I was going to accompany her there with the garment the next day. I don't understand why she was wearing it, she must have forgotten. It was also our misfortune that Mrs Biggs had left for the day, thinking I would be home soon from my errand, and Aunt Millicent was alone in the house.'

Maria said comfortingly, 'That's very sad. I'm sure you gave yer aunt much happiness, and she would want you to be happy as well.'

Nellie continued through muffled sobs, 'I never gave a thought to what would happen to me. I was grieving for my aunt who I had spent the happiest six years of me life with. After the funeral, her solicitor read the will, and that is what sealed my fate. She had no children and the entire estate was bequeathed to a distant cousin called Cedric Parker who spends most of the year in India running a trading company.

'It was a while before he could be traced. In the meantime, the solicitor kindly allowed me a small amount of contingency money from the estate for me needs and to continue paying the housekeeper's wages until this Cedric arrived to sort out matters. I had no idea who he was as I never once heard Aunt Millicent talk of him.'

Ruth's eyes popped. 'If I recall correctly Cedric Parker was a bit of a slimy character and the black sheep of the family. 'E slunk off to India following a scandal of some sort involving his wife's family. I will 'ave to rack my brain to think of it.'

'Having now met 'im, that wouldn't surprise me,' Nellie retorted. 'When the solicitor finally tracked 'im down and he arrived at the house four months after my aunt's death, I felt a shiver run down me spine. 'E looked so haughty and smug and I could tell from his hostile tone and the glint in his eyes, the snooty way he looked down his nose at me, that his arrival would not fare well for me. I was right. He lost no time in making his position clear. 'E ordered me to pack me bags and leave the next day. Mrs Biggs was given immediate notice that her services were no longer required.'

Maria gasped, 'Could he do that? What a horrid man.'

Nellie's eyes locked on to Maria's face. 'I can still recall his exact words. He was standing in front of the fireplace. He leant towards me, puffing on his fat cigar, and said,

"I would like you to leave within twenty-four hours. And don't think you can take anything with you. Every item in this house is recorded on an inventory."

'As if I would ever take anything that didn't belong to me.'

Ruth shook her head. 'What a foul man, to behave in such a cruel way when you were grieving. What did you say?'

'As you can imagine I was afraid of him and didn't know where to turn. Cedric told me I had had more than enough of my aunt's generosity and would be getting no more. I asked him where I was supposed to go. He shrugged his shoulders and said, "You can go back to whence you came from. You came from the gutter and can go back there. It is of no concern to me."

'I had no choice but to leave. I packed my bag that night, gazing from my bedroom window across the sea where the waves were whipping up into a crescendo of huge peaks of white foam. I cried meself to sleep that night and the next day I went back to Pa's in Whitechapel. I didn't even know if he were still living there as I'd not heard from him all the time I was in Margate.'

Ruth groaned. 'Oh no, not back to Whitechapel!'

Nellie nodded. 'I'm afraid so. I was none too pleased about it. I took with me what was rightfully mine, like the clothes Aunt Millicent had bought me. And this little treasure here. I didn't steal it. It was gifted to me by her for me birthday. The last birthday I spent with 'er.'

Nellie stared incredulously at the small image showing the face of England's finest seaman, Admiral Lord Nelson, along with a tiny lock of greying hair, just the size of her thumbnail.

'Aunt Millicent was such a romantic, you know. She would recount her favourite story to me over and over again about Lord Nelson and his love for the beautiful Lady Emma Hamilton. According to Auntie, the lock of hair was taken when Lord Nelson lay dying on his ship at the Battle of Trafalgar, more than one hundred years ago. I can hardly believe it's that old!

'Aunt Millicent would tell me of his bravery on the seas, the kindnesses he bestowed towards the seamen who sailed with him and his love for Lady Emma. She thought the lock of hair was cut by a sympathetic ally who sailed on the ship and gave it to Lady Emma who kept it in the locket close to her heart. Somehow, more than one hundred years later, it ended up in the window of a pawn shop in Margate and Aunt bought it.'

Maria looked incredulous. 'And you say Aunt Millicent gave it to you? But why, if it is such a treasure? Didn't she want to keep it for 'erself?'

'No one was more surprised than me when she gifted it to me on my twenty-first birthday. I was speechless, I can tell you. It's the most precious thing I possess, and I shall treasure it forever. I made her that promise and it's one I intend to keep.'

'I believe you,' said Maria softly, feeling deeply for Nellie.

'That means a lot to me. So will you help me? Will you keep it safe for me, now I have explained how it came into my possession?'

Ruth shook her head. 'I'm not sure we should. I don't think we can get involved, despite our sympathy for your plight. We have to be careful here else we could lose everything. We don't want trouble coming our way right now, not with Joey poorly, and Maria has her job and reputation to consider at the Big House.'

Nellie bit her bottom lip, twisting her fingers in her lap. She returned the locket to its box, her eyes downcast. 'I understand. It is not my intention to cause trouble to anyone.'

Maria muttered, 'If nobody knows it's here, we won't 'ave to lie about it. We'll just keep our lips sealed and not breathe a word. It will be our secret, until Nellie clears 'er name. I can see why Nellie wouldn't want it to fall into the wrong hands and risk losing it forever.'

Ruth pondered. 'Maybe yer right. Nellie is the daughter of me dear friend and brother, the rogue that 'e is, and helping 'er will appease me conscience for not being there when she needed me as a child. Don't worry, Maria, I will make sure yer protected. To safeguard yer position at the Big House, I think the less yer know the better, so I must ask you now to go upstairs while Nellie and I finish talking. I don't think you should hear another word from Nellie's lips.'

Maria resisted at first, but Ruth was adamant. Maria rose reluctantly, left the room and closed the door firmly shut behind her. She noisily climbed the first few steps and then tiptoed back down, pressing her ear against the kitchen door.

Ruth asked, 'There's more to yer story, isn't there? What is yer explanation for the accusation that you're an accomplice for attempted murder? Who is this Stanley Jeacock? And why are yer charged with bigamy? How many husbands have yer had?'

Maria held her breath, keen to hear Nellie's reply. Her response was too faint for her to hear, but she couldn't miss the loud cry from her mother expressing disbelief and shock that made her leap back.

Pressing her ear against the door, Maria heard her mother exclaim, 'That is the most shocking thing I have ever heard. I wish you luck in finding Gus, let's hope 'e is still alive.'

Unable to hold back any longer, Maria burst into the room and stared at them both. Nellie's cheeks were flushed.

'I can never thank yer enough, Aunt Ruth. The next time yer see me I promise you there won't be a stain on my name.'

A knock on the door took them by surprise. 'Quick, hide. Go upstairs,' urged Ruth, pushing Nellie out of the kitchen. 'Go into the front bedroom and close the door.'

She gave Maria the all-clear to answer the door. Beatrice stood on the doorstep and walked straight in as they opened the door. Her eyes fell on Nellie's bag on the floor and she raised an eyebrow. Maria stepped forward. 'It was given to me by one of the maids at the Big House, just in case I need a bag for the fever hospital.'

Beatrice accepted the explanation. 'I'm sorry about Joey. I've just come to say I'm afraid you can't visit Eddie while Joey is unwell. We can't risk you bringing infections onto the wards. In fact, I should keep my distance from you as well.'

Maria stuttered, 'I feared as much but I understand I can't put anyone else at risk. How is Eddie? Is his leg getting better?'

'His mood changed when I told him you couldn't visit for a while. I'm afraid his leg shows no signs of improving. We are waiting for Dr Butterscotch to see him.'

'Tell Eddie I'm sorry. I'm really sorry, and I'll visit as soon as I can.'

Chapter Eleven

After Beatrice left Maria had second thoughts of getting involved with Nellie. She was overwhelmed with feelings of guilt for lying to Beatrice. Maria dreaded the Sawards finding out she had lied about Nellie's bag and feared they would be implicated with her troubles. She was anxious about what Freddie and Archie would think if they saw Nellie standing in their home, but this now seemed to be an inevitability that she could not avoid.

The brothers returned home later that evening, having stayed on later at the station and Lizzie's farm. Maria didn't hear them enter the house and their eyes widened when they stepped into the kitchen and saw Nellie standing there.

Freddie's face reddened. He glowered, 'What is she doing here?'

Nellie stepped towards them and extended her hand. 'Hello, Freddie, hello, Archie. I had to see yer ma. Yer 'ave to believe it ain't true what the papers say about me. I'm innocent and intend to prove it.'

Freddie and Archie moved away from her and stared at their mother. Ruth told them, 'I believe what she says, we should give her a chance to set matters straight. She is yer cousin, after all.'

Nellie stared down at her feet. 'If it's going to cause trouble, I will lay me head in the porch in the church for the night.'

'Oh no,' blurted Maria. 'We couldn't allow you to do that. You can stay just one night, can't she, Ma? Please, Freddie, give her this one chance?'

Archie turned to his brother. 'If Ma believes Nellie, then we should too.'

Freddie shuffled his feet. He bit his lip, before nodding. 'Very well, but I just hope we don't get into trouble.'

Ruth declared, 'Well, that's settled then. I'll find a couple of blankets for you and you can sleep on the armchair.'

Nellie flung her arms around Ruth and hugged her, and then Maria. Her brothers inched backwards.

She told them, 'I only wish we could have met again under different circumstances. I promise I'll leave first thing in the morning.'

Maria barely slept again, and she crept downstairs bleary eyed the following morning as the cockerel's crowing welcomed the start of a new day. Nellie was folding the blankets and greeted her nervously, dressed in a dark blue dress with a white collar. 'Thank yer for taking me in last night. I know yer took a risk for me and I'll never forget it. I shall leave now before yer brothers are down and set off back to London.'

'I hope all goes well for yer. I'm glad to see yer wearing something different that won't attract attention. We need to make sure yer ain't seen leaving.'

Nellie took Maria's hand in hers. 'You're very lucky, Maria, to have such a wonderful family. I shall pray for your Joey and Eddie to pull through.'

A warm rush of sympathy filled Maria's body. 'Times are tough right now, but that's life. I hope you find yer pa and that he does the decent thing for you.'

Nellie threw herself into Maria's arms, almost sending her flying. 'Thank you again, Maria. I meant what I said last night, next time yer see me I'll be able to hold me head up high. I won't be skulking in the shadows.'

'Good luck, cousin,' Maria whispered, walking a few steps ahead and checking the coast was clear as Nellie disappeared out of the back door and down the lane.

∽

Abel collected Maria from the Big House the following Sunday after finishing her duties after lunch and they returned to the fever hospital.

'I know you will make the time up here,' Mrs Pennywick told her kindly, seeing how worried Maria was.

Maria fidgeted on the journey to the hospital, urging Abel to encourage Starlight to quicken his pace.

''E's doing his best, lass. Joey ain't going nowhere.'

As soon as they arrived, Maria leapt out of the cart, ran up to the hospital and flung open the door. She saw the same nurse seated in the corridor and rushed towards her.

'I've come to see me Joey. How is 'e?'

'Hello, it's Mrs Saward, isn't it?'

'Well, it's . . .' Maria began, intending to correct the nurse and tell her she was Miss Saward. Instead, she nodded her head, concealing her ringless finger between the folds of her skirt.

'I can ask the doctor and let you know, but I'm not sure if Joey is well enough for visitors yet.'

Maria's eyes welled. 'But surely, just for a moment, that's all I ask.'

'I'm sorry to disappoint you, Mrs Saward, after you have made this special journey in. We can't make any exceptions and our first concern is for the patient and preventing the spread of this infection. Have you considered too that it would also unsettle Joey if he saw you? It could be traumatic for him and jeopardise his recovery.'

Maria's bottom lip wobbled. 'But he'll be frightened in a strange place, I know he'll want to see me. When will I be able to see 'im? Why isn't 'e better?'

'Please, take a seat and wait a moment while I check Joey's condition with the doctor on duty.'

Maria's heart pounded. She sat where the nurse indicated, twisting her fingers in her lap and biting her lip. A couple approached from around the corner. The woman's shoulders shook as she sobbed loudly while the man fought back tears. The next moment the woman's knees gave way, and the man steadied her.

Maria rushed over to help, taking hold of the woman's arm. She was in her twenties with blonde curly hair pinned back with tortoiseshell hairpins. She wore a pale blue blouse with a crisp white collar and matching cuffs and a dark blue skirt. Her eyes were red and her cheeks were streaked with tears.

'Here, come and sit down for a moment,' Maria coaxed, concerned about the woman's distress.

The woman allowed herself to be led to a chair. She dabbed her eyes with a dainty lace-edged handkerchief and the man reached into his jacket pocket for his handkerchief and did the same.

He stuttered. 'We thank you for your kindness, only our daughter . . .'

Seeing pain etched across their tear-stained faces, Maria jerked her head back at the realisation of what he was going to say.

He stuttered, 'Her name was Rebecca and she was five years old.'

'My darling girl, my poor angel,' sobbed the woman.

'Ah, Mr and Mrs Hope, and Mrs Saward . . .' They all turned to face the nurse. 'I'm so sorry, Mr and Mrs Hope, so very sorry for your loss.'

The woman rose slowly, gripping her husband's hand. Her eyes were filled with sadness. 'Thank you, Mrs Saward,' she whimpered. 'I pray you don't suffer as we are. The loss of a child is unbearable.'

Maria's face crumpled as she watched the grieving parents walk out of the door without looking back, the woman wobbling unsteadily as her husband held her firmly. She couldn't help but think how their name had not lived up to its meaning.

She faced the nurse and spoke falteringly. 'My Joey won't die too, will 'e? He's been here near on a week. What did the doctor say?'

The nurse's face softened. 'These things take time, Mrs Saward. If you return next Sunday, there is a good chance you will be able to see Joey then, unless you have had notification from us before. There is a very good chance he will pull through.'

'Another week!' Maria exclaimed, fighting back her tears.

'It's for the best. Please try not to think of Mr and Mrs Hope. Their little girl was a weak little thing to start with and in a far worse state than your Joey. The doctors tried everything, they even shaved her head to cool her as she was burning such a high fever, but to no avail.'

'Oh no, you won't shave me Joey's head, will you?' Maria bleated.

'The doctors will do what is necessary. Please, Mrs Saward, go home and be assured we are all doing what we can for Joey. My name is Nurse Franklin, by the way. I'll be here next Sunday and will look out for you.'

Maria thanked the nurse and shuffled out despondently.

She paced the grounds outside waiting for Abel to return, knotting her fingers in her hands and trying not to think the worst. A gardener sucking on a clay pipe nodded as he trundled past with his wheelbarrow. She avoided the enquiring eye of the porter on the door. Feeling restless, she walked around the Victorian brick building and stopped in front of a large window.

She peered inside and saw a row of small beds on each side of the room. Standing on tiptoe, stretching her neck to look around both sides of the room, her eyes almost popped out of her head. Joey was in one of the beds in front of her. She had almost missed him as he was no longer her healthy, bouncing little boy full of laughter. She could just about make out his reddened eyes, his blotched torso and two nurses at his bedside with a bowl of water and a razor. The sight of Joey lying there so weak and helpless as he was about to have his head shaved tore at her heart.

A man's voice bellowed. "Ere, what do you think yer up to? This is private property. I 'ave a fair mind to report yer. What's yer name?'

The porter, a square-set man with a round face produced a pencil and notepad from his pocket. 'This is a fever hospital and the bosses don't take kindly to trespassers.'

'I'm not a trespasser! That's me boy in there,' wailed Maria. 'And a nurse there . . .'

The porter put his notepad away and spoke kindly. 'Oh, I recognise yer now. You came 'ere the other day with the young 'un, didn't yer?'

'I did, that was me. And the nurse, she's shaving his head. The nurse is shaving my Joey's head,' Maria cried.

'Now come on, lass, that's what they do 'ere to cool the little 'uns' heads when they burn a fever. They have to bring the fever down, you see. His hair will grow again.'

'But when they did that to Rebecca Hope she died. My Joey must be really poorly else they wouldn't be doing it.'

'All that blubbing ain't gonna 'elp 'im, is it? All yer can do is give it time,' he told her.

The familiar clip-clop of Starlight's hooves, his soft neighing snorts and the sight of Abel at the reins filled Maria with relief and she rushed over to them. She climbed on to the cart and rested her head on Abel's shoulder.

Abel smiled, chewing on a long piece of straw in the corner of his mouth as he flicked the reins. 'My missus used to like doing that too. Go ahead an' catch forty winks if yer can. You'll be all the better for it. There's nowt more you can do.'

∽

When they reached the cottage, Maria could scarcely believe she had nodded off. Abel told her, with a twinkle in his eye, that Starlight must have sensed her exhaustion as he carefully avoided any potholes.

Maria gratefully accepted Abel's offer to take her to the fever hospital the following Sunday. 'It ain't no trouble. I enjoy yer company. You're a plucky lass and I have a fondness for yer lad.'

She stepped into the house and opened a drawer in the dresser, taking out a small bundle of letters. She sat reading through them and even though they were short, and his handwriting just a scribble, Eddie's love for her was clear.

Just imagine us together again, Maria, walking along the lane arm in arm, little Joey with us, without a care in the world.

123

Maria choked as she read his words. 'I haven't forgotten yer,' she whispered, pressing the page to her lips and kissing it softly.

She rummaged around and found a fountain pen and some paper and wrote him a letter, promising to visit him as soon as she could.

Remember what yer said about walking along the lane arm in arm? Well, I want that too. Joey and me, we need yer. Try and picture that in your mind when yer feeling bad.

She signed it with her love and kisses. She checked upstairs and, seeing her mother was having a nap on the bed, decided to cycle over to the station master's house to leave the letter for Beatrice to give to Eddie at work the next day.

She dismounted from her bicycle when she reached Harry's house and noticed a large man's bicycle propped against the side of the house there too. She saw Betty in the garden bringing in the washing, with Leslie running around her ankles. The child ran straight to Maria and she scooped him up and swung him around playfully. Police Constable Rickett stepped out of the house.

Betty approached him and asked if he had got all the information he needed. 'She's asked me to come back in a couple of days, she's too upset to speak to me, so I'll leave it for now and come back later,' he told the housekeeper.

He turned to Maria. 'I'm sorry to hear about Joey. I hope he pulls through, he's a good little lad.'

Maria stuttered, 'Thank yer, Constable, that's kind of yer to say. I've just called in to leave a letter for Eddie at the hospital. I'm hoping Beatrice can give it to 'im.'

'Of course she will, here, give it to me, I'll give it to her later.' Betty took the note and placed it in her apron.

After the police constable left, Maria reached down to cuddle Leslie. Betty commented, 'Leslie is wearing me out good and proper. It will be lovely to have Joey back so they can play together.'

Maria asked Betty why the police officer was there and if he had mentioned anything about the woman who ran away from the station. Betty shook her head and the relief was visible on Maria's face.

Betty's eyebrows arched. 'He came to speak to Ada about that captain's death. It's really shaken her up. She was in no fit state to see him and make a statement so he's leaving it for now. Why should you ask about Nellie? You haven't seen her, have you?'

'Oh no,' Maria lied, walking straight to the gate to make a hasty exit.

Betty's eyebrows furrowed as she watched Maria leave. She mumbled under her breath, 'I hope she's telling the truth.'

Chapter Twelve

Police Constable Rickett returned two days later to speak to Ada. She was still deeply distressed but realised she could put the conversation off no longer. Since she had found the body of Captain Charles Hopkins-Handley slumped over his desk, a gun placed by his hand, she had been unable to remove the haunting image of his face from her head.

She asked the police officer, her voice trembling, 'Do you think he . . . I mean, surely it wasn't . . . ?'

The words stuck in Ada's throat. She couldn't bring herself to ask if the captain, only thirty-two years old, had deliberately taken his own life. It seemed inconceivable to her.

'That will be for the coroner to decide,' answered Police Constable Rickett formally. 'I am here to inform you that you will be required to attend the inquest to present your evidence. I will notify you of the date when it is decided, once the investigation is completed.'

'Evidence? What investigation?' whimpered Ada.

'Yes, of course, we have a duty to gather all the facts regarding the deceased and his untimely death and you will be required to make a statement.'

'How do you mean? What can I say that will help?'

'I can take your statement now, if you wish. And I believe there is a letter from your husband that could be of interest?'

Ada walked over to the oak roll-top bureau and opened a drawer. 'Here, this is the letter Alfie wrote asking me to visit the captain, if you think it will help.'

'It helps to set the scene, if you understand, explaining the process that led to your discovery of his body and the reason you went to his rooms.'

'You mean you can't take my word for it?' asked Ada edgily.

Police Constable Rickett coughed nervously, took the letter without a word and placed it in his jacket pocket. He asked her to recount the events, which she did, her voice croaky. She paused for a while, lowering her eyes, twisting her fingers in her lap, as she saw him staring at her. Finally, after she had told him everything she could recall, the police officer placed his notebook and pen in his pocket and left, apologising for any upset his visit had caused.

Ada had spent the last week in a state of extreme anxiety, unable to sleep and having little appetite. It was the first time she had seen a dead body, and to see one in these circumstances had really shaken her, the terrible events still vivid in her head. Her eyes had shadows underneath them as her nights were spent tormented, reliving the events. She kept asking herself, *Why? Why? Why?* as she reflected on how his death was a terrible waste of a talented young life.

Ada was aware that her husband was in touch with Charles's father, Sir Edgar Hopkins-Handley, through their mutual appreciation of music and the arts. She discovered from Police Constable Rickett that he was married to a talented actress called Annabel, and Ada surmised she must be the beautiful girl in the photograph on his desk. It caused Ada considerable anguish to consider the pain she must be feeling at the sudden death of her husband.

She was still trying to summon the courage to write to Alfie and inform him of his friend's death. She knew she couldn't put it off for much longer, but every time she seated herself at her father's bureau and picked up the fountain pen, her heart lurched against her ribs and scalding tears poured down her cheeks.

Betty put her head around the door. 'It looks like you have a visitor, I can see a well-dressed lady walking down the front path. Are you expecting anyone?'

'No, I most certainly am not, and I have no desire to see anyone either. I can't face anyone else in this state. Whoever it is, Betty, can you please say I am not available. I think I shall rest for a while.'

'Of course. I'm sure they'll understand. I'll explain that you are indisposed. I think a rest is a good idea, and maybe afterwards you'll be able to write that letter you keep putting off.'

'Where's Leslie? I've hardly seen him these past few days. I do feel I am a bad mother for neglecting him.'

'Don't you fret about Leslie. He's happy enough playing on the kitchen floor with the wooden engine that Mr Saward gave him. It's keeping him well occupied.'

'Thank you, Betty. How could I manage without you? You won't leave us, will you, not just yet?'

'No, I'll not be going anywhere.' Betty smiled, as she closed the door behind her.

Ada slumped into the winged armchair and shut her eyes. She saw Charles's lifeless face in her mind's eye, such a handsome young face, an image that sprung into her head whenever she closed her eyes. However hard she tried, she couldn't rid herself of it. Tears welled up and she dabbed her eyes.

The door burst open and Betty stepped into the room. 'I'm sorry, Ada, I did try explaining you were in no fit condition for visitors today, but Lady Appleby insisted and . . .'

A slender, elegantly dressed figure wearing a long mauve skirt with matching jacket, decorated with shiny black buttons over a neat white blouse, swept into the parlour, forcing the housekeeper to step aside.

'My dear Ada, please forgive me for my intrusion. I've heard about the terrible shock you have had and I had to call in and see you.'

Ada smiled thinly. She extended an arm in the direction of the sofa, inviting the woman to take a seat, nodding towards Betty that she could leave them alone together.

Lady Appleby had a youthful exuberance and appeared much younger than her sixty-two years. She was a close associate of Queen Alexandra, supporting her in many of her community endeavours. Lady Appleby shared the Dowager Queen's strong sense of philanthropy.

As soon as it became known that temporary war hospitals were needed in the country for wounded servicemen, Lord and Lady Appleby readily offered the use of their rolling estate, Hillington Hall, retaining a spacious wing at the back of the premises for their personal use.

'I've just called in to see dear Alix, our Queen Mother, and she passes you her warmest regards too. Such very sad news for Charles's family and a terrible shock for you to have witnessed,' the visitor sympathised.

Ada fought back the tears that were welling up.

'You look ghastly, Ada. I imagine you haven't stopped crying since finding Charles's body. How absolutely awful for you.'

Ada gulped. 'What I am feeling must be insignificant compared to the grief suffered by Charles's family. I've just had to relive it all for the police constable, it was upsetting for me, but it needed to be done.'

Lady Appleby rose and walked towards the armchair where Ada was seated. She took hold of her hands and pressed them gently. 'You are right, Charles's family is devastated. I came to inform you that Jonathan and I will be attending the funeral, and to ask if you wished to accompany us there.'

'Why thank you,' murmured Ada. 'That would be a comfort for me.'

'That's settled then. I've just read Charles's death notice in *The Times*, have you seen it? It was a wonderful tribute to his life. It's all so tragic, such a sad state of affairs. Jonathan and I are good friends with Charles's family going back many years. He was their only son, they are naturally devastated.'

Ada's lips quivered. 'I'm curious, Lady Appleby. Tell me, how did you learn that it was me who discovered Charles's body?'

'Beatrice let it slip. I saw her at the hospital two days ago. Our solicitor, Mr Perryman had called on us at Hillington Hall regarding a business matter and he was just leaving when I spotted some papers he left behind. I rushed down with them and overheard Beatrice mention Charles's name to him. I asked her if she knew him and she told me what happened.'

Ada's eyes fell to her lap. 'I blame myself. If I had seen Charles a day earlier, maybe I could have prevented it somehow. Maybe, if we had spoken, I could have seen or sensed his state of mind, I would have known if he was feeling disturbed.'

'Please don't allow yourself to think that. We still don't know the full facts. None of this is your fault. All these ifs and buts will not bring Charles back. Of course, poor Annabel is heartbroken and beside herself with grief. She is pregnant with their first child, you know. I can't begin to imagine what kind of emotional state she is in. I have written offering our sincere condolences.'

Ada's voice was soft. 'Pregnant? Oh, poor Annabel. How will she manage? How terribly sad that their child will never know its father.'

'It's all very tragic, my dear. Annabel's and Charles's family will take good care of them, but my heart goes out to her.'

This latest revelation made Ada snap out of her morose state and count her blessings that Leslie still had a father who would one day come home to him, as soon as he was able.

'Thank you, Lady Appleby. I feel better for talking this over with you. I can't believe Charles would have taken his life deliberately, leaving behind his wife and unborn child.'

Lady Appleby pursed her lips. 'Do not concern yourself with the cause of death, that is for the coroner to decide. It so happens the coroner is a good friend of my husband's and I have every confidence that he will get to the bottom of this and record a, shall we say, favourable outcome for the family.'

Ada merely demurred, unsure what a 'favourable outcome' was. She let it pass, querying, 'Do you feel my presence at the funeral will distress Charles's family?'

'On the contrary, I'm sure they would like to meet you. Charles was such a talented actor, you know, cut off in his prime.'

Ada's eyebrows rose. 'It's so tragic. What kind of actor was he?'

'The classics, mainly. His wife was on the stage with him, that's how they met, she's such a dear soul. While I am here, Ada, there is another matter I would like to raise with you. It will also, I hope, help take your mind off this awful tragedy.'

'I'm not sure I'm up to anything at the moment.'

'Let me be the judge of that, dear Ada. I fear this tragedy has made you too withdrawn. You need bringing out of yourself a little.'

'Maybe you are right. I have been brooding about it and fear it has prevented me from being the attentive mother I should be. I've felt utterly wretched, as if a big stone was weighted inside me that will not shift.'

Lady Appleby thought for a moment, then leant forward. 'Firstly, my dear, I don't believe for one moment that your child has been neglected in any way. Whenever I have seen Leslie he appears a happy little fellow, the picture of good health. You must bear in mind that young boys that age can play up from time to time. But it's a normal part of their growing up, my Tobias used to have the most embarrassing tantrums. Believe me, your Leslie is an angel compared to how my son behaved at his age.'

Ada's face broke into a small smile. 'Really? Betty says very much the same, though I must confess, I do find him totally exhausting at times.'

'I can see you are in need of a tonic. A change is as good as a rest, as they say, and in this case, a diversion of the mind. I hope what I am going to suggest will interest you. In fact, it is a very topical issue that has roused the interest of women throughout the country who are united in their desire for change to be made that will make a very big and positive difference to many lives.'

Intrigued, Ada tilted her head to one side. 'Please, do tell me what you have in mind. I am very curious.'

Lady Appleby fished in her bag and produced a leaflet. 'I'm not sure if you're aware that I am on the committee of National Baby Week. It is to be held the first week of July, and you can be a part of it.'

'National Baby Week? I've heard some mention of it, but not taken much notice. How can I help?' queried Ada.

She had read reports in the paper about the national campaign that was gathering momentum throughout the country, but her own troubled thoughts had prevented her from enquiring further.

'Oh, there's plenty you can do. The facts are quite shocking. Did you know that in 1915 more babies died at home than servicemen at the Front; twelve babies died for every nine soldiers.'

Ada's jaw dropped. 'No, I had no idea. That's absolutely shocking.'

The words tumbled from Lady Appleby's mouth, her eyes shining with passion. 'Because of disease and poor hygiene, because of poverty and overcrowded families living in rat-infested slum dwellings, because of poor midwifery and ignorance. We are campaigning for the government to form a Ministry of Health. We want a free health service for infants, like they have in New Zealand. If it can be done there, why not here?'

Ada perked up for the first time since discovering the captain's body. 'What you are doing is admirable. I would very much like to be involved.'

'I was hoping you would say that. We have many events planned in London and if you could work on a stall for just one of the days, that would be a marvellous help.'

'Of course, Lady Appleby, you can count on me. I had no idea that so many babies were dying in such terrible circumstances. Those poor babies and mothers, what chance do they have unless improvements are made to their living conditions?'

'Exactly. You are my saviour, Ada. One of my ladies had to pull out suddenly as she is going to spend a few days with a bereaved relative in Sussex.'

Ada straightened her back. 'Surely, with the terrible loss of life through war, we need to have a future generation of healthy infants who when they grow up can help rebuild our country when all of this is over?'

'That is absolutely correct. Today's infants and young children will be be the future generation and we need to do the best we can for them. The scheme has taken off better than we could have hoped for and events are being held all around the country, not just in London. The Canon of Westminster will deliver a sermon next week on Baby Sunday, the first of July, and the following day Queen Mary has kindly agreed to open our exhibition at the Methodist Central Hall, Westminster. It will be simply marvellous. In fact, your sister Beatrice may well be there too.'

'Oh really? I had no idea she was going.'

'Apparently, some of her disabled patients have made the most exquisite needlework displays on canvas and they are to be displayed there. She will accompany one or two of the patients to the exhibition, those who can travel best, and they will demonstrate how they do their work.'

Ada's face broke into a small smile. 'Thank you, Lady Appleby. I already feel my mood lifting. Being able to contribute towards something as meaningful as this will give me a sense of purpose and I can see that's what I need right now.'

'Helping others is always good for the soul. I can already see some colour returning to your cheeks.'

After Lady Appleby bade farewell Ada plucked up some courage and took a seat at the bureau to inform Alfie of his friend's death. The words faltered at first, but her flow steadily increased and when she finished she pressed her lips against the envelope as she sealed it, wishing Alfie a speedy, safe return to Wolferton.

Her mind dwelled on National Baby Week. Her eyebrows furrowed as she recalled Lady Appleby's shocking words about the suffering of families whose babies and infants were taken by the Grim Reaper due to poverty and poor education.

Losing men on the battlefields may be beyond their control, but she could, and would, do all she could to help prevent more mothers suffering.

Chapter Thirteen

Ada barely slept a wink the night prior to Charles's funeral. The prospect of facing his grieving widow and family unnerved her. As she pulled her black mourning dress over her head in the morning, she almost had second thoughts about going, but knew she needed to force herself on account of Alfie's affections for his old pal.

Ada's hands shook as she buttoned her gown up at the front, the black fabric making her face appear even more drawn. Jessie had thoughtfully cut a spray of white roses from the garden for her to lay at the grave. Ada tucked two letters in her black embroidered handbag, the personal heartfelt notes of condolence she had written for Charles's widow and parents.

Betty had offered to keep an eye on Leslie, and when Ada made her way downstairs, he excitedly jumped off his chair when the housekeeper mentioned they would picnic in a sheltered spot in the woods.

Beatrice appeared unexpectedly and offered to accompany Ada to the funeral. It was her half-day at the hospital and Ada gladly accepted, rather than impose on Lady Appleby. She asked her mother to call Lady Appleby from the post office to inform her of her change of plans, which she did.

∽

The funeral was to take place at St Margaret's Church in the heart of King's Lynn, close to the location of Charles's death. The church was a fifteen-minute walk from the town's railway station, and as the sisters alighted on the path, Beatrice gripped Ada's hand as she felt her wobble and reassured her sister she would do Alfie proud.

The last time Ada had set foot in this church was to listen to Alfie playing an organ recital, which had been well reviewed in the press. As she walked up the aisle, which was flanked by stone arches on either side, the sound of weeping caught her attention. She saw a woman's hunched figure draped in black, a comforting arm around her shoulder. The pews were packed with sombre-faced mourners, many of them tearful, sobbing into handkerchiefs. Ada and Beatrice took their seats halfway down the aisle just before the church doors opened. They turned their heads as the coffin was carried past by six of Charles's regimental colleagues marching in uniform as the organist thundered 'Jerusalem', a hymn that defined their strong British roots and patriotism. The William Blake tune was intended to lift the spirits of people during the Great War and it tugged at the heartstrings, making mourners even more tearful.

The sight of Charles's coffin, his cap placed on top of the Union Jack, which was draped across the coffin, as the hymn played, made Ada well up and choked cries could be heard from around the church.

The vicar spoke stirringly about Charles's immense power of persuasion to make people believe in him, whether on stage taking on the guise of a character, or as a leader of men in the army.

He told the congregation, 'Charles's desire for peace, for a world where mankind loved one another, is a dream that will one day be fulfilled, we can be sure of that. We pray that Charles has peace now in God's arms.'

Ada's attention peaked when one of Charles's actor friends spoke with a theatrical flourish from the pulpit. He wore a dramatic black velvet cloak and spoke eloquently about Charles's thespian talents, saying the world was a poorer place for his loss. He recited lines from Shakespeare's *Measure for Measure*:

> *If I must die,*
> *I will encounter darkness*
> *as a bride,*
> *And hug it in mine arms.*

The vicar addressed the mourners again, saying God's cloak of love was shrouded around them in their moment of grief, protecting them from the heartaches of sorrow. Few believed it at that moment, weighed down by their grief.

There wasn't a dry eye when the service finished. Charles's widow, her black veil hiding her face, her shoulders visibly shaking, was supported by an elegant older woman who Ada assumed was her mother. The congregation followed behind the coffin to the 'Radetzky March', a poignant tune on this sombre occasion.

Ada was too distraught to join the family at the graveside where Charles was to be buried with full military honours. Beatrice suggested they should go ahead instead to the wake at Duke's Head Hotel. It was a short walk from the church and they could take refreshments there while they waited, giving Ada a chance to compose herself. Many others appeared to have the same idea as they walked in that direction too.

As they arrived at the hotel on the Tuesday Market Place, the same place that had been packed with thousands of families and soldiers who paraded as they marched off to war, Beatrice recognised a familiar figure standing on the front steps outside the hotel.

George Perryman gave a small bow to the sisters and Beatrice felt a warmth stirring inside her. 'I wasn't expecting to see you here today,' commented Beatrice, her heartbeat suddenly quickening.

Her cheeks flushed as she thought back to how she had snubbed George at the hospital when he had asked her out for the afternoon, but he showed no signs of discomfort.

'I represent Lady Appleby's family and the deceased's too. I will tell you more inside, if you ladies would like to join me for refreshments while the burial takes place. I must say that was the most moving funeral service I have ever been to.'

Beatrice and Ada followed George into the hotel's comfortable lounge. He settled them in some plush peach armchairs in front of the window, leaning heavily on his silver-topped stick.

The solicitor's eyes lingered on Beatrice's face, a tender look behind them, making her heart skip a beat. 'What would you ladies like to drink? Some tea? Or something stronger? May I recommend a sherry? It's a delight to see you again, Ada. I'm so sorry it was you who found Charles's body. He was a very decent man. Is there news of your husband with the Artists Rifles?'

Ada's eyebrows furrowed. 'Only to say he cannot take leave yet as they have suffered too many casualties. Thank the Lord he has escaped unharmed, so far. A sherry sounds like the perfect thing to calm my nerves, thank you, George.'

'A whisky for me,' he ordered from the waiter who appeared. 'And two of your finest sherries for my companions.'

As they sipped their drinks, the solicitor explained that he would be acting on behalf of the Hopkins-Handley family at the inquest as they were dear family friends. In fact, he added, his uncle, Sir Henry Perryman, was the coroner.

'Oh, I had no idea you were related to Lord Perryman,' Beatrice commented.

Ada leant towards him, unable to hold back. 'Can you tell me honestly, what do you think, George? Did Charles really intend to take his life? I can't believe he could do such a thing and leave his wife in her delicate situation.'

Beatrice shot her a glance. 'Oh, Ada, I'm sure George is not at liberty to disclose confidential details about this very sensitive matter.'

Mr Perryman's face broke into a smile. 'I quite understand why Ada would ask, and while I am limited with what information I can share, there is a delicate matter we need to discuss while we are alone.'

Ada asked, 'Is it something to do with the inquest?'

The solicitor leant closer towards the sisters. 'It is indeed. I must ask first, can I please rely on your utmost discretion, that you will not repeat a word I say?'

'Of course,' both sisters replied in unison, their eyebrows arched.

'I have Charles's best interest at heart when I ask this of you, as will become evident.'

Mr Perryman cleared his throat and glanced over his shoulder to ensure nobody was within earshot, then leant even closer so his breath could be felt on the sisters' faces. He spoke in a hushed tone.

'I believe there was a pamphlet on Charles's desk about a play called *The Pacifists*. It is currently on stage in London and is due to go on tour.'

Ada confirmed she had seen the pamphlet. 'What about it?'

'Charles's family are anxious that the leaflet is not referred to as Charles having it does not show him in a patriotic light. His parents were frequent guests at Sandringham, invited personally by King Edward and performed for him on the piano on many special occasions.

They are concerned that public knowledge about him possessing this leaflet could suggest he had certain views, which could create a scandal and slur their good name. If people assume that Charles was a pacifist, and, in their eyes, a coward when he was a serving officer, it could be very bad news. I've seen your statement to the police constable and there is no mention of it there. Was there any reason for this omission?'

'That's correct. When I saw the leaflet I did wonder whether it was of any significance, but felt nobody could be sure one way or the other, so felt it was best to say nothing. It has played on my mind since. I must confess I feel in a quandary about it now and I can't lie to the coroner if the issue is raised.'

Mr Perryman took hold of Ada's hand. 'I promise you won't be telling lies. Saying nothing isn't the same as lying, and what purpose would it serve to mention it now? Absolutely none. I should also add that the police officer who attended the scene has disposed of the pamphlet and no mention of it is included in the coroner's papers. Can we forget it ever existed?'

Ada stuttered, 'Well, if you think that's the right thing. What do you think, Beatrice?'

Beatrice paused before answering. 'I think we have to place our complete trust in Mr Perryman. I know from past experience that he has only the best interests of the people he serves at heart, whether they be the likes of Robbie Bucket, or distinguished families like Charles's. They say a man's reputation is worth a king's ransom. If

Charles's parents have faithfully served the royal family in the past and they fear disclosure of their son's involvement with *The Pacifist* would harm their standing, I see no point in adding further to their distress, and George should be commended for his consideration towards a grieving family.'

Mr Perryman's eyes lit up. 'Thank you for your kind words, Beatrice. It is much appreciated. The truth is, Charles was one of the financial backers of the play, he was in partnership with the gentleman who spoke at the funeral. It would break his parents' hearts if it came out that Charles was a pacifist, and I intend to also seek his partner's discretion. This is not a time for making political statements. As far as Charles's parents and Annabel are concerned, he was a hero, and must remain so in their eyes.'

Ada readily agreed.

An hour later, they spotted the arrival of the tear-stained faces of Charles's family being escorted to a separate reception room next to the bar.

'My heart goes out to Annabel. I admire her courage so much,' Ada commented. 'I'm told her baby is due next month. Can you imagine how very sad it will be for her to bring a child into the world who will never know its father?'

Mr Perryman left the sisters to speak to other mourners in the bar's lounge. He was deep in conversation with an older man with thick white hair like cotton wool, a walrus moustache and bushy side whiskers. An elegant woman by his side was dressed from head to toe in black and draped in shimmering jewels down her front and around her wrists. Annabel stood alongside them, her swollen belly clearly evident. George caught Ada's eye and indicated she should join them.

Beatrice had left her seat to tidy her hair and Ada stepped nervously towards the group, still clutching the roses.

'Sir Edgar, Lady Sarah and Annabel, I would like to introduce you to Mrs Ada Heath, the wife of Charles's dear friend, Alfred Heath, and daughter of the royal station master at Wolferton. It was she who discovered Charles's body on a visit at her husband's request.'

Ada felt her cheeks redden. She offered her condolences and presented the flowers to Annabel with her card. 'I'm so very, very sorry for your loss. I believe my husband Alfie knows you through your musical connections, and I am so very pleased to meet you, though I wish it was in happier circumstances.'

Annabel dabbed her moist eyes. In spite of her grief Ada couldn't help noticing the young widow's natural beauty. She had a perfectly formed heart-shaped face with the clearest complexion, rosebud lips and the brightest sapphire eyes Ada had ever seen.

Sir Edgar was a tall man who held himself upright, a silver-topped cane propping him up, like George. He was every inch the distinguished gentleman. He whispered in Ada's ear, his words sticking in his throat. 'I believe Mr Perryman has spoken to you about our . . . rather delicate matter . . . and that we can rely on your discretion?'

His thick eyebrows, which were streaked with grey, lifted as he fixed his eyes firmly on Ada's face.

'Of course. I am so very sorry for your loss,' she replied, knowing that it was what Alfie would have wanted her to do. 'If there is anything else I can do to help during this sad time, please let me know.'

'That's very kind of you. We are all most grateful,' he replied. He then turned to speak to a group of mourners in the corner of the room who were trying to catch his attention.

Lady Appleby spotted Ada and walked over to join her, and after exchanging feelings of sadness for the occasion, she wished Ada well for the forthcoming inquest.

'It's really nothing to worry about. It's just a formality. And then afterwards you will be able to put it behind you and plan ahead to National Baby Week.'

'I'm already looking forward to Baby Week,' Ada replied, observing Beatrice out of the corner of her eye. George was now standing close to her sister, holding her arm with an intense expression on his face as she spoke. He seemed to be enraptured with her.

Lady Appleby spotted the direction of Ada's straying eyes. 'They make a lovely couple, don't they?'

'I was thinking the same,' agreed Ada. 'But does Beatrice think so?'

Beatrice threw her head back and covered her mouth with her hand to conceal her laughter. A moment later, George was swept away from Beatrice by a group of young women. Beatrice, looking on in amazement, made her way to Ada and Lady Appleby.

'It looks like he has some admirers there, judging by the way the Grainger sisters are fawning over him. Their mother and aunt look very pleased to have him in their company,' Lady Appleby murmured with a mischievous look in her eye. 'I have noticed him looking at you out of the corner of his eye. Is there something I should know?'

Beatrice blushed. 'I do like George, but I'm not sure if I like him in that way. Besides, I might have put him off when I turned down an invitation from him not so long ago.'

Ada blurted, 'Are you blind, Beatrice? He is besotted with you, anyone can see that. He's a good sort, a very decent man. Look how the Grainger girls are hanging on to his every word.'

'There's nothing like some competition to discover what the heart desires, my dear Beatrice. What is your heart telling you?' Lady Appleby asked softly, with a kind look in her eye.

Beatrice inhaled a deep breath. She glanced over at George and was surprised to feel her pulse racing and a giddy sensation rising inside her. Ignoring the attention of his company, he returned her gaze. Their eyes locked, telling her the answer within her heart.

Yes, my nursing means the world to me, but I have no intention of being married to it, like Matron.

Chapter Fourteen

Lady Appleby was correct when she said the inquest was just a formality. Ada arrived in good time at the town hall where the hearing was due to be held, hoping it would be over quickly. An official from the coroner's court, wearing a dark suit, showed her to a waiting room.

Charles's parents were already there seated on hard bentwood seats, their faces etched with sadness, deep in conversation with Mr Perryman. Annabel sat with them, her hands protectively across her swollen belly, with Lady Appleby nearby. She looked up when Ada entered the room and glanced at her reassuringly. A couple of army officials sat reading notes in the corner, and a moment later a smartly dressed gentleman wearing a dark grey suit joined them, who turned out to be the doctor.

Police Constable Rickett nodded solemnly as he entered the room, respectfully removing his policeman's hat. A moment later, the clerk stepped into the room and called the group into the coroner's court. The court comprised of wooden benches with a raised platform on one side, an enclosed area for witnesses to give their evidence. The sombre-looking clerk sat at a table at the top of the room and he asked everyone to stand when the coroner walked in.

Ada looked down at her hands and noticed they were shaking. She was relieved to see that Sir Henry Perryman had a kindly face. He explained it was his duty to determine the circumstances and medical causes of sudden, violent and unnatural deaths. Both Charles's mother and widow sobbed at the mention of these words, which sounded so cold and matter of fact spoken out loud. The coroner paused. He looked kindly at them and allowed them a few moments to compose themselves and to take sips of water from the glasses in front of them.

Much to her alarm, Ada was the first witness to be called. She trembled as the coroner read her statement aloud, cross-referencing with Alfie's letter, which suggested she visit Charles, then looked across at her.

'This must have been a distressing experience for you, Mrs Heath. It was very kind of you to follow up on your husband's suggestion to visit the deceased. He was fortunate to have had such good friends as yourselves. Thank you for your statement. I have no questions, that is all I need from you, unless there is anything else you would like to add?'

Ada's heart pounded. This was the moment for her to mention *The Pacifists* if she wished. She paused for a moment, and after a few seconds she raised her chin and answered firmly. 'No, sir, that is all I have to say.'

The maid who was with Ada when Charles's body was discovered suddenly burst into the room. All eyes swivelled in her direction.

'I do apologise for me lateness,' she mumbled awkwardly.

'Miss Curtis, I believe?' enquired the clerk. 'Please come straight to the front and take the stand.'

The maid corroborated Ada's story. After she had finished giving evidence, she asked the coroner, 'Please, sir, may I be excused now, only I've got beds to change and rooms to clean before the new arrivals come tonight.'

Permission was granted and she exchanged a swift glance with Ada as she passed her. Dr Gibson, a small bespectacled man in his forties with a round face, was called next. He confirmed Charles had died from a single self-inflicted gunshot wound to the head. The coroner asked if he could tell if it had been deliberate, or if the fatal wound was an accident. The doctor shook his head and said he could not say for sure.

The two army officers gave their evidence next and told the coroner they had no reason to suspect anything was amiss with Charles's mental state. They described him as a popular officer who had an exemplary military record and was destined for a distinguished career in the army. They insisted his manner appeared perfectly normal and that he was well prepared and looking forward to leading his commission.

The senior officer added, 'Having seen his room it appears to me that Captain Charles Hopkins-Handley was cleaning the pistol at the time and a latch slipped which resulted in the fatality. It was an accident, a terrible tragic accident. We would like to extend our sympathies once more to his family.'

The coroner arched his eyebrows. 'Are you sure of this? There is no doubt in your mind?'

'None whatsoever, sir.'

The coroner demurred. 'Yes, I can see that's quite possible and is the most likely explanation. How terribly unfortunate.'

Having heard from all of the witnesses, the coroner thanked everyone for their thoughtful evidence.

'I have taken everything into consideration and am in no doubt that there is only one verdict I should record, one of accidental death. As stated earlier, it would appear the captain was cleaning his pistol when his hand slipped, causing the bullet to pass through his head. I would like to extend my deepest condolences to his widow and family for their loss.'

Ada saw Annabel and Charles's mother dab their eyes as the coroner described Charles as a hero his family could be proud of, who had served his country well and had fully deserved to be buried with full military honours. His eyes met those of Charles's father and they exchanged a nod.

With the hearing at an end, everyone rose to leave. As Annabel stood, she bent over and gripped her stomach, filling the room with a pained cry. Lady Appleby caught her in her arms as she wobbled. Annabel's face was contorted in pain as she attempted to stand, but she doubled up again over her swollen belly and emitted a piercing scream.

Lady Appleby searched her face. 'Is it the baby?'

Annabel nodded. She cried out again. 'I think . . . it's coming . . .'

The coroner's mouth opened wide. 'You mean to say, you're having your baby now?'

Annabel's face was filled with fear. She gripped Lady Appleby's arm tightly.

'She can't have her baby here. We must get her to the hospital. Is the doctor still here?' Lady Appleby asked in a worried voice.

Dr Gibson had already rushed to Annabel's side clutching his black medical bag. 'I always carry it with me, in case of emergencies. Clear the room everyone,' he ordered.

'This is a first,' the coroner muttered under his breath. 'This room is usually required to resolve issues of sudden death; it's never been used for a birth before.'

Ada bit her lip. Her heart went out to Annabel, who was clearly in much pain. She caught Lady Appleby's eye and was about to make a discreet exit when Annabel turned suddenly to her and gripped her hand. She pleaded 'Stay with me, Ada. Please. I'm terrified of giving birth.'

'Me? But you have Lady Appleby.'

'You're nearer my age, and I like you,' Annabel gasped, beads of sweat dotting her brow.

'Are you sure, Annabel?' queried Lady Appleby gently. 'I can stay too if you like.'

'No, just Ada,' cried Annabel. 'I know you need to leave, you mentioned so earlier.'

'It's true, Ada, I do have a meeting with Queen Mary shortly. She is anxious for the latest news on National Baby Week. I could send word to her . . .'

'There's no need,' wailed Annabel.

'Very well. I would have peace of mind if I knew you could stay with Annabel, Ada.'

'Of course I'll stay,' Ada murmured. She recalled her own experience of giving birth, which had been unpleasant and one she was only too happy to forget. She brushed her own feelings aside and asked in a clear voice, 'What can I do to help?'

Annabel's pained eyes showed her gratitude. Lady Appleby gave Ada a grateful glance, then slipped out of the room as Annabel gripped Ada's hand and squeezed it.

'I know how it feels. I promise you everything will be all right,' Ada said softly.

She quickly took charge, calling out to Charles's parents to fetch towels and hot water. She pointed to a space at the front of the room which would serve as the birthing area. Annabel waddled over to the area, pausing and gripping the side of the bench when a contraction took her breath away.

The towels and hot water appeared within minutes, as well as some sheets, blankets and pillows that had been borrowed from a nearby hotel. Ada spread them out on the floor. She could imagine the shocked expressions of office workers who were told about a baby's imminent arrival in the coroner's court, of all places. Charles's parents were instructed to remain outside the door, to guard it and be sure nobody entered.

Then there were just the two women and the doctor, who asked Annabel to remove her undergarments. Annabel breathed a huge sigh of relief as she was no longer constricted then doubled over as another wave of contractions surged, pain etched on her face, which was now bathed in sweat.

Annabel gasped for breath and tossed her head back, gripping Ada's hand so tightly that she feared her bones would be crushed. The station master's daughter stroked Annabel's forehead, offering soothing words of reassurance and recounting amusing stories of Leslie growing up to distract her from the pain. Ada told her how he would snuggle on her lap and she would read to him and how he loved chasing Magnolia's cats and pulling their tails. Annabel managed a weak smile, then winced in pain. Ada grimaced as she remembered how unbearable she had found giving birth following a pregnancy plagued by sickness and discomfort.

'There, there,' Ada soothed. 'You are doing really well, Annabel. Just take a deep breath, that's better. And again, take another.'

Ada could see Annabel squeezing every muscle on her face and holding back the screams that were becoming more frequent. Dr Gibson urged her to 'Push'; 'Push harder'; 'Just one more push, I can see its head'; 'Push, push, come on, Mrs Hopkins-Handley give me one more big, big push . . .'

A long piercing scream, which must have resounded around the whole of King's Lynn, was followed by the sweet sound of a baby's cry.

Annabel collapsed back on the floor and gave a big sigh. Ada gripped her hand tightly, her face beaming as the doctor announced, 'It's a boy. A healthy boy! Congratulations, Annabel. You have a son.'

Tears cascaded down Annabel's face as she tenderly held her son in her arms. He was wrinkled and curled up tight, slowly stretching out his tiny limbs and crying softly. She stroked his cheek and bent over to kiss him gently. It was a bittersweet moment that tugged at Ada's heartstrings, knowing that this baby would never know his father's love.

Seeing the baby being born, a new life entering the world, filled her with raw emotions. She was transfixed at the sight of him being held in his adoring mother's arms, his eyes staring directly into her face. Annabel placed her son on her breast, moving his tiny lips with her finger to help him latch on.

Annabel looked over at Ada. She whispered in a hoarse voice, 'Thank you, Ada. Thank you so much for being here for me. I have been blessed with the most perfect son. He looks so much like his father.'

Ada was suddenly overcome with feelings of guilt, regretting the moments she hadn't been there for her own son when she found him too much of a handful. She vowed that she would never again take being a mother for granted. She would shower Leslie with the love he deserved.

The words stuck in Ada's throat. 'He's beautiful, Annabel. He's just perfect.'

Annabel continued, her eyes moist, 'When my son grows up, I shall tell him what a hero his papa was.'

Chapter Fifteen

My duty's now done
I gave it my best
Thinking on of our comrades
Still fighting at our behest
I'm left now with one leg
It's not such a to-do
Whatever my future holds
My loyalty to King and country remains true

'Oh, Private Cripps, I think that's wonderful. It's so well expressed. You should submit it to the *Tommy Herald*.'

The soldier turned his face away, but not before Beatrice saw him bite his lip and swallow hard, fighting back the tears.

'I've never written a poem before. I read something like it somewhere and it stuck in my mind, and then I added my own words to it as well. Are you sure it's all right? I did it for you, Nurse Saward, 'cause I know how well you cared for me here and I count myself lucky to be alive.'

'It's just wonderful, Private Cripps. You are a credit to yourself the way you keep your spirits up. I know it can't be easy,' Beatrice told him, her face unable to disguise the pity she felt for this once fit young man, now facing life as a cripple.

Johnnie Cripps gazed down at the floor. She knew he didn't want her to see the emotions etched on his face.

'Private Cripps, please, look at me. Let me help you,' she said in a soft voice.

He nervously raised his eyes and they fixed on her concerned face. 'It ain't easy, truth be told. Matron said to write something positive for the hospital magazine. But look at me. What is there positive to say about my situation? How am I gonna be of any use to anyone with one leg?'

Beatrice shot a quick glance in Eddie's direction. They were seated at a table in the day room and Eddie was at the next one over. She hoped he hadn't heard Johnnie's words, but Eddie appeared to be distracted with a letter he was writing. He seemed to be struggling with it, scribbling out lines and tossing the paper aside, and then starting again.

Johnnie was a new patient who had arrived two days after Eddie. Beatrice had suggested to Matron that Johnnie should be placed further away from Eddie in case the close proximity of Private Cripps' amputation distressed him, but Matron said this was nonsense. Private Cripps' leg was removed before he arrived at Hillington Hall and she could not make exceptions, saying the disabled soldier might be able to help Eddie accept his fate if he too needed to have his leg amputated.

'When they come to us here, it is our job to prepare them for the outside world. Private Herring needs to get used to the idea,' Matron told Beatrice crisply.

Though deemed physically fit, Private Cripps still suffered nightmares from the attack on the Western Front when his leg was blown off and he needed support with rehabilitation, which Hillington Hall was gaining a reputation for excelling at.

Beatrice was concerned to note that Eddie's mood was becoming lower each day, and not just because of the worry about his leg. She knew he was desperate to see Maria. He had asked about her every day in the two weeks since he had been admitted, and his mother's visits were unable to fill the void in his heart. Each day she replied with the same. 'You just need to be patient a little longer, Eddie. Maria isn't allowed to come until Joey is better. Matron would have a fit if she came here with Joey still poorly.'

That morning, Beatrice saw the same crestfallen expression on Eddie's face when she told him Maria would not be coming in; she had taken to stopping off at Honeysuckle Cottage on her way home from work when she could. Maria was usually at work, and Ruth would pass on the message, leaving Beatrice to be the bearer of disappointing news.

Beatrice stared across at Eddie and sensed he was brooding. She invited him to join Private Cripps and herself.

'Private Cripps was just showing me a poem he's written. We're hoping it will be published in the next issue of the *Tommy Herald*. Perhaps you would like to write a small article, or draw a picture, contribute whatever you wish.'

'Na. I'm not educated like that. What could I put in it?' Eddie scoffed.

'I wouldn't say what I've written is going to win prizes, but if I can scribble a few words down, you can too,' Private Cripps encouraged.

'I've just been trying to write a note to Maria, and I've not even managed that. I'm not very good at putting words down on paper.'

Beatrice suggested, 'I'll help you with your letter later, Eddie. To get some writing practice in, why don't you write about Wolferton Station and your work there, the people you meet on journeys up and down the line? By the way, Father – I mean, Mr Saward – sends you his best regards and says he will try to visit you sometime on Sunday afternoon.'

'That would be a treat, I would very much like that. But truth be told, I just don't see why anyone would be interested in what I have to say. And who reads this stuff anyway?'

'You would be surprised, Private Herring. The *Tommy Herald* is very popular and sells more and more copies each month. People enjoy reading stories written by Tommies – ordinary men like you and Private Cripps – about their real life experiences of the war. They want to hear it straight from you, nothing fancy. You could write a poem, like Private Cripps did, or even do a drawing. Then you could show it to Maria when it's printed, I know she would be proud of you whatever you do. If you like, I'll see if I can find you a spare copy from last month and then you will have a good idea what the *Tommy Herald* is like.'

Eddie shrugged his shoulders. 'If you say so. Perhaps I'll give it a go, seeing as I don't have anything else to do.'

Beatrice glanced around the day room where various therapeutic activities were held. It was one of two day rooms situated on either side of the hospital's grand entrance and had formerly been Lord and Lady Appleby's drawing room. It was a light, airy room where the sun streamed in, its vast bay window reaching from floor to ceiling with wooden shutters nailed back and giving glorious views across the immaculate grounds.

With still no sign of the war coming to an end, the demand for more men to sign up was becoming desperate. It broke Beatrice's heart if a soldier under her care was later posted overseas and killed. 'If only they could stay in England once they had patched them up,' she would say.

Matron had first tentatively suggested that the hospital should have its own magazine after hearing of such success in other war hospitals. She broached this with Major Griffiths, the hospital's commanding officer, who readily agreed and set up a committee which he served on with Matron, Beatrice, Lady Appleby, and a couple of other nurses. Major Griffiths had editorial control and the final say on its content, claiming he had enjoyed some moderate success as a writer while at university. His father had had a successful army career and dismissed notions that he wanted to have a writing career, insisting he follow the army life instead.

Beatrice observed the major stepping into Matron's office for a quick catch-up to discuss the paper's next edition. Matron opened her desk drawer and handed the major some paperwork. Beatrice knocked and entered the room and was invited to join the meeting.

'You enquired about the content, Major. With the aid of Nurse Saward, Private Bowers has contributed an excellent article about his needlework. It is indeed most heart-warming. In fact, he is one of our disabled soldiers who will display his fine work at the National Baby Week convention in London next week,' Matron said.

'That's excellent news, Matron. I shall leave this in your capable hands and look forward to reading about it in the next *Tommy Herald*. Tell the lads they are doing a grand job and making their country proud.'

After he left the office, Beatrice turned to Matron. 'I can barely believe the change in Private Bowers. I regard it as a privilege to escort our patients there.'

'This is a golden opportunity for us to show the rehabilitation work we do here. We shall rely on Private Bowers to fly the flag for us. It could help provide sponsors, or even commissions.'

Beatrice's face broke into a smile. 'I'll do my best, Matron. From what Ada tells me, there are going to be hundreds of stalls there. It would really boost Private Bowers' confidence too. He's been feeling very low recently. His family have not been able to visit yet, and although he puts on a brave face, I can see how upset he is about it.'

'Indeed, Nurse Saward. While we are on the subject, I believe Private Herring is still waiting for his young lady to visit. Do you know when she might come? His mood is very low and I'm afraid his leg is not looking too good and the infection has worsened.'

Beatrice's eyes showed concern. 'Oh no, poor Eddie. I was worried that might happen, and after everything he has been through. I know Maria will visit as soon as she can, once her son Joey has been given the all-clear for scarlet fever. We can't take the risk of her bringing the infection here. I'm afraid he took the news badly.'

'That can't be helped for now. Do keep an eye on him, Nurse Saward. My father will see him later this week and can advise us about his leg.'

Beatrice's eyes narrowed. 'I hope there is a chance it can be saved.'

They turned their heads at the sound of cheers erupting on the ward.

'I think your gentleman friend is here,' nudged Matron, with a twinkle in her eye.

Beatrice blushed. 'Oh, but he isn't my gentleman. We're just friends.'

'I can see by the colour of your cheeks that you like him. Take my advice, Nurse Saward, and grab the chance at love while you can. I wish I had. You could do far worse than George Perryman.'

Matron returned to her office leaving Beatrice speechless. She knew Matron was right. Her advice jolted Beatrice into opening her eyes fully and she felt a fluttering sensation ripple inside her as George limped along the ward. He had a big grin on his face and was carrying a bundle of cigarette packets. She blushed as she saw his eyes fixed on her face. Beatrice reddened even more as the cheers from the patients became louder and some wolf-whistled.

George's gaze barely left her face as he dished out cigarettes to raised hands that beckoned him over. As the cheers continued it felt as if George was being greeted with a hero's welcome.

'Isn't he wonderful?' whispered a voice behind her.

Beatrice turned and saw Nurse Jennings tilt her head in George's direction.

Beatrice's heart skipped a beat. Her lips curved up at the corners. 'Yes, he is rather wonderful. You were right, Jemima. I believe I am falling for him.'

Chapter Sixteen

Maria slept fitfully. The anguished expressions on the faces of the bereaved couple at the fever hospital haunted her. Thoughts of Joey having his head shaved made her fear the worst. She buried her face in the pillow.

Please Lord, don't let 'im be taken into the arms of angels, she prayed.

Eventually, her eyes closed, and in what felt like minutes, she was woken by her mother shaking her. She couldn't remember dozing off. 'It's time for yer to get up,' said Ruth. 'Yer don't want to be late for work after the time off you've just had to see Joey.'

'What time is it?' asked Maria blearily, rubbing her eyes. 'I didn't hear the cock crowing.'

'Aye, it did, ten minutes ago. It's now five past five and as yer have to be there at six you need to get up sharpish.'

Maria flung the bedcovers off and quickly splashed her face with cold water. She brushed her hair vigorously and pulled her black dress over her head. After pulling up her grey stockings, she rushed downstairs and thirstily gulped back the cup of tea her mother had poured.

Maria glanced across at her mother. 'Why are you up so early, Ma?'

Ruth coughed, a long phlegmy cough, and looked away.

'Is it yer chest again?'

'It will pass, yer needn't worry about me. Now, off yer go.'

Maria barely noticed the new day breaking with its soft, pastel shades, the pale sun rising in the sky with a scattering of white streaky clouds. She scurried along the lanes taking her up to the woods and onto a well-worn path lined with lacy ferns.

She entered the servants' quarters at the Big House at the same time as Philomena, a new maid and Mrs Pennywick's niece.

Maria greeted Philomena in a friendly manner, but Philomena barely glanced at her, walking in front of her and almost closing the door in her face.

Philomena was tall and gangly with thin eyes and lips. She was a couple of years older than Maria and had previously worked as a maid at Holkham Hall, a vast Palladian-styled country house, which was home to the Earl of Leicester, a close friend of the royal family, just twenty miles away on the Norfolk coast. Her aunt had fixed her up with a position at Sandringham House in the last year as Philomena felt disgruntled, having been passed over for promotion on a number of occasions.

History was repeating itself at Sandringham, with Philomena's nose being put out of joint again when Maria was asked to step up as Queen Alexandra's maid when her usual maid became sick.

When no one was looking Philomena hissed, 'So you think you can waltz around here and get a cushy job upstairs? Let's see what me aunt says about that. Your place is here in the kitchen. Why would our Queen want anything to do with someone like you, what with yer bastard son. I know all about him. You belong in the gutter. This is no place for the likes of you.'

Maria yelped, 'Why, yer nasty, horrid . . .'

'Miss Saward,' a voice barked. 'I will not tolerate raised voices in my kitchen. Come and see me now. I will be in my room down the corridor.'

Mrs Pennywick stood rooted to the spot with her hands on her hips. She glared at Maria who was shaking from head to toe.

Philomena's face was untroubled. She simpered, 'I'll prepare a breakfast tray for Her Majesty if yer like, Aunt – I mean, Mrs Pennywick,' she said smugly.

'Yes, and don't dally. My head can't take this squabbling.'

'Of course, anything to help, Aunt.'

Maria followed Mrs Pennywick down the corridor with a leaden heart. The housekeeper opened the door to her office, which was next to a room occupied by the head butler. A large desk with papers piled was on one side, and filing trays labelled for invoices and staff rotas on the other side. Maria's eyes rested on a shelf on which there was a photograph of Mrs Pennywick and a gentleman she took to be her husband standing together in the grounds of the Big House. A portrait of King George and Queen Mary hung on the wall staring down on them. The housekeeper sighed as she sat down on a padded leather seat, pointing to the bentwood chair on the other side of the desk for Maria.

'So tell me, what made you speak out in such a loud and undignified way to Philomena?'

'I'm sorry, Mrs Pennywick, I know I shouldn't have raised me voice, only Philomena, she said something horrible and I couldn't help meself.'

'This house can only be run efficiently if there is harmony among the staff. What did she say to make you react so angrily?'

Maria inhaled a deep breath and poured out her story, pausing when the words stuck in her throat and she was overcome with emotion. She was surprised to see that Mrs Pennywick showed an interest and did not dismiss her account out of hand.

The housekeeper offered Maria a handkerchief. When she had composed herself she asked in a muffled voice, 'Do yer want me to leave now? I didn't mean to well up, only I couldn't 'elp meself.'

Mrs Pennywick rose and paced around the room, wringing her hands in front of her.

Maria sniffled. 'Please, don't make me leave this job. I give yer me word it won't happen again.'

The housekeeper faced Maria. 'Very well, I will give you one more chance. I know that Philomena can be rather difficult at times. I will speak to her later as well. But if there is another outburst like this you will be sent packing. Do I make myself clear?'

'Oh yes, Mrs Pennywick, I promise, it won't happen again.'

'That promise will be tested now. Her Majesty is hosting tea for some of her distinguished friends tomorrow. She has asked that everything in her drawing room is polished and cleaned to the highest standards. Can I trust you and Philomena to do this together?'

Maria clasped her hands to her chest. 'Oh yes. You can count on me. There won't be any trouble from me. I give yer me word.'

'Very well, you may go. Please return to the kitchen and assist with any chores there until Her Majesty has finished her breakfast and gone out. I believe she has duties on the estate to attend to later and will be going out mid-morning with her lady-in-waiting.'

Maria gave a little bob and walked out of the room, sighing with relief. She met Philomena in the corridor carrying a breakfast tray, her nose in the air, sneering as Maria walked by. Maria was determined to ignore any provocation.

∽

Later, after the breakfast dishes had been cleared away, Mrs Pennywick summoned Maria and Philomena to follow her. They entered the drawing room and Maria's eyes immediately searched for the parrot that had captivated her before.

'The cage needs cleaning. Here are some cotton gloves for you to wear when you put your hand inside, just in case she pecks you,' the housekeeper instructed. 'But be very careful. That bird means more to Her Majesty than any treasure in this room. Emerald is just as precious to her as her jewels after which he is named.'

'Ain't Emerald a girl's name?' Maria queried.

The housekeeper shrugged her shoulders. 'It can be for either sex. I believe one of the young princesses called it that when she first saw it and the name has stuck.'

Maria's face lit up, 'Well, he's a real beauty. I don't mind cleaning the cage. I'll be very careful.'

'Well I'm not going fight you for it. I'm sick to death of its loud squeaking noise. I don't know what anyone sees in it,' retorted Philomena.

'Well that's settled then. I shall be off now to see to the lunches and will return in two hours,' the housekeeper informed them. 'Remember what I said about being careful. Remove one item from the shelf at a time, give it a good dust and be sure you put it back in the same place. We can have no breakages. I suggest you start at different ends of the room first and meet in the middle to minimise any friction between you, and Maria can clean the cage at the end. Is that understood?'

Philomena stared sullenly at her feet while Maria gave her pledge and then headed straight towards the parrot.

'Do yer remember me?' she whispered.

The colourful bird cocked its head to one side and stared straight back at Maria's face, which was pressed against the cage.

169

'You stupid idiot. Do you really think it understands you?' mocked Philomena, who suddenly appeared at Maria's side.

The bird switched its gaze to Philomena and squawked, flapping its wings and hopping on and off its perch. Philomena bent down and poked her finger into the cage, wagging it at the creature. 'Who's a silly bird then? Let me hear you speak. What do yer have to say?'

The bird screeched so loud that Maria leapt backwards as it lurched forward and bit the end of Philomena's finger. The astonished maid yelped in pain while the parrot repeated the taunts Philomena had uttered. 'Who's a silly bird then. Let me hear you speak.'

With a look of thunder on her face, Philomena turned towards Maria. 'This is all your fault. You set that bird against me.'

'Don't be so ridiculous. 'Ere, let me look at yer finger?'

'Don't touch me. Leave me alone. Get out of my sight!'

Before Maria could stop her, Philomena had flung open the cage door, shooing the bird out, poking it with her feather duster.

Maria watched in horror as the parrot flapped its colourful wings and soared towards the ceiling, then swooped low around the elegant room before perching on the top of a portrait of a sombre-looking royal relative that hung on the wall.

'I hope you get your just deserts now, Maria Saward. You won't stay here once my aunt knows you let the Queen's precious bird escape.'

'But I didn't. Yer know I didn't,' Maria protested. 'It's your fault!'

'I'm going to inform my aunt now and will show her my finger and tell her you made the bird attack me. She won't take kindly to this.'

'Oh Philomena, please don't. Yer know I'm blameless. I don't know what I've done to upset yer, but can't we try to be friends. Let's catch the bird and put it back quickly before it does any damage and we get into trouble. We don't need to tell anyone about it then.'

Philomena glared at Maria and wrapped a duster around her finger to stem the blood pouring from the bite. The bird took to the air again and soared towards the window. Unable to fly out, it hovered above the room again, swooping low above an occasional table, its wings clipping a precious ornament. The ornament crashed to the floor and Maria rushed over to pick up the pieces.

'That's done it. Aunt will be furious now.' Philomena flounced out of the room with a triumphant look on her face.

Mrs Pennywick entered moments later as Maria was on her knees retrieving the broken pieces. Maria's heart was beating so fast she thought it would explode out of her ribcage.

The housekeeper's face stared down at her. 'So it's true. You let Emerald out of her cage, in spite of what I told you. Her Majesty will be furious. I can't believe you could do such a terrible thing, especially after our talk earlier.'

Maria rose unsteadily, her elbow sending another ornament flying from the occasional table next to her. It was the delicate Meissen figure of the man in white and gold. As it fell to the ground its head toppled off.

Maria froze, her throat tightening. 'Oh no, I'm sorry,' she bleated. 'I . . .'

She looked over Mrs Pennywick's shoulder and saw Philomena hovering in the doorway, a satisfied smirk etched across her face.

'Please, Mrs Pennywick. Please let me explain,' Maria begged.

'Philomena has already explained what happened. And now I would like you to return to the kitchen. You are no longer allowed in these rooms,' commanded the housekeeper. 'This will be Philomena's duty from now on, until I can decide who else I can spare to work upstairs.'

'But, I didn't let Emerald out, I swear on me life. I swear on me Joey's life!' Maria bleated.

Mrs Pennywick fumed. 'How could you say such a terrible thing! Swearing on your own son's life when he is in hospital and it hangs on a thread. Why it's akin to blasphemy. Please leave now, Maria, before I change my mind and dismiss you altogether.'

Maria trembled, her voice barely audible. She appealed to her adversary. 'Please tell 'er the truth, Philomena. Tell 'er it weren't me.'

The housekeeper ducked as the bird swooped down and up again. 'Did you hear me, Maria? I asked you to leave this room now. And I mean *now*! Report to Cook immediately, she can always do with another pair of hands.'

Maria fought back her tears as she headed for the door. Philomena nursed her injured finger, a grin plastered across her face, which she swiftly switched to a pained expression when Mrs Pennywick looked in her direction.

The parrot squawked even louder and circled the room, then dived towards the door, landing on top of Philomena's head.

'Get orf you bloomin' stupid bird. If I get me 'ands on you I'll make sure you end up in one of Cook's pies. Get orf.'

'Please watch your language, Philomena. Remember how you were brought up,' Mrs Pennywick scolded. 'You really are testing my patience.'

Philomena ran down the corridor as the parrot soared up to the ceiling one moment, then dived low around Philomena's head. Mrs Pennywick followed, crying out, 'Will someone fetch Mr Armitage from the aviary right now? And do not open any doors. We cannot let Emerald fly out.'

Emerald enjoyed his freedom for twenty minutes before being coaxed by the head aviary keeper from the estate. A small, slight gentleman whose duties were tending to the royals' collection of budgerigars and canaries, he was renowned for communicating to them in their own language by whistling commands in various tones. Within minutes, Emerald was enticed onto Mr Armitage's outstretched arms, coaxed by a slice of apple and some nuts, and returned to his royal cage. Emerald continued screeching, 'Who's a pretty bird then. I'm very pleased to meet you. Please take a seat. How do you like your tea? One lump or two?'

As Mr Armitage secured the cage door, he smiled at the bird. 'You are a beauty. But I want no more fooling around, do you hear me? You gave me a right turn then.'

The bird's beady eyes stared straight back at him. 'Get off me, you stupid bird. I'm going to inform my aunt now and will show her my finger and tell her you made the bird attack me. She won't take kindly to this.'

'Ah, so that's what happened,' he muttered under his breath.

∽

Maria's fingers were red raw by the end of the day. Mrs Pennywick had instructed Cook to work her hard as punishment for her misdemeanour. Maria's blood boiled when she saw Philomena standing behind the house-keeper with a smug expression on her face.

Cook was pleased to have Maria back. 'I'm sorry for what happened to yer, but your misfortune is my good luck. I'm one girl down today as poor Annie's had a fall and is on crutches. I do worry about that girl. My guess is that her ole man beat her up again. And to think he's exempt on medical grounds from signing up on account of his hearing, so he'll be at 'ome making her life a misery.'

'Why? What's wrong with his hearing?' asked Maria, her arms elbow deep in water as she scrubbed the pans until they shone.

'His pa belted him around the head when he were a nipper, and he's deaf in one ear, and can barely hear from the other. Annie is a soft-hearted thing and thought she could give him some happiness. But his childhood left him scarred and he has now become the brute his father was, taking out his moods and bad temper on Annie.'

Annie was a couple of years older than Maria and although she was not the brightest girl, she had a good heart and was always kind to Maria.

Cook continued, 'What you told me about Philomena, I wouldn't worry about her. You're not the only one she has schemed against. I know the cook at Holkham and she told me she set everyone against her with her back stabbing and gossip mongering. She even tried to plant lies in the mind of one of the butlers by saying his wife's head had been turned by the groomsman. The final straw was when she was caught red-handed hiding some of the mistress's undergarments in the housekeeper's chest of drawers because she didn't like how hard she was being made to work by her.'

Maria's eyes widened. 'Does Mrs Pennywick know about this?'

Cook wiped her forehead with her elbow and shook her head. 'She knows some of it, but she feels duty bound to take her niece under her wing as her own family are at the end of their tether with her. I don't believe she would have taken the girl if she knew the whole story.'

Maria's mood lifted a little with Cook's revelation. She was thankful to have her as an ally. From now on she vowed to keep her head down and hoped the truth would emerge and clear her in Mrs Pennywick's eyes. She needed to keep her mind set on Joey and Eddie and she would do whatever was asked of her to keep her job in the Big House.

Cook interrupted her thoughts. 'It must have been a funny sight, the parrot flapping about the room and chasing Philomena down the corridor.'

Maria grinned. 'It wasn't at the time, though I can see the funny side now. And it talked. It really talked! Emerald is a real beauty.'

Cook said, 'Oh yes, he is a clever bird. You can count your blessings that Mr Armitage caught Emerald when he did.'

'What will Queen Alexandra say when Mrs Pennywick tells her? She might think I'm careless and too much of a liability to set foot in her rooms again.'

Cook tut-tutted, her crinkly eyes smiling. 'Her Majesty has far more important concerns on her mind at the moment. Queen Alexandra is a very fair woman. As long as her pretty bird is returned to its cage without being harmed, that is all that will concern her. It's not the first breakage and won't be the last. She'll know a good craftsman who can repair the figure so it looks as good as new, so don't fret about that.

'And as for our King and Queen? They are on a tour in the north of England looking at shipyards. Mr Armitage were telling me about it when he stopped here for a cuppa after catching Emerald. He says scores and hundreds of munition girls dressed in blue trousers fluttered handkerchiefs and joined the men with their rousing cheers. Everywhere they went in Tyneside they spoke to people who lined the streets. With the war carrying on and our ships attacked by the Huns, we need our shipyards to deliver more ships, that's why they are there.'

Maria's ears always pricked when stories about the royals were mentioned. Her mind turned to Annie and the cruelty she endured at her husband's hands. She counted her blessings, knowing that Eddie would never lay a finger on her or Joey. As if reading her thoughts, Cook asked, 'What news is there of your young man? How is he faring at Hillington Hall Hospital?'

'Not too good, from what Beatrice tells me. He's suffering with his leg as it's badly infected. With Joey in hospital, I've still not had a chance to see him. I'm worried about him, after all he's been through.'

Cook raised an eyebrow. 'The poor boy, he must be desperate to see his ma.'

'He is, and I feel the same. The fever hospital says I 'ave to wait till Joey has been given the all-clear from his illness, seeing as I were in close contact with 'im, and I don't 'ave that yet.'

Cook pressed her chin into the palm of her hand. She looked thoughtful. 'Seeing as you're not unwell, the chances are you ain't going to get it now. Why don't you just turn up at Hillington Hall and take a chance? They can only say no. Plead your case with Matron and see what she says.'

'Do yer think so? I hadn't thought of that. I shall stop off and see Beatrice at home after work. Maybe she could speak up for me with Matron before I go.'

'That's an excellent idea. Now we have that sorted, can you clean the shelves in the pantry? They need a good going-over.'

∞

Maria arrived at the station master's house later that evening with a spring in her step, feeling uplifted at the thought of seeing Eddie soon. Beatrice was already there.

Maria followed her into the kitchen and spoke excitedly about Cook's suggestion. 'What do yer think, Beatrice? Could yer ask Matron? I'm sure I ain't got the fever. I'm as fit as a fiddle.'

Beatrice's eyes narrowed. 'I think you'd better sit down and read this note first. It's from Eddie. He gave it to me just as I left the hospital today. He spent ages writing it.'

Maria grabbed the note eagerly and ripped open the envelope. She smiled as she anticipated the loving words she would read from her sweetheart.

Within seconds her face crumpled. 'No, it can't be true. Surely 'e can't mean this.'

'What does he say?' Beatrice asked.

'He says 'e doesn't want to see me again, that 'e is releasing me so I can find someone else who can give me a better life. I can't believe 'e would say such a thing. Why is 'e doing this?'

'I'm not sure, Maria. He's badly shaken. I'm afraid his leg has taken a turn for the worse and we don't know if it can be saved.'

Maria's hand flew to her mouth. 'I thought 'e was getting better. My poor Eddie. Does his mother know?'

Beatrice nodded. 'She is putting on a brave face for his sake. I'll speak to Eddie tomorrow, if you like, Maria, and Matron too, asking if you can visit as it might help him.'

'Oh yes, please do. I so want to see 'im.'

'I'll do what I can, but I must warn you that Eddie is suffering from dark moods since learning he may lose his leg. He worries constantly about being a burden on you.'

'But that ain't true! Why do so many bad things happen to me? Joey might die. My name has been disgraced at the Big House. And Eddie, the one person I thought would always stand by me, no longer wants to see me.'

Chapter Seventeen

'How are the new farm girls getting on? The ones on the Sandringham Estate?' Lizzie asked. 'Did you see them in the paper?'

The question was addressed to Jessie, the station master's youngest daughter and a good friend of Lizzie Piper's.

Jessie grinned. 'From what I hear they've taken to man's work without any problems. If they can do it, so can we.'

'I can vouch for that. I've been doing it myself long enough,' grinned Lizzie.

Lizzie was the only woman farmer in the area and the thirty-year-old had raised eyebrows in town when she took charge of Blackbird Farm five years ago.

Lizzie had whooped with delight when she heard that three women had joined Sandringham Estate as farm workers. Sisters Hilda and Phyllis Hobson, and their cousin, Marjorie Maxfield, were showing how they could do the jobs of men, just like Lizzie. Like her, they wore breeches, so she would no longer be the only woman raising eyebrows in this attire.

Jessie chortled. 'Yes, I read about them in the paper, they are causing quite a stir. Good for them, showing the country it's not just men who can use pitchforks.'

'Of course it's not. I've been managing well enough these last few years.' Lizzie smiled. 'If the men aren't here to do do the work, then what other choice is there? The government's doing the right thing asking for women volunteers to work on the land.'

The new female farmhands Lizzie referred to attracted widespread admiration around Britain when their arrival on the royal estate farm made headlines. And to think they were in Sandringham, showing everyone how capable they were. They had also been filmed rolling up their sleeves on the farm and digging up turnips, feeding pigs, milking cows and cleaning out animal stalls as well as any man.

Jessie piped in, 'The girls told Ma in the post office that the film of them is going to be shown in cinemas around the world. Everyone's saying they are an excellent example of what women need to do to save the country from starvation.'

Jessie had proved to be a natural at land work as well, tending Queen Alexandra's garden at the royal station, along with her father. The Dowager Queen frequently commented on how pleasant it was to sit there when waiting for a royal train to arrive, or to rest awhile before continuing her journey on to the Big House.

Lizzie had been widowed when her husband, Wilfred, died fighting the war. He had raised his head above a trench and taken a hit from a sniper. She did not mourn his loss. Shortly after they wed, he told her he had only married her to take charge of the farm, which had been left to her when her father died. Wilfred had said it was a man's job, and a woman's place was being a homemaker and raising a family. He'd tried getting out of enlisting, insisting he was exempt due to being needed on the farm, but a tribunal thought differently and after said Lizzie could manage without him, his fate was sealed.

After this her farm manager, Sid, was jailed for stealing food parcels intended for soldiers serving overseas and Lizzie pledged to take charge herself. Now she was free to run Blackbird Farm her way and she'd brought Jessie on-board to help her. Jessie was a quick learner, and between them, and with Maria's brother Archie helping too, they managed to keep the farm running smoothly; milking Lizzie's two cows and growing her barley crops, knowing she could rely on schoolchildren to help during harvest, with school lessons on hold due to the war.

Lizzie had had a glut of potatoes and turnips this year, and today Jessie was digging potatoes and storing them for the winter so they didn't rot in the ground. The country suffered a severe shortage the previous winter and potatoes were left to rot or were diseased, making them now a sought after crop. Replacements had been suggested for the spud and newspapers recommended families use dried peas, haricot beans, swedes, parsnips, salsify and beetroot for meals instead.

Jessie placed her booted foot on the spade and pressed it down hard, feeling a great sense of satisfaction. She felt her spade hit the vegetable and bent down to pull it out with her hands and shake the soil off. She held it up for inspection, a satisfied smile on her face.

Jessie told Lizzie, 'It feels so rewarding to know I am helping feed the nation. I'd far rather be out here on the land with you than stuck in an office as a Women's Army Auxiliary Corps volunteer.'

'Why, Jessie, you sound quite the suffragette. Maybe one day women will get the chance to vote. I'm sick of men telling us what to do.'

'Perhaps I am that way inclined, but don't let Father know.' Jessie grinned, digging a potato clamp to store the prized vegetable.

Lizzie praised, 'Well, I'm impressed. You can make a potato clamp as good as any man. We should have a good supply this winter.'

'It's simple enough. All you do is dig a hole in the ground and line it with straw, layering the potatoes on top.'

Jessie stuck her spade into the soil and rested her chin on the handle. She allowed her thoughts to drift.

'A penny for them?' said Lizzie. 'Or can I guess? Is it Jack?'

Jessie smiled. 'I can't help thinking what he would say if he saw me wearing breeches. Ma keeps telling me they're not very feminine, but the aunt of the land workers at Sandringham was in the post office the other day and told her they are a necessity.'

Lizzie chuckled, 'Does she expect you to wear pink petticoats and your best soft cream leather shoes to dig potato clumps?'

'I wouldn't be surprised.' Jessie grinned, recalling Sarah Saward's shocked expression when she saw her daughter wearing breeches for the first time.

'I could see how well Hilda, Phyllis and Marjorie took to them, so I thought why don't we try them here at Blackbird Farm? They are so much more practical than a skirt.'

'Those girls are a credit to female farm workers. We live in different times now,' Lizzie commented.

Jessie agreed. 'Once I tried the breeches I was glad not to wear long skirts. My boot would get caught in the hem of my skirt making me trip up. Betty used to complain how filthy it was at the end of the day, caked in soil from when I crouched down and my skirt dragged on the ground.'

With four-fifths of the country relying on wheat imports, and increasing enemy attacks on ships bringing food, home food production was more essential than ever. Every minute was squeezed out of land workers following the introduction of British Summer Time to maximise working hours.

∞

Later that evening, back in the station master's house, Sarah enquired about Jessie's day.

'Lizzie says she's never known such a year for potatoes. We could end up with a glut,' Jessie told her mother.

Sarah straightened her back. 'Funny you should say that as I was speaking to a knowledgeable gentleman at the post office yesterday, a chemist. He was saying how the starch from potatoes can be used for all sorts of things, such as laundry starch, which is scarce, and even in the production of high explosives. Who would have thought it?'

'I must tell Lizzie. It never occurred to me potatoes had these other uses.'

Sarah added, a hint of sarcasm in her voice, 'I hope she isn't one of those farmers who withdraws potatoes from sale to increase prices due to government price fixing? That's what some greedy farmers are doing. It's all people are talking about in the post office.'

Jessie's eyes widened. 'That's outrageous. I hope you will set people straight. Lizzie is far too decent and would never consider doing such a thing. Whatever she gets from the land she sells on for a fair price. She has to make a living too, and I know she would never do anything to hurt the people here, they are her friends. She knows how families are struggling with rising prices.'

'You can say that again,' Sarah retorted. 'Old Betty Bartram went to her usual grocery store in King's Lynn to buy a small tin of tongue. It used to cost her two shillings and she stormed out empty handed when she was told the price had increased to four shillings and sixpence.'

'That's outrageous. She has cause for complaint there. I can't believe that shopkeeper isn't profiteering.

'You can trust that Lizzie would never hold back on her crops, like some grasping farmers do, to get more money. She knows two or three that have, but says she would never be able to walk through the village and hold her head up high. It's not in her nature to resort to underhand profiteering tactics.

'Her sole intention is to bring good food to people's tables, not to exploit crop shortages to line her own pockets.'

'We can rely on farmer Lizzie, that's what I tell everyone who comes into the post office and moans about farmers,' Sarah retorted.

Jessie walked into the hallway and the evening light from the parlour, its door open, shone through like a beacon onto the tiled flooring; although fading, it was still luminous. She stepped into the room, positioned in the corner of the house. She always marvelled at the far-reaching view from here of a perfect English countryside setting. The view stretched across to the church spire and she inhaled a deep breath. A blackbird swooped ahead and rested on an oak tree, staring at her with its beady eye. It was a still, calm evening with the odd sound of passers-by on the path going to and from the station. Standing here, in this English idyll, it was impossible to imagine the killing fields stained crimson from the bloodied, mangled corpses of young men who died horrible deaths in order for them to retain their freedom. Yet the realities of the carnage was that here in Wolferton, every home had a son, father, brother or relative away fighting for King and country, their broken-hearted loved ones grieving an all too soon death.

The three Saward sisters had found their calling during the war. Beatrice had proved to be a dedicated nurse, Ada was becoming involved with improving living conditions for the poor, while Jessie was doing her bit to put food on the table.

The war was making the sisters and women of Wolferton stronger and more resilient, proving their strength and courage.

∽

With the King inspecting troops in Britain, and rarely spending time at Sandringham as he attended to war duties, Queen Mary judging a baby show and children's fancy dress competition at a summer fete in London, and Queen Alexandra attending to charity functions to support the war effort, Cook informed Maria she could leave early that day if her work was finished to her satisfaction. Maria's face beamed. She scrubbed harder to make sure there was no cause for complaint. All the copper pans shone and gleamed on the shelves and the wooden work-tops and tiled floor were spotless, leaving Maria's hands red and blistered.

Two days had passed since the incident with Philomena.

Cook confided, 'Don't waste your time worrying about her. What goes around comes around. I overheard Mrs Pennywick telling her that she's on her last warning, so she's being watched.'

Maria sighed. She didn't wish Philomena any harm, but the injustice she had suffered through her spitefulness still made her blood boil and she hoped she would own up to it.

Cook believed every word Maria told her about what had happened. Over a steaming cuppa, Maria had blurted out her worries about Joey. She couldn't stop her eyes from welling up, and the words stuck in her throat when she told Cook how Eddie didn't want to see her again.

Cook sympathised. 'Keep your chin up and your nose clean and you'll get through this, you mark my words, Maria. This time next week your troubles could all be forgotten.'

Cook always had a kind word for Maria, keeping half an eye on her while running the kitchen like clockwork.

She told Maria with a twinkle in her eye, 'I hear Abel has just finished shoeing a horse. Why don't you take him a slice of fruit cake, and seeing as all is done 'ere, why not ask him if he will drop you off at Hillington Hall so you can try to put things right with Eddie. You need to talk to clear up your misunderstandings, and the sooner it's done the better.'

Maria leapt up, giving Cook a hug and peck on the cheek. She wondered if Beatrice had spoken to Matron about her calling in, but decided to take a chance anyway.

Just as expected, Abel gladly offered to take Maria to the hospital. 'That poor lad, after what he's been through, you're bound to cheer him up.'

'I hope so.' Maria smiled, feeding the horse a carrot which Cook had left out with the fruitcake, from her out-stretched hand. Starlight tossed his head back and neighed appreciatively, after munching loudly on the carrot.

'You've a friend for life now. 'Op on, lass,' Abel grinned, holding out his hand. Maria took it and yanked herself up, sitting on the front next to Abel. He flicked the reins, whistling softly under his breath, as they set off out of the stable block in the courtyard, trotting down the meandering lanes.

'Any news yet of young Joey?' Abel enquired, tilting his head towards her as the horse moved into a gentle trot.

'No, nothing yet. All this waiting is tearing me apart,' she replied. 'We should know on Sunday, when I see him next.'

'I expect no news is good news. Did you 'ear about little Gregory Fisher? 'E has scarlet fever and is in the fever 'ospital too. 'E's in a bad way with it.'

'Poor little boy. I wonder if he's with Joey.'

Twenty minutes later, Maria's insides lurched as the cart swayed suddenly into a drive and pulled up outside Hillington Hall. A handful of patients were sitting in deckchairs in their pyjamas, reading books or chatting to loved ones. Some nurses made their way out of the front door and walked past her on the drive.

'I'm feeling nervous now. Don't go far, please, I don't even know if I'm allowed in,' Maria said to Abel in a soft voice, as she clambered down from the cart.

Abel pointed to the side of the building indicating where he would wait for her and trotted off with Starlight.

She walked tentatively up the steps at the front of the grand building, two large bay windows on either side of the front door, which was ajar. Maria stood in the hallway and gawped at the sweeping marble staircase and shimmering crystal chandelier. A grandfather clock struck six times as a nurse wheeled a patient out of the room facing her. She rushed over to assist her.

She observed the patient. He was smiling and joking with the pretty nurse who admonished him. 'Get away with you, Bertie Bowers. Wait till I tell Matron you've been trying it on with the nurses. You won't have any trouble finding a sweetheart when you leave here. Even with only one arm you would be a fine catch for a young lady and keep her in good spirits all day with your positive outlook.'

Maria shook inside as she looked down at the soldier's missing arm and noticed his pyjama sleeve folded over and pinned up down his side.

'Maybe I've found her here,' he laughed, taking Maria's hand and holding on to it with his one good arm.

Maria stuttered, shaking herself free. 'I only . . . only wanted to 'elp with the door. I'm looking for Eddie. Eddie Herring.'

'Eddie Herring? 'E's a sly dog.' Bertie grinned. ''E never said you were so pretty.'

Nurse Jennings joked, 'Leave the young lady alone, Bertie. You can see how uncomfortable you've made her feel.'

Private Bowers raised his left hand to his eyebrow in a mock salute. 'I consider myself well and truly put in place. March forward, one, two, three . . .'

The nurse shook her head. She spoke softly to Maria, 'Take no notice of him. Making jokes is his way of coping

190

with his disability. You'll find Eddie in the third bed on the right as you enter the ward. Can you report to Matron at the end of the room first? It's not strictly a visiting day, though she will sometimes make an exception, and seeing how Eddie's mood has been, she may agree.'

'I 'ope so. I'm a bit nervous of seeing Eddie.'

'Matron will put you right if she doesn't think it's a good idea. And best of luck.' Nurse Jennings winked.

'Thank you, Nurse, I need all the luck I can get,' Maria replied softly.

Feeling embarrassed about her clumsy behaviour towards Private Bowers, Maria leant forward and took his hand. 'I'm sorry, I didn't mean to be rude. It's a pleasure meeting you.'

Private Bowers replied, 'That's all right, I have to get used to it, I suppose. Tell me, are you Maria? Are you really Eddie's sweetheart?'

Maria shrugged her shoulders and inhaled a deep breath. 'I have no idea, but I'll soon find out.'

Chapter Eighteen

Maria stood at the end of Eddie's wrought iron bed. Her heart pounded so hard she thought it might wake Eddie from his sleep. She gasped when she saw his bandaged leg, which lay on top of his bedding.

She shuffled towards Matron at the end of the ward, ignoring the staring eyes that bored into her back and the sound of wolf whistles. Matron glanced up from her paperwork and Maria was about to introduce herself when Beatrice appeared at her side.

'This is the young lady I was telling you about, Matron. Maria Saward, Private Eddie Herring's young lady.'

'Ah, yes, Maria. Nurse Saward has informed me about you and Eddie's letter. This is a very delicate moment for him and his future recovery. I'm sorry to say that Private Herring's condition has deteriorated in the last day with the infection worsening. Our big fear is that it could become septic and blood poisoning will set it. As well as this, his state of mind is declining. We are waiting for my father to come here tomorrow. He is a specialist surgeon working with trauma from the battlefields and can advise us. He keeps abreast of all the latest treatments and if there is anything he can do to save Eddie's leg he will do it.'

Maria's voice wobbled. 'Septic? Blood poisoning? Yer never told me that, Beatrice. That sounds horrible. Please, Matron, I hope yer father can save his leg. I can't bear to think of Eddie suffering.'

Matron replied stiffly. 'We try our utmost to save all our patients' limbs. And if we can't, we offer the best rehabilitation so they can live as normal a life as possible once they leave us. We even teach them a trade, the patients who are willing and able to learn are given the utmost support. The last thing we want is for them to end up begging on street corners.'

Maria's face showed alarm. 'It will never come to that. Will it? I won't let it.'

Beatrice intervened, 'Matron is just preparing you for the worst, should it happen.'

Maria was shaking as she absorbed Matron's words. Her voice wobbled. 'May I speak with Eddie? I want to cheer 'im up and clear up any doubts in his mind so 'e knows I will still be his girl, whatever happens.'

Matron spoke crisply. 'I'm afraid Private Herring is not allowed visitors at the moment. He was very agitated a short while ago and we gave him a strong sedative to ease the pain. He'll sleep through it, and hopefully all night. You can be assured that I will let him know you called in to see him.'

Matron turned to Beatrice. 'Please show Miss Saward out. She is causing quite a stir, and our patients need their rest.'

'I'm sorry,' said Maria. 'I didn't mean to cause any trouble, Matron.'

Beatrice held Maria's elbow as they walked away. 'Come on, Maria. I will make sure Eddie gets your message. It should lift his spirits and I'm sure he'll want to see you. And try not to fret about Matron. She isn't as harsh as she sounds and only has Eddie's well-being uppermost in her mind. She's just tired. She barely leaves the hospital. Dr Butterscotch is excellent and after he has seen Eddie we should have a clearer idea about his progress.'

Maria walked past the beds trying to ignore the occupants as they made soft whistling sounds and called out some raucous comments. She tried to hide her dismay at seeing various parts of their young bodies covered in reams of bandages, while others suffered from the loss of a limb. Some had pained expressions and turned their faces away from her, while others beckoned her over to their beds, making her cheeks flush.

She paused at the end of Eddie's bed again and gripped the bedstead. She whispered his name and her eyes moistened, seeing him lying there in his drugged sleep. Seeing Matron busily occupied with her paperwork, she walked softly to the side of his bed. She kissed her index finger and pressed it on his cheek, whispering, 'I love you.'

She turned quickly and followed Beatrice out of the ward.

'What can I do?' asked Maria. 'It breaks me heart to see 'im like that.'

'There's nothing you can do. Eddie is convinced he is going to lose his leg, and a part of me is worried about that too. I didn't want to say anything that would upset you and Eddie's mother until we knew for sure, but you need to be prepared for the worst, Maria.'

Maria's head was in a spin when she stepped out of the hospital. Abel saw her stumble down the stairs in a distressed state. He was only a few feet away and steered Starlight over towards her.

Maria climbed up into the cart, her mind in a daze, as Matron's and Beatrice's words sunk in.

Abel commiserated with Maria on hearing what had happened, steering Starlight carefully around any bumps they passed.

'I'm sorry to hear this, lass. I'd hoped you would have better news.'

Maria sniffed all the way back to the cottage as she agonised over Eddie's dire situation and the anguish it would cause his mother. Abel glanced at her from the corner of his eyes from time to time, and Maria found his quiet and undemanding presence comforting.

It was early evening when he dropped Maria off, arranging to return in two days to take her to the fever hospital. As she entered the house, she was surprised to be confronted by her two brothers, their jaws set tight, her mother by their side biting her lip.

Freddie asked. 'That detective from London stopped off at Wolferton again today. 'E gave Harry a poster to hang up saying that Nellie is wanted by police. There's now a thirty pound reward for information about 'er whereabouts. I couldn't look Mr Saward in the face. Have you 'eard from Nellie?'

Maria slumped in a chair. 'No, not a word. All I know is that she returned to London to find 'er father to clear her name. I just hope no harm has come to 'er.'

Maria was keen to protect her brothers from the full truth, but Freddie pressed her, 'So she ain't a thief or a murderer? Or a bigamist? That is what people are saying. Imagine what they would say if they knew she stayed here the night.'

Maria's lips pursed. 'Well, they ain't going to know, and it's what we must expect, I suppose, but who is saying this?'

'I've heard it being whispered on the station platform while people wait for their train. I see them point their finger at me saying we're related. Then they say, "There's no smoke without fire."'

'People will talk, but remember she is innocent until proven guilty. We owe it to 'er to give her a chance to prove her innocence.'

Her brothers eventually accepted this and as Maria climbed the stairs wearily for bed, she stopped with a jolt. The thought of a bounty on Nellie's head and her picture plastered on a poster meant she could be arrested before she had a chance to clear her name. She decided to speak to her mother and ask what else she knew. She recalled Nellie confiding in Ruth after she was asked to leave the room and felt uneasy.

Maybe it would make sense for them to take Beatrice into their confidence. She had a solicitor friend and might be able to help.

∽

Nellie lifted her skirt and clutched her bag close to her chest as she clambered over the rubble, glancing down at the remnants of what was once someone's home. She almost tripped, being careful to avoid stepping on shattered glass and twisted metal, catching her shoe on the broken brickwork and pieces of furniture shattered into tiny pieces. She looked across the street and recognised a large oak tree that had stood at the end of the passage where she had lived with her father. She screwed up her eyes and looked around, her jaw dropping as she realised this was the spot where her house had once stood – 9 Bull Terrace, Whitechapel. All that remained were dust and fragments of personal belongings poking up among the plaster and rubble.

She wobbled slightly as she lost her footing and steadied herself, her gaze falling to the dusty remains. She bent down, spotting a tiny hand reaching up towards her. She pulled it out of the wreckage and shook it free of dust. She could scarcely believe she was holding the precious doll that her ma gave her before she died that she had treasured. She had named the doll Rose and taken her to bed with her every night, whispering all her secrets in her ear. She placed the doll in her bag and inched her way carefully to a path clear of rubble.

Nellie's bag contained all that remained of her worldly possessions, which amounted to very little: a change of clothing, nightwear and undergarments. She felt bewildered as she looked around her. What chance did she have of finding her father now? Was he killed in the air raid? Who could tell her what had happened to him?

She knew she had to be on her guard too, having seen a poster at St Pancras Station offering a £30 reward for information as to her whereabouts. She almost collapsed from shock when she saw her face staring back at her. She felt her body stiffen and her face reddened in embarrassment in case someone recognised her from the picture.

She almost leapt out of her skin when a voice from behind called out. "'Ere. Don't I know you?'

Nellie spun around, afraid she had been identified and was about to be handed over to police. She screwed her eyes and cautiously eyed up the woman who had spoken and shook her head. 'I don't think so.'

A moment later the penny dropped. 'Wait a minute, aren't you Doris?'

She shook her head in disbelief as she stared at a stout woman with grey curls wearing a tight blouse, with buttons almost bursting open, her shabby boots visible under her skirt.

'Yeah, that's me. I'm Doris. I just 'ave to work out who you are.'

Looking Nellie up and down, she exclaimed, 'Well bugger me. If it ain't Gus's girl.'

Nellie trembled. 'Oh Doris, do you know where Pa is? I've been worried sick about him since I 'eard about the air aid. It's important I see 'im.'

'Is it now? It would take more than a bloomin' bomb to finish him off, though I know a few who would like to get their 'ands on 'im.'

Nellie feigned shock. 'Is 'e all right? I must see him, if you know where 'e is.'

'I tell yer what, lass. Why don't yer buy me a nice shot or two of gin and that might 'elp me remember where 'e is.'

Nellie pressed her lips together and fumed. A sick feeling in her gut warned her against her father's lady friend. But before she could object, Doris grabbed her arm. 'Now tell me where you've been since I last clapped sight of yer? I wanna 'ear all about it. I always did 'ave a soft spot for yer, you ask yer pa.'

It was only a five-minute walk to The Black Cat, which had miraculously survived the overhead raids. They stumbled past more demolished homes where families were scouring the wreckage for any possessions they could salvage. One two-storey house still had the mirror fixed on the upstairs bedroom wall without a mark on it. It was the only wall remaining in the house.

Doris barged into the Black Cat as if she owned the place. A few rough-looking men were propped against the bar and they eyed Nellie with interest. Doris pointed to a seat in a quiet corner away from prying eyes. Nellie thought it peculiar that anyone would want to go out drinking when their city had been bombed and so many

199

innocent lives lost, carrying on as if nothing had happened. And surely it wasn't right for women to be out drinking in the day? The landlord of this inn didn't seem to care, with his dirty sleeves rolled up and his trousers stained at the front.

Her ears pricked at a couple of drinkers berating the government for not protecting them better against the Hun, before ordering more ale and carrying on complaining. Nellie shifted uncomfortably on the wooden seat, turning her face away from their curious eyes.

'Yer sure yer don't want anything?' queried Doris, tipping a generous glug of gin down her chunky throat. 'Another one will do the trick. And then yer Auntie Doris will tell yer where yer old man is.'

'Are yer sure you know?' asked Nellie tentatively, carefully handing over some coins. Doris wet her lips as her eyes fixed on Nellie's money pouch. Nellie had little money left and needed to take care of every farthing.

Doris rose noisily from her seat, the chair legs scratching against the floor, and stared straight into Nellie's face. She smelt Doris's gin-soaked breath and recoiled. Doris tapped her nose and winked. 'Yer Auntie Doris knows, me pretty little thing. But it'll take more than a couple of gins from yer if yer want me silence, if yer get me drift.'

Nellie recoiled, her face reddening. 'What do you mean? What do you know? I have no idea what yer talking about.'

'Yer old man, he spilled it all out one night when he were intoxicated. He ain't a good man and I wanna see it's put right for yer. Maybe I can 'elp? I can tell the coppers what he let on to me, but it comes at a price if yer want me to remember. That's only fair, ain't it?'

'I don't have any money, not the kind that you might ask for.'

'It's negotiable, as they say. I can 'elp clear yer name. I want yer to remember Doris when yer get what's rightfully yours.'

Nellie furrowed her brow. 'How do I know I can trust you?'

''Cause yer father's a nasty piece of work and deserves what's coming to 'im. Yer not the only one that wants to see 'im skinned alive.'

Nellie thought for a few seconds. What choice did she have? 'I don't know what the future holds for me, but I give you my word that should I be successful and come into some money as a result of yer assistance, and me name is cleared, I shall see that you are well rewarded.'

'You'd better, lass, else yer'll regret it. I'll be keeping me eye on yer. I just need to wet me whistle one more time and then I'll take yer to him.'

Doris staggered to the bar again, and Nellie watched as the landlord filled her glass with a double. Nellie felt uncomfortable waiting for Doris to finish her drink and, as she became raucous, drawing attention to herself, Nellie feared her unguarded mouth would let slip her secrets.

She urged Doris to sit next to her and finish her drink, feeling uncomfortable at the attention shown her by a scruffy bearded man at the bar who was staring intently at her. Doris threw her head back and tilted the glass until every drop of gin had slid down her throat. She wiped her mouth with her sleeve before burping louder than any man Nellie had ever heard. Nellie's eyes strayed down to Doris's hefty bosom as she took her breasts in her chubby hands and wiggled them in an attempt to make them sit more comfortably in her straining blouse. Nellie looked away, feeling disgusted.

Doris chuckled. 'These have got me into trouble a few times, I can tell yer. Me old man never minded if a bloke wanted to feel them, asking them to cough up some brass for the privilege. Then the buggers wanted more, but I drew the line there. The only time I agreed was with yer pa. I genuinely had a soft spot for the geezer.'

Nellie shifted uncomfortably. 'You don't need to tell me this. Are yer ready to leave now?'

Doris heaved herself up from her seat and Nellie followed. They had only walked a few paces when Doris suddenly grabbed Nellie's arm and pulled her into a passageway.

She pressed her fingers against her lips and warned Nellie to be quiet. A few seconds later the shabby bearded man walked quickly past.

'I thought as much. That's Slipper Joe, so called on account of taking the slipper to his ol' lady. I thought 'e had his eye on yer at The Black Cat. He's one of Gus's pals, always up to no good. We've shaken him now. Come, follow me quickly before Slipper Joe comes back looking for us.'

'Where are we going?' asked Nellie.

'I'm taking yer to yer pa, as I said I would. Just be patient, we'll be there soon enough.'

Nellie's heart pounded harder with each step she took, her head spinning in all directions looking out for Slipper Joe. She was surprised at the pace that Doris sprinted, considering the amount of alcohol she had consumed.

Doris led her down a couple of terraced streets, veering right down a passage that led to a small square.

'We're almost there,' Doris panted between deep breaths, her hand resting on her chest.

'I don't recognise this area. Where are we?'

'Just trust Doris. Yer safe with me.'

They continued their pace, diving up and down a couple of alleyways for ten minutes and then stopped at a dilapidated terraced house on a corner, its front door step on the pavement. The grubby curtains on the windows were shut and the house appeared to be unoccupied. Doris yanked Nellie's hand and led her down the side passage. They stopped outside a wooden gate where Doris slowly lifted the squeaking latch.

'You go first,' urged Doris, looking behind her. 'This is my 'umble 'ome. Yer pa has been lodging 'ere since the bombing. Just take a peek in the back window and let me know if yer see him while I keep an eye out for Slipper Joe in case he followed us.'

Nellie's stomach hardened. She suddenly felt nervous. 'You did mean what you said about helping me prove my innocence?'

Nellie felt a chill in Doris's voice. 'That's what I said, didn't I? So get on with yer.'

Nellie froze. She was too scared to move. Suddenly the gate was forced open from behind and Doris pushed her inside. A man's hand reached out to grab her.

As Nellie opened her mouth to scream a rough cloth was stuffed into it.

Her eyes widened and she swooned, her legs giving way as she drifted into darkness.

'Silly ol' lass believing me,' chuckled Doris. 'Leave 'er in the shed while I get 'er room ready.'

Chapter Nineteen

Maria wiped her hands and removed her white apron. 'I've finished everything yer asked me to do, Cook. May I leave now please?'

'Yes, I can see everything's done to perfection. You're going to the fever hospital now, aren't you?'

'I am. I'm 'oping Joey's made good progress. I've not had word from the doctor or hospital, so that must be a good sign.'

'That's the spirit.' Cook smiled, rolling out some pastry. 'I'll bake a nice little cake for him when he's back home.'

Maria had worked tirelessly in the kitchen, pausing only to wipe down her sweaty brow, doing her best to avoid Philomena. She commented to Cook that she hadn't seen her the last couple of days and asked if she was unwell.

'More likely she's unwanted rather than unwell,' Cook told her, with an air of mystery.

'What do yer mean?'

'Don't breathe a word to anyone, but Mrs Pennywick told me she was going to have a word with me about her niece later. I'm as much in the dark about it as you, but it seems something is amiss.'

Maria shrugged her shoulders. 'We'll find out in good time, I expect. Well, good day, Cook. I'll see yer tomorrow. I'll bring Joey back 'ome with me, all being well.'

Starlight and Abel were waiting outside the stable yard for Maria. Abel was propped alongside the cart speaking to one of the stable lads as Maria approached. She stroked the back of Starlight's head affectionately and the horse neighed gently.

Maria leapt up onto the cart and sat next to Abel. 'Orf we go then, lass. Let's hope you 'ave good news waiting for yer today.'

'Oh Abel, I've prayed morning an' night for Joey, and all the other sick children there too.'

'Well, God willing, yer prayers will be answered.'

The journey passed quickly as Maria told Abel the stories she had picked up from Cook. Abel had heard them all before, but enjoyed hearing them again in his good-natured way.

They drew up outside the hospital.

''Ere we are then,' Abel said, dropping Maria off at the front door.

'I'll wait for yer around the corner,' he told her, saying he would make the most of the pleasant weather by walking around the grounds. A number of flowers in the borders had been supplanted with an assortment of vegetables that were doing very nicely, with runner beans reaching towards the sky on their wooden poles alongside the sweet peas and pretty pink carnations.

A different nurse was seated at the desk at the corridor when Maria entered the hospital. She was in her mid-twenties and had an authoritative air about her. Maria introduced herself. 'Ah, Mrs Saward, isn't it? I'm Nurse Jepson. The doctor would like to speak with you. Please follow me.'

Maria's brow creased. 'What is it? Has something happened to Joey?'

The nurse replied firmly, 'The doctor will explain everything. Now please, follow me. I'd be grateful if you were quiet and don't disturb our patients.'

Maria's pulse soared as she imagined the worst. She followed the young nurse along the corridor. The nurse stopped when they reached the end and she knocked on the door, entering after the voice inside invited them in.

Nurse Jepson introduced Maria and excused herself as the tall, thin doctor, who was in his sixties, stopped writing at his desk and rose, extending his arm towards a seat for Maria.

'Why do yer want to see me, Doctor? What's all this about?'

'I'm Dr Fountain and I'm sorry to tell you this, but Joey took a turn for the worse last night. The next forty-eight hours are critical and will decide if he pulls through.'

Tears filled Maria's eyes and she buried her face in her hands. 'But I don't understand. You shaved his 'ead. I thought that would 'elp.'

'I assure you we are doing everything we can. Joey was doing nicely, but then his temperature soared again yesterday. He has a nurse at his side now and there is still hope he will pull through. A lot of other children couldn't have survived this long, but Joey, well I can see he's a tough lad and a fighter.'

'Can I . . . Can I see him?' Maria pleaded, her shoulders shaking.

'I'm afraid not. We can't risk visitors coming in from outside and taking infection onto the ward. I will keep Dr Fletcher informed of Joey's progress. I'm sorry I don't have better news for you.'

'So that's it? I have to go back home now?'

The doctor's face softened. 'I'm afraid so. Don't let Matron hear me saying this, but if you take a stroll in the garden and turn left, the second window along is the one for his ward, you might be able to look in. You'll need to stand on your toes, but you should be able to see him. We wouldn't normally encourage this, but in these circumstances.'

The doctor stepped over to Maria and rested a consoling arm on her shoulder. 'I'm sorry you've had a wasted journey. I promise we are doing all we can.'

Maria's eyes welled. 'This has all come as a terrible shock, seeing as I hadn't had word to cause me alarm.'

She stumbled out of his office, her mind spinning, running blindly into the garden, tears streaming down her cheeks. She recalled seeing Mr and Mrs Hope, the grieving couple, and she feared Joey would die like their daughter had.

Maria knew the spot the doctor suggested as she had looked in on Joey from there before, but wasn't going to let on to him about this. Abel saw her. 'I wasn't expecting you out so soon, lass.'

She stifled a sob. 'Joey's not coming home yet. The doctor says he's taken a turn for the worse. I'm frightened. I thought 'e were going to be better today. The doctor says I can look at him through the window.'

'I'm sorry to hear that lass. I'll come with yer and give you a leg up.'

Maria found the window and Abel bent down, cupping his hands to steady her foot. She wobbled slightly and pushed herself up, placing her elbows on the windowsill. Her eyes scanned the row of beds in front of her. She screwed her eyes up and, for a moment, she thought Joey must have been moved – and then she spotted him.

She almost toppled backwards, seeing him lying there with a shaven head, his eyes shut. He was the smallest child on the ward and a nurse was mopping his fevered brow. He turned his head towards her and his eyes flickered open.

Maria knocked on the window and cried out, 'Joey, Joey, it's me, yer ma.'

Abel warned her, 'Shush, lass. He can't hear yer. Don't go getting yerself in a state.'

Maria knocked on the window again and cried his name out louder.

The nurse looked towards her and made a pitiful face. She whispered to Joey, perhaps telling him to look towards the window, but he closed his eyes again, and the nurse shrugged her shoulders and continued to attend to Joey.

Abel helped Maria down. 'I'm sorry for yer, Maria. Joey's still alive, hang on to that and remember, while there's still breath in his tiny body and a beating heart, then there's still hope.'

Maria stifled her sobs all the way back to Wolferton, the cart rocking gently from side to side. She rested her head against Abel's shoulder feeling some comfort from his quiet presence and Starlight's gentle trot.

As they turned into Wolferton, they passed Kitty Cottage, where the Greenstick sisters lived with their family of cats. Magnolia was standing by the front gate, wearing an outlandish purple flouncy dress with pink bows down the front. She was talking animatedly to a well-dressed gentleman who Maria did not recognise. Magnolia tossed her head backwards and laughed at his comments. She seemed different somehow, her face was softer and she appeared happier than Maria had seen her before. Abel nodded politely to them both and tipped his cap as they approached. Magnolia waved her arms frantically and signalled them over.

'My dear Maria. How are you? What news of Joey?'

She stepped over to the cart, her expression full of concern upon seeing Maria's downcast face. Maria was in no mood to chat, but Magnolia and Aggie had been so kind to her, they were almost like adoptive aunts, and she appreciated she had Joey's best interest at heart.

She blurted out what had happened at the hospital, and once she started she couldn't stop. She bit her lip, fighting back tears. Magnolia rested her hand on Maria's. 'It must have been a terrible shock for you seeing Joey like that. He is still with us, and he will get over it, I'm sure of it.'

Starlight suddenly became unsettled, his hooves digging into the ground and kicking up dust. The sound of a sharp bark made the horse even more agitated. He shook his head and edged away from the gate, while Abel attempted to rein him in. 'Hey, boy. Steady now.'

Maria pointed to a small straw-coloured terrier who had just run around the legs of Magnolia's friend, his lead twisting around him. Magnolia smiled, moving next to him.

'Maria, Abel, I don't believe you have met David. This is David Fellowes. He is an old friend who has just moved back to Wolferton.'

Mr Fellowes moved closer to the cart and greeted Maria and Abel with exquisite politeness. 'And this is Rufus, my friendly hound. Please take no notice of his bark, it's not as bad it sounds. He's just being friendly,' he said with great charm.

Rufus eyed them suspiciously and barked again. Mr Fellowes raised his finger to his lips and ordered him to be quiet. The dog obeyed, sitting on his hind legs, yelping softly.

Maria's lips curled slightly. She realised this must be the gentleman Aggie had told her about. The man Magnolia had once loved and lost.

'I'm pleased to meet yer, Mr Fellowes, and Rufus too. My Joey would like him, he is very fond of animals.'

Mr Fellowes raised his cap. 'I'm very sorry to hear about your lad, Maria. Maybe, when he's better and returns home, he'd like to come and play with Rufus. He's very good with children.'

Maria's face brightened for a moment. 'Oh yes, 'e'd like that very much.' Her eyes filled with sadness. 'That is, *if* he comes home.'

He continued, his voice soft and kind, 'My cousin, Frederick Rumbelow, is the vicar here, and you can be assured that I will mention Joey to him and special prayers will be said on Sunday.'

Rufus made a sudden leap towards Starlight, but was yanked back by David. 'I do apologise about Rufus. He is not usually this excitable. He has already met two of Magnolia's cats and scared the living daylights out of them and now he is unsettling your fine horse. We're not going to make many friends this way.'

Abel stroked Starlight's head and mane until he had quietened. 'Yer don't need to worry about Starlight, he's used to dogs, we always had our own. As long as they don't try to nip him.'

Magnolia's cheeks were flushed and her eyes shone as they barely left Mr Fellowes' face. Aggie knocked on the front window and waved at them, a tabby cat in her arms. A black cat leapt up from nowhere and climbed on to her shoulder. They had been locked into the house, well away from Rufus. Despite her sadness and preoccupied thoughts, Maria couldn't resist a smirk, wondering if Magnolia would convert her friend to a fondness for felines rather than canines.

Magnolia gushed, 'Mr Fellowes used to be a teacher here. He is an accomplished singer too. He has joined the church choir and will take part in our next concert. We are very fortunate to have him as we are in dire need of more tenors.'

Mr Fellowes threw his head back and chortled. 'I think Miss Greensticks is way too complimentary about my voice. I allowed Frederick to twist my arm.'

'Maybe yer can sing a duet together?' Maria suggested.

Maria thought Magnolia almost looked pretty. Her hair was piled on top of her head and a few loose strands cascaded down the sides of her cheeks, which highlighted her high cheekbones.

As they departed, Maria turned to Abel. 'So it's true. Magnolia's gentleman friend has returned. What do yer make of him?'

'Aye, I remember him from afore when he taught at the school, he is a true gent.'

'Who would have thought it, that Magnolia would find love at her time of life?'

'She's a bit unusual, I'll grant you that. But she has a heart of gold, and he can see that. With what's happening in the world now, you have to grab what affection you can when yer have the chance.'

'I know, and that's what I will tell Eddie when I can see him,' replied Maria softly.

∞

Harry Saward called in to see Maria that evening to enquire after Joey. Ruth made a pot of tea while Maria told him what had happened, and also mentioned Eddie's cold shoulder towards her.

He listened sympathetically and frowned. 'You will get through this, you know, Maria. I heard about Eddie from Beatrice, she told me he is in a bad way. He doesn't deserve this, but none of our men do.'

Ruth said, 'I've said the same, Harry. I can't offer you much, but I do have some trench cake.'

'Ah, my favourite.' Harry smiled, his eyes twinkling. He picked up a slice of the dark, dense cake, which Ruth had put down in front of him. The cake was made without eggs, as everyone had been urged to donate their eggs to the National Egg Collection to be shipped to wounded servicemen in hospitals in France and Belgium. Vinegar was used to react with the baking soda to help the cake rise.

'You're in luck, I used the last of my nutmeg in this cake. I'll 'ave to do without until I can get some more. The cakes won't be as flavoursome for a while.'

'Tell me Harry, have you heard news of Nellie? I do worry about 'er, seeing as she is my niece, and I don't believe what the papers say.'

Harry shook his head. 'None at all. There is a poster up offering a reward, but I can't see her coming back. Is there any news of that brother of yours, Gus?'

'Nothing at all. None of our family 'ave had anything to do with him after his shameful treatment of Freddie and Archie.'

Harry sighed. 'She seems so young and desperate, running off the way she did from that detective. Why would she come to Wolferton? Surely it must have been to try to make contact with you. Are you sure you haven't seen her?'

Ruth and Maria glanced at each other and feigned ignorance, shrugging their shoulders in conspiratorial silence. Their cheeks flushed and they looked away.

'Hmm.' Harry pondered, scratching his head wondering if they were concealing information from him. 'If you agree, I suggest we wait another day or two, and if there is no news then I will ask my brother Ronald to call in at Gus's address. He's a special constable and he'll put the word out for Gus Harper. It's a bonus that Ronald lives in London and we can rely on his discretion. The sooner this is resolved all the better for her, and for us too. I've noticed some people pointing their finger at me saying we are related to that woman who is on the run from the police. And the last thing I need is that detective returning to Wolferton and pestering me.'

Ruth readily agreed and slumped in her chair, twisting her hands anxiously. She appeared nervous.

When Maria slipped out of the room Harry asked Ruth if anything else was troubling her.

'I didn't want to say anything in front of Maria, but yes, there is something on my mind.'

The station master moved closer towards her. Ruth was his stepmother, although she was five years younger than him, but looked older and looked up to Harry for advice.

'Can you tell me what it is?'

'It was something I overheard the other day, about the terrible things the Huns are doing.'

'What is that?'

'Some people in the butcher's were whispering about terrible things they have done to children.'

Harry's eyes narrowed. 'I think I know what you refer to. Sarah said people were talking about this in the post office too.'

Ruth bit her lip. 'Is it true, do yer think? They said the Hun were cutting off babies' hands and impaling their bodies on bayonets, that they were snatching children as they clung to their mothers' aprons, and even eating their hands. That's what they say is being done on the Continent. It's barbaric and I can't sleep for thinking about it. What if the Hun invade us and do these terrible things here?'

'The damned Hun will never set foot on our soil, so put such thoughts out of your mind. Think how it would upset Maria if she heard this. She has enough to worry about right now.'

'I know yer right, but that's not the only thing they're saying.' Ruth grabbed Harry's arm. 'Did yer hear about the corpse factory?'

'I did, and I cannot believe they would commit such an atrocity,' replied Harry, who had heard rumours himself that the Germans were boiling down bodies for munitions and pig and poultry food, with one Fritz calling his margarine 'corpse fat'. Harry had shuddered when he heard this and could barely believe it was true.

216

'My view is, Ruth, that as this war continues there is more and more scaremongering, so we shouldn't believe all we hear. If rumours of these atrocities are intended to cause alarm here in Blighty, to stir up hatred against the Germans, then they have succeeded. I find it hard to believe anyone could be capable of such terrible acts, and we cannot believe such terrible things unless they are proven. The Germans themselves have said these reports are loathsome and ridiculous and even though they are our most hated enemy, I don't believe they would act so atrociously.'

Ruth scoffed. 'How can we be sure what to believe these days? Ada's husband is on the Continent and Jack Hawkins travels wherever he is sent as the King's Messenger. Imagine what would happen to them if they were captured. I'm scared rigid when I hear such terrible things.'

'We all are, Ruth. How about calling in one evening with Maria? Sarah's always saying she doesn't see enough of you. Leslie and Joey can play in the garden together.'

Ruth gulped. 'I'd like that. Thank yer, Harry. Thank yer for being so good to us after all the trouble we seem to cause yer.'

'We are all Sawards, it's what Pa would have wanted. We'll always stick together,' he told her.

Chapter Twenty

'My father is here tomorrow and Private Herring is first on his list,' Matron informed Beatrice. 'He has a new technique he would like to try out on Private Herring's wound to help it heal and save his leg. By all accounts it has proved very successful previously.'

Beatrice's face brightened. 'Oh, I do hope it will work. Eddie is very down at the moment.'

Matron's eyes creased. 'Father has asked for you personally to assist him again. You must have made a lasting impression before.'

Beatrice's cheeks flushed. 'It is an honour to assist Dr Butterscotch and I shall do my best, Matron. I'll let Maria and Eddie's mother know, they're bound to be anxious about him, and interested to know about this new technique the doctor will be using.'

'Do inform them that Dr Butterscotch would only use it if he was confident of its success. He will need Private Herring's permission too, of course.'

co

The following morning, when Beatrice arrived at the hospital, Dr Butterscotch greeted her in the operating theatre. He was consulting Eddie's notes.

'I understand you know our first patient. Will this affect your professionalism in any way? If the operation isn't successful we will have to amputate. I'm hoping it won't come to that, but I want you to be prepared for the worst scenario.'

Beatrice's eyes widened. She had never assisted with an amputation before, and the thought of assisting with Eddie's, if he should need one, made her stomach churn.

Her eyes met the doctor's intense gaze. 'What do you think his chances are, Doctor? Can you tell me about the treatment you will be using?'

Beatrice wanted reassurance that Eddie was not being used as a medical experiment. As if reading her thoughts, the doctor told her, 'I have had a high degree of success using this novel method and hope to achieve this again today. Have you heard of the Bipp Treatment?'

Beatrice shook her head. 'In technical terms, it's a bismuth iodoform paraffin paste that I shall smear over the wound after cleaning it out thoroughly. I need to see how bad the wound is and can get into it this way. The paste is then used to cover the wound and has healing properties.'

'I see. I badly want this to work. If you think it will help Eddie, then of course I want to assist you.'

'It's a method that has been well tested on severe gunshot wounds, gangrenous and septic wounds and compound fractures of arms and legs. In every case the condition of the patient has benefited greatly and been spared painful daily dressings.'

'Oh, that does sound very impressive. We are so fortunate that you can be here to attend our patients.'

Matron stepped into the operating theatre at that moment. 'Are you ready for the patient?'

'Very soon. I was just telling Nurse Saward about the Bipp Treatment and she is now going to scrub up.'

Matron smiled. 'Ah yes. Did you know, Nurse Saward, that this treatment was pioneered by the remarkable women at Endell Street Military Hospital in London? It's a hospital staffed and run solely by women after being set up by the remarkable doctors Flora Murray and Louisa Garrett Anderson.'

Beatrice's face shone. 'That is incredible. I've heard of the hospital and am in full admiration for the women who run it. I'm familiar with the treatments they use but wasn't aware that they were using new antiseptic treatments for war wounds.'

Matron continued, 'Indeed they are. Infections from war wounds have led to the deaths of thousands of soldiers and amputations that could now stand a better chance of being avoided. I read in a medical journal how the Bipp Treatment has significant antimicrobial properties and was invented by Professor James Rutherford Morison. The Endell Street doctors contacted him and started using his formulation on patients, and the first hospital to do so.'

Dr Butterscotch added, 'We are extremely fortunate that this formulation has been shared with me too. We are ready now to apply it to Private Herring.'

Beatrice, once she had scrubbed and was gowned up, greeted Eddie with her best reassuring smile when he was wheeled into the operating theatre on a trolley. He looked terrified as he stared around the room full of sterile medical equipment.

The doctor said. 'Eddie and I have already met and he is willing for me to use the new treatment on him. Shall we start?'

Eddie's frightened eyes stared up at Beatrice's face. 'Beatrice, promise me, if I don't make it, tell Maria I didn't mean what I said. Tell her . . . Tell her I love her.'

'She knows that and you'll be able to tell her yourself afterwards. You are going to pull through this operation, and before long you'll be walking tall again. I have total faith in Dr Butterscotch.'

The doctor said, 'Right, young man, let's put this mask on you. There's nothing to be afraid of. You'll be able to see your Maria soon. But first, you need to breathe in the chloroform. Just close your eyes and relax, count to ten, and you will soon be asleep.'

Within a few moments Eddie's eyelids closed. Beatrice passed the scalpel to Dr Butterscotch who expertly slit open the wound. 'Yes, just as I thought. Here's a piece of shrapnel, just below the knee. I'm going to remove it and give the area a thorough clean and then apply the Bipp formulation.'

Beatrice's face brightened. 'Does this mean you can save his leg?'

'I've treated worse than this, so I very much hope so.'

Dr Butterscotch held up a tiny piece of shrapnel with a pair of thumb forceps and placed it in a bowl. He removed some damaged tissue and Beatrice remained calm, passing over the required gauze soaked in methylated spirit and tincture of iodine used to clean the wound. The Bipp formulation was then applied and the wound dressed.

'He's lucky the gunshot missed his bone. The dressing will need changing again in four days. I'll leave some Bipp for your use. When I return next week, I will see how it is healing.'

Beatrice wheeled Eddie into a recovery room, breathing a sigh of relief. Nurse Jennings was waiting for her. 'How did it go?' she asked.

'I have a gut feeling that it went well and the doctor seems confident. Have you heard about the Endell Street Military Hospital run by a group of dedicated, pioneering women?'

Nurse Jennings shook her head. Beatrice said, 'I'll tell you about it later. I've decided I want to work there one day. But, I have to go now, the next patient is waiting for me. Can you let me know when Eddie wakes?'

∽

Magnolia's rekindled connection with David made Aggie hanker back to memories of Percy. She thought of him constantly. She could see her sister's growing affection for David and was happy for her. Although there was just the slight problem of Rufus to overcome as Kitty Cottage was no place for playful terriers.

Without children to fuss over, the Greensticks had showered their affections on their cat family. It had started after a stray cat adopted them. Oscar was only a kitten when they found him hiding in a bush in their garden. They began feeding him with tasty morsels of scraps and the ginger cat soon became a resident. They were astounded to discover later that Oscar was not a tomcat, but a female, and he was promptly renamed Victoria. Their feline family grew to include Jasper, a playful tortoiseshell tabby; Helena, plump and glorious with her shiny black and white fur; and Maud, a beautiful white moggy with deep green eyes, named after the youngest daughter of King Edward, and the Queen of Norway, who stayed at Appleton House on the Sandringham Estate every year.

Aggie knew the cats still meant the world to Magnolia, who at that moment was brushing their fur, one by one. Helena nuzzled up against Magnolia's arm and meowed contently, her jewel-like eyes gazing up into her face.

After breakfast Aggie announced, 'I'm going to the milliner's in King's Lynn today. Is there anything you would like from town?'

Magnolia raised an eyebrow. She knew this was the day of the week that Aggie usually avoided going into King's Lynn, ever since the last time she had seen Percy there.

'Not today, but do hurry back if you can. If you recall, David has invited us both to his house for tea this afternoon. He would very much like it if you could come.'

'That's very kind of him, and do thank him for his invitation, but we are not of the age where a chaperone is needed. I'm sure you will have a far better time without me.'

'Are you all right, Aggie? You seem to be distracted by something. You know how welcome you would be.'

'Of course I'm allright, but you know what they say about three being a crowd. We see so much sadness and heartache with this war that if there is a chance that David has genuine affections for you, and you return his feelings, I want you to know I won't stand in your way.'

Magnolia's cheeks reddened. 'Oh Aggie. I couldn't possibly entertain such a thought. I will never leave you alone.'

Aggie's voice was tinged with emotion. 'If I were to see Percy again, if he was still a free man and had a desire to rekindle our friendship, I wouldn't hold back. I wish I had another chance, like you.'

Magnolia's mouth dropped open and before her sister could reply the back door was slammed shut and Aggie was walking down the path.

∾

Aggie had no intention of seeing a milliner but wanted to keep secret the true nature of her outing. She had thought about it for the last couple of days and decided to go through with it.

After arriving in King's Lynn, she made her way to the market place and queued outside the meat pie stall. She made her purchase, though the pies contained more vegetable than meat these days, but she was accustomed to this now. Her reminisces aroused a tenderness within her as she walked with the pie to the park where she used to walk arm in arm with Percy. Children were playing with a ball and a love-struck couple strolled past gazing into each other's eyes, the man dressed in an army uniform, home on leave. A woman dressed in black scuttled past, her face grim, and Aggie was struck by her sorrow.

Aggie walked to the bandstand and paused. Her pulse quickened as she spotted the bench where they would sit together. She recalled the tender look in Percy's eyes, the womanly sensations fired up within her when his hand took hers, or he stroked her arm or cheek, when they sat close to each other on the bench.

She sat on their favourite seat as her mind drifted to happy memories of their time together. Her wistful thoughts were suddenly interrupted. 'Excuse me. Is this seat free? I won't disturb you.'

Aggie glanced up and saw a friendly faced woman. She was in her fifties and wore a smart dark-green skirt and matching jacket with a shiny brooch on the lapel. She smiled warmly as Aggie nodded.

'Please do. This is my favourite bench. You can still smell the heavenly scent from the roses, even though there are cabbages and runner beans growing among them.'

The woman laughed. 'It's becoming a more common sight, and one that's certainly needed right now.'

Aggie nodded politely and turned her head away.

225

'Excuse me,' interrupted the woman. She stared intently at Aggie. 'You say this seat is special to you. If you don't mind me asking, why is that?'

Aggie gulped. She struggled to answer, not wishing to divulge her innermost thoughts to this stranger.

The woman's voice was soft. 'I apologise, I can see my question has upset you.'

Aggie's voice wobbled. The woman seemed kind and she felt she could confide in her. 'I used to come here a long time ago to meet someone. A gentleman. We would sit on this bench.'

The woman tilted her head and stared at Aggie. 'Really? I wonder . . .'

Aggie's eyebrows arched. 'What do you mean?'

'My brother Percy used to come here every Tuesday lunchtime. He was fond of a certain lady and they would meet here for lunch.'

Aggie's heart thumped hard. 'Do you know the lady's name, by any chance?'

'Why yes, it was Aggie. Her real name was Agatha, but he said she detested it, preferring to be known as Aggie.'

Aggie sobbed. 'I can't believe it. That's me. I'm Aggie! And was your brother Percy a clerk?'

'That's correct. But I don't understand. Why are you here today?' stuttered the woman.

'Please tell me, where is Percy? Can I see him?'

The woman answered slowly. 'My name is Margaret Woods. Oh, Aggie, it is so good to meet you after hearing so much about you. Percy spoke of you with the greatest

226

affection. I'm sorry, Aggie, but I'm afraid I have some very sad news.'

Margaret paused, edging closer to Aggie and taking her hand in hers. Aggie's eyes were wet. She spoke falteringly. 'Oh no, please don't say he's dead.'

Margaret nodded. 'I'm so sorry. Percy passed away two weeks ago from kidney disease. He collapsed in great pain a few days after your last meeting and became delirious. I thought he would die then, but he miraculously pulled through, though he was much weakened and later suffered a stroke. He spoke your name and I couldn't make sense of what he was saying when he mumbled about meeting you on the park bench, but gradually I put the pieces together and tried to find you here. Sadly, Percy spent the rest of his days in a wheelchair and lost his ability to speak.'

Aggie buried her face in her hands. 'Percy, my dearest Percy! How I wish I could have been there for you!'

Margaret placed a consoling arm around Aggie's shoulder that shook. Aggie mumbled, 'I tried to find him, but his office wouldn't tell me his address.'

'They have strict rules not to pass on personal details to strangers. The last time he saw you, when your sister turned up unexpectedly, he was planning to propose marriage to you, but it wasn't meant to be, sadly.'

Aggie gasped. 'I came here today looking for Percy, and felt he had abandoned me when he didn't show up. And you tell me he wanted to propose marriage? I had no idea he loved me so much.'

Percy's sister continued, 'Yes, he did. Before he lost his power of speech his dearest wish was that should I pass here on a Tuesday afternoon, I should search you out on this park bench and sit here for a while in case you appeared. I'm so glad I passed this way today, Aggie. Percy hoped that our paths would cross here one day. It was important for him that you knew his feelings towards you were honourable. He said you were the finest woman he ever met.'

Tears gushed down Aggie's cheeks and she fumbled for a handkerchief. 'He said that? Nobody's ever said that to me before. If only I could have told Percy I returned his affections, that I would have been honoured to be his wife.'

Margaret consoled, 'You must take comfort from knowing that you were loved by the purest of hearts. Many women never experience that.'

Aggie rose, her voice choked. 'Yes, I was well loved by Percy, the most honourable of men. Knowing this has somehow made me feel different. I feel complete as a woman knowing I've been so well loved.'

Chapter Twenty-One

Three days had passed since Maria's last visit to the fever hospital and worries about Joey's well-being filled her head as she worked harder than ever at the Big House to take her mind off it. Philomena had still not returned to work, and Mrs Pennywick was absent too following an accident.

Cook had informed her. 'Mrs Pennywick fell down a stepladder and badly sprained her ankle the day she was going to speak to me about Philomena, so I'm none the wiser as she is still at home resting it on doctor's orders.'

'Oh dear, I wonder what she was going to say.'

'I've heard it rumoured that Philomena isn't coming back to Sandringham – and good riddance to bad rubbish.'

Maria raised an eyebrow. If this was true, there might be a chance she could return to her duties in the Queen Mother's drawing room. She was peeved when Maisie, a timid maid, had taken over there for the time being. Maisie had told her she was nervous of the parrot when it screeched and was even more flustered than Maria had been about touching the precious porcelain, afraid she might break a royal heirloom. Maria couldn't see Maisie objecting if she were asked to return to work upstairs.

❧

At the end of the day, Maria scurried through the woods as she made her way home, her mind fixed on anxious thoughts about how Joey was doing at the hospital. She was relieved to hear that her problems with Philomena were likely to be over if what Cook said was true. When she reached Honeysuckle Cottage, she paused at the gate, seeing Joey in her mind's eye running along the garden path towards her, his arms outstretched. A tear trickled down her cheek, and she brushed it away with her sleeve.

The garden had never looked better than it did that day and she was pleasantly surprised to see Ruth had laid tea out in the garden, having hauled an old wooden table from the shed and thrown a cloth over it. She had even placed a spray of pink carnations into a vase and laid three place settings.

'What's the meaning of this, Ma? It isn't anyone's birthday. Are we expecting a visitor?'

'We are indeed. Aggie is coming. She has something important to tell us and seemed very excited when I saw her earlier in the post office.'

At that moment, Aggie skipped down the garden path carrying a tin. 'Oh, this looks so lovely and it's a perfect evening to sit out for tea. I thought you might like some shortbread I just made. I'll make some more for Joey when he comes home. And he will, Maria, I can feel it in my bones.'

230

Maria replied, 'I hope and pray you're right, Aggie. Your cheeks are flushed. I've never seen yer so excited before. Has something happened?'

Aggie's lips trembled and she pressed her hands against her chest, gazing up at the sky.

'Yes, it certainly has. I have been loved by a man!' she declared.

Maria's eyes widened. 'What are yer talking about?'

'My Percy, who I told you about. He loved me. He wanted to propose marriage. I have been loved! And it feels so wonderful.'

Ruth took hold of Aggie's hand. 'Calm down, Aggie, and tell us from the beginning what's made yer so jittery.'

Between gulps of breath, Aggie poured out her story of meeting Percy's sister. 'It really felt like his spirit was there with us,' she said with a wistful air. 'His sister was so lovely and kind. I'm so happy to know that I have been truly loved by a wonderful man. I would hate to have passed to the other world without knowing what it felt like. Even though he is sadly no longer on this earth, I can still feel his love deep in here,' she gasped, thumping her fists against her heart.

Maria, Ruth and Aggie were talking so animatedly that they didn't hear a car pull up outside.

'Good evening, ladies. I hope I am not intruding.'

Maria rushed over to Dr Fletcher. 'Is there news from the fever hospital? How is Joey doing?'

'Yes, there is. I had to come straight away to tell you.'

Maria's expression showed concern. 'It's not bad news, is it?'

'On the contrary. I was at the hospital today and saw Joey. He is on the mend. He has turned the corner and his condition is improving.'

Maria flung her arms around the doctor's neck and hugged him. 'Oh thank you, Doctor. This is the best news I could have wished for. When can I see 'im?'

'He ate a few spoons of porridge this afternoon and tomorrow the nurses will see if he is strong enough to take a few steps around the ward.

'If Joey continues to make good progress, he could be home at the end of the week. I always knew he was a fighter, just like his mother.' The doctor grinned.

Maria stepped back and pulled a face. 'Whatever do yer mean?'

'I know what a tough life you've had and I'm impressed to see how well you are doing for yourself, and what a grand lad Joey has turned out to be.'

Aggie piped in, 'I couldn't agree more. I shall very much look forward to being Joey's godmother, that is, if the offer still stands.'

Maria beamed. 'Of course it does. You would make the most wonderful godmother, Aggie. After Joey is back home I shall start making plans for his christening.'

∞

Maria spent every spare minute scrubbing Joey's bed with washing soda, laying out freshly laundered bedlinen, scrubbing the walls and floor and airing the room, even though it had already been done when he went into hospital.

When Sunday finally came and she was due to collect him, she could scarcely contain her excitement. She packed a bag of clothes for Joey to change into and stood by her front gate, shifting from one foot to the other, brimming with excitement, and waiting for Abel and Starlight to pull up.

When they arrived and Maria had scrambled onto the cart, she mumbled, in a moment of panic, 'The doctor says Joey has turned the corner. It would tear me apart if it weren't true. What if . . . ?'

'There's no *what if*? to worry about, lass. I saw Dr Fletcher on me way 'ere and he says he ain't heard anything to the contrary. He's over the moon for yer. Yer Joey's on the mend. There, I told yer not to fret. You need to listen to yer old Abel.'

'I hope so, Abel. Oh, I do so hope so. Can Starlight go any quicker? I don't mind the bumps if it means we'll be there faster.'

'Let's give it a go.' Abel grinned, flicking his wrist as he mastered the reins, to little avail. Starlight had his own pace and was not going to be rushed.

Maria sat impatiently, and leapt out of the cart the moment it drew up at the fever hospital. She rushed to the building, flinging open the front door.

Nurse Jepson, who Maria had seen during her last visit, greeted her with a smile. 'How are you today, Mrs Saward? I'm happy to inform you that your little Joey has surprised us all.'

'Do yer mean it? Are yer saying he's better and can come 'ome?' Maria asked falteringly.

'Yes, indeed, that's what I'm saying.'

'Oh thank yer. I feared for the worst. Thank yer. Thank yer from the bottom of me 'eart.'

'You have no need to worry anymore. If you follow me, I will take you straight to the doctor. He can tell you himself.'

Maria's heart pounded and her eyes searched in all directions. The door was slightly ajar when they reached the doctor's office and he was speaking to Matron.

'Do come in,' he beckoned, hearing Nurse Jepson knock on the door.

'Take a seat Mrs Saward. I have good news for you today.'

'I hear Joey is better. Is that right?'

'Yes, indeed he is. And he is quite a character too, telling us all stories about bears running loose at Sandringham. He has been most entertaining.'

Maria gulped, her eyes filling. ''E likes to 'ear those stories. They're all true. Can I see him now, please?'

The doctor rose from behind his desk. 'You can, and not only can you see Joey, but you can take him home today. He has made such a speedy recovery, though I do urge caution. Do allow him time to rest more until he gets his strength back.'

'Oh thank yer, Doctor. I was so worried I was going to lose him.'

'You have the dedication of Matron and her nurses to thank, and the fact that your boy is a fighter. Matron will see to everything now. Good day to you, Mrs Saward.'

Maria felt she was floating on air, her feet gliding along the corridor following behind Matron, who told her they had a list as long as her arm of poorly young patients in need of Joey's bed. 'It won't stay cold for a moment longer than necessary,' she told her, walking through the ward and passing the beds filled with sick patients.

Maria's heart sang when she reached Joey. He was sitting in a chair next to his bed and his eyes widened in disbelief. 'Mama? Is it really you?'

Maria sat on the edge of his bed and reached over, gently brushing her lips against his soft cheeks. She stroked his bare head, which showed signs of new hair growth. 'Yes, my darling boy. It is. I'm taking you home now.'

His face brightened. 'Really? Today?'

'Yes, that's right. Abel is here with Starlight.'

His face saddened as he patted his head. 'I didn't want me hair cut, but they made me.'

Maria clutched him in a tight embrace. 'They did it to help make yer better. It will grow soon enough.'

Maria's eyes filled as she saw his eyes gaze up into her face and he smiled. He snuggled against her.

'I love yer, Joey Saward. Don't go giving me a scare like this again!'

Maria wiped her moist cheeks with the sleeve from her blouse. Joey was wearing short grey trousers down to his knees and a shirt that Maria didn't recognise. Matron approached and explained, 'They belonged to another little boy who sadly didn't make it. His mother left them here, just in case another child needed them.'

'I've brought me own clothes for Joey, do yer want those back? We don't want to leave yer short.'

'No thank you, that's all right. You keep them, Mrs Saward.'

Maria glanced around the ward. Each bed was occupied by a sick child. 'I hope the other children here will pull through too. There are so many of them.'

Joey slipped his tiny hand into Maria's and dragged her to the next bed. A young girl a couple of years older than Joey with bouncy red curls lay there with her eyes shut. 'That's my friend Abigail. She used to tell me ghost stories. I saw a ghost at the end of me bed one night. Abigail said it was going to take me to heaven. But I said, "No, I want my mama." I kicked and kicked at it until it let me go.'

Maria bent down and stared into his face. 'What happened to this ghost, Joey?'

'There was a bright light, like the brightest sunshine and moon all in one, and a big hole at the end of it and the ghost sort of floated into it like magic and disappeared. Abigail said if I had gone with the ghost I would have been in heaven now. What did she mean, Mama? I don't understand.'

Taking Joey in her arms and squeezing him tight, Maria told him, 'It means yer place is here on earth. It wasn't yer time to go to heaven. The angels want you to get better, to be strong and 'ave a happy life. And that's what's going to happen.'

He stared solemnly at his little friend. 'I'm glad the angels let me stay. I hope the ghost doesn't take Abigail.'

∽

Joey had been home for three days and was getting stronger all the time. Three weeks had passed since Nellie had left Wolferton and there hadn't been any word from her. 'Perhaps she really is a bad 'un after all, like her pa,' muttered Ruth.

Maria looked doubtful. 'Or perhaps something has happened to her. She surely wouldn't have left her precious locket with us if she didn't plan to return.'

A knock at the front door halted the conversation. 'I wonder who that could be?' Ruth asked, heading out of the room to answer it.

Joey was happily playing with his soldiers on the floor and the colour was beginning to return to his cheeks. Suddenly the door was pushed open and Maria's hands flew to her mouth as she saw who was there, then dropped to her knees, smoothing down the folds of her skirt as she did so.

'Yer Majesty.' She curtseyed low, her eyes lingering on Queen Alexandra standing before her.

Ruth stood beside her and did the same, shooting a sideways glance at Joey to stand up.

'Yer Majesty,' Joey said, in a faint child's voice, and then covered his pink face with his hands in embarrassment.

Queen Alexandra was accompanied by Jane Rumbelow, the vicar's wife, who busied herself in the community to help her come to terms with her grief following the death of her son, Piers, who had been killed in France.

Jane empathised with families losing their husbands, sons and fathers and drew a measure of comfort from taking food parcels to residents of the town. She also joined Queen Alexandra on some of her visits around the royal estate if her private secretary, the Honourable Miss Charlotte Knollys, was unable to accompany her.

The Queen, now in her early seventies, stood tall and had a regal air about her, her head held high. She was wearing a dark blue skirt and a high-necked cream blouse, the neck and sleeves edged with lace. A choker was fixed to the top of her blouse, matching her earrings, and a string of pearls hung down her front. Her sparkling rings glistened as they caught the sun's rays through the window. Her lustrous light auburn hair was swept up on top of her head in soft curls.

Although Maria had seen the Dowager Queen before at the Big House, it had always been from a distance. She had had it drilled into her not to speak to her unless spoken to first, but here she was now, standing just inches away from Maria, and in her home.

Mrs Rumbelow held out a basket. 'We are so thankful to hear of Joey's good progress and have brought these for you.'

Joey's eyes widened. 'Gingerbread men! Oh Ma, can I have one now?'

'Have you forgotten yer manners? We say "please" and "thank you", don't we?'

'Oh please, don't admonish the boy on my account. I'm sure Joey knows his manners perfectly well.' Queen Alexandra smiled. Despite her advancing years, she retained a natural beauty formed from her high cheekbones and large eyes.

'Thank yer,' Joey said shyly, hiding behind Maria's skirt. 'Please, Ma, may I have one now?'

'Very well. And I'm a fine one to talk about manners. May I offer you some refreshments, Yer Majesty? Mrs Rumbelow?'

Ruth had been speechless up until this point, staring in awe at their royal guest, her jaw almost reaching the floor. She pulled out two chairs for them and then went to fill the teapot with steaming water that had been boiling on the range.

'Thank yer so much for all this. It's so thoughtful of yer. We'll eat like kings tonight, I mean . . . we'll eat well,' said Maria, her cheeks colouring, as she unpacked the contents of the basket, which included a jar of chutney, half a dozen scones, a meat pie, a bottle of fresh lemonade and a bag of humbugs.

Ruth clasped her hands and bobbed. 'Yer Majesty, Mrs Rumbelow, this is so unexpected. It is very kind of yer to take an interest in Joey.'

'Can you speak up? My hearing is poor. Here, on the royal estate, we look after our own,' said Queen Alexandra. 'I like to visit the sick and be kept informed of what's happening on the estate.'

She turned to Maria. 'Tell me, haven't I seen you some-where before? Your face looks vaguely familiar.'

'Yes, Yer Majesty. I work at the Big House. I'm working in the kitchens right now.'

'Speak up, will you? What did you say?'

Maria raised her voice. 'Yes, I work at the Big House. I were an housemaid in yer drawing room, only Emerald escaped from his cage. It weren't my doing, but I got the blame. I wouldn't do anything to upset Emerald, I ain't seen anything like 'im before, he is just wondrous.'

Maria's face reddened as she caught her mother's warning glance.

Queen Alexandra raised her chin. 'Yes, I was informed about that unfortunate incident, and the broken figurine. But tell me, when you say it wasn't your fault, then whose was it?'

Maria knotted her fingers nervously and bit her lip. 'If I tell yer what really happened, I won't get into trouble, will I, Yer Majesty? I don't want to get Philomena in trouble either by snitching on her?'

Mrs Rumbelow's eyebrows furrowed. She addressed the Queen Mother. 'If you wish your Majesty, we can leave now for our next call.'

Queen Alexandra sipped on her tea and waved her hand dismissively in the air. 'I would like to hear what happened under my own roof. Carry on, Maria, and don't worry, no one will get into trouble.'

Maria glanced at her mother, who nodded her head. She spilled out everything and when she had finished she clasped her hands over her mouth.

'What's going to happen to me now, Yer Majesty?'

'I like your spirit, Maria. I will speak to Mrs Pennywick and I'm sure we can come to an arrangement. I've seen Maisie tiptoeing around the rooms and she makes me nervous. I would much rather have someone with spirit like yourself, especially someone who appreciates Emerald and I can trust him with.'

'Oh I do, Yer Majesty. Thank yer. Thank yer so much.'

Joey held up one of his toy soldiers towards the Queen Mother.

'Tell me Joey, do you want to be a soldier when you grow up?' she asked.

'I do,' he replied with gusto.

'That's very good.'

The Dowager Queen rose then and swept out of the room with Mrs Rumbelow behind her. Maria and her mother bobbed down to one knee, with Joey behind imitating their actions.

After their guests had left, Maria chuckled. 'It's time you learnt how to bow properly, Joey, seeing as you'll more than likely cross paths with more royals in the future. None of yer bobbing, this is what yer do,' and she proceeded to show him how to bow.

∽

Two hours later Maria was still pinching herself. 'Ain't we expected at Harry's this evening? It's almost six o'clock, shall we go now?'

'By Jove, so it is,' replied Ruth. 'Wait till they 'ear who called round today.'

'Can I take me soldiers with me?' asked Joey.

'Of course you can, and we'll take one of yer ginger-bread men for Leslie. He'll enjoy that.'

When they reached the station master's house, Maria paused at the gate and reflected back to the day when she had plucked up courage and asked the Saward family to take her in as she had nowhere else to turn. Who would have thought then that the day would come when she would welcome the Queen Mother in her home, and receive gifts from her. The kindness of folk on the royal estate never failed to touch her.

They walked around the side path and saw Betty bringing in the washing. 'I'm almost done. Why don't you go straight through? Harry and Sarah are there, and Ada too with Leslie.'

Maria stayed in the garden. She gushed, 'You'll never believe who just walked through our front door,' and proceeded to tell her.

'She was so kind and interested in Joey, and I told 'er about Emerald and working in the kitchens. I ain't ever spoke to 'er before.'

Ruth added, 'For a woman of a certain age, she certainly has a fine head of hair.'

Betty threw her head back and roared, placing her hands on her hips in a toby-jug fashion. 'Why it's not real hair. Anyone can see she wears a wig. Miss Knollys sees to it. They call it a toupee, and they have their own person at the palace who makes it, a perruquier, I believe he's known as . . .'

Ruth's jaw dropped. 'Never. I don't believe it!'

'What does it matter, Ma. I've seen Miss Knollys, she's a very fine lady and Cook told me how Queen Alexandra owes her life to 'er.'

Ruth exclaimed, 'You've not mentioned this before. What 'appened?'

'One night there was a terrible fire in her apartment. Miss Knollys rushed through the smoke and flames and dragged 'er to safety.'

Betty nodded. 'That's true, and she was rewarded by the King with a special medal for her bravery. She's a fine and devoted woman to our Queen Mother, is Miss Knollys, and clever too, being the first female private secretary to Her Majesty. She's no youngster either, she has a few years on the Queen she serves.'

'Well, I never knew that,' muttered Ruth.

Their conversation came to an end as Leslie ran out into the garden followed by his mother who greeted them. Joey stepped forward shyly holding out his soldiers. Harry joined them outside where Ruth and Maria spoke excitedly about their royal visitor.

Harry smiled. 'Our Queen Mother is very generous. Let's go to the front parlour. We need to talk in private. I'll ask Ada to keep an eye on the boys while Betty finishes her jobs. Sarah has some post office paperwork to see to, so we can talk undisturbed.'

'Is it about Nellie?' asked Maria.

Harry nodded, and they followed him through the kitchen where Sarah had papers spread across the kitchen table. 'Excuse me while I finish this. I want to get it done before Beatrice is back from the hospital and Jessie has finished at the farm.'

Maria handed the gingerbread biscuit to Ada, who stayed in the garden to keep an eye on Leslie and Joey.

Harry cupped his chin in his hands and stared at Ruth. 'I've been making some enquiries of my own about Nellie. Her poster is attracting a lot of attention, with folk wanting to know what her connection is with the Sawards. I couldn't sit back and do nothing any longer. As you know, I have an upstanding position and reputation to maintain, as the royal station master.'

Ruth's cheeks flushed. 'I do know that, and I'm sorry, we don't mean to cause yer any embarrassment. I'm sorry for this trouble, only Nellie swears she is innocent, and I'm afraid to admit it, but I think my brother might be involved. We have no idea where Nellie is and are worried sick about 'er.'

'I see, and what makes you think she is innocent? From what you say it sounds like she has spoken to you.' Harry quizzed, staring directly at Ruth.

Her hand flew to her mouth as she realised that she had let on more than she intended. She proceeded to blurt out how Nellie had called to see her in a desperate state. She finished by asking, 'What enquiries have yer been making? Has Ronald found her?'

Harry shook his head. He had a look of thunder on his face. 'I can scarcely believe you concealed this information from me.'

Tears sprung to Ruth's eyes. Harry's voice softened as he passed Ruth a handkerchief from his jacket pocket.

'I suppose she put you on the spot. I phoned Ronald at the station this morning. It's fortunate the station sergeant allows the odd personal phone call, though I can imagine his ears pricked up when Ronald said he would keep it unofficial for now and do his best to get to the bottom of the matter.'

Ruth said, 'Thank yer, Harry. I know it's the right thing. I'm sorry for keeping yer in the dark. I didn't know what to do for the best.'

Harry rubbed his chin. 'I've been thinking the same. If Ronald can't find Gus and get the proof he needs of Nellie's innocence, she is the one who will suffer. Trust me, if anyone can get to the bottom of this Ronald can, and he'll do his best to keep this between us, for now.'

Ruth bowed her head and nodded. 'I'm very grateful to you Harry for yer understanding and I'm very sorry for the trouble and embarrassment this has caused you.'

Chapter Twenty-Two

'Help. Help. Let me out.' Nellie banged on the door with her fist and screamed as loudly as she could.

'Shout all yer like. Nobody will care what happens to yer here. I'd save yer breath if I were you,' Doris yelled back from the yard.

'Where's me pa? When he hears about this 'e'll be furious.'

'Oh yeah. 'E will, will 'e? Here he is now, so yer can ask him yerself.'

Nellie peered through a tiny crack in the door and immediately fell backwards. She could scarcely believe her eyes. Standing right in front of her was her father, alongside Doris. They were rummaging through her bag, tossing out her possessions to the ground.

Gus flung open the shed door. 'Where is it then? Where's that locket yer nicked?'

'Why are yer doing this to me? I ain't nicked anything. I came to find you to help me prove me innocence against these terrible charges. You know I've done nothing wrong.'

'Yer should count yerself lucky I ain't marching yer straight down to the nick. Yer a wanted woman with a price on yer head. Thirty quid would suit me nicely right now.'

Nellie's legs wobbled. 'But Pa, I'm innocent. You know it. Don't yer want to help me clear me name? I'm sure it's all a misunderstanding. We can go to the police together and sort it out. I never tried to kill me husband either. And you know it. Stanley was a good man. Do yer know what happened to him, 'cause yer were the last person to see him alive?'

Doris snuggled up against Gus. Her father's paunch hung over his trousers and the bottom of his shirt flapped open, too tight to button up. Nellie was shocked at her father's hostility towards her. He had always been difficult to live with and had done his fair share of wrongs to her, but she'd never expected him to be so cruel. Her heart pounded and she inched away from him.

Doris mocked, 'She's such an innocent, bless her. Did I do good bringing her to yer?'

Gus grabbed hold of Doris's ample buttock and gave it a squeeze with a lecherous grin. 'Yer did well me little dumpling.'

Nellie's jaw dropped. 'Yer mean, you planned it all between you? Neither of yer care what happens to me?'

Gus sniggered. 'Of course we care, my precious daughter. In the meantime, 'and over that locket, there's a good girl, and then we can talk about what to do next.'

247

Nellie gasped, the words sticking in her throat. 'What's that locket to you? It was my birthday present from Aunt Millicent. It's all I 'ave left to remind me of 'er and I shall treasure it.'

His face darkened and he raised his hand to strike her. Doris pulled him back. Nellie shook. 'I don't 'ave it. I swear to you I don't 'ave it. Search me if yer like.'

Doris made a grab for Nellie, pinning her against the wall, feeling her body all over. She forced open the buttons on Nellie's blouse and plunged her thick fingers into her bodice, feeling around her soft breasts.

Nellie spat at her. 'Don't you dare touch me. Get off me this minute.'

She kicked out and opened her mouth to scream, but Doris clasped it shut with her ham-like hands.

'Shut it, yer bitch.'

Nellie froze, her eyes widening and filled with fear. She felt the hairs rising on the nape of her neck. Her heart pounded so hard she thought it would leap out of her chest. Gus dragged Doris off her and Nellie attempted to rush out past them, but her father grabbed her arm.

'Steady on. Where do yer think yer orf to? I can't risk yer dobbing me in it with the coppers. We've got a nice little room for you in the attic.'

Before she could resist she was dragged by them both into the back of the house and forced up two flights of stairs into the attic. Gus threw her inside the room, slammed the door and then she heard the sound of the key turning in the lock.

Nellie picked herself up and glanced around the room. It was small and airless with one tiny window that was boarded up. The ceiling sloped down under the eaves of the roof making the room appear even darker. The only flash of daylight was beamed in through tiny cracks in the boards across the window.

She turned her nose up in disgust at the stained mattress on the bed with grubby crumpled linen heaped on top. There was a marble-topped washstand against the wall with a cracked jug and bowl resting on the surface, a chest of drawers with some of its handles missing, a rickety chair and a stained chamber pot that stank.

Nellie pressed her ear against the door and heard raised angry voices coming from below, followed by a door being slammed. Gus and Doris had been at each other's throats by the sound of it.

She slumped to the floor and wept, trying to fathom how her father and Doris could do this to her. It must be all about the money for them. She thought back to her happy days in Margate, reading to her beloved Aunt Millicent and walking arm in arm together along the promenade. She thought about her husband Stanley and wondered what really happened to him that last night out he spent with her father. Stanley was a good man she had married as an escape from her unhappy life with Gus, and, although she couldn't imagine the worse, the question crossed her mind more than once about how he could have fallen into the River Thames. Thankfully, he was alive, but it was unthinkable that she should be charged as an accomplice to his attempted murder when she never wanted any harm to befall him. Would her Aunt Ruth and Cousin Maria give her another thought? She had burdened herself on them, and Freddie and Archie too, or would they all think, *Good riddance.* She couldn't blame them if they did.

After an hour, Nellie's ears pricked at the sound of footsteps stomping upstairs. There was a pause and then the sounds of someone clearing their throat and a key turning in the lock. Doris thrust a plate of dried bread and cheese into the room, made a snorting sound and left, locking the door behind her.

Nellie banged her fists on the door and begged her to let her out. 'Please, Doris. Please let me go. I ain't done anything to you.'

Doris shouted, 'There's no point yelling, no one is gonna 'ear yer up 'ere, so yer may as well belt up.'

As the evening drew in, Nellie lay on top of the bed, and wrapped her arms around her chest, unable to bring herself to pull the filthy sheet up to her face. She leapt up at the sound of screams from below. Her father had returned and Doris was really laying into him, warning him that her ol' man would be back soon from his brother's place in Wolverhampton and would be none too pleased if Gus hadn't paid any rent since he moved in after the air raid.

She just about made out her telling him, 'Remember what he said, yer don't get nought for free.'

The row became fiercer and Nellie heard the sound of crockery being smashed, followed by heavy footsteps stomping up the stairs. She backed into a corner of the room as the sound of the footsteps came closer and Gus unlocked the door. He stormed in, and she stared at his reddened cheek, which he covered with his hand, but she could see the injury from where Doris had clearly struck him.

'Just tell us where the locket is and then yer can go,' he slurred. 'Yer see, I know someone who wants it for a good price.'

She recoiled, pressing her back against the wall, shaking from head to foot. He repeated his demand, his face growing angrier.

'I don't have it, that's all I can say . . .' she stuttered, her words trailing off as Gus pressed his hand against her throat. His expression had a wildness she had never seen before and she thought his eyes were going to pop out. The stench from his foul breath made her flinch and she tried to turn her face away, but he swung it back towards him.

Fearing for her life she blurted, 'All right, I'll tell yer. Ruth and Maria 'ave it. It's in Wolferton. Will yer let me go now? Please? I beg yer, Pa.'

'Tell me where they are,' he demanded. She whispered their address, immediately regretting it the moment the words had slipped from her lips, fearing she had put the safety of her family at risk.

Gus tossed Nellie aside and she crumpled to the floor and drew away from him, bringing her knees up to her chin to protect herself. Was he intending to keep her here until he had the locket in his possession?

A sense of relief washed over her as he stomped out of the room, turning the lock in the door.

Nellie shuffled around on the floor, frozen with fear. She could not believe the monster her father had turned out to be. The floor was thick with dust and Nellie was about to pick herself up when her eyes were drawn to an object under the bed. Curious, she reached underneath, taking hold of the object.

She screwed her eyes up as she turned the item in her hand. It was a small wooden carving, the like of which she had never seen before. It was about fourteen inches long and very narrow with a pointed end in a triangular shape. It had small carvings on one side, while the other side was plain.

In a flash it came to her. She'd seen something similar in a curiosity shop in Margate with Aunt Millicent and she had asked her about it. It was called a stay busk and resembled a long pencil. It was used as a support in women's corsets, making bosoms appear shapely and flattening the stomach. The one Nellie had seen before had carvings of love hearts and a declaration of love from a husband to his wife and was intended for her to wear close to her heart.

The one in her hand was much more macabre and she shuddered as she screwed up her eyes and scrutinised it more closely. The grisly carving showed a man meeting his death by hanging from a giblet. In small writing the name John Doe was carved with the date 1795. There was also a picture of a man and woman holding hands, the man presumably being John Doe and the woman his wife or sweetheart. She felt oddly drawn to the object.

What could this man have done that was so terrible that he had to be hanged? Who was John Doe and why was this carved into a stay busk? And why was it lying on the floor here?

Nellie's mind spun as so many unanswered questions filled her head. She sat on the floor, her back pressed against the bed as she mulled over everything.

One thing was for sure, she had no intention of suffering the same fate as John Doe and would somehow clear her name.

∽

Ronald Saward clambered over the dust and rubble of what was once Gus's home. He shook his head and swore oaths about the enemy as he surveyed the devastating damage around him. The London mayor's emergency fund to help the poor homeless souls was much needed. The air raid had hit London hard, with other cities around the country fearing the same fate would befall them.

For those who survived these terrible attacks, times were harder than ever for ordinary families who had to dig deeper into their pockets to pay the soaring price of food.

Bread was rationed and laws had been introduced banning food hoarding. You could even be fined for throwing food away. Butter was hard to get, and if word got around about a delivery, stores could be looted.

Ronald spotted a couple digging into the rubble of what had once been their home with their bare hands. He asked if they knew of Gus's whereabouts and they shrugged their shoulders and carried on with their search for any personal belongings they could salvage, their faces lighting up when they retrieved a child's teddy bear.

Ronald continued walking and paused when he spotted a church steeple in the distance. He rubbed his chin and looked thoughtful. *What would Sherlock Holmes do in my shoes?* Ronald mulled. He was a devotee of the writer Arthur Conan Doyle, whose crime stories which were serialised in *The Strand Magazine*, and modelled himself on the fictional detective. Dressed in a tweed jacket with black trousers held up with braces, he fancied himself as something of a sleuth. He followed Nellie's case with great interest and although he was still employed by the railways as a transport police officer, his bosses agreed he could spend time as a special constable for the Met as they were short of men.

He wrinkled his nose. Ronald felt he had a knack for sniffing out criminals. His instincts told him that Gus Harper was more involved than he was letting on and had implicated his own daughter to save his skin. He knew Gus was a slippery, unsavoury character and he remembered him well from when two years before Harry had asked him to check up on Freddie and Archie, and he had discovered they were being exploited by Gus for his own ends. Ronald spotted a lad aged around twelve hovering nearby. The boy's chestnut hair fell to his shirt collar and was wiry and unkempt, his grey shirt and black shorts hung from his thin frame; probably hand-me-downs from an older brother or donated by a shelter if his clothing had been destroyed in the raid. Ronald observed the boy watching his every move from the corner of his eye as he poked a stick into the rubble.

'The best of the pickings will have gone by now,' said Ronald, walking towards him.

The boy's face reddened. 'I ain't no thief. I'm looking for me grandpa's pocket watch. 'E said I could 'ave it one day. And now, 'e's dead. I want to find it to remember 'im by, but I expect someone has nicked it while salvaging metal for the war.'

Ronald ruffled the boy's hair. He recoiled. 'Don't touch me. My grandpa used to do that. 'E were like a dad to me since me own dad died when I were only two.'

'I'm sorry to hear about your grandfather. What's your name lad?'

'It's Peter. That's all I'm telling yer as I don't know who you are, or anything about yer and I ain't supposed to talk to strangers.'

Ronald smiled. 'That's true, fair enough. How about if I tell you I'm a copper?'

The boy's eyes widened. 'Never. Are yer really?'

Ronald introduced himself, pleased the boy was impressed. He moved closer towards him. 'Tell me, Peter, did you know Gus and his daughter Nellie who lived in the vicinity of where we are standing right now?'

'I might have done. What's it to you?'

'I'm family and we are keen to know they came to no harm in the raid. There's threepence for you if you tell me what you know.'

Ronald fished the coin out of his pocket and tossed it in the air from hand to hand. Peter's eyes followed it hungrily. He reached up in the air to snatch the coin after Ronald flicked it upwards, but it was out of the boy's reach.

'I did sort of know them. We kept well clear of Gus Harper as he were always in a bad temper. We didn't see much of the girl. Ma said she felt sorry for 'er, but didn't want to interfere.'

'That's a start, but I need to know more. Can you tell me where the man might be now? Then the money is yours.'

The boy scratched his head. 'He used to 'ang around with a woman called Doris. Ma says she's an ole slag, if yer pardon me language. Why're yer asking? Only, I'm worried 'e might track me down and give me a good walloping if he knows I told yer.'

Ronald put on his best Sherlock Holmes air. 'He won't find out from me, lad, I can promise you that. The truth is, Peter, we are very concerned about his daughter's whereabouts and want to be sure she has come to no harm. As you might know she didn't have it easy with her father.'

Peter looked uncomfortable and scratched his head. Ronald tapped his nose and warned, 'I'm sure I don't need to remind a bright boy like you that withholding information from the police will get you into trouble. Serious trouble.'

The boy considered what he had been told. 'I want to be a copper when I grow up.'

'Well then, tell me what you know and I'll put in a word for you when the time comes.' Ronald smiled.

'Will I still get yer threepence?'

'You will. But will it be worth it?'

'It will, cross me 'eart. I can take yer to where his lady friend lives, but I can't say if 'e'll be there. I ain't seen him for days.'

Ronald tossed the coin in the air and Peter leapt up and grabbed it. 'Very well. Take me there, Peter. You can be my Watson.'

Peter's eyes looked quizzical. 'Er? What do yer mean? Who is Watson?'

Ronald threw back his head and roared. 'You don't know who Dr Watson is? If you want to be a copper, you should know who Sherlock Holmes and Dr Watson are. Come along, I'll tell you on the way.'

Chapter Twenty-Three

Lady Appleby fussed over Ada. 'Have you recovered now from your terrible shock? It was such a frightful ordeal for you.'

Ada sighed. 'I can't help but think of poor Annabel. And how sad it is that her little boy will never know his father.'

Lady Appleby agreed. 'These must be very difficult times for her. But we can take comfort from knowing that she is being well looked after by her family. They will never go without.'

Ada bit her lip. There were some things money could never buy. She couldn't bear the thought of Leslie being brought up fatherless.

As if reading her mind, Lady Appleby said softly, 'Money cannot buy love, but she will always have a roof over her head and her family's support, and not all widows have that.'

The hostess pulled a sash by the wall and a maid scurried into the drawing room at Hillington Hall. She gave a small bob and brought in a tea tray, which she placed on a small round table, a delicate lace tablecloth covering its surface. The walls were hung in an elegant pale blue and white paper with matching drapes and a chandelier shimmered from the ceiling. The room was tastefully furnished, yet retained a homely, comfortable feel with soft cushions.

Lady Appleby and Ada sat on a deep blue velvet sofa. The hostess placed her hands in her lap and leant forward. 'I thought it would be a good idea if we met one last time before National Baby Week to discuss our plans. It is admirable that you have persuaded so many young mothers from the estate to participate.'

She briefed Ada about the exhibits that would be displayed at the week-long event at the Methodist Central Hall close to Parliament.

'Baby Week has been getting a lot of notice in the newspapers, and we are so fortunate to have the support of Her Majesty, our Queen Mary and Lloyd George as our esteemed president, as well as Lord Rhondda.'

Ada agreed. 'That is simply marvellous!'

Lady Appleby continued, 'We are indeed most fortunate that so many influential people are behind this. Only a week ago I attended a fabulous concert at Sunderland House arranged by the Duchess of Marlborough which was hugely successful for topping up our funds. Lady Chetwynd was incredibly generous in auctioning off her frocks, hats, coats and lingerie and raised £250 for our funds, a truly staggering figure, and it even made a few lines in *The Times*. Her satin and velvet gowns were in great demand and the bidding was quite fierce.'

'I can believe it, I hear the gowns were stunning. We must hope some good comes out of all this, that as many mothers and society in general gain knowledge about improving their health and conditions in the home to prevent disease and save babies' lives. While we can't be active in saving men's lives on the battlefields, at least we can save our babies at home. They are the next generation.'

Ada accepted a refill of tea in her bone china cup, her eyebrows pinched together. 'I do have a suggestion I would like to share with you. It's something you mentioned earlier, about the Canon of Westminster speaking at his service about Baby Week.'

'Oh do tell me,' her hostess encouraged.

'I thought we could have a guard of honour at Wolferton church with mothers standing at the entrance holding their babies as the congregation arrives for the Baby Week service. A number are disappointed they won't be able to manage the journey to London for the parade through the city's street, but this way they will still be a part of it.'

'That is a splendid idea. I also understand from Matron that your sister will be there with two patients who are being rehabilitated and excel at needlework, despite their disability.'

'Yes, they are such an inspiration to us all. I will call in downstairs and see them when our meeting has finished.'

'That's an excellent idea. I do believe Matron mentioned she has a special visitor today who is bringing in some new needlework patterns. I'm sure she won't mind if you go down and have a look.'

Ada swept down the vast sweeping staircase, the heels of her shoes making a clicking sound on the steps. Matron was with a gentleman who was talking animatedly. He was in his late thirties and holding a leather briefcase. He had an aristocratic air about him that was instantly recognisable. His blond hair was foppish and his thin face had angular features. Ada was intrigued by his manner, which was theatrical, and he made exaggerated movements. He was very different to the usual men she saw on the royal estate.

'We can't thank you enough,' Matron gushed, captivated by her visitor's charm.

He bowed slightly, taking her hand and lifting it to his lips. 'The pleasure is mine and I am delighted your father is so enlightened and suggested I call in and offer my services.'

Ada took a few small steps towards the pair and the man turned to face her, giving a small bow, his eyes dancing mischievously.

Matron, her cheeks flushed, lightly touched the side of her face with her hand. 'Ernest, may I introduce Ada Heath, her father, Harry Saward is the royal station master who you met briefly at Wolferton Station. And Ada, we are most fortunate to have Ernest Thesiger with us today. Ernest is a distinguished artist and actor who is pioneering the benefits of needlework for disabled servicemen.'

Ada felt her pulse quicken when the visitor lifted her small white hand to his lips, his eyes fixed on her face. She inhaled a breath and returned his smile, surprised, yet unable to resist feeling attracted towards him.

'I'm very pleased to meet you, Mr Thesiger. Needlework was actually what I came to talk to you about, Matron, to ask how your patients' work is progressing for display at the exhibition.'

'In a word, excellent. I was just taking Mr Thesiger to meet the men. He has kindly brought some new needlework patterns for them to use.'

'After you.' The visitor beamed and stretched his hand out for Ada to go first. She did as instructed and noticed, as she passed him, that his other hand was scarred.

His unusual presence created a stir among the nurses, all vying to catch a glimpse of this dashing visitor from London. He had a slender physique and piercing blue eyes, soft full lips and the most attractive dimple on his chin. As he walked, he had an upright, elegant posture and was brimming with confidence. He lapped up the attention from the nurses and patients, smiling and giving a courteous nod to those he passed.

Ada overheard Matron whisper to him, 'I did so enjoy the play you were in, *Alice in Ganderland*. It really is so inspiring to see the wit and satire of suffragists performed so well on stage.'

'Thank you for your kind words, Matron,' he replied softly, patting her arm. 'It did cause quite a stir and I'm delighted to hear you have sympathies for these courageous women.'

Ada's lips slightly curled. She was unaware that Matron was a suffragette supporter and it pleased her to discover she was a very modern woman of the day. She followed them into a side room where the needlework was laid out on a table. As they waited for the patients to join them, Ada asked the dashing actor how he became interested in needlework.

'Doesn't it seem, well, unmasculine?' she enquired, raising an eyebrow.

He shook his head, his expression serious. 'That is the antiquated way of thinking. We have women today doing men's work because without it this country could not survive. So who can judge a man for taking up a needle and thread to create a work of beauty? How is it different from a man painting a portrait or a landscape?'

'I didn't see it like that. You must think me dreadfully old fashioned.'

He continued. 'I myself, being an artist, had a keen interest in needlework before the war. You may have noticed my left hand is badly scarred. I almost lost it after it was badly injured in a battle. I was serving in France and my battalion took refuge in a deserted barn which was shelled. I was one of the lucky buggers; I survived. I took up needlework to keep the muscles active and I have that to thank for my rehabilitation. I have seen it work wonders with other disabled soldiers. It quietens the mind and makes them focus on a task that requires their full attention, as well as keeping the muscles active. And as a result they have skills they can use when they are discharged.'

Nurse Jennings tapped on the door and led in a group of four disabled soldiers. One had lost an eye and the side of his face and head were heavily bandaged, another had had a chest wound and suffered terrible shell shock. Private Bowers walked in while Private Cripps hobbled in on crutches.

'We hope to have you fitted with your new legs soon,' Matron said to Private Cripps, going on to explain they were waiting for the latest style of wooden legs, which were being made especially for disabled wounded soldiers. Demand for them was higher than had been anticipated by manufacturers. 'They are the finest available, my father assures me,' she told them.

Mr Thesiger unclasped his leather briefcase and fished out some examples of needlework.

Ada gasped. 'You did that? Why it's exquisite.' She took it in her hand and stared at it closely. 'Why I couldn't do better myself.'

He smiled. 'The one you are holding is our family crest. And this one is of my battalion crest. But this is my favourite,' he said, holding out a third. 'It's one I made for my dear wife, Janette. We married in May. I thought some of the men might like to do something similar for their wives or sweethearts.'

'What a wonderful idea,' Ada smiled wistfully, fingering the delicately stitched bouquets of roses and forget-me-nots and love hearts, the newly-weds' names entwined in among the flowers. 'Janette is a very lucky lady. This is so touching and romantic. You are extremely talented, Mr Thesiger.'

Ernest's passion for his needlework was infectious. He passed samples of his work around the group and encouraged the men to create something similar. The rest of the afternoon passed in a flash and Ada left with the group still deeply engrossed in their intricate cross-stitching. She hoped to speak to Eddie while she was at the hospital. Matron pointed him out where he was sitting beside his bed, instructing Ada not to excite him.

She warned, 'He is still very low. We will remove his dressings tomorrow for the first time since his operation and will know then how successful it has been.'

Ada stared at Eddie from the end of his bed. She barely recognised him as the once happy-go-lucky boy he was when he portered at the royal station. Where was the cheery Eddie with his cheeky ways, his winks and whistling under his breath while Harry Saward was not in sight? *Poor boy, he's suffered so much.*

She sensed the deep despondency that filled his being. The haunted look in his eyes cut right into her. She made her way to him and reached out to take his hand in hers, but he recoiled from her grasp, turning his face away when she asked how he was.

'Joey's back home now and on the mend,' she told him gently.

'I'm really pleased to hear that, he's a grand little lad. You don't have to try and cheer me up though, Ada. I'm a useless wreck.'

She reached out to him again and he recoiled. 'No, please don't touch me. And I don't want to do any sissy sewing either. I heard that's what you are here for. Beatrice tried to involve me as well, but it's not for the likes of me, the no-hopers.'

'Eddie, please don't be like that.'

'Like what?' he asked, turning towards her.

'We all care for you, Eddie, but if you prefer to be on your own, I'll leave now.'

Eddie turned his face away again. Ada thought she heard him stifle a sob.

'Good day then, Eddie. I wish you well.'

When Ada returned home she spotted a large envelope on the hallstand. Her name was written on it, but she didn't recognise the writing.

She ripped it open and stared in confusion at the bundle of letters that fell out. They were her letters that she had sent to Alfie, as well as two photographs of her, one with Alfie and the other with Leslie.

Dear Madam,

I am returning your letters and photos which were found in a ditch here in the battlefields of France. Despite our best efforts, I am very sorry to say I could not find the owner. I cannot say if he has been wounded or killed. We have made a note of your details and will continue enquiring about his whereabouts. We send you our prayers and urge you to keep your resolve during this difficult time.

With God's blessing.

Yours most faithfully,

Revd J. W. Hammer, the Soldiers' Christian Association

Ada's cries could be heard throughout the house. Her mother rushed to her just as her knees buckled. Harry dashed to the hallway and picked up the letters that fell from Ada's hand.

They led a weeping Ada through to the parlour. Harry read the accompanying letter and gasped, then handed it to Sarah.

Ada sobbed, 'What does this mean? I don't want Leslie to see me like this. Where is he?'

Sarah placed a comforting arm around her daughter's shoulder, her forehead furrowed. 'Don't concern yourself about Leslie. He's playing in the garden with his wooden engine. What does the letter say to have upset you?'

Sarah's eyes scanned the letter. She placed it in her lap. 'This is just terrible, but it doesn't say he's dead. Alfie's no fool. He can speak some French too which could help. Maybe he's in hospital or been found by some French people who have taken him into their home. It doesn't do us any good to fret when we don't know for sure what's happened.'

'What if he's dead?' blubbed Ada. 'Or he could be missing for months and months, like the Sandringham Company.'

Leslie burst into the room at that moment. 'Why are you crying, Mama? Is Papa dead?'

Sniffling, Ada scooped Leslie onto her lap and rubbed his cheeks. 'No, he's not dead. But he is missing. A kind man found his letters and photos in a ditch and returned them to me. We must pray for him every night.'

Poor Leslie, he had barely spent time with his father since he was born. He recognised him by his photographs and Ada regaled him with stories about their life in the seaside town of Cromer, which was fast growing into a popular up-and-coming resort.

As they retreated to bed that night, Ada leant over her son's small cot bed and kissed his forehead. His eyes were wide open, his hands clasped together across his chest in prayer. 'Please God, let the angels bring Daddy home,' he whispered. 'I promise I'll be a good boy.'

'Shush, sweet boy, you are good. Tomorrow we will be strong together. We must carry on living our lives as your dear papa would want us to, and make him proud of us.'

By the time she had finished speaking, Leslie's eyes were clasped shut, his chest swelling gently with his soft breaths.

Ada knelt by her bed and prayed. 'If there is a God, please listen to my heart crying and bring my Alfie home to his family.'

Chapter Twenty-Four

Ronald had just finished explaining to his young guide about the Sherlock Holmes mysteries when the boy stopped at the entrance of a narrow passage. Peter pointed to a wooden gate at the side of a dilapidated house. 'That's the place, I saw her go through there once.'

'Are you sure, lad?' Ronald asked, and Peter nodded vigorously. 'All right, scarper then.'

The boy vanished quick as a flash, keen not to be seen with a copper by the criminal types that lurked nearby. A plump woman with her womanly assets clearly displayed walked towards Ronald swaying her hips.

'Yer looking for Doris, are yer?' The woman eyed Ronald up and down. 'You ain't her usual type.'

'I'm looking for a relative, actually,' Ronald replied.

'Oh yeah, pull the other one, me love. I can look after yer just as nice as Doris, if you fancy a bit of slap an' tickle. She ain't got anythink I ain't.'

Ronald puffed his chest out. Surely Sherlock Holmes would approve of his next cunning step. 'Doris is exactly my kind of lady. I prefer to be discreet and call in the house through the back entrance.'

'Just as well you didn't come 'arf an hour earlier. That Gus of 'ers was in a filthy temper and stormed out, almost knocking me over on the corner where I was promoting me assets.'

'I see, well you shall be rewarded for your very helpful information. I ask one favour of you, that you do not say a word to anyone about my presence. I wouldn't want Gus to get wind that I'm here.'

The woman nodded, thrusting out her chest, tapping her nose with her finger. 'I get yer meaning. Now how much do I get for me trouble?'

Ronald fished out a shiny shilling from his pocket and pressed it into her palm. 'That's all for today. And remember, not a word to anyone.'

The woman whistled softly, placing the coin deep between her cleavage. 'Ta, love. That's the easiest job I've had.'

Ronald watched the woman wobble down the alley and turn the corner. The next moment a half-starved cat rubbed its head against his leg, meowing softly. He kicked it off, whispering, 'Scram.' The cat persisted in snuggling against Ronald's calf, becoming increasingly louder, its large green eyes staring up at him.

He became impatient, not wishing to draw attention to himself. 'I said *scram*. Now beat it.'

Surely Sherlock Holmes had never been held back in his pursuit of justice by a scraggy-looking cat. But then this was a black cat. Wasn't it supposed to bring you good luck? Or bad luck? Ronald couldn't remember which. He wasn't going to take any chances. He shook his leg again and swung it back when the cat made a yelping sound and scarpered up the wall into the yard that was under his surveillance.

'Darn it,' he muttered under his breath.

He could hear the cat meowing louder as he inched closer towards the house. He glanced upwards and saw a woman's figure at the window. She pushed the window open and looked down, speaking to the cat. 'Stay there. I'm coming for yer. We have some tasty mice here if yer fancy catching them.'

The hairs pricked on the back of Ronald's neck. 'That must be her. Doris!'

He flung open the gate and dashed to the back of the house, pressing his back against the wall. The cat screeched and leapt over the wall just as Doris stepped into the yard.

'I want a word with you,' Ronald told her.

'Who the bleedin' 'ell are you?'

'My name is Ronald Saward and I am a police officer. Shall we discuss this inside?'

Before she could answer, he took a firm grip of her arm, but she flung it off and kicked him in his groin. It was a ferocious kick and Ronald doubled over, the sharp pain taking his breath away.

'Ouch, you bitch,' he yelped.

She picked up a discarded wooden washboard, which had been lying on the ground, and held it in both hands above her head. As she brought it down, her eyes filled with fire. Ronald swiftly moved aside and kicked his leg out. Doris crashed to the ground, her skirt flapping above her waist and showing off her underwear, her legs akimbo. He placed his foot on her chest and looked down at her.

She spat at him, 'You could 'ave killed me. I'll 'ave yer for assault.'

'It is you who will be charged with assaulting a police officer. Now are you going to behave yourself? Or should I whistle for assistance? Do you want your neighbours to know what's going on?'

'What do yer want with an ole lady like me? I don't know anything.'

He knelt down, covering her chunky stockinged legs with her skirt. 'Tell me woman, where is Nellie?'

'Nellie? I've no idea. Now get orf me. I'll tell the justices I thought yer were a burglar and I was within me rights to protect me 'ome. Get orf me,' she spat, refusing his hand to help her up.

She attempted to rise unaided, wincing in pain, holding on to her hip. Ronald was still smarting from her kick and he pulled a face, rubbing the injured area.

He stood slightly stooped, keeping a close watch on Doris. 'Come, give me your hand, unless you want to stay there all day.'

Scowling, Doris pressed per pencil-thin lips together, a look of thunder on her face. She heaved herself up and Ronald reached out to catch her as she wobbled to one side.

'After you,' he said, pointing to the back door. They stepped into a scullery with a kitchen piled high with dirty pots and pans. Every inch of the room was filthy, with bottles, food wrappings and paper strewn in a corner on the floor.

The sitting room was dark and damp, the floor covered with stained linoleum which was ripped at the edges. The oak table was covered with faded newspaper. He picked up a cup and turned his nose up in disgust at the sight of mould growing inside.

'Let a woman have a seat,' pleaded Doris, her face contorting. She plonked herself in a tatty leather chair by the fireplace. The hearth was overflowing with ashes and the mantelpiece was thick with dust.

Ronald reached into his pocket and produced a set of handcuffs. She recoiled. 'Yer not using them on me? I can 'ardly move. I ain't going anywhere in a rush.'

Ignoring her protests, he grabbed her thick wrists and locked them inside the cuffs, placing the key in his top pocket. 'Tell me, Doris, where is the girl? You're already in deep trouble. Do you want to be locked up for the rest of your life?'

'What girl? I've no idea what yer talking about.' She stared at him defiantly.

'I think you do. Don't play the innocent with me.'

He opened the door and looked up the stairs. Doris shuffled uncomfortably.

A loud thud from upstairs made his ears prick. It was followed by a softer thud.

He raced up the stairs, two at a time, stopping first to search two rooms on the first floor on either side of the stairs. He retched as he entered the main bedroom. The air was filled with the stench of urine. Once he was sure nobody was in there he left and entered the smaller room across the landing. It was piled high with old furniture, bags of clothing and boxes. He called out Nellie's name, but there was no reply, just a thudding sound that seemed to be coming from another room above him.

He spotted another door at the top of the stairs and dashed up towards it. He turned the handle, but it didn't budge. He heard the thumping sound again, as if something was knocking against the door.

'Move back. I'm going to kick the door in.'

Taking a big gulp, he pressed his shoulder against the door and pushed hard. After two more big heaves the door sprung open.

'Heavens no!' he cried. A young woman's body dangled from behind the door.

'Nellie!' he cried, standing on a chair to untie the sheet from around her neck.

He lifted her body down gently and placed it on the bed. 'Nellie. Nellie. What have you done? Please, don't die. I've come to help you.'

He felt for a pulse in her limp wrist and stared into her pale face. Her eyes were open, staring upwards. He leant over and pressed his mouth over hers to breathe life into her. Her body remained still. He stood up and paced the room, rubbing the back of his neck. His throat was tight and he undid his tie. Beads of sweat were plastered on his forehead and his lips were dry.

I'm not giving up on you, Nellie. Sherlock Holmes wouldn't. I'm here to save you, and by darned I will, he vowed.

He leant over and slapped her cheek. One side, then the other. He slapped them again, harder. He pressed his hands over her sternum, between her ribs, and pushed down. 'Don't die, Nellie. Your father's going to pay for this. I'll make sure of it.'

He pushed his hands down again on her chest, for the umpteenth time, muttering, 'I won't give up. How could I tell Harry that Nellie is dead? He'd never forgive me.'

'Suddenly a small spluttering sound from the lifeless figure gave him hope. 'Nellie? Come on, Nellie. Breathe. Please breathe.'

He pressed down on her chest again, his heart racing. She spluttered again and she opened her eyes slightly. He gasped, his face lighting up. Tears pricked the corners of his eyes and he took her hands in his and rubbed them hard. She spluttered again and large gasps of air came out of her mouth.

'Thank God you're alive.' He wept with relief as he lifted her head, gently stroking her hair and cheek.

Nellie screwed up her face and stared at him. She spoke falteringly, through gasps of air, her eyes fearful. 'Who are you? Are yer with them?'

'If you mean your father Gus and that despicable woman Doris he associates with, I most certainly am not. I'm a policeman. My name is Ronald, and I am Harry Saward's brother. He was worried about you and asked me to find you I know the trouble you're in and I'm going to help you.'

Nellie lowered her gaze. Her bottom lip trembled. 'He did? I wish I were dead. My life is over. I'm a wanted woman with a price on me head.'

'I believe you're innocent. So does Harry. I shall not rest until I find your father and bring him to justice. I'll help you clear your name.'

'You will? What about Doris?' she quavered. 'She brought me 'ere.'

'She's downstairs, cuffed. She has what's coming to her.'

Nellie turned her head and closed her eyes. 'Thank yer for saving me, Mr Saward.' Do you really think you can help me clear me name? She spoke softly, the words sticking in her clenched throat.

I do. I model myself on the greatest sleuth, Sherlock Holmes. You gave me a right scare though. 'I really thought we'd lost you. You poor thing, you must have suffered if things were so bad you wanted to die.'

'It might sound strange to yer but I felt a dark cloud swarm over me and wrap me inside it. As the room filled with darkness and me head began to spin, I saw death beckoning me as a release. Nobody believed I were innocent and I had no future trapped in this room.'

She turned on her side and her hand felt under her pillow, feeling for the macabre stay busk. She slipped it between her fingers and glanced at it without Ronald seeing. A shiver rippled down her spine as she remembered the man dangling from the noose. As her finger traced over the doomed man swinging by the neck, she trembled. Had this been the reason she had momentarily lost hold of her senses?

I don't know your story, but I feel you are a curse and connected with something terrible, *I want nothing more to do with you.*

Ronald said softly. 'I'm going to help you clear your name, Nellie. You can come home with me. Matilda, my missus, will take care of you while I sort this mess out for you.'

Nellie turned and rose off the bed slowly, deliberately letting the stay busk slip from her fingers. 'How can I ever repay yer for what you've done?'

Ronald spotted the strange object on the floor and, without Nellie seeing, he slipped it into his pocket.

∽

Harry could scarcely believe what Ronald was telling him on the telephone. His face reddened and his eyes bulged when he was told that Nellie had attempted to take her own life.

Once Doris was banged up in Whitechapel Police Station, it didn't take long for her to spill the beans and point the finger at Gus.

Ronald warned Harry, 'My concern is that he will head your way. He wants to get his hands on a locket Nellie left with Maria and Ruth.'

'A locket? Ah, yes, the one mentioned in the court case. It contains Lord Nelson's hair. What's all the interest in that?'

'It has a significant value and was stolen a few years ago, but was later gifted to Nellie by her aunt. The original owner is offering a substantial reward for its return, and says no questions will be asked as they are desperate to have it back. You can see why Gus would want it, so do warn Ruth and Maria that Gus knows they have it and where they live.'

'I see, and yes, I will most certainly tell them. By the way, did Nellie say anything to you about the bigamy and attempted murder charges?'

'Not yet, all in good time. She was very shaken and I shall do so when the time is right. The good thing is that Doris has been most helpful. She corroborates what Nellie says and blames it all on Gus. The sooner we find him all the better for Nellie so we can help prove her innocence.'

Chapter Twenty-Five

Nellie had taken an instant liking to Matilda. She had walked into her home a stranger, as a frightened injured bird who thought her life wasn't worth living any more, only to be taken in and looked after like her own. Ronald and Matilda were childless, and within a few moments Nellie couldn't help but think what wonderful parents they would have made.

Matilda's warm smile and kind face brought a lump to Nellie's throat. It was like she finally had a mother's love. Matilda had rosy apple cheeks which were framed by dark bouncy curly hair and Nellie could see that Ronald and Matilda were clearly devoted to each other. They smiled a lot and, even though they were no longer a love-struck couple, being in their fifties, they held each other's hands across the table and gazed adoringly at each other.

On her first evening with them, Matilda pushed a plate of food in front of Nellie. Nellie hungrily devoured the tasty kidney pie – packed with heaps of carrots and swede to make up for the lack of beef – mashed potato and rice pudding. After a steaming cup of tea, the colour returned to her cheeks and she relaxed.

'How can I ever thank yer? You must wonder how I got meself in this mess and have nowhere else to go. I can't express me thanks for yer taking me in.'

'I'm happy to go along with whatever Ronald says. He's always right.'

'Not always, my dear, but thank you all the same,' Ronald replied affectionately.

'But I feel I owe yer an explanation,' Nellie faltered.

'You don't have to say anything yet, pet, if you don't want to,' Matilda told her softly, taking hold of her hand.

'I feel I must. I've stopped running now and I am in a safe place with good people I can trust. I need to unburden myself, else how can I prove my innocence?'

Matilda moved her chair closer to Nellie's. 'Well, if you're sure, pet.'

'I am. I had no idea what a troubled man me pa was and the pile of debts 'e had when 'e told me to marry Stanley Jeacock. 'E said 'e was an old man with a bad 'eart who wouldn't live long and I would be set up for life once 'e passed on. I agreed because Pa threatened to throw me out on the streets if I didn't go along with it. I feel so ashamed now, but I had no choice.'

Ronald shifted in his seat and leant in closer.

Nellie's body tensed and her chin and lips trembled. She covered her face with her hands and sobbed. Matilda placed a comforting arm around her shoulders and let her cry. When the tears subsided, Nellie looked up. 'Please, yer must believe me. I had nothing to do with Stanley's death. It saddened me greatly when I 'eard as 'e was a good man and me husband. Looking back now, I wonder if Pa planned it from the beginning.'

Ronald rubbed his chin and looked thoughtful. 'Why do you say that? I give you my word, you can trust me, Nellie, I will get to the bottom of this. Don't hold anything back.'

Nellie's body tensed and she bit her lip, her eyes becoming moist. She sipped the glass of water Matilda pressed into her hand.

'I think that's enough for one day. This is very upsetting for you.' Matilda said.

Nellie rubbed her neck. 'Just speaking about it to you is hard as I'm reliving it again, but I will press on.'

'Well, only if you're sure,' Ronald said gently.

'Before I married Stanley I lived with Aunt Millicent in Margate as her companion, and she gifted me the beautiful locket with Lord Nelson's hair as my twenty-first birthday present. I was heartbroken when she died and knew my future was uncertain. Then Cedric turned up suddenly, her cousin who is a solicitor, and he informed me he had inherited everything and slung me out.'

Ronald stroked his chin thoughtfully. 'Cedric, you say? Do you know his last name?'

'Yes, it's Parker. His name is Cedric Parker.'

Ronald looked thoughtful. He rubbed his chin. 'I think I know that name. It will come to me later. Do carry on.'

'As I said, I was slung out and had nowhere to go, so I returned to Whitechapel. I kept a tidy house for Pa and scrubbed it from top to bottom. I tried to find work, a respectable job. Pa said I was to put ideas out of me 'ead of being a lady's companion as he was asking around. The next day 'e announced I was to work in a pie shop run by his drinking chum, Wesley. This Wesley complained how a new pie man had started trading down the road and that his pretty daughter was attracting a lot of his customers by displaying her feminine charms, if yer get me meaning.

'Pa told Wesley I was prettier than the other girl and would pull in more customers. 'E forced me to go along with it. No respectable girl would wear the kind of clothes I was forced to wear.'

'You poor girl,' Matilda said softly, shaking her head. 'What kind of father could make his daughter behave in such a way?'

Nellie bit her lip. 'One day, Pa brought Stanley to the pie shop with him, that's how we met. I could see 'e was a gentleman, not the usual company my father kept. He said 'e had bumped into him around the corner when Stanley was asking for directions to some place, and Pa asked him if he was hungry. He almost dragged him in, saying he looked like 'e needed a good meal inside him and could take him to the best steak and kidney pie shop in London.

'It turned out he had met Stanley a few months before on his rag and bone rounds. He gave Pa a bundle of good quality women's clothing after his wife died. I could tell Stanley was lonely by the faraway look in his eyes. He seemed easily led and good natured. Stanley enjoyed his pie and agreed it was the best he'd ever had. Pa laughed and arranged to see him there again and he soon had him wrapped around his finger.'

Nellie paused and inhaled a deep breath. Matilda smiled encouragingly. 'Poor Stanley, it's like your father was a spider and lured him into his web.'

Nellie continued, 'That's exactly how it was. Pa encouraged Stanley to call into the pie shop and told me to be friendly with him. I could see Stanley was flattered by my kind words and 'e soon took a shine to me.

'One evening, Stanley invited me out for a walk. Pa wasn't around and I had finished at the pie shop, so I agreed. He was easy company and a good listener and I confided in him about me early life and the sorry circumstances I was in. It didn't seem to matter that 'e was old enough to be me father. He said my story touched his heart and 'e took me hands in his and smothered them with kisses. It was music to me ears when 'e said I deserved a better life and needed taking care of properly.

'I must admit I encouraged his attention and a genuine affection grew between us, though I can't say it was love. It was good to feel protected again, like when I was with me aunt.'

'I can understand that,' Matilda said.

'One Sunday, Stanley invited me for afternoon tea at his house. He wanted me to meet his daughter. I was that nervous. He lived in a respectable street with tall white houses. I wore me best dress in pale blue that Aunt Millicent bought me and his face shone with pride when

283

'e introduced me to Connie. I could see straightaway that she didn't take to me, and I could hardly blame her as I was only a couple of years older than 'er. Later, when Stanley and I walked along the Embankment, his eyes were filled with love and when I placed me arm in his and 'eld me 'ead high I felt like a lady, not a common pie seller.

'Pa rubbed his hands with glee seeing how well we were getting on, telling me to ignore Connie's disapproval. He encouraged me to get a ring on me finger, else some scheming woman would have their eye on Stanley.'

Nellie paused and glanced at Matilda and Ronald's astonished expressions. 'I can see I've shocked yer both.'

Matilda murmured. 'These are not our ways but carry on. What happened next? Stanley sounds a very nice gentleman.'

'Oh yes, he was, and I won't have a bad word said about him. Stanley and I wed within six months. It was a quiet affair. He tried his best to persuade Connie to come to the wedding, but she refused, though she continued living in the house with us afterwards, keeping herself as much to 'erself as possible.

'Pa suddenly started appearing at the house making demands on me, saying if it weren't for him I would still be selling pies instead of living a comfortable life, and how I owed him. I know Connie overheard him a couple of times and I felt nervous whenever she was around. I managed to entice some money from Stanley, saying I needed to pay off the dressmaker for some new gowns, and I gave the money straight to Pa to pay off his debts.

'One afternoon, Pa waited for me around the corner. He grabbed me arm and dragged me down a passage. He kept looking over his shoulder saying his life was threatened by money lenders and had to pay off gambling debts within three days. He asked me for one hundred pounds.

'I told him I couldn't find that sort of money, that it would arouse Stanley's suspicions if I asked for more, especially as I had Connie breathing down me neck. I dug in my heels and refused, saying I owed him nothing more and made it clear 'e would have to sort out his own mess.'

Matilda spoke in a gentle tone. 'You did the right thing, Nellie.'

Nellie gulped in a deep breath and sipped some more water. 'Little was I to know the consequences of that. The next evening Stanley told me Pa had invited him out for a tankard of ale down by the river in Tower Hill saying 'e would appreciate Stanley's advice about a property he was thinking of buying there. Alarm bells rang in me head when Stanley told me this as I knew Pa didn't 'ave two pennies to rub together, but I didn't know what to say, and I couldn't have foreseen what was to happen. I honestly had no idea.'

Ronald pressed her. 'What happened? Is that the night Stanley died?'

Nellie sniffled. 'My husband didn't come home that night. I should have stopped him going out. I believed Pa when he told me Stanley had had an accident. He said me husband tripped and fell into the river and his body was swept away by the fast current.'

Nellie wept into her handkerchief. Matilda's eyes widened. 'Are you saying that maybe it wasn't an accident?'

Nellie nodded, her voice shaky. 'I didn't know what to think. I couldn't believe my father could sink to such desperate depths for his own ends. I found out later that Pa expected me to inherit everything and give him whatever he asked for. Only, it didn't work out that way.'

Ronnie and Matilda exchanged glances. 'What do you mean? Why not?' asked Ronald.

'Unbeknown to me, Connie had insisted that her father should include a clause in her father's latest will stating that if 'e died within one year of our marriage, everything would go to her, and I was to be allowed to stay on in the house for as long as I wished, along with an annual settlement of five thousand pounds.'

Matilda's hand flew to her mouth. 'You can hardly blame her. How did you feel about that?'

'It was difficult, as yer can imagine. Because Stanley's body wasn't found, I was still legally married to him. The atmosphere in the house with Connie and 'er housekeeper constantly staring at me with their accusing eyes was unbearable. I gave Pa what I could manage, but it wasn't enough, he always came back asking for more. After a few months, the tension with Connie was too great and I decided I would seek a position as a lady's companion.

'The following week, after I had been out to buy a newspaper to look at advertisements for these positions, I met Adam. He was home on leave from the army. He was the most handsome man I ever saw, tall with fair hair and eyes that danced when he smiled. His family lived a few streets away and our paths crossed when 'e bumped into me while 'e was distracted in conversation with a friend. It was love at first sight and, for the first time in my life, I came alive inside, I felt like a woman in love.'

Matilda handed Nellie a handkerchief as her eyes began to well up. She continued, panting, 'I 'ave to confess he aroused strong passions in me that I never felt before. I sneaked him into the house when Connie was away visiting a cousin and told the housekeeper to take her day off then. We just kissed and clung to each other, I'm a good girl in that respect.'

Nellie paused. 'Adam never tried to take advantage. He begged me to marry him before 'e returned to his regiment. Although Adam knew about my circumstances, that I was still legally wed, we withheld these details from his parents who accepted me with open arms as we were desperate to be together. We convinced ourselves that as Stanley's body was still missing, 'e must surely be dead as six months had since passed without any sign of it.'

Ronald frowned. Nellie bit into her bottom lip.

'I know it was wrong, but telling everyone about Stanley would only have complicated things, especially as we had no death certificate. Adam was being recalled to the front line. We were in love and wanted to wed and live as man and wife for a couple of nights before he left the country.

'I'd naturally kept my relationship with Adam a secret from Connie and was planning to tell her about it after our wedding. I often wonder if she had her suspicions as she commented that I had a spring to me step and seemed much more cheered.'

Matilda questioned. 'So you married Adam? Without burying your first husband?'

'I did. We didn't have a body to bury. We were so in love. We wed in a church four streets away with just his family there. I certainly didn't tell Pa. My heart burst with joy and love. I felt giddy and excited about the new life I was starting to being Adam's wife. It was arranged I would move in with his parents until we had a chance to find our own home. I was walking on air.'

Ronald shook her head. 'But not for long, hey?'

Matilda sent a warning glance at her husband, holding her fingers to her lips. There was a long pause. Nellie nervously twisted her hands in front of her. She shook her head, her eyes filled with sadness.

'We walked down the steps outside the front of the church after our wedding, laughing and holding each other's hands, our hearts overflowing with happiness, thinking we had our whole future ahead of us. But our happiness was shortlived, for waiting at the bottom of the steps was Connie – and Stanley. My husband was alive!

'I thought I was seeing a ghost and felt my legs give way. Adam caught me and stared at Stanley, unaware he was staring straight at my husband.'

Ronald and Matilda's expressions were incredulous. Their eyes widened. 'But if he was pushed in the river, how did he survive?' asked Ronald.

Nellie paused, sniffing as she spoke. 'I discovered later that a fisherman saw Pa push Stanley into the river and leave him to drown. He was hauled into the boat barely alive and taken to hospital. He couldn't remember what happened, having hit his head badly when Pa pushed him to the ground before he ended up in the water. I hope he believes I had nothing to do with it, and, when the time is right, I hope he will let me make amends.'

Matilda's jaw dropped. 'Well what a story that is! I've never heard anything like it before. What a mess this is. Can you sort this trouble out for Nellie, Ronald?'

He pondered. 'It's not going to be easy. We need a confession from Gus, unless Stanley can recall now what happened. Or maybe I could find the fisherman who saw Gus push Stanley in the river and leave him to drown. As things stand the only person who could confirm that you knew nothing of the plan would be Gus, and how willing will he be to tell the truth?'

Nellie sniffled. 'That's what worries me. Maybe you could find Stanley? I wouldn't blame him if he hates me after what 'appened. Adam was shocked when 'e discovered Stanley was alive and watched as the police turned up and arrested me for bigamy, on me wedding day. Cedric had already reported the theft of the locket, me name was blackened and I was charged with that too.'

Matilda queried, 'What a terrible thing to happen. What a shock for Stanley too, I imagine. So how was he found, after all these months?'

Nellie twisted her fingers in front of her. 'It was thanks to Connie. I was told later that Connie searched everywhere for 'er father. She scoured all the hospitals in the area and eventually found him in St Thomas's, just a month before my wedding to Adam. She never gave up looking for him. Poor Stanley was suffering from amnesia and couldn't tell her what had happened. It turns out that the maid at Adam's house was on good terms with Connie's housekeeper and told her about the wedding. Connie followed me a few times and saw me with Adam. I think the only way she could convince Stanley that I was marrying someone else was to make him turn up at my wedding.'

Ronald paced the room shaking his head. 'Stanley is one hell of a lucky man to have been fished out of the river and to have a resourceful daughter like Connie.'

Nellie pleaded, 'You have to believe I had nothing to do with it. I would never harm Stanley. I could never hurt anybody.'

Matilda placed a comforting arm around Nellie's shoulder. 'We do believe you, pet, don't we, Ronald?'

Ronald paused before answering. 'I do, and your wicked father will to answer for this. You will need to come to the station with me and make a statement. Doris might not come across as the most reliable witness, but she's all we have right now. Hopefully, her conscience will trouble her enough to tell the truth and Gus's whereabouts.'

Nellie raised her face towards Ronald. 'Thank you for believing me. I can see now that Doris was in fear of Gus, and that's the reason she treated me as she did.'

Ronald rubbed his chin. 'He can't hide forever. Our boys will catch him, you can be sure of that.'

She begged, 'But they have to, before 'e arrives in Wolferton and snatches the locket.'

'I've sent word to Harry, so don't worry yourself about that.'

I can't leave it to Ronald. I must return to Wolferton and warn Maria and Ruth that Gus is on his way there.

Chapter Twenty-Six

Matron examined the dressing on Eddie's leg and smiled broadly. 'I have good news for you, Private Herring. The operation was a success. In fact, it was a great success.'

Eddie jerked his head. 'Yer mean, I'm not gonna lose me leg?'

'No, you most certainly are not. You have Dr Butter-scotch to thank for that, though knowing my father, he won't want any thanks. He'll just be delighted for you.'

Eddie wept tears of relief. 'I can't wait to tell Maria. I did her wrong in pushing her away and I need to put it right.'

Eddie glanced at Bertie in the bed next to him and felt ashamed. Bertie had lost an arm and yet he was rarely seen without a smile on his face, while Eddie had allowed himself to wallow in self-pity.

Bertie's needlework was admired by everyone at the hospital. Despite his handicap he skilfully managed to balance the wooden frame of the canvas between his chin and the table and sew two hearts with the name of his sweetheart and his own entwined. And always with a smile on his face.

Bertie had persuaded Eddie to try needlework too once he was feeling better. It was true what everyone said about it calming the mind. Eddie was now sitting in the back seat of Lady Appleby's Daimler, stroking the plush leather seat, on his way to the Methodist Central Hall in Westminster for National Baby Week, while Bertie was in the front aiding the chauffeur with directions.

Ada, bleary eyed after a sleepless night fretting about Alfie, had almost pulled out of going, but was persuaded to attend by her family, while Betty kept an eye on Leslie. She insisted on travelling there alone by train. She wanted to be alone to dwell on her thoughts, and was conscious there might be a crush in the car with Beatrice there too.

The sleek car cruised through the countryside, turning heads as it glided past pedestrians at what seemed like a great speed to those unfamiliar with automobiles, reaching London after three hours. There were long queues outside grocery and food shops, and Beatrice hoped supplies would not run out before patient families reached the counter. It was the same scene she had witnessed at home, but here, in London, the queues seemed to snake longer around street corners and police stood by to manage some unruly people who were trying to jump the queues. It was sadly an all too familiar scene in Britain where, despite food shortages, rationing had not yet been introduced.

As the chauffeur approached the city centre they recognised some familiar landmarks, sweeping along Pall Mall, passing the ornate gates of Buckingham Palace, where potatoes and turnips were now growing in the flowerbeds in front of the palace. The distinctive dome that perched on top of St Paul's Cathedral was spotted in the distance and within minutes they were gliding along the Embankment and heading towards Westminster, where Parliament stood.

Beatrice drew in a sharp breath as the car swept through the city's streets. Buildings here reached to the sky, but the streets, though wider, were similar to those in Norfolk, occupied by busy office workers, servicemen on leave jostling along the pavements in their uniforms and bereaved families, their arms covered in thick black bands. Horses pulled carts through the streets alongside automobiles, more than she had ever seen before, including an automobile bus with seating upstairs. There were so many different sights to behold that her head spun around from one side to the other.

The large number of beggars on street corners caught her eye, many with limbs missing, some blind, others just crumpled in heaps on the ground, too weak to move. Urchin children in rags held out their bony hands to passers-by. Young girls proffered posies of flowers or bunches of freshly picked watercress for a few pence.

As the car made its way around the corner, it suddenly pulled up outside the newly built Methodist Central Hall, another marvel to behold, as impressive as the landmarks they had passed. The white building was constructed in an elaborate Viennese baroque style to mark the centenary of John Wesley's death, the founder of Methodism. It had a spectacular domed ceiling and was regarded as an architectural marvel when it opened in 1912.

As Beatrice stepped out of the car, she saw hundreds of mothers, many with tired, worn faces, walking briskly towards the venue and march up the steps arm in arm. They came from all sections of society and all wearing their finest. Lady Appleby smiled and led the way inside. Beatrice took Eddie's arm and assisted him up the steps slowly.

Once inside the main hall their jaws dropped at the grandeur of the room. It had a spectacular ornate ceiling with exquisite carvings and sweeping arches framed tiered seating on the first floor. The hall was a teeming hive of activity with dozens of stallholders and visitors of all classes. Lectures and conferences on welfare issues were billed for the week and a slum house had been created to highlight the dangers they posed to health and well-being. There was much excitement about Queen Mary's arrival later that afternoon to officially open the event, with a parade of mothers and babies due to be held and a guard of honour to welcome Her Majesty on the steps outside the front of the building.

Beatrice followed Lady Appleby with her patients in tow in search of their stall advising on cleanliness to prevent childhood illnesses. Leaflets had been prepared for them to give out. Lady Appleby paused to speak to a lady she recognised, a well-dressed woman in a dark-green dress with white collar and cuffs. She was positioned at the front of her stall and raised her arms. 'Isn't this wonderful? National Baby Week has begun, and not just here, but in every town and village in the country. It's a national tragedy that disease is killing fifty thousand children a year – many preventable. I hope the government is listening.'

She introduced her friend, Lady Jane Fowley, a no-nonsense kind of woman with a confident manner who offered Bertie and Eddie seats to rest for a moment and poured them glasses of water. Eddie's eyes widened and he tugged at Beatrice's arm, pointing up at the ceiling.

'Look over there, there's a giant fly hanging from the ceiling.'

'Well, isn't that the strangest thing,' Beatrice replied, staring at it intently.

'It's marvellous, isn't it?' marvelled Lady Appleby. 'It's a giant fly magnified two hundred and fifty-two times.'

Bertie and Eddie whistled softly, their eyes fixed on the fly that was attracting many enquiring glances. Lady Fowley continued, 'It has a span of fifteen feet across its wings and is intended to demonstrate that it is a poisonous and dangerous household pest that causes infant diarrhoea and spreads other life-wasting maladies through germs.'

Eddie commented, 'I will certainly mention it in my write-up for the *Tommy Herald*.'

'Oh how splendid,' gushed Lady Fowley. 'I shall look forward to reading your report. Beatrice, would you be a darling and send me a copy?'

'Of course,' replied Beatrice, who had spotted Ada and a group of mothers she recognised from Wolferton walking along the aisle. They bade farewell to their new acquaintance and followed Lady Appleby who warmly greeted Ada and the Wolferton arrivals and allocated voluntary marshalling positions to the group.

'Oh Ada, I was so very sorry to hear the news about Alfie,' consoled Lady Appleby, taking Ada aside. 'It's very good of you to still come today when you are understandably upset.'

'There's no point staying at home. Yes, it is upsetting, but until I hear news to the contrary, I shall believe my Alfie is still alive.'

'That's admirable, Ada. I totally agree. Look, Ernest is over there, next to our stall, he is promoting the rehabilitation of disabled servicemen. Hasn't he done a wonderful job in displaying their needlework?'

Ada caught Ernest's eye and he greeted them enthusiastically. 'I have given pride of place to the beautiful needlework done by Bertie and Eddie. It is quite extraordinary what they have accomplished in such a short time, and will inspire others, I am sure.'

Eddie blushed as Ada picked up his needlework. The cross-stitching was exquisite, and very similar to Bertie's, both having their names entwined with their sweethearts' names in two love hearts, surrounded by spring flowers. 'Maria likes daffodils,' he said softly.

Ada praised Eddie, 'You have surprised us all, and to think it has helped still your mind is wonderful. It seems that you are on the path to recovery, Eddie Herring. Maria will absolutely adore this.'

Eddie brushed a tear away and gulped. 'I just hope I haven't messed things up.'

'I'm sure it's nothing that can't be fixed, try not to fret about it.'

Ernest's stall was adorned with a collection of other disabled servicemen's work and they all marvelled at the intricacy of some pieces with a religious theme and others that featured regimental banners and colours.

Suddenly, the room quietened as the sound of aircraft and bombings could be heard.

'Oh no! This is outrageous. The blasted Hun, bombing us again, in broad daylight.'

Bertie's face paled and Eddie gripped his arm. 'It's all right, matey. They'll not bomb us here.'

'I hope you're right,' retorted Beatrice, covering her ears to the sounds of the air attack.

∽

Planned processions around London with mothers and their infants were hastily cancelled on safety grounds as the attack from the air continued, but word spread that Queen Mary's visit would go ahead.

One hundred mothers excitedly assembled along the aisle, their babes clutched tightly in their arms. These were the model babies brought up following new healthy guidelines at the city's infant welfare centres, all of them the picture of health. A resounding applause and cheers filled the hall as the Queen arrived and walked along the aisle, commenting on how healthy, well cared for and beautifully dressed the babies were. Most of the women were wives of men who were away fighting. Despite the air attack, the women heartily chorused 'God Save the King' accompanied by the Ladies Orchestra, under the direction of Mabel Seeley, singing as loudly as they could to drown out the sounds from the air.

Ada was enthralled by it all, a slight colour returning to her cheeks, and congratulated the orchestra of women on playing their string instruments so beautifully.

'This really is the most wonderful sight. I wonder if they would come to Wolferton,' she mentioned to Lady Appleby afterwards. 'I so enjoyed their rendition of Elgar's "The Spirit of England".'

'I'm sure they would. Just leave it to me,' Lady Appleby replied. 'Mabel is a family friend.'

Ada felt her spirits lift. The day had been an outstanding success and ended with Lady Appleby declaring she would open an infant welfare centre on the Sandringham Estate.

'Can I count on your support?' she asked Ada.

'You most certainly can.'

'I was hoping you would say that. I think it's time to leave now. Would you like to join us on our journey home? I'm sure we can squeeze you in.'

Ada gladly accepted. Bertie and Eddie squeezed alongside the driver on the front padded seat as Ada, Beatrice and Lady Appleby huddled together in the back.

As the Daimler drew into Wolferton an hour before midnight, Lady Appleby gently pressed her hand on Ada's arm. 'You dozed off and I didn't want to disturb you.

299

Thank you again for coming today, my dear. I appreciate how very difficult it must have been for you.'

Harry was still awake when Ada opened the door at eleven o'clock, followed by Beatrice. She said, 'I didn't expect you to still be up. Is everything all right?'

Harry pulled out his pocket watch. 'Is that the time already? I was going to turn in and thought you would be back very soon, so I waited up for you. I have some news.'

Ada's face brightened. 'Is it Alfie? Has he been found?'

'Oh no, Ada, I'm sorry, I didn't mean to raise your hopes. No, I am referring to Nellie. Ronald has found her and believes she really is innocent. She is staying with Ronald and Matilda while he gets to the bottom of her story and tries to find Gus. There are rumours he might head for Wolferton, so we need to be on our guard.'

Tears welled in Ada's eyes. 'Oh, Father, I really thought for a moment there had been news about Alfie.'

'I'm so sorry, Ada,' Harry replied softly.

Tears trickled down her cheeks and she threw herself into her father's open arms. He stroked her hair, letting her cry until her tears had dried up.

∞

Mrs Pennywick was fit to return to work and called Maria into her office. She sat behind her large desk and pointed to the chair opposite. Maria sat down nervously, her hands gripping the edge of the seat.

'Relax. You're not in any trouble. Firstly, may I say how delighted I am to hear that Joey has pulled through and is making excellent progress.'

Maria's face lit up. 'Thank you, Mrs Pennywick. Joey is doing nicely.'

The housekeeper rested her elbows on her desk, her fingers pointing up in the steeple position. 'There is something else I need to say. Please accept my apologies for what happened to you.'

'Is it something to do with Philomena and the parrot?'

'It is, and you have Mr Armitage to thank for reporting to me what happened after we left the room. He said he'd never heard anything like it and brought it to my attention.'

'Why? What happened?' asked Maria, her eyes wide.

'Emerald is renowned for being chatty and repeating what he hears, but I have never known him recite so many words in full flow, and several times too, squawking and gabbling away as if desperate for people to understand.'

'Well I never. What did Emerald say?'

'Words to the effect, "Get off me, you stupid bird. I'm going to inform my aunt now and will show her my finger and tell her you made the bird attack me. She won't take kindly to this."'

Maria stifled a giggle as Mrs Pennywick continued, 'It was clear Emerald was referring to Philomena. Fortunately for you, Emerald is an excellent mimic.'

Maria covered her hands with her mouth. 'So does this mean . . . ?'

301

Mrs Pennywick smiled. 'Yes, you can start upstairs in Her Majesty's rooms again straightaway. I am sorry it has taken so long for you to be reinstated while I was away recovering from my fall. I have a new scullery maid starting tomorrow, and I think I can depend on Emerald to keep me reliably informed on what happens upstairs!'

'You mean, like a spy?' Maria grinned.

'Exactly!' chortled Mrs Pennywick. 'You can go there now and start by tidying up the trays and newspapers in Her Majesty's drawing room.'

Maria rose and shuffled her feet. 'Er, do yer mind me asking, did Her Majesty mention anything about this at all? Only she called in to see Joey with Mrs Rumbelow and I mentioned it.'

'I couldn't possibly divulge the nature of my private conversations with Her Majesty.' The housekeeper smiled and gave Maria a wink.

Walking to the door with a spring in her step, Maria turned and smiled. 'Thank you, Mrs Pennywick. I swear I won't let yer down. Or Her Majesty.'

Chapter Twenty-Seven

Lizzie Piper paced the courtyard gripping a letter in her hand, an anxious expression on her face.

'What's happened? Why are you so upset?' Jessie asked.

Lizzie thrust the letter at her. Her hand was shaking and she bit her lip. 'How dare they!'

The station master's daughter took the letter and read it, her hand flying to her mouth. 'No! It can't be true.'

'I'm afraid it is. The army is taking my horse from me. They say they're coming for Gilbert and he'll no doubt be shipped off to France and marched across the front line. Then who knows what will happen, but I know one thing for sure, I'll never see him again.'

'Oh Lizzie, isn't there anything we can do to stop them?'

Lizzie shook her head. It had crossed Jessie's mind that this might happen. It was well known that the army was increasingly taking horses from owners and using them to pull artillery guns and carry supplies.

Lizzie's face reddened. 'Gilbert is eighteen years old. What use is he going to be to them?'

'It doesn't make sense. I can't imagine an officer riding him across a battlefield. I can't see Gilbert pulling heavy army equipment on a battlefield. He's used to country ways and will be scared to death.'

'That's what worries me,' Lizzie choked. 'Oh, Jessie, what am I to do?'

Gilbert had been born on Blackbird Farm and knew no other life than pulling a plough in Norfolk fields. Admittedly, he was still good at it, albeit a little slower in his older age.

Jessie read on. 'It says they're coming today. They've contacted all the farmers telling them to be prepared to do their duty and give up their horses. That's no warning.'

Word had spread quickly that the army's district superintendents were on a recruitment drive in the area and were commandeering horses and baggage wagons from whatever source they could. It had been a rolling out programme since the beginning of the war and was now on their doorstep.

Only last week they heard how Philip Bagshott's horse, which pulled the grocery van, was stopped by soldiers when it was making deliveries around the neighbouring village of Dersingham. Their superintendent inspected the horse closely and announced they would take it. The grocer swore blind the horse had bad feet and kicked like a devil, but his words fell on deaf ears.

'We'll soon take that out of him,' barked the superintendent.

What chance would Lizzie have of keeping Gilbert? Jessie knew any appeals for him to stay would be futile. They could only hope and pray he would survive the challenges that lay ahead and somehow return to Wolferton at the end of the war.

Archie ran over to them and pointed to the gate. The words stuck in his throat and he spoke in short, fast breaths. 'It's the army. What do they want here? Why are they carrying harnesses?'

Maria's younger brother had spent many hours rubbing down Gilbert and mucking out the stable. Although only fourteen years old, laws had been passed to release school children from the age of twelve to become substitute land workers and Archie spent every spare minute on the farm. He had proved an invaluable pair of hands, willing to learn all the tasks, and working happily alongside Lizzie and Jessie, who enjoyed teasing him for his shyness.

Lizzie grabbed Jessie's hand. 'I'm afraid they've come to take Gilbert. There's nothing we can do to stop it. Let's go and say our goodbyes.'

Archie burst into tears. 'No! Never! Over my dead body. You can't let them take Gilbert. Please. Stop them. It ain't right.'

He ran into the stable and threw his arms around Gilbert's neck. He stroked the horse's chestnut-coloured mane and clung to him, scalding tears cascading down his cheeks.

Lizzie and Jessie's eyes moistened as they said their farewells, pressing their faces against the faithful horse's head and neck. The stomping sound of heavy army boots in the stable made them look up.

Jessie stared at the hard, unfeeling expression on the superintendent's face, his thin lips pursed and his cold grey eyes making a shiver run along her spine. He ran a horse whip along Gilbert's back and walked alongside him, raising his chin with the whip.

Gilbert kicked up his rear hooves and moved away from the army official.

'Yes, he'll do nicely,' said the officer, a satisfied smirk across his face.

'Leave him! Don't you dare touch him with that whip again!' yelled Archie, facing the officer, his eyes bulging.

The officer placed his whip on Archie's shoulder and hissed, 'Move out of my way, boy, else you'll get a whipping. This horse has war work to do.'

Lizzie pushed herself forward, raising her chin. 'Don't you dare lay a finger on Archie. He's doing his share of war work here on the farm. We all are. So I request you show some respect towards us all, else . . .'

'Else what?' the officer sniggered.

'Else . . . I'll report you to your superior officer.'

A coughing sound from the stable door made them turn their heads. A junior army officer spoke, 'Sir, if you excuse me for saying, we need to press on if these horses are to be transported by train later today.'

The superintendent stepped back, looking down his nose at Archie. He grunted, instructing his junior officer to take Gilbert. 'You'll be paid a fair price for him. He's in good shape and I can see he's been well looked after. After some training, he'll be ready to do his job.'

The unsmiling officer nodded curtly and walked off brusquely. His junior patted Gilbert on his flank and told Archie, 'Don't worry, lad. I promise I'll do my best to take good care of him while we are together. I can see he's a fine horse and means a lot to you.'

There was nothing more anyone could say. Archie clung to Gilbert's neck as he was led away. The horse turned his head, neighing and kicking out his rear hooves. Archie fought back his sobs, whispering softly to Gilbert, telling him to go safely, promising he would be back on the farm one day and that he would never forget him.

As they reached the gate, Jessie gently pulled Archie's arms off Gilbert's neck, the kindly officer allowing them one last moment to say farewell. Archie followed after Gilbert as he left, stopping abruptly at the end of the lane. In front of him were two more horses that had been commandeered. He recognised one of them as Starlight and called his name, but Starlight trotted away with Gilbert.

'Poor Abel. That horse was his best friend. They went everywhere together,' Archie whimpered to Jessie. 'It ain't fair.'

Jessie saw Starlight being led away too. 'Poor thing, he looks so downcast and can't keep up the pace. What use will Starlight be to the war? He's older than Gilbert, and much slower.'

'Can you check in the barn and see how much straw we have left? I might be able to sell some of it,' Lizzie asked Jessie.

The far side of the barn was piled high to the roof with straw and Jessie was counting when she heard a scuffling sound.

She straightened, and thinking it might have been a mouse, she ignored it and carried on totting up the bales. The sound became louder and Jessie jerked her head and pricked her ears. Picking up a pitchfork and gripping it tightly, she tiptoed behind the bales and her mouth fell open. An elderly man crouched on the floor, his eyes fixed on her face with a frightened look. He raised his hands slowly above his head. She shuffled back a few steps and yelped, 'Who are you? What are you doing here? Lizzie, come quickly!'

The man rose bit by bit, keeping his hands raised. He stuttered, 'Please. No need to be afraid. I no harm you.'

Jessie pointed her pitchfork at him and shouted, 'Stay there. Don't you dare move an inch. Lizzie!'

Lizzie rushed in, her face incredulous. 'What the . . . ?'

'I just found him, hiding behind the straw. We must report him to police straightaway. He could be a spy,' Jessie told her, her eyes fixed on her hostage.

'Me, no spy. I beg you to listen to me. Please.'

Lizzie picked up a spade from the ground and pointed it at him. 'Keep your hands up,' she ordered. 'You're German, aren't you?'

'Yes, but I am no spy. I am peace-loving German,' he gulped.

Jessie scoffed. 'There's no such thing. We know what you lot are like.'

Lizzie gasped. 'Just imagine if the soldiers found you here. Do you know the army has just left? They would have dragged you off and shot you for hiding out! We could have been charged with being accomplices and shielding you!'

The man lowered his gaze. He spoke softly in a heavy guttural accent. 'Yes, I hear them and am afraid. I hear they take your horse. I'm sorry. I no mean to cause you trouble.'

Lizzie slowly walked around the man, eyeing him up. He was in his seventies, with thinning fair hair, tall, with angular features, hollow cheeks and glassy grey eyes filled with sadness. He was well dressed, wearing dark grey trousers, a blue waistcoat, white shirt and dark green tie. A checked jacket lay at his feet, along with a leather holdall. Lizzie noticed his shoes appeared to be of very good quality.

She picked up the bag and tipped out its contents. 'We'll soon find out.'

Spread on the ground was a change of clothing and a bundle of letters addressed to Klaus Schmidt with a German postmark.

'I thought as much,' said Lizzie, her face jubilant.

She ripped open the letters. 'These are all in German. Are these your instructions to cause harm and destruction to our men. Perhaps I should ask Archie to chase after our soldiers and bring them back.'

The man fell to his knees and burst into tears. 'No. No. Please don't do that, I beg you. Please, you must believe

I am no spy. I am a cobbler and the letters are from my daughter, Helga. She was a servant for your gracious queen for many years. If you look in the front of the bag, you will see a letter addressed to Her Majesty. I come to ask for her help.'

'Why would our queen help you?' asked Jessie, her eyes widening. 'You're the enemy.'

Lizzie fished around and found an envelope addressed to Queen Alexandra. 'Here it is. This should tell us one way or another what his business is here.'

She opened the letter and her eyes devoured its contents, her expression confused. She tossed it to Jessie. 'This is astonishing. What do you think?'

Jessie screwed up her eyes as she read. 'Is it really true? You are hoping the Queen will help secure your release out of the country? Why would she do that?'

The man gulped. 'Because she knows I am good man and I throw myself at her mercy. I met her when she came to my shop in King's Lynn with my daughter. I made beautiful shoes for the King. The Queen told Helga to tell me they were the best shoes the King had ever had, made from the softest calfskin with the strongest stitching. After the war began, the Queen was sad to lose Helga, but said she must leave Sandringham immediately and return to Germany.'

'Why didn't you go with her?'

Klaus's eyes saddened. He crumpled to his knees. 'I am old man and do not have good health. I was going to leave, but my heart gave me great pain the day of our planned departure. I told Helga to go on alone, and I would catch

310

up with her, but I did not have the strength. Now, the time has come and I must leave here. My shop has been destroyed by people who hate me for my German blood. My assistant had good heart and took me in and suggested I change my name to English name, but it is of no use now. It's too late. I still have my German voice. I've lost everything here and want to be with Helga, she beg me to come.'

Jessie tossed her pitchfork down, her voice softening. She knelt down beside the man. 'Have you been to Sandringham yet? Have you seen the Queen?'

Klaus shook his head. 'I walked there from the station this morning and realised my stupidity. I read in the paper on the train coming here that Queen Alexandra is in London doing charity work. I was thinking of going to the post office to leave the letter there for them to post, but knew my German accent would attract attention.'

He paused, his eyes brightening. 'Will you help me? Please, will you take my letter to her?'

Jessie shook her head. 'I knew Helga, she was a good person. But we can't do that. We would be considered traitors if we helped you now, and we certainly can't involve Her Majesty. Oh Lizzie, what are we going to do?'

The man had a forlorn expression. 'Please believe me, I want no part of this war. We were friends, and now we kill each other.'

Lizzie tossed her spade aside. 'He tells a good story. Cobbler or not, I don't like this one bit. I think we should keep this to ourselves for now.'

311

Chapter Twenty-Eight

Harry Saward traced the lines of tiny print in the newspaper as he scanned the names of those reported killed or missing. Two pages were filled with rows of tiny black print naming people's loved ones, but none that he knew from the Sandringham Company in which he had held the rank of sergeant before the war.

How was it possible that still no one could say where Captain Beck and a large number of his men were? The battle in Gallipoli, almost two years ago now, had been a disaster for them, ill prepared for the Turks with their snipers, some said to be women. Despite pressing enquiries by the government, foreign diplomats, and even the King, many men remained unaccounted for. Deep down Harry sensed it could only be bad news, but without proof there was still hope that they were alive, maybe captured and held as prisoners somewhere.

It had been a terrible blow to receive news that his son-in-law, Alfie, was missing, and for Ada to have her letters and photographs returned. Ada did her best to put on a brave face to keep Leslie in a cheerful mood, like other women on the royal estate who were waiting to hear the fate of their missing men.

Betty pushed a plate of food towards him. Harry stared at the slice of hard bread, a boiled egg and slice of tongue, which he knew he was fortunate to have. He picked up the dark-coloured bread and wrinkled his nose. The shortage of wheat forced bakers to use potatoes and other bulking agents to make up the shortfall. He tried not to remember how delicious a freshly baked white loaf tasted. Furthermore, new regulations made it illegal to sell bread until twelve hours after it had been baked, with the government stating that stale bread was more nutritious and would be consumed less hastily than fresh bread, making it last longer.

Harry bit into the stale bread and pulled a face. He was chewing on it when someone knocked on the front door. Betty answered it and returned to the room with the vicar.

'Ah, I see you're breaking bread,' the Reverend Rumbelow commented, the corner of his lips slightly curling.

Harry grinned and pushed the plate away. He offered the vicar a seat. 'It's not more bad news, is it?'

The vicar shook his head. 'It's Ada I've come to see. I may have some good news about Alfie.'

Harry's face brightened. 'Really? What is it? I'm afraid Ada is out at the moment, but she should return soon. I believe she has taken Leslie to see Magnolia. He enjoys feeding the cats and playing with them.'

The vicar's eyes shone. 'I can wait a while. The good news is, Harry, that I think Alfie has been found. I think he's alive!'

Harry's eyes widened. 'Thank God! That's the news we've all been waiting to hear. I'll ask Betty to go to Magnolia's and bring her home if she isn't back in a couple of minutes. I hope you are right, Vicar. I wouldn't want Ada's hopes raised if it turned out to be a false alarm.'

'I'm fairly certain. A fellow vicar I trained with by the name of Winston Bakehill is based in a military field hospital in France. He has been in touch to tell me that one of the patients there came in recently with memory loss. The loud shelling explosion blew him to the ground and he hit his head badly. When he came round, he couldn't remember his name and they couldn't find any papers on him.'

Harry leant closer. 'Poor man. But why do they think it's Alfie?'

At that moment, Ada stepped into the room, her cheeks flushed. Leslie followed, hanging on to his mother's skirt. She stared at the vicar and her father sitting together, a confused expression on her face. Before she could speak Reverend Rumbelow rose. He blurted, 'I have what I think is good news, Ada. It's Alfie, I believe he's in a military field hospital suffering amnesia.'

Ada's face shone. 'Oh thank the Lord. My prayers have been answered. Are they sure it's Alfie, if he has amnesia?'

'We are certain it is. I know the vicar there, who put the pieces together and he contacted me to enquire about the chances of it being him. He was with a new patient recently who was just coming round from an unconscious state in a field hospital. He had no papers on him, so nobody knew who he was. At night, he becomes delirious, calling out for Ada and Leslie. It would be an incredible coincidence if another injured soldier had a wife and child by the same name.'

Ada's eyes filled with tears of joy. She scooped Leslie into her arms and cried, 'Daddy's alive. He's alive!'

The vicar smiled. 'Yes, your prayers have been answered, and we have the Lord to thank that Winston was there for Alfie. He heard him mumble Wolferton over and over again, saying he had to go back to Wolferton. That's when Winston's ears pricked up as he knew I had a position here and, even though we haven't been in touch for a while, he wrote to me asking if this man could be connected with my parish, and if I had any idea who he might be.'

Ada's eyes shone. 'I'm so thankful. Alfie must have had a guardian angel looking down on him. I couldn't bear the thought of Leslie being a fatherless child.'

'It is indeed fortunate. Alfie was on the brink of death and suffering from concussion, I am told, but he is gradually recovering. We have much to be thankful for.'

The vicar paused. 'I hope you don't mind, Ada, but I took the liberty of writing back immediately to confirm that Alfie fitted the description. I've asked Winston to pass on details of his home to his regiment. I have the address of the field hospital, if you would like to write to Alfie there.'

Ada felt her heart would explode. She squeezed Leslie tight and smothered his face with kisses. 'I can't wait. I shall write tonight. When can he come home?'

Reverend Rumbelow smiled. 'As soon as he is well enough to travel. I'm sure once Alfie is informed by Winston that I have been in touch with you, the wheels will be put in motion for his return home, to a hospital.'

Ada broke the news to Jessie as she returned home. 'Oh, Jessie, Alfie's alive. The Germans didn't kill him! He's alive.'

Jessie's stomach clenched as she pictured Klaus in Lizzie's barn. Innocent or not, he was still a German. He was the enemy that threatened the future of her family and loved ones. Seeing Ada's relief consumed her with guilt. She decided what they must do. Tomorrow, she would tell Lizzie that Klaus must be handed over to the police.

∞

Leslie chanted, 'Papa's coming home, he's coming home,' in an excitable state the day after hearing his father had been found. Ada and Leslie sat in the garden of the station master's house picking fresh white daisies from the border, then placing them firmly in a chunky flower press, screwing the bolts down at each corner.

Leslie was gleeful when Ada then took his small hand and placed it on a sheet of writing paper, her brows knitting together as she drew in pencil around it. He giggled as she drew the outline of his stubby fingers to send to his father, who had only seen him twice since he was born.

Ada then left Leslie in the kitchen with Betty while she went to the parlour and opened a drawer in the bureau, taking out writing paper and an envelope. She dipped a pen in ink and thought for a moment. There was so much she wanted to say, and the words poured from her, telling him of their delight that he had been found and would be coming home soon, how excited Leslie was to see him, as well as news about Beatrice working at the hospital where she hoped he would be sent to, Jessie's life as a land worker on Lizzie's farm, and how well Maria was doing at the Big House. She omitted mention of Nellie, feeling the situation was still too uncertain. She rambled on about Joey and Eddie's recovery, how busy Sarah and Harry were and plans for a new infants' welfare clinic in Wolferton following the success of National Baby Week.

She put down her pen and folded the letter neatly, five pages in all once she had signed off with her love. She placed it in an envelope and included the sheet of Leslie's hand outline and the pressed flowers which she placed gently between tissue paper, thinking how much he would enjoy holding a flower from her family's garden.

She missed the wifely comfort of being held in her husband's arms. Sometimes at night she would imagine he was there with her as she slowly unbuttoned her blouse, then unclasped the front of her corset underneath. She closed her eyes and remembered the thrill that coursed through her body when he aroused her passions with his caresses and gentle lovemaking, his eyes filled with tenderness. She saw him watching her in her mind's eye as she removed the hairgrips that held her neat knot in place behind her neck and let it tumble down her back, imagining Alfie taking the hairbrush from her hand

and running it slowly through her hair, pressing his lips to the back of her bare neck. She flushed with delight at the memory.

She sealed the letter and kissed it softly, placing it on the hallstand, ready to post when she went out.

∽

Later that evening, Ada pressed Beatrice about Alfie being given a bed at Hillington Hall Hospital.

'We could fill each bed ten times over, but the army medics try to send their men to local hospitals when they can.'

The sisters were sitting in a shaded corner of the garden, sipping glasses of lemonade and chatting idly.

Beatrice told her, 'You have surprised me, Ada, becoming so involved in issues to improve welfare and housing for the poor. And there is Jessie, dressing like a man in her breeches and working on Lizzie's farm. The war has certainly changed us.'

'You're right. I would never have thought myself so capable before the war. It little compares to your nursing though. I hope Alfie will be placed under your care as I feel he would be in the best possible hands.'

Beatrice placed an arm around Ada's shoulder. 'That's very sweet of you to say and I appreciate it. I will ask Matron if I can be assigned to Alfie. We must hope we have a spare bed when he arrives. We are now being sent soldiers suffering from the effects of mustard gas and their injuries are horrific and take time to heal. It makes me sick to see people developing weapons of war to destroy human life.'

Ada shuddered. 'I've heard about this mustard gas and the terrible burns and blindness it causes. People say it's a slow, painful death and I'm too scared to think about it. What if Alfie . . .'

'I'm sure Winston would have mentioned if that was the case. From what he says, it sounds like Alfie has concussion; it's quite common following a head trauma. I know it's easy to say, but try not to become overly anxious until we know for sure.'

'Of course, you're right, Beatrice. I promise not to worry, it's not good for my nerves. Tell me, how is Eddie doing? The trip to London must have tired him out, though he seemed to really enjoy it. I hear there was great interest on the embroidery stand.'

Beatrice grimaced. 'Physically, Eddie has had a setback and is on bed rest. It's fair to say the exertions did tire him and we are treating his infected leg with a tincture of iodine as it appears inflamed again. Perhaps, with hindsight, he shouldn't have gone. On the other hand, his mind is stronger. The trip lifted his spirits and I feel that in part this is thanks to him taking up embroidery, which has calmed his restless mind. He is also writing about the exhibition for the next issue of the *Tommy Herald* and Matron thinks it's an excellent report.'

The conversation turned to Maria. Beatrice said, 'Eddie has confided that he plans to make up with Maria once he is well and on his feet. We have Private Bowers to thank for this too. He encouraged Eddie to declare his true feelings for Maria. If ever there is a young couple meant for each other, it is them. He just dotes on Joey, and adores Maria too. We have to hope she will give him another chance and realise he was not himself before.'

Ada hesitated. 'I'm pleased to hear that Uncle Ronald is sorting out Nellie's problems.'

The sisters gossiped, their heads locked together. 'And what do you think about Magnolia's gentleman friend . . . ?'

∞

A new influx of patients was due to arrive at Hillington Hall. Matron declared that more rooms were needed and it was decided that the library would become an additional ward.

The plan was hastily put into action. Bookshelves lining the walls that reached from floor to ceiling were covered with sheeting. Iron bedsteads were wheeled in and positioned along each side of the long room and made up.

The new ward filled rapidly with wounded servicemen, some limping on crutches, others with their arms or heads covered in bandages or slings. Others were pushed in wheelchairs, their rotting limbs heavily wrapped up – the result of trench foot – hoping to avoid amputation.

Beatrice's attention was focused on a patient whose eyes stared blankly at the ceiling. His thin body shook as he gripped the blanket tightly, pulling it over his head, then ducked underneath the covers. He cried out, 'I'm not a coward, I'm not!' None of the patients took a blind bit of notice. Other patients made similar moans while some were able to sit in chairs by the beds and read the papers or huddle in the side room and play cards.

It was Sunday, visiting day, and relatives were drifting in.

Beatrice stopped by Eddie's bed to share the news of Alfie's return. He sat on the edge of his bed looking into his lap. Bertie was speaking to him, but Eddie turned his head away and bit his lip.

'What's happened, Eddie? You haven't had bad news, have you?'

Bertie told her, 'I told him to take no notice. This girl came in and told him a pack of lies. She looked like a mischief-maker to me.'

Beatrice was confused 'What girl? What on earth are you talking about?'

Bertie shrugged his shoulders. 'I've no idea. She was here a few minutes ago. I was telling Eddie what a wonderful girl his Maria is and how proud he must be of her, working at Sandringham House with the old Queen, and all that. This girl must have heard me 'cause she came straight up and asked Eddie, very direct like, "Are you talking about Maria Saward?"

'He should have told her to mind her own business, only Eddie said, "Yes, she's my girl, or I'm hoping she will be again. We had a silly fall out."'

'What was wrong with that?'

'This girl asked questions about Maria and Eddie told her everything, he even showed her the needlework he did for her. I could see she didn't like it. Her face became hardened. She told Eddie that he was wasting his time as Maria has another fella.'

Beatrice's jaw dropped. 'But that's ridiculous. What other fellow? I'm sure I would know if that were true. And how would she know?'

Beatrice sat on the bed next to Eddie. She coaxed gently, 'You don't believe this girl, surely, Eddie? Maria is devoted to you.'

Eddie wiped his damp cheeks with his pyjama sleeve. 'She made it sound so true. She told me she worked at the Big House with Maria and had seen her being overly friendly with a groomsman.'

'That's outrageous!' Beatrice protested.

Eddie bit his lip. 'She said she saw him kiss Maria and she kissed him back.'

Beatrice snapped, 'I don't believe a word of it. Maria wouldn't behave like that. The Maria I know is working hard for her family and hasn't put a foot wrong since she moved to Wolferton.'

Eddie's bottom lip juddered. 'There's more. She said the groomsman touched Maria's chest and she let him. She let this other fella touch her there. I respect her too much to take advantage like that. She would only let him do that if she loved him, so I've lost her. And it's me own fault for giving 'er the brush-off.'

Eddie reached into his bedside cabinet and removed his exquisite embroidery. Tears streamed down his cheeks. Before Beatrice could stop him he pulled at it, tearing it apart, throwing the shredded pieces on the floor.

⁓

The following day, Eddie was signed off by the doctor and told his bed was needed and he would be well enough to return to his regiment after a two-week rest at home.

'I'm glad I'm going back to war. I don't care if I live or die now,' he declared.

Chapter Twenty-Nine

After staying with Matilda and Ronald for three weeks, Nellie told them, 'I shall be forever thankful. I'm feeling stronger now and there is something I need to do. I feel the time is right now, especially as Pa is still at large and may be spreading falsehoods about me.'

Matilda's face showed concern. 'What is it, pet?'

Nellie inhaled a breath. 'I owe Stanley and Adam an explanation. I want to write and tell them what happened. In the eyes of the law I am still Stanley's wife, and though my heart was never truly his, he deserves to know the truth as Connie will have poisoned his mind against me. Though it was Adam who won me heart, I suspect 'e will want nothing to do with me now and his family will have washed their hands of me.'

Matilda wrapped her arms around Nellie and stroked her hair. 'I reckon you're right to try and make amends. It's a big weight you carry around with you. And how will you know how this young Adam will feel towards you, once he knows the truth? There's nothing to be lost in dropping him a line.'

Matilda left the room for a moment and returned with a pen, some ink, a jotter and several sheets of writing paper. Nellie decided she would write to Stanley first. She struggled for a while to find the right words to put down on paper, but once she formulated her thoughts, her shoulders hunched over the table, she wrote line after line, page after page, until finally she placed the pen down and stopped writing.

Nellie stared at the lines in front of her and sighed. 'I hope Stanley finds it in his heart to forgive me. I don't have the strength to write to Adam as well, not right now.'

Matilda murmured, 'I'm sure they will understand, pet, given time. There is nothing more healing for a wronged person than telling the truth.'

'Will you glance your eye over this, and tell me what yer think?'

Nellie thrust the letter into Matilda's hands. Her eyes widened and her chin dropped as her finger followed the words. She gazed up. 'I'm sure Stanley will believe you and will realise you had no part in what happened. I know Gus is your father, but it beggars belief . . .'

Nellie raised a hand. 'I 'ave to start afresh and can only do so if I put this behind me. That includes forgiving Pa. I want to remember him with some fondness. Now I feel stronger, it is my intention to restore my reputation and make amends with Stanley and Adam and hope they won't think too badly of me.'

Matilda swallowed. 'You're a plucky one, that's for sure, and with a heart of gold. Gawd knows, you didn't get that from your father. Your mother must have been an angel.'

Matilda took the letter and placed it in the deep pocket of her skirt. 'I'll post it tomorrow. Once you've put matters to rest with Stanley, then you can put your mind to writing to Adam.'

∞

Ronald returned home that evening with a twinkle in his eye. Matilda greeted him with her usual warm smile, placing a steaming cup of tea on the kitchen table, but he ignored it.

Ronald cleared his throat. 'I have some very good news for you, Nellie.'

Her face showed interest and she exchanged glances with Matilda who took her arm in hers. 'There you are, pet, I knew your luck would return soon enough.'

Ronald continued, 'It's as I suspected. Your Aunt Millicent's so-called cousin is a fake. When you mentioned his name I knew I had heard it before. I don't come across that many Cedrics. I asked around and then recalled the reason my suspicions were aroused.'

'Well, go on. Put us out of our misery,' Matilda chided.

'I'm afraid you were not the only one to have been duped by him, Nellie. There was another young lady called Ruby who is around the same age as yourself. She turned up at the police station one day with a very similar story to yours, having been encouraged to do so by a close friend of her grandmother's who had her own suspicions about the sudden change in her will.'

Nellie said falteringly, 'But I don't understand. What are yer saying?'

Ronald fixed his gaze on her. 'It turns out that this young lady's grandmother, a Mrs Phoebe Carrington, resided further along the Kent coast of Margate in the town of Broadstairs. She passed away recently and Ruby had expected to inherit the entire estate. She was brought up by her grandmother after her parents died in a tragic boating accident when she was only three and Ruby's grandmother doted on her.

'After she died, Ruby was deep in mourning when a solicitor called to see her, stating his firm had been given instructions by her grandmother about her wishes, explaining that she had revised her will a few weeks leading up to her passing.'

Matilda asked, 'But what's this got to do with our Nellie?'

Ronald twisted his thumbs behind his braces and pulled his shoulders back. 'Because it's the same solicitor, the same Cedric Parker, who turned up out of the blue and swindled Nellie out of her inheritance. There is even a connection between these two cases because while it is true that Cedric Parker certainly is a distant cousin of your Aunt Millicent, he met Mrs Carrington at your aunt's house and secured her personal details on the sly, after discovering she was a widow of not insubstantial means. Just as in your aunt's case, the swine fabricated both wills, naming himself as the main beneficiary.'

There was a stunned silence as Matilda and Nellie processed the information.

Matilda's voice wobbled. 'So you're saying, Aunt Millicent left everything to Nellie? Her house and everything in it?'

'That's right. Everything is Nellie's. She is an heiress of substantial means.'

Nellie gripped Matilda's arm. 'I can't believe it. It can't be true. Me, an heiress?'

'It is absolutely the truth. I can't claim all the credit. I had some assistance from a solicitor in King's Lynn who Harry put me in touch with, a Mr George Perryman. He made enquiries too on my behalf with the legal fraternity and confirmed what I had discovered. This Cedric Parker has been struck off for malpractice. He is banned from working as a solicitor, but continues to act as one to dupe innocent people. All the pieces came together when I heard Ruby's story. I couldn't be more pleased for you, Nellie.'

Matilda gushed, 'Oh, Ronald. You should give up the railways and become a full-time detective. If it hadn't been for you then Nellie and this other young lady would have lost everything. So where is this Cedric Parker now?'

Ronald rubbed his chin. 'It's very kind of you to say so, my dear. As far as that swindler goes, we passed on word to our boys in Margate, who raided his house. He had made attempts to burn both wills, but they were able to retrieve enough fragments to piece them together. We have Mrs Carrington's friend to thank for insisting that Ruby go to the police and report her suspicions.

She sensed Cedric Parker was up to no good when she met him as he fawned over Mrs Carrington in the most unprofessional way. I'm afraid there is no sign of Parker. We fear he may have already fled the country and be on the continent somewhere.'

Matilda probed, 'But Nellie will still get her dues, won't she? Or has he already got his thieving hands on the money?'

'It appears he has, though we can't say how much at the moment. We have put out word at the ports. I can't imagine he would want to flee by boat, not with the bombardments happening right now. Never fear, we'll catch the scumbag sooner or later. And you still have the house and contents, Nellie, as well as a large proportion of her shares.'

Matilda nudged Nellie. 'So you're a little heiress then. That's a turn up for the books, I'd say. I'm very happy for you, pet.'

Nellie blushed. 'I still can't believe it. Anything I have I will share with yer both to repay yer for yer kindness. I can never thank you enough for believing in me and taking me in.'

Matilda retorted, 'There's no need for that. We're happy that you are getting what is rightfully yours. I'd like to see your father's face when he hears about this. And what about Doris? Ronald says you're not pressing charges against her for kidnap and imprisoning you against your will? And to think you almost died!'

'Oh no, I couldn't possibly press charges. I believe Doris when she says she was under Gus's thumb. Her 'usband used her too in the most appalling way. I don't see what good it would do to press charges against her. I hope she can put this behind her and keep away from men who use her for their own means.'

'That's very good hearted of you, pet.' Matilda smiled, staring at Ronald, who nodded.

Nellie's smile dropped the next moment when Ronald fished out an object from his pocket and held it in front of her face. She recoiled, as if she were a vampire and he was pressing the crucifix against her face. 'What can you tell me about this? I spotted it in the attic that day I found you.'

Nellie's face paled. 'Seeing it brings back painful memories. I found it under the bed in Doris's house and felt drawn to it. It has carvings of a man hanging by his neck, and that's what I did to meself. It gives me the shivers. Take it away.'

Matilda shuddered. 'I feel a chill course through my body. It looks evil.'

Ronald tapped his nose. 'I don't mean to distress you, Nellie. I wanted to find out what I could about it. I had to apply some less traditional sleuthing to practise here and tracked down an old woman who lives in a shack at the end of Oil Drum Lane down by the river. Some folk say she knows a thing or two about the supernatural, so I showed it to her.'

Matilda's jaw dropped. 'I never thought you believed in such things!'

Ronald stared at her. 'I don't usually, but it's a strange tale. She told me to speak to the person who owned it, and as it was found in Doris's house, I asked her about it.'

Nellie whimpered. 'I'm not sure I want to know.'

Ronald reassured her. 'You have nothing more to fear. Do you mind if I carry on?'

Having been given the nod by Nellie, Ronald continued, 'This old peculiar item is a wooden stay busk that was used by women in their corsets to enhance feminine assets, if you get my meaning.'

'What's that got to do with the poor fella hanging by his neck?' asked Matilda.

'I'm telling you now. I turned to Doris for information about it and was surprised how much she knew and was willing to disclose. When I showed it to her I thought she was going to faint. She threw it to the ground, saying words "vengeance" and "curse" over and over again.'

Nellie shuddered. 'What did she mean? How is it cursed?'

'That's what we have to work out. From what Doris has told me, many years ago this man Barney Pritchard was arrested with another fella called Bob Frisk for holding up a stagecoach and shooting dead the driver. Barney always insisted he was innocent. He'd got into trouble with Frisk over a game of cards and ended up losing twenty pounds. He had no means of paying it. Frisk was a bully and card cheat and everyone knew he set Barney up to lose.

'Barney had only played in the misguided hope of winning a few extra shillings to start off married life, having planned to wed the following week, but he was doomed the moment he sat down with Frisk. Frisk threatened to kill Barney and then if he didn't do as he ordered to pay what he owed.'

Nellie held her hand up to her mouth. 'What's this got to do with the stay busk and Doris?'

'Patience my dear, patience. Frisk ordered Barney to meet him the following evening at the Scissors Crossroads in Wolferton. He told him there was a job he wanted him to do and it would be over in minutes, robbing some rich folk travelling through in their coach. Barney resisted, but Frisk threatened Barney that he would kill his wife-to-be, Jane, if he didn't go along with it.

'As you can imagine it didn't turn out that way. The coach driver put up a fight and was shot dead by Frisk. A gun was pointed at the heads of an elderly couple who were forced to hand over their jewellery. It didn't take long for Frisk to be arrested, but he pinned it all on Barney, who had fled.

'Frisk's cronies turned up at Barney's house and beat him, saying they would kill Jane unless he confessed to the shooting. Terrified of the harm that might befall the woman he loved, Barney confessed to it all, and only blurted the truth to Jane the night before the noose was tied around his neck.'

Nellie's jaw dropped. 'That's shocking. Poor Barney. What a terrible injustice. Did Bob Frisk get away with it? Couldn't the couple in the coach identify the real villain?'

'They were too terrified and held their hands over their eyes, as instructed by Frisk. I'm sure you would have done the same if you had a pistol pointing at your head. And Frisk did get his comeuppance. He was killed the following year in a drunken brawl with a fella he had wronged.'

Nellie frowned. 'This is the most dreadful tale. I'm glad to hear that Bob Frisk got what was coming to him in the end. Poor Jane, what a terrible burden for her to carry for the rest of her life. But I don't understand, what's the connection with Doris?'

Ronald's lip curled slightly. 'Barney Pritchard's sweetheart, Jane, was Doris's great-grandmother on her father's side. Jane was with child when Barney went to the gallows, though neither knew it at the time. She was heartbroken by Barney's death and how he had been wronged. She made the stay busk and wore it every day to remember him. The tragic story has been passed down by the family over the years. Doris blames the stay busk for her bad fortunes and says everyone who takes possession of it suffers some terrible misfortune. Her father was kicked in the stomach by a horse and died under the wheels of a cart carrying barrels of ale, and her grandfather was struck by lightning as he sheltered from a storm under an elm tree. She can't bring herself to destroy it, fearing what will happen to her if she does. She believes its curse on her was putting her under Gus's spell, She never wants to see the stay busk again and asks that I destroy it.'

Nellie spoke sharply. 'You can't do that. It's not ours to destroy and maybe it could backfire against us if we are not careful. Maybe there's another way to break this curse, if that's what it is.'

Matilda looked thoughtful. 'Yes, you could be right, pet. Let's not act too hastily, Ronald. We don't want this to come back on us. You've seen how it made Nellie act.'

Ronald rubbed the back of his neck. He walked slowly towards the dresser, opened a drawer and placed the stay busk there, covering it with a napkin. 'I suggest we leave it here and forget all about it.'

Chapter Thirty

In bed that night Jessie tossed and turned thinking about Klaus, concerned for her friend's safety at being left with him. Lizzie assured her the next day, 'I know he's German, but I think he's harmless. I've kept the barn door shut and he has stayed inside, and I brought him some food when no one was around.'

Jessie urged, 'But he can't stay here. He's an illegal alien and you'll be in serious trouble if he's found.'

Lizzie told her. 'I know that. He could also be taken away and shot as a spy or sent to a prisoner of war internment camp. He's too old and wouldn't survive. When I saw him last night he spoke about Helga and said how much he missed her, how she wants to care for him. I felt sad for him, but I know I shouldn't as he's the enemy.'

Jessie's eyes creased. 'I think Klaus should leave tonight, under the cover of darkness. Shall we tell him?'

They found Klaus huddled behind the bales, his eyes closed. 'Is he . . . ?' asked Lizzie anxiously, staring at the motionless figure.

'Good Lord, I hope not,' exclaimed Jessie, bending down and touching the man's shoulder.

Klaus jerked and inched away, his face filled with fear. He relaxed when he saw the two women.

He attempted to rise, but his legs gave way and Jessie reached forward to grab hold of him. His breathing was heavy. 'I make up my mind. I leave today. I do not want to cause you trouble. I shall figure out a way to make it to Germany.'

His face was ashen and he was bent over, his arms folded in front of him.

Lizzie said softly, 'That's what we came to discuss. You may stay here and rest today, Klaus, as long as you stay out of sight and leave when it turns dark tonight. I will bring you something to eat when I get a chance. You will need to summon all your strength for your journey.'

Jessie and Lizzie left him there to go about their day's work on the farm. Outside the barn, Jessie's hand flew to her mouth. 'I have something to tell you. I forgot to mention it earlier.'

'I can't take any more shocks. You're not leaving me, are you?'

Jessie's face brightened. 'Oh no, it's nothing like that. It's Jack. He will be in London later this week and asks if I can meet him there on Friday. Do you think . . . would you mind if I had the day off?'

'Of course, you must go. If all goes to plan, Klaus will have left tonight. I have Archie and some of the older children from the school helping out, so off you go, and have a splendid time. You deserve it.'

The following day, Lizzie told Jessie 'He's gone. 'He left before I had a chance to say goodbye or take a small food parcel I prepared.'

'Oh, well he's off our hands then. What a relief,' sighed Jessie. 'I am so looking forward to seeing Jack, but I won't breathe a word about this.'

'Don't you dare!' Lizzie said. 'Come on then, let's go and see to the hens.'

∽

Jessie could think only of Jack over the next three days, when she was squatted down on the three-legged wooden stool milking the cows or tending to Lizzie's vegetables.

Archie whooped with joy when Jock, an old shire horse from a neighbouring farm, was led into the farmyard.

Lizzie smiled. 'You have a new friend. Jock was going to the slaughterhouse, and even though his best days are over and he was rejected by the army, he can still pull the weight of a cart or furrow, even if he is slower and needs coaxing.'

Archie threw his arms around the horse's neck and nuzzled his face against Jock's head. 'This is your new home, Jock. We'll take care of you now.'

Lizzie smiled. 'We can't force him too much. He can only do what he can with his arthritis, poor old thing.'

∽

When Friday finally arrived Jessie rose early and drew open her curtains just as the sun was rising. She carried a jug of warm water to her room and hummed the popular song 'Keep the Home Fires Burning' under her breath, feeling both nervous and excited about her reunion with Jack after a year apart.

She picked out her best lilac skirt to wear with a pretty white georgette blouse with a deep lace collar and flouncy sleeves edged with lace. She brushed her toffee-coloured hair and swept it up, piling it into a knot on top of her head, allowing a few loose strands to dangle down the side of her cheeks.

Her violet eyes sparkled and she smiled back at her reflection in the mirror. She couldn't recall the last time her heart had beat so fast, or she had dressed so finely, the breeches being her most frequently worn clothing nowadays. She traipsed down the stairs with a light step and burst into the kitchen as Betty arrived and the family were tucking into breakfast.

The housekeeper remarked, 'Oh you do look a picture. Jack will be proud to have you on his arm.'

Harry gazed approvingly. 'You do look lovely, Jessie. Do you know your plans for the day?'

Jessie's face shone. 'Not exactly. He wants it to be a surprise. I only know that Jack will meet me at St Pancras Station.'

Betty smiled. 'I'm sure he'll have a nice treat planned for you. I've packed a few rock buns for you both, in case you get peckish.'

Ada came down a moment later. 'I say, Jessie, you look absolutely beautiful. I didn't know you could scrub up so well after seeing you dressed in manly clothes for so long.'

'I really don't mind wearing breeches. They are perfectly practical for farm work. But I must admit it does feel lovely to put a pretty dress on.'

Harry cleared his throat. 'Jessie, promise me one thing.'

'Of course. What is it?'

'That you will take very good care of yourself and be watchful of strangers who appear over-friendly.'

'I promise. You can be sure that Jack and I will keep out of harm's way. And thank you Betty for your bakes. Jack would have been disappointed to have missed out on them.'

Harry stepped into the hallway. He slipped on his dark blue jacket, closing each button carefully, and straightened his tie. He pulled his cap on his head and turned to Jessie.

'If you have everything, we can walk to the station together. Your train goes in fifteen minutes.'

Jessie felt a glowing sensation swarming insider her as she imagined Jack taking her into his arms for an embrace. Her head was still in the clouds as she followed her father out of the house and didn't notice heads turning from passers-by, making admiring comments. She quickened her step as a cloud of smoke belched a short distance away and the train pulled in at the platform.

'Oh, Father, I'm feeling nervous. What if Jack no longer feels the same way as me? It's been so long, almost a year, since we were together.'

339

'Don't be so daft. I don't believe that for one moment. I'll see to your ticket, you get yourself a comfy seat and I'll come and find you.'

Harry was as good as his word and found Jessie in a compartment, already engaged in conversation with a mother and her young girl, who were also travelling to London to visit relatives. The girl was around six years old, with bouncy red curly hair, and she shyly held out a knitted doll to show Jessie.

The journey passed in a flash and the distraction of her companions helped take Jessie's mind off her fears about Jack's feelings towards her. Her stomach tightened as the train pulled into St Pancras and she stepped onto the platform. Everything seemed so much bigger here, there were more trains and platforms, it was noisier, and the black engine smoke made it impossible for her to see far up the platform. She walked anxiously to the end, her eyes searching in all directions for Jack.

As the passengers thinned out, she continued looking in vain. She began to panic and felt a lump in her throat. A thought flashed through her mind that he wasn't coming. Then a voice in her head told her he would never let her down so cruelly. She could only imagine that circumstances beyond his control had detained him.

She spun around again, pacing the platform, glancing anxiously in all directions. 'Can I help you, ma'am?' enquired a guard.

Jessie didn't hear his words but read the guard's lips. 'There's a gentleman walking in this direction. He's calling out for Jessie. Is that you, by any chance?'

'Why yes, it is.'

Her heart skipped a beat as Jack ran towards her, his face beaming. Her shyness melted away as he opened his arms and she pressed herself against his chest, his arms tightening around her.

She gasped, 'Oh Jack, I thought you weren't coming.'

He pulled away. 'Oh, sweet Jessie, I'm so sorry to be late. I was detained unexpectedly with His Majesty. Please forgive me. I've never seen you look so lovely. We can relax now and enjoy our time together. We have the whole day ahead of us. I can't tell you how happy I feel seeing you again, how much I've been looking forward to this moment.'

Jessie's heart melted and her eyes shone. Jack looked more handsome than ever in his smart dark blue and maroon striped jacket teamed with dark trousers, a white shirt and blue tie. He had shadows under his eyes, but brushed off Jessie's concerns, telling her his work as the King's messenger was an honour-bound duty. His moustache seemed thicker than before and his fair hair thinner on top. His blue eyes were as soft and loving as ever.

'It is so wonderful to see you again. I have taken the liberty of planning a day's enjoyable activity for us. The King is conferring military honours today so I managed to take the day off. It's so very humbling when I learn of the brave deeds of these men. It makes me think that I should offer to . . .'

Jessie stopped dead in her tracks. 'If you are about to say you wish you could enlist and fight on the front line, then I urge you to put such thoughts out of your head. The King would have suggested this himself if he felt it the right thing for you to do. There are many ways of fighting this war, and they are not all on the battlefield.'

'That's very true, my love. But not everyone regards my royal work in the same light. The topic inspires strong feelings, and rightly so. Why, only the other day I heard of a colonel who was court-martialled for allowing certain non-commissioned officers and men fit for service to remain in the regimental band and football team. That's hardly an excuse not to fight, yet he had signed a War Office certificate to the effect that they were not fit for fighting in France.'

Jessie paused. 'What happened to the colonel and his men? Was he right to keep them back? I know it weighs heavily on Beatrice's heart when she makes her patients better, only for them to be posted back to the front line and killed.'

'If they're fit they have to go back. As to the colonel's fate? He appealed and was cleared after proving the men's unfitness for war. Some say he must have found a sympathetic doctor. We urgently need every man we can get at the moment. Tell me, how are you faring on the farm? You look so fine and elegant today, my dearest Jessie, that I can hardly imagine you wearing breeches and digging up potatoes that you described in your letter.'

Jessie winked mischievously. 'Mother says I look a dreadful sight in breeches, but I'm hoping you will find it pleasing. I am curious, Jack, what do you have planned for today?'

'It is a day filled with surprises. As it is a fine day I thought we could take a bus to St James's Park and enjoy a stroll there, and then, if you agree, I thought you might like to see the Royal Academy of Arts Summer Exhibition in Piccadilly, followed by afternoon tea at a fine eating establishment close by.'

Jessie's face shone. 'That all sounds just perfect, a day to remember for ever, though I don't mind what we do, as long as we are together. Just being with you is enough.'

'I feel the same way,' Jack replied, taking her hands in his and brushing his lips on them, gazing into her eyes. Jessie's face flushed and she tilted her head.

Taking her arm, Jack led her outside the station where they joined a queue for a bus.

'Our first stop is St James' Park. Have you ever been?'

Jessie shook her head. Jack told her, 'You will so enjoy it. I hope we won't wait too long for the bus, but you can never tell as there is a shortage of drivers.'

An older man nearby gave up waiting and whistled outside the station for a cab, and was immediately cautioned by Jack. He apologised. 'Oops, I keep forgetting that's not allowed, though I don't see how my whistle could be mistaken for an air raid warning.'

Unlike the corner of Norfolk where Jessie lived, Jack informed her that Londoners were constantly on the alert for an air raid warning.

Jessie was on cloud nine and didn't mind how long the wait took. She barely heard a word Jack spoke, straining to hear his voice above the comings and goings around them, his kind eyes speaking volumes to her, more than any words he could say.

The bus finally pulled up and Jessie gawped. She had never been on a double-decker motorised bus before. An unsmiling woman conductor took their fare and they climbed up the narrow spiral staircase, finding seats together at the front. It gave them a bird's-eye view of London. The streets seemed so wide and the brick buildings so tall, compared to those back home in Norfolk. Her head spun around as they passed piles of rubble and wreckage, and the sight of children and disabled men begging on the streets tore at her heart. Every other person wore a black armband or were dressed in mourning.

As they reached St James's Park they passed uniformed servicemen on leave strolling with their sweethearts, one pushing a perambulator with one hand while his other arm was around his wife's waist.

Jack led Jessie to a seat by the lake where the heady scent of perfumed roses wafted under their noses. She spotted a corner in the garden that had been turned over to a makeshift allotment, with a poster encouraging folk to turn their flowerbeds into vegetable plots, just as they were doing in Wolferton.

She suddenly remembered the rock cakes Betty had given her and fished them out of her bag and the two of them munched happily on the baked goods. Jack reached forward to brush away some crumbs from the corner of Jessie's mouth and her cheeks flushed as a wave of emotions stirred within her. Embarrassed by the intimacy her cheeks flushed and, she turned her face away.

Jack apologised, but she could not hear his words. She stared upwards as a loud humming sound in the distance, that even she could hear with her impediment, made her afraid. She clung to Jack's arm. 'What's that sound? Should we take cover?'

Jack gazed up at the cloudless sky, shielding his eyes from the bright sun with his hand. The eerie sound was heard again and Jessie clung tighter to his arm.

'The War Office is trialling new air raid warning alarms today at the Horse Guards Parade. It's a terrible sound, but you have no need to be alarmed. What you can hear is a cannon being used to fire detonators. It seems to be most effective, especially if you can hear it.'

Jessie sighed with relief. Jack rose and offered his arm. 'Come, let's walk to the Royal Academy, and afterwards we will have a special afternoon tea.'

The sound of the air raid trial was still ringing in their ears as they walked to Piccadilly, the grand buildings they passed making Jessie want to stop and ogle them.

'Life in the capital is so different from the quiet country ways of Wolferton. I pride myself as something of an artist. I enjoy painting country scenes in watercolours when I have a chance,' he told her.

'I had no idea,' Jessie replied. 'I would very much like to see your paintings.'

'They are amateurish, but I find it relaxes me if I am away and have a moment to myself. The Summer Exhibition is always my favourite. It's held each year, even throughout the war, for anyone to exhibit, as long as they meet the required standards. It means any amateur with talent can see their work hanging in the galleries where our grand masters are shown.'

'And you, Jack? Are you going to surprise me and say one of your paintings is on show here?'

'Oh no. Absolutely not. I paint merely for my own pleasure.'

The stone building was vast at three-storeys high with life-size statues standing in recesses. Jack paid the one shilling each admission charge for them, free to service-men wearing their uniform. He collected a programme of the exhibits and seemed to know his way around. Jessie followed him up a grand sweeping marble place.

They followed signs directing them to the Summer Exhibition and finally entered the first gallery, a light airy room covered from floor to ceiling with paintings of varying sizes. Jessie's eyes absorbed the astounding range of talent and subject matter before her. As they stepped into the next gallery, she felt an elation and sorrow at the same time; while many of the titles indicated the breadth the paintings covered, offering a much-needed distraction during these difficult times, such as *The Sunlit Sea*, *Going to Pasture*, *Ullswater*, *Nymphs Bathing*, and even *Mrs Scrope*, it was the more contemporary works showing the horrors on the battlefield that her eyes lingered on the longest, depicting the brutality of war, raw carnage there for all to see in vivid colours. She wondered who had wit-nessed the terrible atrocities they painted, with titles such as *A Stray Shot*, *The Wrecked Zeppelin*, *200 yards from the Bosch*, and *The Captain's Dug-out*.

After strolling through ten galleries, Jack declared, 'I'm afraid that's all we have time for. We are expected elsewhere soon for our refreshments. It's not far from here, but I want it to be a surprise. I hope you've enjoyed it here.'

'Oh Jack, I really have. I would like to come every year. I've just loved it all. How clever of you to suggest coming here.'

'It is I who should thank you for your delightful company. I hope you will like my next surprise just as much. Come, let's go.'

Jessie spontaneously reached forward and stroked his golden moustache and lips before kissing them softly. She pulled back and covered her face with her hands, looking around her. 'I can't believe I did that,' she said. 'Do you think anyone saw?'

'I don't give a damn. I've been wanting to kiss you all afternoon. You are a woman of many surprises, Jessie.'

Jessie felt reckless, unable to resist the simmering passions within her. She was falling in love, and she didn't care who knew it.

Jack took her arm and she snuggled against him as they gaily traipsed downstairs and outside into the afternoon sun. She felt guilty to be feeling so euphoric at a time when so many families' lives had been torn apart by the war. They walked arm in arm across the road, and along Old Bond Street until Jack stopped outside an elegant shop, its windows filled with the most exquisite handmade chocolates.

'I've booked us afternoon tea here. I hope you approve.'

Jessie gasped. 'But, it must cost a fortune!'

'It's a special day and I've taken the liberty of booking us a table. The selection will be smaller than in normal times, but Charbonnel et Walker are the best chocolatiers in London and have been granted the royal warrant, and if they meet the approval of our King and Queen, I'm sure they will be to our liking too.'

Restaurants in London did brisk business during the war and were popular with servicemen on leave looking to relax, and if you had the money, most treats were still available.

A selection of dainty handmade chocolates and truffles with decorative boxes to be tied with satin ribbon and gifted were displayed in the front window. 'I've never been to such a lovely place,' Jessie said as she followed him inside, her eyes on sticks.

A young smiling waitress in a black dress and long white frilly apron showed them to a small round table in the corner, removing the white card displaying the word 'Reserved'.

Jack pulled out the soft cushioned chair for Jessie as her eyes feasted on her elegant surroundings; a sparkling chandelier overhead and pretty sidelights and ornate gilt mirrors on the wall. Aspidistra and palm plants added a splash of colour to the restaurant and elegant figurines were placed on a sideboard with gold edging.

The circular tables were laid with dainty lace-edged tablecloths and matching napkins, silver cutlery and a small bouquet of fresh flowers placed in the centre. She observed the clientele, either uniformed officers out with their wives or sweethearts, or well-to-do ladies accompanied by their affluent friends or family, their heads close together as they savoured the mouth-watering delights in front of them.

The waitress handed Jessie a menu and she opted for a hot chocolate drink and a small round of egg and ham sandwiches made with brown war bread. Most of all she looked forward to sampling the rose and violet creams that Charbonnel et Walker was famed for. After finishing her sandwiches, she slowly devoured three of the chocolates, savouring the sweetness of the floral perfumed cream. Jack entertained her by telling her how Prince Francis of Teck, the younger brother of Queen Mary, gave the Teck Emeralds to his mistress after courting her with delicious Charbonnel et Walker chocolates. The Queen was furious and had to pay the mistress £10,000 to recover the family heirlooms.

'And to think it all started here,' exclaimed Jessie, her eyes bright. 'Is that your plan too, Jack? Are you courting me with Charbonnel et Walker chocolates? You can rest assured I don't need jewels to entice me, these three delicious rose and violet creams have done the trick. My heart is yours.'

Jack smiled and took Jessie's hands in his. He raised them to his lips. 'You make me the happiest man in the world, Jessie. I would shower you with jewels if I had them.'

Jessie laughed. 'They would sparkle rather nicely on the farm and make me stand out, me in my breeches and emeralds. What a hoot. Oh Jack, I don't want this day ever to end.'

She rubbed her stomach. 'I really can't eat another morsel, though, I am fit to burst. If only time could stand still at this very moment for me to savour for ever and ever. It's been the best day of my life.'

'I've had a wonderful time too.' Jack smiled, his eyes twinkling. 'I'm sorry it has to end now as I need to report to the King shortly to discuss my duties for the morning.'

He called the waitress over and asked for the bill, which he settled, being sure to leave a generous tip, which Jessie noticed, a little shocked at the larger than usual sum he was leaving.

'Is that really necessary? It's already cost you so much.'

'Well, no, I suppose not. But every farthing was well spent and I have no qualms about showing my thanks. Now, it's important I get you to the railway station, else I'll have your father to contend with.'

Jack topped the day off by insisting on buying a small box of chocolates for Jessie to take back to her family. She had resisted, saying he had been more than generous already, but he led her to the counter to choose from the collection before her. She selected mouth-watering rose and violet creams and crème cassis, insisting firmly that six was enough. She left the shop clutching the box tied with a pale mauve satin ribbon.

Jack placed a protective arm around her shoulder on the return bus journey to St Pancras Station. Her train was due to leave in fifteen minutes and was already on the platform when they arrived. The same guard recognised her, ushering her through.

'Just the lady, is it?' he asked.

Jack nodded, taking hold of Jessie's hands and gazing deeply into her eyes.

'Thank you, my darling, for the most wonderful day. Even though I can't say when I will be able to see you again, I will remember this day forever.'

Jessie threw herself into Jack's arms. He stroked her hair, and as she looked up at him, he took her chin in his hands and lifted it so he could kiss her lips.

'Promise me you'll stay safe,' she begged, as he opened the carriage door for her.

'I promise, my love, my darling Jessie. We have a lifetime ahead of us when this war ends. Please never doubt for a moment how sincere my feelings are for you, however long it takes for my letters to reach you.'

Jessie wound down the window. 'I believe you, Jack Hawkins. Take good care. I shall miss you.'

The guard blew his whistle. 'All aboard!'

Slowly, the engine pushed forward, covering Jack in a cloud of smoke. Jessie reached out of the window and waved until he was out of sight, her heart fluttering as he faded from view.

The return journey home was a blur. By the time Jessie was seated in her compartment, she already missed him. She relived every conversation they had had during the day, the thrill of seeing the paintings at the Royal

Academy and the delicious creamy taste of the rich choc-olates still in her mouth.

It was ten o'clock when Jessie walked through the door at the station master's house. She saw the light in the parlour and burst into the room, desperate to tell her family about her day, but the expressions on her parents' and sisters' faces cautioned her to be silent. 'Has something happened?'

Ada blurted, 'Oh Jessie. It's Alfie. He's coming home. He's coming to Hillington Hall Hospital.'

'That's wonderful news, Ada. Do you know how he is?'

Beatrice answered, 'Not exactly, though I believe he has a head injury, which has affected his memory. We are fortunate we have some available beds for these new arrivals. The doctors have discharged those they've done all they can for, including Eddie. He was discharged this afternoon. There are several first aid carriages arriving in the morning from France and I'm told Alfie will be travel-ling in one of them.'

Leslie blearily rubbed his eyes and tugged his mother's skirt. 'Can I see Papa tomorrow, Mama? I want to see my papa.'

Ada scooped her tired son into her arms and brushed her lips against his cheeks. 'He was caught up in the excitement of our news and couldn't sleep so I brought him downstairs. And yes, Leslie, you most certainly can see your papa tomorrow. We'll go together and greet him when he arrives at the station. Papa will be so pleased to see you.'

Chapter Thirty-One

A meeting was planned to discuss the opening of the new infants' welfare clinic in Wolferton.

Lady Appleby bristled with excitement when she spotted Beatrice at the hospital. 'I have some wonderful news, Beatrice. You'll never guess who I have arranged to come to our first welfare clinic.'

Beatrice raised an eyebrow. 'Is it Queen Mary? Or Queen Alexandra?'

'I mean as well as our Majesties, though it is not yet certain if they will be available. I am referring to Lady Plunkett.'

'How marvellous. I do recall she spoke at the National Baby Week exhibition. She is quite a pioneer in promoting infant welfare, I believe.'

'We couldn't have anyone better. Her husband was the governor of New Zealand a few years ago, and through her good deeds, free healthcare and advice was given to all mothers of new-born infants in New Zealand.

'If free healthcare can be provided in New Zealand for new mothers and infants, we should offer state support here too. We have much to thank Lady Plunkett for. I look forward to hearing how she made this happen.'

Beatrice was truly impressed. 'You are so generous with your time and sharing your contacts.'

'I won't detain you. I'm sure you have important work to do.'

Beatrice was thinking the same thing. Her mind dwelled on Eddie's discharge a couple of days before. She thought it had been sudden and queried it with Matron, who assured her that his leg had healed better than expected, though his mood was still low at times and he had insisted he wanted to convalesce at home.

∽

Beatrice called in on Ruth when she finished work, propping up her bicycle against the back wall.

'This is a nice surprise,' greeted Ruth. 'There's just the two of us here. Maria is still at work, if it was her you wanted to see.'

She was washing the dishes in the kitchen and dried her hands on her apron. Joey ran up to Beatrice and he held out his wooden engine. She knelt down and played with him for a moment, rubbing his head affectionately.

'It's good to see how well Joey is now. I've come to talk to you about Maria and Eddie.'

'What about them?'

'What do you know of this Philomena?'

Ruth told her what had happened in the Queen Mother's drawing room, adding that Maria's position upstairs had been reinstated. When Beatrice told her what Philomena had told Eddie, Ruth was knocked sideways.

'What a minx. Of course our Maria isn't playing the fiddle. You know Maria, there's no way she would be interested in another fella. Groomsman or prince, she would never let a man touch her the way that girl said.'

Beatrice looked thoughtful. 'That's just as I thought. Now Eddie regrets breaking it off with Maria. I wonder if there is a way we can bring them together again?'

'If only there was,' Ruth mumbled.

Beatrice looked up. 'I have an idea. I'll arrange to go with Maria to the infants' clinic meeting. Matron would like a representative from the hospital to be there and has asked me to attend.'

When Maria returned Ruth broached the idea with her. Maria had been told that day by Mrs Pennywick that some staff could have time off to go to the meeting as it was so well supported by both Queen Alexandra and Queen Mary. Maria was thrilled to be granted permission and her mother mentioned that Beatrice could stop by on her way there after work and they could go together.

∽

Two days later, Beatrice put her plan into action, stopping off at Honeysuckle Cottage where Maria had just arrived and was changing out of her work clothes. Little Joey tagged along as Maria and Beatrice left and ran down the garden path in front of them, pulling his mother in the direction of the Greensticks sisters' house, begging to see their family of cats.

'Very well, but only for a moment, else we'll be late,' Maria agreed.

Aggie was standing by the front gate and her face brightened as Joey ran towards her. She lifted the latch and Joey ran inside their garden, tickling tabby Maud's tummy as she lay on her back in a sunny spot. With Maria distracted keeping a watchful eye on Joey, Beatrice took Aggie aside and told her about her plan. With time running on, she told her, she hoped to entice Maria to stop off at Mrs Herring's house after the meeting and see Eddie there.

Aggie instantly agreed to be part of the plan and suggested to Maria, 'Seeing as I'm on my own today, with Magnolia and David out in King's Lynn, I could do with some company. Do you think Joey would like to stay on for a bit and feed my little fluffy family?'

Joey jumped up and down and squealed. 'Please let me stay, Ma. I would love to feed the cats with Aunt Aggie.'

'I can hardly refuse, can I? I'm sure Joey would rather be here than at a meeting to discuss the new welfare clinic.'

Aggie gushed. 'Very well, that's decided then. I may not be a mother, but as Joey's future godmother, there is much for me to learn, as well as our hard-pressed young mothers. Anything that can help save their young lives from disease and ignorance has to be welcomed. Now come along, Joey.'

Joey didn't need asking twice and gleefully ran towards the back door. The sound of cats meowing around his feet could be heard from inside the house as he entered through the back door.

Women were still arriving at the meeting room when Beatrice and Maria got there. There was good attendance and roles were to be assigned and plans for the official opening discussed.

Beatrice caught Lady Appleby's attention and introduced her to Maria. She was instructed to pass on her thanks to Mrs Pennywick that she had been given time off work to attend the meeting. Maria assured her she would, and she would pass on the information to other young mothers with infant working at the Big House. Lady Appleby moved away she spotted Eddie's mother seated towards the back of the hall. She was engaged in conversation with Jane Rumbelow. The vicar's wife was listening to her with one ear, while at the same time occupied with her stitching, which drew admiring glances from those close to her. The needlework was dedicated to her beloved son Piers. His name and date of birth and death had been exquisitely stitched in gold on a dark green background and were framed in a pretty border of white Christmas roses, their son's favourite bloom.

Lady Appleby stood at the front of the hall and raised her arms in the air. The hall fell silent.

"Today we are laying the foundations for our children's futures. May they live long and happy lives free from infection and disease. It is our intention to have healthy children growing up in Wolferton, and lots of them.'

'That's if we are fortunate enough to have our men back to make them. You don't get babies from under goose-berry bushes,' one disgruntled woman heckled.

'That's true,' another voice piped up.

Hands were raised by women willing to volunteer on the day, and as the meeting came to an end, Beatrice suggested they speak to Mrs Herring to enquire how Eddie was doing.

They approached Mrs Herring as she was about to leave. Maria felt a twinge of nerves wondering if Eddie had told his mother about them, but Mrs Herring greeted her in a friendly manner and she felt relaxed enough to enquire, 'How is Eddie?'

'He's been better, truth be told. You're looking well though, Maria. Can I ask you, is it true what I hear, that you have another fella, some groomsman at the Big House?'

Maria's face reddened and her jaw tightened, 'I most certainly am not. Who's been telling such wicked lies? I'd never do that to Eddie. I've never looked at another man.'

'Eddie mentioned it when I last went to see him. He told me a girl had put these ideas in his head, but I couldn't believe it. I told him not to be so daft.'

Maria blurted indignantly. 'Well it's not true. Not a word of it.'

Beatrice suggested in a soft voice, 'Seeing as we are just a few steps from your house, Mrs Herring, maybe Maria could see Eddie and tell him herself? I think he also regrets acting so swiftly and breaking it off with Maria, and they need to spend some time together to resolve these matters.'

Maria's gaze fell to the floor. 'But do you think he wants to see me if he was so ready to believe this girl? He's the one that pushed me away. I do miss him though. I think about him all the time.'

Beatrice held Maria's expression. 'He thought he was going to be a cripple and didn't want to burden you as an invalid. But we know that's not going to happen. Shall we call in and see how he is, just for a moment?'

Maria fumbled with her hands in front of her. Maria nodded. 'I would like to see 'im again. He has gone through a lot, it can't have been easy for 'im.'

Mrs Herring nodded approvingly. 'That's settled then. While you are talking to Eddie, maybe Beatrice could lend a hand in the yard and feed the chickens.'

Within a flash, they were stepping along the cobbled path at the side of Mabel's cottage. The back door was ajar. Maria popped her head in and called out Eddie's name. It was a faint call and there was no response. She called out again, louder, and a moment later, she heard a slow thud and shuffle of a foot being dragged along the floor.

Maria sprang back when Eddie flung the door open. Her eyes narrowed as they fell to his crutches. He leant on his good leg. He was wearing a white collarless shirt and grey trousers held up with braces. He stuttered, 'What . . . what the . . .'

Maria's eyes searched his face. 'How are yer, Eddie? I've been worried about yer.'

Eddie averted his gaze. 'Maria?'

'It's so good to see you again. I missed you. I'm so glad your operation was a success.'

Eddie bit his lip, his eyes downcast.

'Can you look at me, Eddie? I thought we were friends? I waited for yer as I promised.'

Eddie stuttered. 'I 'eard from a maid at the Big House that you were seeing Douglas, the groomsman.'

Maria threw her head back and laughed. 'No, I've been seeing Mr Armitage from the aviary, if you must know. Who's been telling yer these wild stories?'

'I shouldn't have believed, it but I wanted to hear it from yer own lips that it weren't true.'

Leaning towards him, she scolded, 'I thought yer knew me better than that, Eddie Herring.'

Shamefaced, Eddie bit his lip. 'This girl told me who was visiting at the hospital. She said she saw you kissing and you let him touch you intimately . . .'

'Bah! If you weren't on crutches I'd be tempted to clip you round the ear to knock some sense into you. How could you believe that of me?'

'Well, she said she saw you . . .'

Maria demanded, 'So what did she look like, this girl who has made up this pack of lies about me?'

'She's tall and thin and a bit older than you. I can still see her narrow eyes and thin lips twitching as she spoke. She seemed ever so concerned for me.'

'I bet she was, the strumpet. The girl you describe is Philomena, who was sent packing from the Big House for letting Queen Alexandra's parrot free from its cage, for

360

which she blamed me. She's set against me, for some reason. She's out to cause me trouble whenever she can.'

Eddie's face reddened. 'I've been a stupid . . .'

'Yes you have, Eddie Herring. Don't yer know Douglas is pledged to wed Winifred, the dairy maid?'

Eddie faltered. 'Oh Maria, can you forgive me for being such an idiot? The truth is, I've missed yer so much, and little Joey too. Will yer be my girl again?'

Before Maria could reply, Beatrice approached them clutching a basket of freshly laid eggs, with Eddie's mother chatting alongside her.

Maria was oblivious to their presence as she stood on her toes and kissed Eddie softly on the lips. 'You can take that as your answer.'

Eddie's face broke into a big smile. He dropped his crutches and spun her around in his arms, almost falling over.

'Careful, Eddie Herring. I'm counting the days till we can go out walking together again. I don't want to push you in a wheelchair.'

'We'll have lots of walks together, Maria, and picnics and trips to the seaside when this blasted war is over. There's something I have to tell you.' Eddie's face showed concern.

'What is it?'

'As soon as I am up on my feet properly again I'll be posted to France. They need all the soldiers they can get.'

Maria's face crumpled. 'You'd best not get better too quickly then.'

Eddie's eyes were moist. 'They're not going to let me off for long, else I'll be accused of being a malingerer. And you wouldn't want that, would you?'

'Then we must make the most of what time we have together then. Shall we sit out in the sun for a while and you can tell me about your time in hospital. I hear you're quite a writer and an embroiderer.'

∞

Magnolia and David were passing Mrs Herring's cottage with Rufus at their heels when they spotted Maria standing on the doorstep saying farewell to Eddie after they had made up. Beatrice had already left and the two had spent the last couple of hours rekindling their affections for each other.

Magnolia paused at the Herring's front gate, her hand on David's arm. She told Maria, 'I'm glad you've made up. Life is too short for silly misunderstandings.'

Maria smiled. 'We intend to make the most of what time we have together before Eddie rejoins his regiment. I'm on my way to your house to collect Joey. Aggie was kind enough to care for him this afternoon. May I ask a question?'

'What would that be?'

'How does Rufus get on with your cats? Surely he must scare them.'

'That is a problem we have to address. We try to keep them apart, but animals being what they are, they have their own ways. I'm afraid David is very attached to his terrier, just as I am to my little feline family.'

David rubbed his chin. 'I have been giving this some thought, Magnolia. I know how you'd prefer it if Rufus did not join us on walks and that he makes you nervous when we approach your house.'

Magnolia replied slowly, 'Maybe, in time, I will get used to Rufus, but his barking does make me a trifle edgy and this prevents you from coming in for tea and cakes.'

David nodded. 'I think it's because he can sense your unease, my dear. Which is why I have been giving this some thought. I wondered if Joey would like to care for him?'

Maria looked surprised. 'What are you saying?'

'I've seen how fond Joey is of Rufus. I wondered if he would like to keep him. I will help with the dog food, of course. But it makes good sense to me as I will still be able to see him.'

Magnolia interrupted, 'But, David, that is far too big a sacrifice for you to make. I would never dream of asking you to give up Rufus for me.'

'Rufus wouldn't be far away, and I'm sure I'd be able to see him when I wish.'

'Of course, Mr Fellowes. You could see him any time. Joey loves all animals, he has a way with them and I'm sure he'll work with them one day.'

They walked on and were almost outside Kitty Cottage when Rufus began to quicken his pace and bark, his tail wagging furiously. Maria stifled a laugh, her hand covering her mouth.

Joey spotted them from the side of the garden. He skipped along the path with Helena and Maud scampering alongside his heels, making playful meowing sounds. Aggie called the cats in and they disappeared obediently inside the back door in the flash of a tail.

Joey called out Rufus's name and the dog became increasingly excited. Maria told him about Mr Fellowes' offer. Joey's face brightened. 'Please let Rufus stay.'

Maria faced Mr Fellowes with a grin. 'I think Rufus has a new home.'

Magnolia's grin was even bigger. 'Oh, David. I didn't realise you cared for me so much.'

Chapter Thirty-Two

Ada stood anxiously at the station platform, one hand firmly clutching Leslie's, who could barely contain his excitement. He jumped up and down calling out, 'Papa.'

She tried to explain to her young son that Papa was not well and wouldn't be able to play with him straightaway because he was going to a hospital to get properly better before coming home. *Or more likely he will be sent back to the front line, like Eddie,* she thought with a heavy heart.

Ada overheard snippets of conversation from families waiting alongside her, many concerned at how different their men's lives would be now, worried how they would cope. Some described how their husbands had lost limbs or their eyesight, while others were recovering from burns and gunshot wounds. *How hard would it be to recover from amnesia?* Ada wondered. A handful of well-wishers had turned up too, laden with cigarettes and sweets to welcome the soldiers home. They were heroes in everyone's eyes.

Soon all heads were drawn towards the end of the line at the sight of the black engine pulling in, belching its belly full of smoke, its brakes screeching as it came to a halt. Families were asked to stand back as the train doors were flung open. Red Cross nurses stepped off carrying wheelchairs, the patients looking anxiously around.

Porters who had been sent from Hillington Hall Hospital stepped up briskly to the plate, some carrying stretchers. Slowly, more injured occupants disembarked, either carried off on stretchers, lifted out on wheelchairs, and transferred to a waiting ambulance, or hobbling out to face a row of onlookers. Some women were unable to suppress their shock at seeing their once strong, fit men returning in such a state. On top of their injuries, all of the men looked much thinner than when they had left home to fight the war.

Families searched for their loved ones, holding back their tears at the sight of the broken men who had returned home.

'Where's Papa?' begged Leslie, becoming impatient, grabbing hold of his mother's hand and tugging it.

'He's here, somewhere,' Ada muttered, shaking herself free of Leslie's grip.

Ada walked anxiously further along the platform, craning her neck and staring hard at every patient that disembarked. She spotted one being helped into a wheelchair by a nurse. Half his face was covered in bandages and his left arm was in a sling. She stood rooted to the spot. Her pulse began to soar, and as she walked towards the man, he turned his face towards her.

'Alfie?' she cried, rushing towards the wheelchair.

He looked straight at her and showed no emotion. His expression was blank. He stared at her showing no sign of recognition. She took his hand in hers. 'It's me, Ada. I'm your wife. And this is our son, Leslie.'

He stared right through her. 'Ada? Leslie?'

'Yes, my darling. I, your wife this is your son. It's so wonderful to have you back home.'

The nurse told her, 'I'm so sorry, but your husband is very tired and suffering from amnesia still. I'm sure after he has settled in at Hillington Hall, he will be more responsive. Just give it time.'

Ada bit her lip as she stepped back, fighting back the tears, while Leslie slipped his hand out of his mother's grip and ran to his father, throwing his arms around his chest.

'Papa, welcome home. I hope you get better soon.'

Alfie looked down at his son. 'Leslie? How are you, old chap?'

'I'm almost three.'

'I hope you are looking after your mother.'

Ada gulped. 'Oh, Alfie, do you remember us? I'm sure you will now you are back home.'

She reached down and kissed him on the cheek. The nurse smiled. 'Come on now, it's time to go. Let's get you to hospital, Lieutenant Heath. You've had a long day.'

Ada wanted to ask the nurse about Alfie's wounds and how long it would take for him to remember his family, but she cut her short, explaining that the ambulance was waiting for him. Ada felt like a heavy stone had been placed inside the well of her stomach. She felt tears welling up as the ambulance departed, wondering how their future would unfold. Leslie jumped up and down, excitedly waving off the ambulance.

Ada resolved to be patient. They had their whole lives ahead of them. She counted herself lucky that her husband was home again, and alive. And he had recognised them, which was more than she had hoped for.

She brushed aside a tear that escaped. 'Come along, Leslie, it's time to go home. You can draw a picture for your papa.'

Leslie scrambled around the ground and picked up a stick. He pointed it in front of him, as if it were a pistol. 'I hate the Germans for what they did to Papa.'

∽

'What do yer make of the King's new name?' Maria asked Cook over lunch.

'It's less of a mouthful than what they had before. I could never get my tongue around that long foreign name,' she replied, referring to the King's former name of Saxe-Coburg-Gotha.

'Windsor is a good strong name, like Saward. I don't ever want to change me name.'

'Not even when you marry?'

She joked. 'I will then, as long as I like me husband's name.'

Strong anti-German feelings throughout the country had meant the King and Queen were keen to distance themselves from their German ties, and just weeks before had renounced their name.

The King was also troubled by his cousin's problems in Russia and feared being tainted by association and the impact this could have on his country. The two men bore a striking resemblance to each other, and Tsar Nicholas II and his family had enjoyed visits to Sandringham House, his children paddling in the sea on the Norfolk coast. But in March, Tsar Nicholas II had been forced to abdicate by the rampaging Bolsheviks, having been dethroned by the Revolution in February, and growing labour unrest and the rise of socialism in Britain were a potential risk for the royal family.

Cook commented, 'I don't get involved with politics, but what I do know is that honest folk want to earn an honest wage and be able to put food on their tables, which is beyond the means of many at the moment.'

'We're all having to make do. But what choice do we 'ave? We can't let the Hun invade us.'

Cook wiped her hands on her apron. 'When will it all end? We are meat-eating people and all the substitutes in the world will not make up for the loss of beef and mutton. Mothers are going without to give their children what food they can. And paying more each time for it.'

Mrs Pennywick entered the kitchen then and sat with them at the table. 'You are correct, of course. I think it's commendable that our royal family are making sacrifices too by cutting back. Gone are the glory days of the lavish dinners and now they are eating much more frugally. The King says that his guests should be grateful for anything and he is keeping his word to refrain from alcohol while the war continues.'

Maria pulled a face. 'I can't wait for a good crusty loaf again. I'll never take to the heavy war bread, and neither will Joey.'

'How is young Joey doing now?' enquired the housekeeper.

'He's made a full recovery and I am planning to have him christened in the church later this month. I almost lost him and want to thank God for saving him.'

Cook raised an eyebrow. 'Excuse me for asking, but is that possible, seeing as he was born out of wedlock?'

Maria flushed. 'The vicar says it's up to his discretion. He asked the Bishop about it and 'e says the Lord forgives those that 'ave been sinned against, and that was me. I was sinned against.'

An awkward silence followed, broken by Mrs Pennywick. 'Of course you were. We are not here to judge you, my dear. What are your plans for the christening? Have you decided who Joey's godparents will be?'

'I've asked Aggie Greensticks, as she is very fond of Joey, and he of her, and I thought of asking Eddie and Mr Saward too. Aggie has accepted and I hope she will spend more time with us, especially now Magnolia has found a gentleman friend.'

Cook chortled. 'I never thought she had it in her, to find a nice gentleman like Mr Fellowes.'

'They appear very happy together. Mr Fellowes seems to be smitten with Magnolia and has given his dog to Joey as Magnolia has no liking for him, which is no surprise as she has a house full of cats.'

Cook clasped her hands in front of her chest. 'Well that says it all. I say good luck to them both. And, Maria, if you need a hand with food for your christening party, you've only to ask and I'll see what I can put together. It won't be anything fancy, mind you.'

Cook gathered the plates as Maria and Mrs Pennywick made haste to the royal rooms. A feather duster in her hand, Maria almost skipped along the corridor.

Could her life be any better, she wondered. She was reunited with Eddie, Joey was back to his old self and work was going well. Then she stopped in her tracks as she remembered Nellie.

When would she return to Wolferton for Lord Nelson's locket? And even though there'd been no sight of Gus, surely it was only a matter of time before he made his way to Wolferton. Maria shivered at this.

∞

Nellie announced that it was time for her to leave. She told Matilda, 'I've been here over a month now and need to return to Margate to sort out the paperwork regarding my legacy.'

'Why don't I come with you, pet?' offered Matilda. 'Some sea air would do me the world of good.'

They agreed to leave for the Kent coast in two days. Nellie accepted the offer of company gratefully, but her mind was also on Wolferton and she hoped Harry had managed to warn Ruth and Maria about Gus's plans to snatch Lord Nelson's locket.

She could still scarcely believe the wealth she suddenly had at her disposal. She had given it some thought and decided she would live in Aunt Millicent's house and reinstate the loyal Mrs Biggs as housekeeper. She planned to use her fortune to help young women in dire straits, as she had once been herself, and was still mulling over the details in her mind.

When the time came for Nellie to leave and she had packed her bags, she sighed deeply, taking one long last look at the room that had once been a welcome refuge. She straightened the embroidered 'Home Sweet Home' canvas framed on her wall and folded the bedlinen neatly at the end of the iron bed.

As she descended the stairs with her bag, she heard loud voices coming from the sitting room. Hearing Gus's name mentioned, she pressed her ear against the door.

'A grass told me Gus has been lying low with an associate, figuring he would stay in London until things quietened down as he knew we would be on the lookout for him in Wolferton. That's why there's been no sight of him there. But I'm reliably informed he's on his way there now.'

'Are you sure? We don't want to give Harry another false alarm,' Matilda pressed.

'This fella I know was told so by the landlord of The Black Cat. Gus owes the landlord a tidy sum and swore that he would clear his slate in the next few days, and give him a bonus on top.'

'How's he managing that?' asked Matilda. 'He doesn't have two pennies to rub together.'

'Gus told the landlord he was collecting a handsome reward any day for returning a valuable family heirloom to its rightful owner, and that he was on his way to Norfolk to seal the deal.'

Matilda fumed. 'The scoundrel! The locket is Nellie's by rights. He must be found as soon as possible to help clear Nellie's name.'

'It's best if we don't let Nellie know, it will only alarm her. I'll pass on word to Harry that Gus could be on his way at any moment and he can arrange for the police to lie in wait.'

'It's just as well we will soon be leaving for Margate. We'll be as far away from Wolferton as we can be,' Matilda replied.

Nellie stayed rooted on the spot, her mind in turmoil. Her visit to Margate no longer interested her, not if her father was heading for Wolferton. She knew she had to warn Maria and Ruth and prevent Gus from stealing the locket.

She stepped into the sitting room and pretended she knew nothing of their discussion. Matilda and Ronald exchanged glances and the room fell silent. Matilda pointed to the bag Nellie was clutching.

'It's not long now till we leave, pet. I must first look in on Flossie who has been poorly. She lives two streets away and I want to make sure she has everything she needs before I leave. I'll only be twenty minutes, then all being well we'll catch the 10.40 a.m. to Margate. I'm looking forward to a brisk walk on the beach.'

After Matilda left to see to her neighbour, Ronald told her, 'You take good care of yourself. I shall want to hear that you have arrived safely. I wish you every happiness and good fortune for the future, Nellie, and I'll be over to see you too once you have settled in.'

Nellie felt a lump rising in her throat. She threw her arms around Ronald's neck. 'You've been like the father I never had. I shall always remember what you have done for me.'

As she pulled away, her eyes lingered on the drawer of the dresser. It was open a couple of inches and she saw the stay busk inside. She had all but forgotten about it, and seeing it there that moment made her heart pound and beads of sweat dotted her forehead.

Alone in the house, Nellie paced around the room, wringing her hands in front of her. A voice in her heard warned her, leave it well alone.

Leave it well alone. It will only bring evil to those who possess it.

She pressed her hands to her head as another thought occurred. *I have to do something. I can't leave it here and put Matilda and Ronald at risk. I must take it and destroy it.*

In a lightning flash she snatched the object from the drawer and stuffed it into her bag. She fled out of the house without a backward glance, leaving the front door ajar.

I'm going to Wolferton. I have to stop Pa. Whatever he has planned, I must to stop him.

Chapter Thirty-Three

Gus leapt off the train as it began to slow down a mile outside Wolferton. He lost his footing and rolled along the grass bank, grabbing a large branch which was over-hanging. The branch snapped off and he rolled alongside the track, until finally stopping.

His face was unshaven, the beginnings of a beard show-ing, and his clothing was unwashed. He groaned, then pulled his black cap down over his face and hauled him-self up. His dark eyes searched furtively around, but there was nobody in sight. He brushed himself down and took a few steps, relieved he hadn't broken any bones. It was early morning, and as the clock struck seven times he sat under the tree and pondered his next move while munching a piece of stale bread that he retrieved from his pocket.

He was making a promise to himself that he would snatch the locket, claim the reward, and afterwards turn over a new leaf. He was too old for all the ducking and diving and running from the police, and wanted to live a quieter life. He was so deep in his own thoughts that he didn't hear footsteps approaching.

'Gus? Uncle Gus?'

Gus leapt up. He rubbed his hands over his moist eyes and scanned the face of the young fair-haired figure in front of him.

He edged backwards and said falteringly, 'I know you. Aren't you ...?'

The boy eyed him suspiciously. 'You look different with yer beard. What are you doing here?'

Gus scratched his head. 'Which one are yer? Is it Archie? Or Freddie?'

'I'm Archie. I can't believe it's you.'

'I was always getting you and yer brother mixed up. You've shot up since I last saw yer. How long ago was that? A couple of years?'

Archie wavered. 'You were horrid to us. You used to scare us. Does Ma know you're here?'

'No, she doesn't. But I should like to see 'er. She is me sister. How is she? I don't intend her any 'arm.'

'She's not in the best of health as her chest troubles her. I don't want yer to upset her or Maria, like before. I 'eard Ma talk about some terrible things you did to Nellie. They say you're a bad man, Gus Harper. That's what Ma says. I'm going to tell her you're here.'

Archie turned to flee but stopped, rooted to the spot, as he saw something. He pointed to the railway track. 'That large branch is covering the track, we have to move it quickly, before the next train comes and crashes into it. It could be derailed.'

'That must have been me. Quick, let's get down there and move it.'

Archie followed Gus along the steep bank and stopped abruptly. He pointed to an object further along the track, beyond the branch.

He cried, 'Uncle Gus, look, over there. It looks like a man's body.'

And then he yelped, a pained look on his face, as his foot caught under the side of the metal railway track. 'Ouch. I can't move. I must 'ave twisted me ankle.'

He attempted to get up, but fell again, wincing when he tried to put his weight on his injured ankle. Gus rushed to Archie's side and scooped him up, hauling him over his shoulder, walking a few steps and lying him down gently in a safe clearing further along the bank.

Gus screwed up his eyes and looked towards where Archie had pointed. 'Bugger me. I think yer right. I'll go down and look, but I'd better clear the branch first. There's no time to lose, this is a busy line.'

He darted fifty yards along the track and grabbed the branch, yanking it inch by inch until it was cleared from the track. He collapsed in a heap gasping for breath, his fore-head glistening. He mopped his brow with the back of his hand and glanced at Archie, who gave him the thumbs up.

He scurried a few yards further along the bank and reeled backwards when he saw the object that Archie had spotted. It was indeed a man's body. 'Poor bugger. How did he end up 'ere?' Gus asked himself.

He nudged the crumpled figure lying face up on the grass, but there was no response. Gus searched the man's jacket pocket and found a letter with a German name on the envelope. His eyes narrowed and he bit his lip. 'A German bastard, here in Wolferton,' he exclaimed. Was he a spy? He decided to conceal the man's possible German connections from Archie so as not to alarm him. He looked around for any other strangers lurking around, but saw nobody.

'Well, Fritz, or whatever yer call yerself, whatever filthy deeds yer were planning, you ain't going nowhere now, so yer can stay 'ere a bit longer till the police come.'

He rose as he saw grey clouds of smoke in the distance, coming closer and closer, the hiss of the steam engine louder and louder.

A thought flashed through Gus's head. All he need do was take a few steps onto the track and that would be the end of his worries. He would no longer have the police on his back or worry about his debts. And Nellie wouldn't have to deal with him anymore. He'd done so much wrong to that girl.

Should I end it all now and be reunited with my dear wife Maggie? My one true love.

He stepped towards the track, about to place a foot on the sleeper. Archie saw what his uncle was about to do. '*No!*' he screamed.

As the train passed him, Gus glanced at the window and stared in disbelief at a face staring straight at him.

Nellie! And to think just a second ago I wanted to end it all. He fell to his knees. *I shall do right for yer now, Nellie. I'm sorry for all the wrong I've done yer.*

☙

The porters at Wolferton Station rushed to the assistance of the Ladies Orchestra as they stepped onto the platform. Their cases containing their musical instruments were piled onto a luggage trolley. There were six musicians and Queen Alexandra had graciously offered the use of the royal retiring rooms ahead of their afternoon performance.

Nellie arrived in Wolferton on the same train. She recalled the fuss she had caused the last time she was there and hoped to avoid another scene. She mingled with the musicians as her eyes searched for Harry or Gus.

She saw the lady musicians enter the royal retiring rooms where, to their great surprise, Queen Alexandra was in her royal suite sitting on a sofa with Miss Knollys, sipping tea.

While Nellie paced anxiously along the platform, Sarah Saward was on hand in the retiring rooms, having closed the post office for lunch. Extra seating was hastily brought in from the King's suite of rooms to accommodate the group. They chatted as Sarah brought in two steaming pots of tea on a tray and an exquisite set of fine bone china cups and saucers decorated with pink and gold rosebuds, and a plateful of mouth-watering Empire biscuits that Betty had made the day before; two shortbread biscuits sandwiched together with jam and topped with icing and a glacé cherry.

As the orchestra were taking their refreshments, Nellie spotted a dark-green door with the sign 'Station Master' on it and knocked. The door was ajar and she walked in without waiting for a reply, glancing behind her.

Harry rose, astonished. 'Nellie? This is unexpected. Do Ronald and Matilda know you're here?'

She shook her head. 'I came 'ere without telling them. I had to be here, in case Pa . . .'

Harry offered her a seat. 'I know what you're going to say, that Gus is on his way here. Ronald called to tell me and Police Constable Rickett is on the lookout for him. I'm afraid the police couldn't spare any more men, but I've made my staff aware. If he is here in Wolferton, he will be found and handed over to the police.'

Nellie slumped into a chair. 'You won't hurt him, will you? I know he has to answer to the law, but he's still my pa. What do yer think will happen to him?'

Harry spoke softly. 'You've a soft heart, Nellie, after everything that's happened, but the law will take its course. Ronald told me everything that happened to you, but that's in the past now. With your inheritance, once your name is cleared you will be a woman of substantial means and have a chance to make a new life for yourself.'

'It's all come so unexpectedly. All I can think of now is my father. Please promise no one will hurt him. That's all I ask. I know he's done some awful things, but he wasn't always like this.'

'Very well, I give you my word. We must hope he doesn't resist arrest once he is apprehended.'

Nellie lowered her eyes. 'I understand. I must go and see Aunt Ruth and retrieve my locket. She has been so kind looking after it for me.'

'Ah, well, there's something you need to know. After you left the locket with Ruth she brought it to me and asked if I would keep it for you, knowing it has a high value. I have it here, in my office safe. I believe there is a reward for its return. If that's the case, and it can be proven this other person who states it is theirs is the rightful owner, you will have to give it up. They will want to know how it came to be in your possession and trace its origins back to the shop in Margate where you say it was purchased. Going back over this chain of events will help clear your name, as I'm sure the shop would have kept paperwork showing your Aunt Millicent purchased it from there. Can I suggest I keep it here until this is all clarified?'

'I think that would be for the best. I don't want it if it was taken from someone else. It makes sense now why Pa wanted it so much, he wants to claim the reward.'

'I'd better let Ronald know you are here.' Harry telephoned him at the police station. 'I see,' Harry muttered. 'Very well, thank you for letting me know.'

When he replaced the phone he told Nellie, 'Ronald is on his way here now. He's been very worried about you after you disappeared without a word.' Harry's eyes narrowed. 'Now it's my turn to ask you to make a promise.'

'What's that?'

'That you won't do anything foolish if you see Gus. Let me know the moment you see him.'

'I promise,' she said. 'I'm sorry for any trouble I have caused. I'll keep out of everyone's way. I would like to call in on Aunt Ruth and later I will return to London with Ronald.'

'That sounds an excellent idea. Hopefully this trouble will be over then,' Harry said, walking to the door with her.

Nellie stepped outside and pressed her back against the wall.

Please forgive me, Mr Saward, but I couldn't hand in my father. I couldn't tell you he's here already. I couldn't tell you I've seen him.

Chapter Thirty-Four

Archie winced, his twisted ankle making him cry out. 'It's no good. I'm never going to make it.'

'Just lean on me. It's best not to put any weight on it,' Gus told him. 'Where were yer off to anyway?'

Archie pointed to a building in the distance. 'Across that field, see, that's Blackbird Farm. Lizzie will be wondering where I am.'

'I can take you there if you like, or back home so yer can rest it. That ankle is going to swell and be sore in the next few hours.'

Archie eyed him suspiciously. 'I want to go home, though I'm not sure what Ma will say when she sees yer.'

'Don't worry, I won't come in. I'll just get yer back there.'

Only a few minutes before Gus had been on the brink of death. He'd closed his eyes as he stood on the track, wishing for an instant release from his torment. *Can bad men like me ever be good?* he had asked himself.

He recalled the words Maggie had spoken to him before she died. *It's time for you to be the father you were meant to be.* He realised in that moment that he wanted to live, and be a proper father to Nellie, if she would let him.

Would she ever forgive him for the despicable way he had behaved towards her?

Gus had come back to his senses and opened his eyes just in time. After hearing Archie's cry he leapt off the track with just a fleeting few seconds to spare before the train shot past. As he stared up at the train, he saw a girl's face staring out of her carriage window. She'd caught his gaze and their eyes locked. She pressed her cheek against the glass as the train passed him and looked back as he faded from view, suddenly recognising the figure. She mouthed the word, *Father*.

Gus had felt a shiver run along his spine and broke out in a cold sweat. Seeing Nellie on the train, his mind was made up. Even if she wanted to wash her hands of him, he would feel better for trying to make amends, and would turn himself in to receive his punishments.

Archie interrupted his thoughts. 'You did a good job there, clearing the branch in time, Uncle Gus. I hate to think what would have happened if you hadn't.'

It gladdened his heart that instead of being a villain he was now a hero in Archie's eyes, and his words made him feel as if he had been reborn.

Gus held out his hand. 'It was nothing. Now come on, we can get to yer house if we take it easy. Keep all yer weight on me.'

'What about the man you found on the bank? What do yer think happened to him?' Archie asked.

'I dunno. Don't think wrong of me, but seeing as he is dead, there's nowt we can do and I don't want to get involved. It ain't nothing to do with me, and you can bear witness to that. Can I rely on you to report it as soon as you're home?'

'I will, Uncle Gus. Poor man, I don't like leaving him there like that, even if he is dead.'

Archie's face was pained as he took hold of Gus's outstretched hand. He managed to get upright and hobbled on one leg.

'Now take it easy. Just one step at a time. Put your arm around my shoulder. You'll have to tell me the way.'

Archie did as instructed. 'Why are you doing this for me? Why are you being, well, nice?'

'I gave you and yer brother an 'ard time in the past, and I'm sorry for it. You're a good lad, and I want to make up for the bad way I treated yer. Will that do you?'

After hobbling for twenty minutes, they stopped. Archie pointed. 'There, that's the lane to our house.'

'I'll leave you here then. I'm afraid I need to be getting on me way now. If you take it slowly, you should be able to get back in one piece.'

'Won't yer come in? Ma will want to thank yer. She'll be over the moon to know you are changing your old ways.'

Gus shook his head. He now needed to find Nellie. 'Nah, I'm sorry, lad, I'll see her next time I'm here. I'm a wanted man and I don't want to put 'er in a difficult position. Don't forget to report the man's body. As you spotted it, let's keep matters simple and leave it at that. I'd best be on my way now.'

Gus placed Archie down carefully, leaning him against a fence. He found a branch, strong enough to act as a walking stick. He broke off the leaves and tested it for its strength.

'This should get yer home. If by any chance you should come across Nellie, will you give her a message?'

Archie hobbled up, standing on his good leg, supported by the stick. 'Nellie ain't here, is she? But I can tell 'er if I see her.'

'Tell her her pa is sorry for what he's done and he's going to put matters right.'

Archie looked solemn. 'I'll tell her, though I don't know when I'll see her. Can you tell me where you are going now?'

'I'm going to take the train back to London and give meself up to Ronald Saward. I've caused enough trouble.'

Archie watched Gus walk off until he turned the corner and vanished from sight. Ruth was in the garden hanging out the washing when he hobbled up to the gate.

'Ma, you'll never believe who I've been with. And I found a dead man's body on the bank by the railway track.'

The words tumbled out of his mouth as she helped him inside the cottage and he collapsed onto a chair. 'You're telling me Gus is here? And you found a man's body? Whatever are yer talking about? We must inform Police Constable Rickett.'

A voice in the corner shrieked, 'No. Please don't do that. Let me see him first.'

Archie's eyes narrowed. 'Nellie?'

'From what you have recounted my father did you a good deed. Not only that, but he saved many lives on that train. It could have derailed if he hadn't removed the branch. I was on that train, along with a group of lady musicians from London. We owe our lives to Pa.'

Ruth gesticulated with her hands. 'I don't know what to do. You say he's going to give himself up? Can we believe him?'

'He says he's changing his old ways and had a message for you, Nellie.'

She grabbed his arm. 'Tell me, what did he say?'

'He said to tell you he's sorry for what he's done to yer. And he's going to put matters right.'

Nellie's eyes moistened and she fought back tears. She picked up her bag, walked to the front door and opened it.

Ruth tried to stop her saying, 'But you've only just arrived.'

'I'm going to look for him. I must find my father,' said Nellie, a determined look on her face.

Chapter Thirty-Five

A sea of new faces, broken limbs and minds, awaited Dr Butterscotch at Hillington Hall. He examined Alfie, who could only recall a fierce succession of explosions and gunfire as he fell to the ground, landing hard on his left side. An injured comrade fell on top of him, his full weight landing on Alfie's head – and then there was blackness. Alfie had been lying there, covered by a corpse, for two days until soldiers searching for survivors saw his fingers move.

Sitting in a chair by the side of his bed, Alfie told the doctor, 'The next thing I recall was waking up in the field hospital. I have the poor blighter on top of me to thank for my life as his body gave me the cover I needed, though I didn't realise it at the time.'

'You were most fortunate, and it's a good sign that you are beginning to recall what happened. Your arm needs resetting, I'm afraid they didn't do the best of jobs in that field hospital. Fortunately, your eye has not been damaged after that wound on the front of your head. Concussion is common when you lose consciousness, and it can affect your memory but it should only last a few weeks. It sounds like you are making improvements there, but I'd like to keep you under observation for a while as concussion can cause temporary disruption to brain function. If you continue to make good progress, which I'm hopeful you will now you are back in old Blighty, then I can discharge you into the care of your wife.'

Alfie beamed. 'I can't thank you enough, Doctor. I was so disorientated when I arrived. I feel a world of difference being back in England.'

The doctor smiled. 'Promise me one thing. When you are back on your feet you will invite me to hear you play. I believe you are quite the musician.'

'So I will still be able to play? I'm so relieved. I would be delighted if you could join me at my next performance, and Matron too. In fact, I would like to hold a concert for everyone here, as soon as my arm heals and I feel I can recall the notes well.'

'Of course you will, just give it time. All being well, there's no reason why your fingers shouldn't glide along the ivory keys like an old pro again.'

Beatrice approached Alfie after the doctor had finished with him. 'Judging by the look on your face, all went well?'

'That's right. I'm one of the lucky ones. When can Ada and Leslie visit? I hope I didn't scare my boy at the station.'

'Of course you didn't. Leslie can't stop talking about you. We are all so happy you are home again. Ada and Leslie can come on Sunday, but I can let her know your good news in the meantime. She'll be thrilled.'

'I've missed them both so much. I am so looking forward to seeing them.'

'Today we have a new welfare clinic for infants opening in Wolferton and Ada will be there. A group of lady musicians from London are playing. It's quite a coup for us.'

Alfie squeezed Beatrice's hand. 'When you see Ada, tell her I love her. Tell Leslie his old man will soon be playing cricket with him.'

George Perryman walked past at that moment, holding on to his cane for support. 'Did someone mention cricket? Alas, that is one activity I leave for others.'

Beatrice felt a fluttering sensation inside her at hearing his voice. She introduced George to Alfie. Although they had never met before, they chatted away as if they had known each other for years.

Beatrice smiled at their easy comradeship and spotted Alfie wink at her while George turned his head.

Matron approached and scolded, 'This isn't visiting day. Nurse Saward, please attend to your duties elsewhere.'

George smiled sheepishly. 'May I say how very charming you look today, Nurse Saward?'

Beatrice giggled behind her hand and went to change a dressing, her mind on George and the feelings she was developing for him.

∞

The Ladies Orchestra were smartly attired in black skirts, crisp white blouses and small black bow ties. They were positioned at the front of the meeting room with their string instruments in position, four playing the violin, one the viola and another the cello. The seats in the audience rapidly filled with mothers from the royal estate. They chatted among themselves as they waited for the event to begin.

'Have you heard any news about the Sandringham Company?' one woman whispered to her friend next to her.

'Not a word. I was in the family way when they disappeared, and it doesn't look like Emily will ever get to meet her father. It's a struggle just to get by.'

Her friend replied, 'How can we keep hoping they're still alive?'

'I've resigned meself to the worst. My Emily deserves a good start in life, that's why I'm 'ere today.'

'As long as this doesn't cost us. I don't have a spare farthing at the end of the week.'

Aggie and Mrs Herring had offered to take charge of some of the younger children in a side room. Wooden building blocks, puzzles and some books were provided to keep the children entertained. Leslie was in his element playing with the other children, teasing Joey, who gripped his toy soldiers tightly, refusing to share.

Suddenly there was a pause in the music as the doors opened and everyone rose. Heads spun around as Queen Alexandra entered the room, her head held high, followed by her lady-in-waiting, Miss Knollys.

When they were seated, Miss Knollys whispered to Lady Appleby, who was seated across the aisle with Ada. 'Queen Mary sends her regrets. She is visiting a munition factory in Norwich today. Women there are doing a splendid job.'

'So I've heard, and some of the work can be quite dangerous too,' replied Lady Appleby.

Lady Appleby gave the orchestra the nod and they started playing. The musicians began playing movements by Elgar and Mozart and their performance had the audience spellbound. They included a few jaunty tunes from Gilbert and Sullivan too.

As the music finished and everyone was seated, the door creaked open. Everyone's head turned once again as Dr Butterscotch entered the room, closing the door noisily behind him. Lady Appleby rose and beckoned the latecomer to join her at the front.

'We are most fortunate to have Dr Butterscotch with us for a short time. He will speak now, explaining how we can all help the prevention of disease in infants.'

You could hear a pin drop as the doctor spoke. He commended Lady Appleby and the women of Wolferton for being at the forefront of action to give their children long and healthy lives. When he finished, he was given a rousing applause.

He made a polite excuse to leave and returned to the hospital. Another speaker followed, an eloquent woman from London who said she was pressing the government to introduce formal midwifery training. Finally, a stout authoritative woman, with a loud voice, demanded that slums should be demolished. She pronounced that babies of today deserved better homes and urged women to support her protest.

As the meeting drew to a close, Lady Appleby thanked everyone for attending and repeated her call for free child care in Great Britain, like they have in New Zealand.

A rapturous applause followed and the Ladies Orchestra took to their instruments for their final piece, playing a composition by Strauss. Lady Appleby thanked them warmly at the end, telling the audience that each member of the orchestra was a mother who passionately supported the cause. Ada glanced across at Her Majesty and thought she saw her nod approvingly as the speakers made their comments. The Queen had stayed longer than expected and Ada took that as an encouraging sign.

With the formalities over and a rousing rendition of National Anthem finishing the afternoon's programme, Leslie was allowed to rush into the meeting room. He found his mother talking to Emily's ma and her friend. He tugged impatiently at her skirt. 'Mama, please can we visit Papa.'

Emily's mother said, 'I heard your husband was home. I'm so happy for yer, Ada.'

'Still no news of Tom?'

Emily's mother shook her head. 'No. Nothing.'

Ada placed a hand on her shoulder. 'I'm so sorry to hear this. Tom is a good man. If there's anything I can do . . .'

'Come on,' urged her friend, placing her hand on her arm. 'Let's get out of here. Yer Emily's by the door. These are just a bunch of do-gooders here. They don't know what it's like to be down to yer last farthing.'

Affronted, Ada replied, 'I meant what I said. I'll help you if I can, just let me know. Today's meeting is the start of giving every baby the chance of a longer and healthier life.'

∞

Nellie hot-footed it back to Wolferton Station and arrived panting. She nodded at the porter, who stared at her curiously. She could see no sign of Harry or Ronald and she paused as she reached some sheds at the furthest end of the platform. One of the doors was slightly ajar so she looked in and jumped back when she heard a sound.

'Psst. Over here.'

She stepped inside and heard the sound again. She looked around. 'Pa?'

She barely recognised Gus as he stepped out from behind a pile of glistening coke. His face was covered in soot.

'Pa! I can't believe it's you. I heard you were coming to Wolferton. I came here looking for yer.'

Without a care for his filthy state, she threw her arms around his neck. It had been a spontaneous reaction, with no thought of the appalling way he had treated her.

Gus's eyes were moist. He stroked her hair and his voice wobbled. 'Oh Nellie. What terrible trouble 'ave I caused yer? How can yer be so kind as to hug me as if yer really cared? I don't deserve it. I've been rotten to you, to Doris who deserved better, and even me sister's own boys.'

The words stuck in Nellie's throat as she fished out a handkerchief from her pocket. 'Stop crying, Pa, else yer'll set me off. Of course I love yer. Yer me pa.'

'I don't deserve yer love, Nellie, but I'll make it up to yer, I promise. I'll say anything to get yer out of this trouble that I caused.'

They embraced again. Nellie pulled away and asked, 'I saw yer from the train, Father. I thought I saw a man's body nearby. Was that right?'

'That were nothing to do with me. I just found him lying there, I cross me heart. Archie spotted him and he is letting the police know. He can vouch that I had nothing to do with his death. The truth is, I came here to snatch the locket and claim the reward, but I've changed me mind. I don't want that kind of life anymore. I'm done with running away. I'm handing meself in to the police.'

Nellie's face showed concern. 'Oh, Father, you will go to prison, for sure. When it's all done, we can start afresh. Will yer come and live with me in Margate? Aunt Millicent has left me her home and everything. We can be together and you'll never 'ave to worry about money again. I'll have enough for us both.'

Gus's eyes moistened. 'I don't deserve yer kindness. You take after yer ma, she had a kind heart.'

'Uncle Ronald is on his way here, Pa. Harry told me.'

'Before I see them, there's something I need to give you.'

He fished into his pocket and produced a crumpled piece of paper. 'Read this and hang on to it. It's about the locket. The rightful owner is offering £100 reward for its return. I was planning to claim it after returning it to them, but I want nothing to do with it anymore. Maybe you can return it to them.'

Nellie took the paper and placed it in her pocket without reading it. 'That's not important now. Cedric Parker is being pursued by police for forging wills and he made up a pack of lies about me stealing the locket. I am happy for it to be returned to its rightful owner as it has caused me nothing but trouble. I can't tell you how happy I am that you are giving yourself up, Pa.'

Gus lowered his eyes. 'I'm truly sorry for everything I did to yer, and to Stanley too. I've been a right monster.'

'Everyone deserves a second chance, Pa. As Stanley is still alive, you won't face a murder charge. I've told Ronald I have no intentions of pressing charges against you or Doris for my imprisonment. Your sentence may not be as harsh as you believe, especially if the court sees you are a changed man and that I am standing by you.'

Gus looked a pitiful figure. He sat on a pile of coke and placed his head in his blackened hands. Nellie rooted around in her bag and brought out a handkerchief. Gus blew soot into it and mumbled incoherently. Nellie made out her mother's name between sniffles. She could scarcely believe that the man who had once been such a cruel bully was now snivelling in front of her.

'We can't let Ronald and Harry see you in this filthy state. If you follow me, I know somewhere you can tidy yerself up.'

Gus rose obediently and shook the soot off his clothing. She stared at the broken man before her. She asked falteringly, 'Tell me, Pa. Do you really mean what you say, about wanting to change?'

'I do, and I don't blame you for doubting me. I'm an old dog now. A foolish old dog who has come to his senses.'

'It's never too late to change. Just think, you're a hero. You saved the train from derailing and crashing down the bank. You saved my life, the women from the orchestra and dozens more and I'll make sure I tell the police. That should stand you in good stead when you go to court.'

She tentatively poked her head out of the shed and glanced in both directions. A handful of passengers stood a few feet away, chatting idly, but nobody was looking in their direction. It was a thirty-foot dash to the royal retiring rooms where she had spotted a lamp glowing on a table in front of the window. If they were in luck, the room might still be unlocked.

'Come on, let's go.'

She grabbed his hand and they sprinted across the platform, ducking under cover of the entrance that separated the King's royal retiring rooms side from the Queen's suite of waiting rooms.

Gus stared in disbelief. 'What are yer doing? We shouldn't be in 'ere.'

He stared in amazement at the finery around him. The old Gus would have been tempted to slip a few of the precious objects into his pocket. 'Are these the Queen's waiting rooms? I don't want to be done for treason too.'

'Shush. You can clean yerself up here. Just hurry,' Nellie urged, placing her bag on the floor. 'I'll see what toiletries I have in me bag for yer.'

She fished out a bar of cold tar soap and a flannel and handed them to Gus.

'I can't use the Queen's towels.' He said. 'Have you got something in your bag that will do instead?'

Before she could answer, Gus had grabbed the bag from Nellie and fished around inside, but as he did so he tripped over Tommy, the station cat, who had emerged from the corner of the room. Gus produced an object from the bag as he fell sideways, catching his foot on the table in front of the window, hitting his head on the corner of the table and, sending the gas lamp on the table flying.

Flames instantly burst out from the lamp and Nellie stared in horror as they quickly made their way up the bottom of the velvet curtains and spread upwards.

She pulled at Gus's arm. 'Pa, get up. Please, please, get up. We have to get out of here and raise the alarm.'

Gus lay on the carpet motionless, his eyes were fixed wide open staring up at the ceiling. In his hand he gripped the stay busk. Nellie took it from his hand and threw it into the flames. 'That's put an end to the curse,' she cried. 'I wish I'd never set eyes on it.'

Very quickly the fire spread to the sofa and the room filled with acrid smoke. She pounded on Gus's chest, begging him to get up, but there was no response.

'I'm not leaving you here to die,' she choked, grabbing his legs and dragging him towards the door. His weight was too much for her. Her lungs filled with smoke and she staggered over. She heard Harry shout her name and her eyes closed as she collapsed and drifted into unconsciousness.

Chapter Thirty-Six

The following day, Harry surveyed the damage inside the Queen's suite of retiring rooms. His expression was grim. How had Gus and Nellie managed to gain access to the Queen's private rooms? And why was the gas lamp left on? His neck would be on the block.

Ronald, who had arrived from London was there with him. 'The estate manager says we saved it just in the nick of time. If it wasn't for the quick thinking of the porter spotting them going in and the fire brigade's swift arrival from Sandringham House, it could have been much worse,' Harry said.

'Thank goodness they did. I hope it can be restored,' Ronald replied.

Harry stroked his moustache and looked closely. 'Fortunately, only one side of the panelled walls were burnt, and the furniture that was destroyed was not of significant value. We were able to retrieve family portraits and valuable objects. The carpet will need replacing and the rooms will need a good airing to clear them of the foul stench of smoke.'

'If only I'd got here earlier. Maybe I could have reached Nellie and Gus and prevented this,' Ronald replied, holding his head in his hands.

'What's done is done. Her Majesty is furious and wants to know how two uninvited guests gained access to her private rooms. I will have some explaining to do as I have no idea myself.'

'I don't envy you that, Harry. How is Nellie?' enquired Ronald.

'She was still unconscious when I left a moment ago. It's touch and go. How terrible this whole business has been, after everything she's been through.'

Ronald shook his head. 'Matilda is beside herself with worry and wants to come here. I need to get word to her. Seeing as there's nothing more we can do here for the moment, can I suggest we return to your house and see if there is any change in Nellie's condition?'

They returned to the station master's house where Ada was sitting with Nellie. She had been carried there on a stretcher by railway staff and laid gently on the padded sofa in the airy parlour.

As they stepped into the room Nellie's eyes fluttered open.

'Nellie,' Ada whispered. 'Would you like a drink of water?'

Nellie blinked as she stared at the stranger's face. 'Who are you? Where am I?'

'Shush now, take a sip of water. Gently now.'

Ada propped a cushion behind Nellie's back. Nellie took a few sips of water, her eyes looking around the room.

She jerked. 'The fire. What 'appened to Pa?'

Ronald stepped forward. 'Thank goodness you've come round. You had us all worried, Nellie.'

'Ronald? Why are you here? Will someone tell me what's appened?'

Ada soothed, 'Shush now, Nellie. You mustn't overly excite yourself.'

Ronald knelt beside her and whispered, 'I'm sorry, Nellie. But your father . . . I'm afraid he died.'

Nellie cried, 'Oh no. It's my fault. I took the stay busk. It was cursed. That's why the fire happened. That's why Pa is dead.'

Harry shook his head. 'Stay busk? I know nothing of that. I can tell you Dr Fletcher came straightaway. He thinks Gus had a heart attack. I'm sorry, Nellie.'

Nellie whimpered, 'A heart attack? My poor father, dead? Just as he was going to give himself up. We were planning a new life together once he'd served his time.'

'I'm afraid there was nothing you could have done. He didn't die as a result of the fire. His heart could have stopped at any time,' Ronald consoled.

Nellie sobbed. 'Father wasn't all bad. He was a good man once and wanted to be good again.'

'I'm sorry for your loss Nellie. We saw today that he had a good side to him. There's something else,' said Harry.

'Thanks to Archie, we alerted police to the body on the bank. They confirmed he was a German spy.'

'Is that the man Pa saw?' she asked tentatively.

Harry nodded. 'It is believed he had plans to derail the train by shooting at the driver in the belief that the King and Queen were travelling on it. In fact, they arrived on an earlier train. It's usual for decoy trains to be announced, and this man, Klaus Schmidt, was unaware of this. Thanks to Gus and Archie, the lives of dozens of innocent people were saved. Your father was a hero, Nellie.'

Harry continued, 'According to Dr Fletcher the German had advanced cancer and died from natural causes. If he hadn't died then, he would have faced the firing squad.'

Harry smiled. 'Nellie, His Majesty would like to award a posthumous honour to Gus for his part in averting a major disaster on the royal estate. Would you like to accept it on his behalf?'

Tears streamed down Nellie's cheeks. 'I'd be honoured. I think he would like his sister to be there with me.'

∽

When Jessie and Lizzie heard of Klaus's death and his true identity they were shocked to the core.

'Can you be a good, loving father and a spy?' Jessie asked.

'Only an English one. I don't think we should tell anyone how he came to us. We'd be scorned for the rest of our lives, or worse, if they accuse us of harbouring a German spy.'

They swore each other to secrecy, mortified they had been taken in by a smooth talking elderly German.

They discovered that although it was true Helga had been a much-loved servant of Queen Alexandra, her father had died when she was a child. Klaus Schmidt was one of the most wanted German spies, his advancing years and frail demeanour being part of his cover story.

∽

A week had passed since the blaze. Ronald had returned to the station master's house and was sitting in the parlour. Nellie was there with him. She had almost made a full recovery and was planning to leave Wolferton in a couple of days.

Harry leapt up at the sound of the door knocker. 'Ah, that will be Lady Appleby.'

Nellie rose as the visitor swept into the room wafting of lavender toilet water.

'I don't understand, why do yer want me to see this lady?' Nellie asked.

'I was wondering the same,' replied Lady Appleby, taking the seat indicated by Harry.

The station master produced a small box. 'I believe you recognise this, Nellie? It was left in my safe keeping, if you recall.'

Harry opened the ebony box with a shiny gold clasp and held up the locket. Lady Appleby stared in astonishment as he opened it to reveal the fragment of greying hair with a hint of auburn cut from Admiral Lord Nelson's head on his deathbed. 'That's mine. I never thought I would see it again. How did it come to be in your possession?'

Nellie was astonished. 'It's yours? I had no idea. Aunt Millicent gave it to me for my last birthday and I treasure it.'

'It's most definitely mine. It is the only one of its kind. May I enquire, where did your aunt purchase it from?' asked Lady Appleby.

'From a pawn shop by the seafront in Margate. How come if it belongs to you it ended up in Margate? I don't understand.'

'It was stolen from me by a butler years ago. I believe he has family there. We could never prove it was him, alas, and the last I heard he was in France. We are distant descendants on Lady Hamilton's side. The lock was cut by one of Lord Nelson's seamen and given to her. She kept this with her to her dying day. It's such a treasured possession. After I noticed it was missing, we offered a reward, but nothing has been heard about it, until now.'

Ronald held up a crumpled piece of paper. Nellie nodded, lowering her gaze. 'Father gave this to me. He was planning to claim the reward but had a change of heart and asked me to give the locket back to its rightful owner. I didn't know it belonged to you, Lady Appleby, I swear. I never knew.'

'I believe you, Nellie.' She smiled, placing her hand on Nellie's arm.

Nellie's heart pounded. 'I'm not a thief, I swear I didn't know.'

Lady Appleby announced, 'I owe you an apology, Nellie.'

'Me?' she queried. 'You ain't done me wrong.'

'I may have done, without realising. You see, it was me who hired the private detective. We had just discovered from the shop in Margate where the locket had changed hands and he tracked you down. It was my instruction to recover the locket from you without any fuss, and to recompense you for having to give it up. But it became complicated after these other charges were made against you, though my primary interest was the return of the locket. The detective felt it would further his career if the case against you escalated and he became overenthusiastic. I hear he made quite a scene at the station, but it was never my intention to prosecute you.'

Ronald raised a hand. 'So you see, Nellie, it's all been taken care of. The charge of theft has been dropped. I will arrange for you to meet the police inspector and discuss the outstanding charges. I'm sure they'll be dropped against you. Harold mentioned that the family knows a very good lawyer, someone by the name of George Perryman, who will be able to represent you. There will be a court hearing for all the charges against you to be dropped, so it will just be a formality. I will be there by your side.'

Nellie stuttered, 'So I will be able walk with my head held high again?'

'You will indeed,' chorused Lady Appleby and Harry.

Ronald added, 'There's more, Nellie. These letters came for you.'

He handed over two letters. Her heart pounded as she ripped open the first. She glanced up. 'It's from Stanley, I recognise his writing.'

Her bottom lip trembled as she read the words on the page. She placed the letter in her lap when she was finished and stared at Ronald. Her voice wobbled. 'He says he believes me, he knows I had nothing to do with throwing him in the river and insists no charges are brought against me.'

'So your name is cleared?' Harry asked.

'I think so. Stanley wants a divorce and will give me a generous settlement. It seems he has met another lady closer to his age who is the mother of his daughter's friend. He wants to forget what happened and start afresh. He says there are no hard feelings.'

'Well that's good news, surely? Why do you look so glum?' asked Ronald.

'Because Stanley is a good man and didn't deserve any of this. I'm pleased though that he has found someone who truly loves him.'

Her hand shook as she held up the second letter. 'I think it's from Adam, but it doesn't have a stamp,' she whispered. 'I don't have the courage to open it.'

'But you must. He is a fine, upstanding man,' Ronald said gently.

'How do yer know?' asked Nellie, perplexed.

'Matilda took it upon herself to write to him after the fire. He called straight round to our house as he was on leave and she told him everything that had happened. He declared his love for you, and Matilda was quite overcome with emotion by his concern for you.

'He asked for a pen and paper and wrote to you from our house, expecting you to read it on your return. But as I am back here now, I brought it with me.'

Nellie slid her finger along the opening of the envelope. Her eyes shone as she started reading. 'He says he misses me. He wants to see me again. He believes I am a good-hearted person and will wait until I am free to marry properly.'

'Well this calls for a celebratory drink,' chortled Harry.

'Indeed it does,' chorused Lady Appleby.

EPILOGUE

As Maria prepared for Joey's christening, news about the fate of scores of men from the royal estate was still unknown, two years after the fierce battle in Gallipoli.

Harry insisted that on this day of Joey's christening, they should not dwell on the uncertainty.

Reverend Rumbelow stood at the church entrance waiting for Maria to arrive with Joey. Jessie had decorated the church with a colourful blaze of carnations, lilies, roses and delphiniums from the garden at the station master's house.

Aggie had already arrived and was sitting in the front row. Harry and Eddie were alongside her.

'I feel so honoured. I've never been a godmother before,' gushed Aggie.

'Me neither,' added Eddie, who arrived at the church without the aid of crutches. 'Well, godfather, that is.'

Magnolia reached over from the pew behind where she sat with David and whispered, 'He is a lucky lad indeed to have you. You'll be a good influence on him.'

Eddie blushed. 'I feel choked up. I'm so happy for Maria.'

Mrs Pennywick had managed to take the Sunday afternoon off and sat with Mrs Herring and Betty. 'It makes such a pleasant change to attend a christening rather than a funeral,' she muttered. 'We've had far too many of them.'

Nellie, Ronald and Matilda were there too, sitting close to Archie and Freddie. Beatrice had special permission to attend, promising to make up the time at the hospital, and was accompanied by George Perryman, who could barely keep his eyes off her. Ada and an unusually quiet Leslie made up the Saward family, and Ada reflected on how wonderful it would have been if Alfie could have joined them at this happy family gathering. All being well, he would soon be fit enough to return home. Sarah sat on the other side of Leslie, retrieving his stuffed bear as it slipped to the ground.

The larks soared overhead in the clear blue sky as Maria stepped onto the church path, her mother walking alongside her, gripping Joey's wriggling hand. Maria's hair hung loose down the back of her white dress with a pretty pale blue bow tied at the waist and she radiated an inner glow. Ruth had brushed up well in her Sunday best plum skirt, which she teamed with a cream blouse.

Joey tugged at his mother's hand. 'Let me go, I'll walk proper.' His hair was neatly brushed into a side parting and with his sapphire blue eyes and cherubic cheeks, and wearing a sailor suit that had been loaned to Maria by Ada, he looked every inch a young prince.

Maria felt a lump rising in her throat as she walked along the aisle, the organist raising his pitch as he played 'Lord of All Hopefulness'. She spotted Aggie, Harry and Eddie sitting at the front and they smiled encouragingly at her, giving a little wave to Joey. Ruth and Maria slid into the front pew on the other side of the aisle. Reverend Rumbelow smiled kindly in her direction. Maria listened entranced to the words of the christening service, her heart fit to burst. She was one of the Sawards, accepted and loved by the royal station master and his family, it was everything she had dreamt of.

Joey began to fidget with his shoes trying to remove them. Maria lifted him onto her lap and whispered into his ears, 'Shush. This is yer special day. Show everyone what a good boy you are.'

The godparents were invited to stand by the font at the back of the church, its elaborate wooden carved cover gifted by the parish of Wolferton in commemoration of Queen Victoria's golden jubilee in 1887, placed carefully on the side.

Joey wriggled when Maria passed him over to the vicar. He soothed him by allowing Joey to splash his hands in the water, scooping some up himself in a small silver bowl to dribble over the top of Joey's head. He read out the solemn words, saying slowly, 'I hereby name you Joey Harry Jack Saward, Amen.'

The godparents held Joey in turn in their arms and repeated the godparents' oath, then returned to their seats for prayers and finished by singing 'All Creatures Great and Small' with great gusto.

Maria and Eddie led the party out of the church, allowing Joey to run ahead of them. Maria laughed at Eddie's slow pace. He no longer needed his crutches to steady him, but still couldn't move quickly.

Eddie couldn't hold in his feelings for Maria. 'I've never seen you look so pretty, Maria Saward. I'll always be there for Joey, you know that, don't yer?'

'I do. I have to pinch meself how well everything has turned out. It's impossible to believe that I can be so contented here in this small green corner of Norfolk while the battlefields are stained red with blood, and while so many of our Sandringham Company are still unaccounted for. I feel guilty for feeling so happy.'

Eddie told her. 'Don't ever feel guilty for feeling happy. You deserve every happiness that comes your way.'

He shuffled his feet. 'Maria, there's something I have to tell you. I'm returning to my regiment tomorrow. I've been signed off by the doctor as fit to fight. I'll be posted overseas again. I don't know when I'll see you again, or Joey.'

Maria gasped. 'Oh, surely not so soon, Eddie.'

'I'm afraid so, Maria.'

She linked her arm in his. 'I shall miss you, Eddie Herring, and Joey will too. Please promise me you'll come back home in one piece. Don't go getting yourself shot again.'

'I promise I won't. And I promise you the next time I come home you will walk down the aisle as my bride. If you want to, that is?'

Maria flung her arms around his neck, her heart pounding so hard she felt it was going to burst from her chest. Streaming tears trickled down her cheeks. Eddie gently wiped them dry with his hand and raised her chin, their eyes locking.

'Don't cry, Maria. This is Joey's special day. And it is one I will remember when I'm lying in a filthy field in a foreign land. Your sweet face, your love and knowing you are waiting for me will give me the strength to take on anything.'

'I didn't know such happiness existed.'

'You deserve it more than anybody, my sweetheart. Come on, we'd better hurry along and join the others.'

Maria linked arms with Eddie and noticed everyone else had walked ahead, leaving them to talk alone. Harry and Sarah led the procession back to their house where tea and cakes were prepared for the christening celebration. Ada and Jessie rushed ahead to make sure everything was in order at the house. Lady Appleby and Nellie followed, chatting amiably to Ronald and Matilda. Maria's brothers chided each other over a girl one of them was keen on, while Betty, Mrs Herring and Mrs Pennywick cooed over what a wonderful service it had been.

Aggie kept a close watch on Lesley and Joey, who were playing tag, while Magnolia and David happily strolled arm in arm. Magnolia giggled girlishly at something David whispered to her and had never seemed happier. Beatrice and George stood close together under a tree staring intently into each other's eyes as George tenderly stroked her cheek.

Maria nudged Eddie. 'Mrs Maria Herring? Yes, I like the sound of that. But seeing these other lovebirds here, I don't think we are the only ones with wedding bells to look forward to.'

Acknowledgements

Writing *The Station Master's Daughters at War*, the second in my trilogy, has been a dream come true.

I have my wonderful editor at Zaffre, Claire Johnson-Creek, to thank for her unfailing support and encouragement. Her skilful insights helped make my characters and stories leap from the pages. I could see she cared about them as much as I do.

Her belief in me as a new novelist was shared by my lovely agent, Hannah Weatherall, at the Northbank Talent Agency, and I would be lost without her words of wisdom.

I love that the Zaffre team are caring towards me, never pushy, but understanding when my energy sapped following the loss of my beloved mother, Loula, giving me time to grieve and re-energise.

The marketing and social media team have been terrific at promoting the series on their Memory Lane Facebook page, attracting dedicated new readers and considerably raising its profile. It's been a great joy to meet readers on Memory Lane and respond to their comments. I look forward to meeting many more with this sequel.

The Royal Station Master's Daughters trilogy would never have happened if Brian Heath, Harry's great grandson, hadn't so generously shared his ancestor's story with me, who was aided by his family, including Penny Coe, Sue Dingle, Shirley Brittin, Lynda Prior, Richard Saward, Chris Burrell-Saward, Helen McFarlane and Alison Heathorn.

The one man I rely on to check for factual accuracy is historian Neil Storey. There isn't anything Neil doesn't know about the WWI era and the ill-fated Sandringham Company. His seal of approval assures me that all is good as far as that is concerned, which makes me sleep better at night. I have also found my online and digital subscription at the London Library an invaluable source of information so I can place my characters in the right place at the right time, working from home while I do so.

Richard Brown, who restored the royal station at Wolferton, always welcomes me with open arms when I call in to see him, and proudly displays my first book there for visitors to see. It has meant a great deal to me to have his approval and support for which I am immensely grateful.

I also greatly value the support of Ben Colson, who resides in the splendid royal retiring rooms opposite Richard's, on the other side of the track. I doubt anyone can know more about Sandringham's royal history than Ben. He is a senior guide at Sandringham House and generously shared all he knows with me.

I must also thank the countless families from Norfolk who have shared their ancestors' stories with me about their time with Sandringham Company and working on the royal estate back in the early 20th century. I have Graham Peters to thank for telling me about the eerie stay busk he stumbled across with a hangman's noose carved on it which inspired one of my story lines. As they say, truth can be stranger than fiction, and I do try to stay as close to the truth as I can and weave my characters around them.

My family have shared this journey with me and I thank them for their patience when I am stuck to the computer, deep in my thoughts, in another world. A writer's life can be solitary, but knowing they are there for me at the end of every day gives me total happiness.

Betty's Gingerbread Biscuits

A recipe that Betty knows off by heart. Why not try this tasty treat with a cup of tea and your favourite book?

Makes approximately 14 biscuits

Ingredients

- 360g flour
- 1 tablespoon ground ginger
- 1 teaspoon cinnamon
- 1 tablespoon bicarbonate of soda
- 1 teaspoon nutmeg
- A pinch of salt
- 170g butter, room temperature
- 150g brown sugar
- 120ml treacle
- 1 egg
- 5ml vanilla extract

Recipe

1. Preheat oven to 180 degrees. In a large bowl, combine flour, ginger, cinnamon, bicarbonate of soda, nutmeg and salt.

2. Using a stand mixer fitted with a paddle attachment cream butter, and brown sugar on medium. Mix until fluffy.

3. Add in the treacle, then the egg and vanilla and mix until combined. Scrape the bowl down and mix once more.

4. Add in flour gradually while mixing on low until a nice dough form until combined.

5. Divide dough into two portions and roll into disks. Cover with plastic wrap.

6. Refrigerate for about 4 hours or overnight. This step is important because the dough gets soft quickly and really needs to be thoroughly chilled.

7. Roll out chilled dough to about ¼-inch in thickness.

8. Cut out shapes with a biscuit cutter. Carefully transfer to a baking sheet.

9. Bake the biscuits for 10 minutes. Let cool.

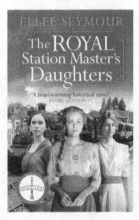

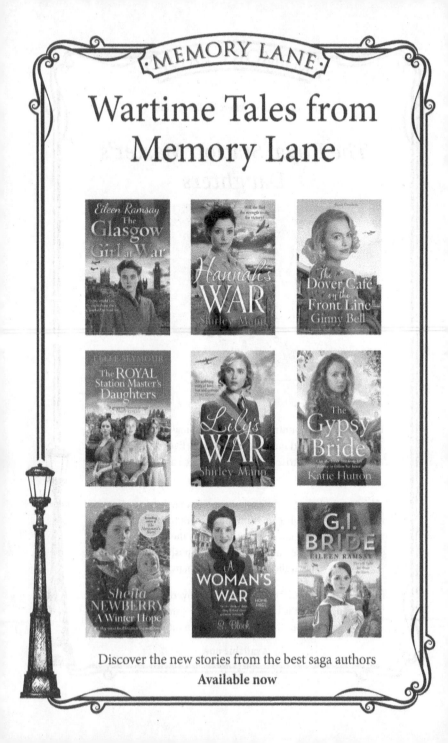

·MEMORY LANE·

Wartime Tales from Memory Lane

Discover the new stories from the best saga authors

Available now

·MEMORY LANE·

Introducing the place for story lovers – a welcoming home for all readers who love heartwarming tales of wartime, family and romance. Sign up to our mailing list for book recommendations, giveaways, deals and behind-the-scenes writing moments from your favourite authors. Join the Memory Lane Book Group on Facebook to chat about the books you love with other saga readers.

·MEMORY LANE·

www.MemoryLane.Club
www.facebook.com/groups/memorylanebookgroup